Chill Factor

Chill Factor

STUART PAWSON

First published in Great Britain in 2001 by
Allison & Busby Limited
Bon Marche Centre
241-251 Ferndale Road
London SW9 8BJ
http://www.allisonandbusby.com

Reprinted in 2005, 2006

A catalogue record for this book is available from
the British Library.

10 9 8 7 6 5 4 3

ISBN 0 7490 0549 1

Printed and bound in Great Britain by
Bookmarque Ltd, Croydon, Surrey

STUART PAWSON had a career as a mining engineer, followed by a spell working for the probation service, before he became a full-time writer. He lives in Fairburn, Yorkshire, and, when not hunched over the word processor, likes nothing more than tramping across the moors, which often feature in his stories. He is a member of the Murder Squad and the Crime Writers' Association. *Chill Factor* is the seventh novel to feature Detective Inspector Charlie Priest.

www.meanstreets.co.uk

Also by Stuart Pawson

Scott Walker had just reached the poetic bit – *Loneliness…is the cloak you wear* – when a movement in the wing mirror caught my attention.

"They're here," I said. *Emptiness…follows everywhere.* I reached out and cut him off before he could break my heart.

"Aw, I like the next bit," Detective Constable Annette Brown complained without conviction, twisting round in the driver's seat to see through the back window.

"I'll sing it to you later." I clicked the transmit button on my RT three times and spoke into it: "Charlie to Young Turks. Wake up, we're in business."

"Promises, promises," Annette mumbled quietly.

"And you can put it back on Radio Four," I told her. We were sitting in my car in the short-stay car-park outside Heckley station – that's railway, not police – with Annette in the driving seat. It's fifty pence for twenty minutes, except that the barrier was fixed in the upright position with all the covers off the electrical boxes so that it looked as if it were faulty. There were five other unmarked police cars nearby, including a couple of hastily arranged armed response vehicles, awaiting the connection from Manchester that had just arrived. It would have looked bad if we'd all had to stop, one by one, and put a fifty pence piece in the box before we could follow our suspect, so I'd arranged for the barrier to be out of order for an hour. That's the sort of power I have. Impressive, eh?

A trickle of people were leaving the concourse: businessmen with briefcases; younger people with sports bags, heading for the taxis and buses or looking for somebody meeting them. "Hey," Annette suddenly remarked. "You never told us about the sales conference. Did you learn anything?"

"Some," I replied. "It was interesting to see our man in action, and I'm now an expert on how to sell double glazing."

"Which might come in handy," she reminded me, "after today."

The warbling of my mobile phone prevented me from dwelling on that prospect. "Priest," I said into it.

"He's off the train and will be with you any second," a voice with a London accent told me. "He's wearing a blue leather blouson, fawn slacks and carrying a huge Adidas bag. I suggest you lift him as soon as he's clear of the building."

"Understood," I replied, and broke the connection. "And ignored," I added, quietly.

"Boss…" Annette began, "are you sure this is wise?"

"Oh, it's Boss now, is it?"

"Charlie, then."

"Um, Sugar Plum?" I ventured.

"Get stuffed."

"Here he comes." I put the radio to my mouth again. "Young Turks, Young Turks, Robin leaving concourse now. Wearing a blue leather blouse and carrying a big Adidas bag." The most wanted man on our books stepped through the automatic doors and looked around him. "And," I added, "a suntan like George Hamilton III."

Six cars along from us a blue BMW moved forward. "We were right," Annette said. "It's the BMW."

The telephone was warbling again. I switched it off and threw it in the glovebox.

Annette started the engine. "Charlie…" she tried once more.

"I know, I know," I told her. "You're right, it's not *wise*. But what's *wise* got to do with it? I didn't get where I am today –" I gestured expansively towards the raised barrier, symbol of my power, "– by being *wise*, so let's do it." The BMW had pulled out of the car-park and stopped at the kerb in front of the station entrance. Robin exchanged a quick word with the driver and climbed in the back, throwing his bag in first. I clicked the RT. "Charlie to Jeff and Pete," I said, more urgently than before. "Robin just leaving in blue

BMW. We'll do it my way, so he's all yours."

"Got him," and "Understood," came back to me, and a motorbike and a rusty Ford Fiesta parked in the road outside the station moved off. The car looked grotty, but there was a turbo-charged sixteen hundred engine under the bonnet, and the tyres were extraordinarily wide.

"Besides," I said to Annette, "we don't have enough firepower. He wasn't expected to get off at Heckley, and he wouldn't hesitate to shoot himself out of trouble."

"Oh God!" she exclaimed. "I've just seen Batman."

Batman was our contact, and he'd been following Robin for the last eight hours. I turned to look. A big man with the beginnings of a beer gut had emerged from the station. He was wearing Burberry check shorts that came to just below his knees, a Desperate Dan T-shirt and some chunky sandals that could have been made by Land Rover. With socks.

"Jee-sus," I hissed.

Batman stabbed a finger at the mobile phone he was holding and shouted something at it. My phone, in the glove box, remained resolutely silent. He did a little war-dance, shooting glances from one side to the other, as if his feet were on fire and the man with the bucket of water hadn't turned up.

"Charlie…" Annette tried again.

"No," I told her.

Batman pushed a woman away from the door of the first taxi in the queue and climbed in. The Asian driver tried to remonstrate with him but Batman was in no mood for an argument and the force of his personality, reinforced by a warrant card, prevailed. Besides, the driver had always dreamed of the day that a top cop would climb into his cab and tell him: "Follow that car."

"Flippin' 'eck, I've always wanted to do that," I declared. Annette looked across at me, sighed and shook her head. She's shaken her head quite a few times, recently. "Charlie to Young Turks," I said into the radio. "Move off, move off. ARV1 in front, ARV2 behind me. Let's go, and note that it's the taxi we're stopping. Have you got that?"

The ARVs were an afterthought, at the super's insistence, and not completely in on the plan. "The taxi?" one of them queried. "You mean the BMW?"

"No, the taxi. Not the BMW. Understood?"

"Batman? We're stopping Batman?"

"Affirmative, Batman."

After a long silence one of them said: "Understood," and the other grudgingly admitted: "You're the boss."

It almost went perfectly. When I gave the signal we boxed-in the taxi and forced it to a standstill. Annette squealed to a stop alongside him, leaving my wing mirror parked neatly behind his, but with no room for me to open the door. She leapt out, slamming the door at her side behind her. As I unbuckled my seat belt the driver glared across at me, his eyes wide with fright.

I had to climb over the centre console, avoiding the gear lever and handbrake, and slide the driver's seat back before I could push the door open, so everything was under control when I finally arrived on the scene. The ARV gunmen had Batman spread-eagled across the bonnet of the taxi, their Glock 9mm self-loading pistols aimed at his head. They'd pulled on their chic little baseball caps with the black and white checks, especially for the occasion. "OK, boys," I said as I negotiated my way around the jammed-together cars, "put them away, he's one of us."

The ARV officers lowered their guns and stared at me, mystified. Batman stretched upright and turned round. He looked a lot uglier than before, and had developed a twitch at the corner of his mouth. From the colour of his face his blood pressure wasn't too good, either. I said: "DI Charlie Priest, Heckley CID," by way of introduction, but decided that a handshake was probably a trifle over-familiar.

For a few seconds he couldn't speak, his breath rasping in his throat as if he'd just completed the four hundred metres hurdles, his shoulders rising and falling as he fought to drag air into his lungs. When he did his voice had a cracked, bluesy tone, a bit like Tom Waits. "Detective...Chief Inspector...Moynihan," he eventually gasped as he turned in my direction. "Metropolitan Police...Regional Crime Squad." His arm slowly raised until it pointed straight at me, his fingertip an inch from my nose. I stared along the length of it, straight into his piggy eyes as he hissed: *"And if it's the last thing...I ever do...I'm going to have...your fucking head on a plate."*

Chapter Two

It is a truth universally acknowledged that if a man wishes to maintain a long and happy marriage he should refrain, as often as is possible, from arriving home from work early.

He was having a sod of a week. It wasn't just a sod, it was a complete meadow of sods of a week. Like the one before it and all the ones before that since the government brought in the new legislation. He was Northern Area manager – "Uh!" he snorted at the thought of it – of Trans Global Finance, and he'd spent all week on the road, chasing clients when he should have been chasing sales staff.

TGF, as the company was known, was formed by the few directors of a Far Eastern bank who were still free to walk the streets undisguised after the bank crashed and left thousands, some say millions, of their customers penniless. As most of them were of Oriental extraction the collapse caused academic concern in the financial pages of the heavier papers but aroused no desire among the greater public to help out. The CEO and mastermind behind the bank received a derisory jail sentence but fled abroad while awaiting his appeal hearing, and two of his co-conspirators vanished without a trace. Not to be deterred by this small hiccup, and seeking a new venture in which to invest their ill-gotten millions, the remaining European directors created Trans Global Finance.

Thanks to aggressive sales techniques and a range of financial products that regularly invoked the comment "too good to be true," which was an accurate description, TGF blossomed like a garden centre on Good Friday. Salesmen – sales *executives* – made money to match their mobile phone numbers, and spent it as quickly as they earned it, because, they were told, the good life was theirs for the taking and success breeds success. Nobody loves a loser. To them that have, it shall be given. If you've got it, flaunt it.

Then came the pensions scandal, and they were in the

thick of it. Thousands of working people with perfectly good company pension schemes were exhorted to change to TGF, with promises of higher, index-linked pensions when they retired. Promises that nobody, particularly a company that paid its directors and sales people like TGF did, could keep.

The government, in an uncharacteristic fit of guilt because it had led the exhortations to change, ordered the financial houses – and there were several of them – to pay heavy compensation. TGF was nearly crippled, but not quite. They pulled in their horns, downscaled, rationalised and regrouped. It was going to be a long slog, but for those who stayed the rewards could be immense. The days of Rolexes and Porsches, if not Ferraris, would be back.

But not just yet. It's the manager's prerogative to see the most promising clients. The riffraff are sent to talk to the ones that the tele-sales girls churn out: the ones who reluctantly agree to let a financial consultant call at their homes – without obligation – because the girl on the phone has a come-to-bed voice and there's always the chance she will visit you herself. The manager calls during office hours on the small and medium-sized companies who are thinking of expanding and might be interested in a variety of packages that are on offer. And on the lottery winners whose only previous experience of investment has been via the little shop on the high street with the sporting prints on the blacked-out windows.

But even these were wise, nowadays. Three hundred and twenty miles of driving and four appointments had left him with two *I'll think about it*s, one *I'll have to ask my brother in law, who works for Barclays*, and one *Are you that lot who went bankrupt? The Sunday Times says you are.* Cruel experience, fashioned in the crucible of double-glazing selling, had taught him that all of these were just variations of a straight forward *No way, Jose*.

"Closing," he said to himself. That's what it was all about.

Closing a deal. Backing the punter into a corner by asking him what he liked about the product, what he was looking for, and then giving it to him in such a way that he couldn't retract. Once he'd been the master. He'd sold double-glazing to people who lived in council flats and to people who lived in caravans. He'd sold double-glazing to people who already *had* double-glazing.

"Do you prefer the aluminium or the UPVC, Sir?"

"Oh, the UPVC, don't we, Elsie?"

"That's right, Joe. Easy to clean, eh?"

"Precisely my sentiments, Elsie. Life's too short for cleaning window frames. And you won't say no to the free patio door, will you?"

And they didn't. And they signed the bottom of the complicated form that was hastily explained to them and slid across the table, pen laid invitingly across it. And when the windows and the "free" patio door were fitted they thought they were wonderful, because double-glazing in a climate like Britain's is essential. And they never knew that they could have bought the same deal for a third of the price if they had shopped around, because they were lazy, and inexperienced, and kind, and he'd been such a nice man. And they didn't discover until it was too late that the ten-year guarantee was worthless, because it was the company's policy to go bankrupt every five years.

The Prince of Closing, someone had christened him at a conference, and he was regularly asked to lecture on the subject. But times change, and punters were becoming streetwise to the language of the salesman. Say one wrong word, a single misrepresentation, and they'd have you on some consumer programme, explaining that it was a simple oversight not to mention that the quoted interest rate was monthly, not annual. A change of tactics was required; the books needed re-writing. He burped and tasted bile. He'd grabbed a ham sandwich for lunch, gulped down with two pints of Tetley's – beer, not tea – and his stomach and bladder were protesting. The big roundabout was approaching. Left for Heckley and home, right for the next appointment, another twenty miles away. He glanced at the clock: nearly half past three. The sixth form college would be letting out soon and he hadn't seen her for three weeks. He turned left, reaching for the phone to cancel the appointment, and slowed to a crawl.

Schoolchildren were walking towards him, some purposefully, some in desultory groups; and others, the smaller ones, fooling around. The girls wore blue skirts and white blouses, the boys grey slacks, with a few of them carrying blazers. She'd be going in the opposite direction. He drove past the end of the street that led to the school and hoped he hadn't missed her.

There she was. Her skirt was grey and short, a gesture of defiance against a school regime ill-equipped to deal with young women like her, and her blouse hung outside it. She was tall, about five eight, he guessed, and stacked like whoever made her enjoyed his work. Black tights held legs that would never have to do the chasing, and her skirt curled under her bum so that the afternoon sun's shadows delineated its curves. He imagined his hands resting on those hips, holding her close, before sliding upwards on to the arch of her waist and her cool, young skin.

He squirmed in the driving seat, making himself more comfortable, and cast a sideways glance at her as he drove by. The expression on her puffy face was miserable or sultry, depending on your standpoint. As he watched her hand came up to her mouth and she took a puff of a cigarette, rocking her head back in pleasure as she drew upon it, her breasts rising as she inhaled. He swallowed and reluctantly looked back at the road. In ten years, perhaps less, she'd be over the hill, he thought, but right now she was perfect. Just perfect.

A hundred yards beyond her there was a small shopping precinct. He swung into it and jumped out of the car. As she reached the precinct he was coming from the newsagent's shop, peeling the cellophane off a packet of Benson and Hedges. He walked out on to the pavement on a collision course.

"'Scuse me, love," he said to her. "I seem to have lost my matches. Could you give me a light, please?"

"Mmm, 'course I can," she replied, raising her stunted cig to the fresh one between his lips. Glowing tip met tobacco and transferred its fire as he inhaled, his eyes on her. Her lashes were short and brown, and there were whiteheads at the sides of her nose. She was wearing cheap perfume, lots of it, and he wondered what a classroom full of that would do to a man.

"Thanks," he sighed, smoke streaming from his nose and mouth. "I was ready for that."

"No problem," she replied with a smile. She looked radiant when she smiled.

He turned, as if to leave, then said: "Sorry, love, can I give you one?" and held the packet towards her.

"No, I'm all right," she told him, blushing ever so slightly.

He walked in the wrong direction, away from his car, for a few yards, then turned in time to see her cross the road and walk up a street on the right. Her feet were walking, but her arse was doing the samba. She vanished into a development of houses built at the height of the boom: all Elizabethan gables, Georgian windows and Thatcherite mortgages.

Back in the car he wound the window down and lit another B and H. They were shorter than they used to be, he thought. Once they were a luxury cigarette, the epitome of coolness, but now they were just a device for getting nicotine into your system as economically as possible. He held it outside in a half-hearted attempt to stop the car's interior smelling like a public bar.

It had been a long time. He inhaled deeply, wrapping his tongue around the smoke like a grazing cow, and felt it fill his lungs, inflating every little bronchiole and alveolus, finding its way into corners where oxygen had never ventured.

Distillations of nicotine were absorbed into his bloodstream and transported to the brain, where receptors, lying redundant for millions of years until Sir Walter Raleigh brought tobacco from the New World, eagerly latched on to them and converted them into an electro-chemical signal. A signal that said: "Ah! That's good."

Yes sir, it had been a long time. But the urge never left you. Once tasted, you were hooked. He remembered the date and did a quick calculation. Fifteen years and six months, almost to the day, since the last time. It hadn't been easy, for the yearning, the hunger, was always there, waiting to catch you out. And lately it was stronger than ever. He'd allowed the genie out of its bottle, and once on the loose he knew it had to be obeyed. The thought scared and excited him. He flicked the smouldering stub on to the car-park and started the engine.

Home was a four-bedroomed detached house built with just six others on a spare patch of land between a farm and the canal. The service road was block-paved, with speed humps, and the gardens were open plan. There was a paddock to the rear, but his neighbour had jumped in first and bought that, much to his annoyance. Each house had a double garage but they all left their vehicles outside. It's not conspicuous consumption if you hide it away. On a Sunday morning, when everyone was at home, the development resembled a four-wheel-drive regatta, just before the judging of the *concourse d'elegance*.

His wife's Suzuki Vitara was on the drive, with a Citroën Xantia behind it. "What's he doing here?" he wondered, parking in the street and swinging his legs wearily out. He collected his jacket from the Armani hanger behind the driving seat and his briefcase from the boot.

The wind chimes welcomed him as if he were entering a Buddhist monastery, but he broke the illusion by shouting: "I'm here. Cut it out, whatever you're doing," as he moved through the kitchen and hallway, towards the parlour.

His wife was sitting on the settee and the visitor in an easy chair, an empty cup and saucer perched demurely on his knees. A compilation CD of music from television adverts was playing in the background, very softly. The track was *Bailero*, from the *Songs of the Auvergne*, but he only knew it as the Kenco coffee tune.

"Hello, darling," his wife said. "You're home early."

He stooped to give her a peck on the cheek and turned to the visitor. "So this is what you get up to while the boss is working his butt off, eh?"

"Oh, not every week," the visitor replied with a grin.

He placed his briefcase on the floor and draped his jacket over it. "Will you excuse me," he asked them, moving back towards the door he'd just entered through, "but I'm bursting for a piss."

They listened to his footsteps climb the stairs, looking at each other. She with an expression of relief, he guiltily. The bathroom door closed and he opened his mouth to speak, but she silenced him by putting a finger to her lips. It was possible, she knew, that her husband had closed the door but remained outside it. It wasn't until she heard the sound of flushing that she dared to whisper: "Phew! That was close."

"What are we going to do?" he hissed.

"I'll ring you," she replied.

He placed the cup and saucer on a low table and rose to his feet as footfalls sounded on the stairs again. The husband went straight into the kitchen and was looking in the refrigerator as the visitor passed through. "I'm off," he said.

"Why not stay and eat with us, Peter," the husband offered.

"Thanks all the same, but no," he replied. "I've things to do. I was in the vicinity so I thought I'd come and have a cuppa with the little woman."

"OK. See you tomorrow, then."

"God willing. Bye Margaret," he called. "Thanks for the coffee."

"You're welcome," she called back.

When he'd gone the husband poured himself an orange juice and rejoined his wife. "What did he want?" he asked.

"You've been smoking," she accused, ignoring the question.

"Just the one," he replied. "A client...you know how it is."

"Good God, you're pathetic," she told him.

"I asked you what he wanted."

"Nothing," she replied. "Like he said, he was just passing."

"Does he make a habit of just passing?"

"That's about the second time this year, but Peter's welcome any time. He's a good friend."

"He's a bloody awful salesman. What time's supper?"

"I haven't thought about it. I wasn't expecting you for another two hours."

He resisted the temptation to say: "Evidently." Scoring meaningless points wasn't his style. "Let's eat out, then," he suggested.

"We can't afford it."

"It's two for one at the Anglers before six."

"The Anglers!" she sniffed.

"Well bloody-well cook something. I'm starving."

"Oh, very well," she said, standing up. "Let's go to the Anglers."

Chapter Three

Nine o'clock Wednesday morning somebody mugged a *Big Issue* seller in Heckley town centre. He'd never get rich that way but he made four pounds – enough for a heroin wrap or a few tueys; or some bush, bute, bhang, boy, blow, Bolivian or B-bombs to see him through the day. I ticked the report and slid it into my You'll be Lucky tray.

I was reading the list of overnight car thefts when there was a knock at the door of my partitioned-off domain in the corner of the CID office and big Dave "Sparky" Sparkington walked in. He's a DC and my best pal.

"It looks lovely out," he announced.

"Well leave it out, then," I told him. We'd lost a Fiesta XR3 and an elderly Montego to enemy action. Both crashed and burned, both somebody's pride and joy. Two more people would be braving the rigors of public transport this morning, or arranging for neighbours to take the kids to school and grandma to her appointment at the hospital, while they sorted the insurance.

"Somebody mugged a *Big Issue* seller," he said.

"I know. I've seen the report from downstairs. Any ideas?"

"No, but I could borrow a couple of bags and a dog, and we could have a day in the field, undercover, while the weather's nice."

I looked down at my jeans and check shirt. I dress the same nowadays as I did when I was an art student, before the Flood. "I wouldn't have to borrow any clothes," I said, before he could.

"That's true," he confirmed, adding: "or have a haircut."

I changed the subject. "Where's young Jamie Walker these days?"

"Ah," Dave began. "You've noticed the small blip in the stolen vehicles chart, with the emphasis on older cars with low-tech ignition systems."

"So where is he?"

"He finished his youth custody yesterday. Jeff and Annette have gone round to his mam's to see if he's there."

"The little bastard," I hissed. "We could do without him ballsing up all our figures and budgets."

Jamie Walker was fourteen years old and weighed seven stones. Our file on him was so thick he couldn't see over it. He'd spent nearly all his short life in care and his disregard for the law was total. We couldn't touch him, couldn't hurt him. He'd never had anything so he didn't know what loss was. His mother was a slag who only remembered his dad as an obligatory but unsatisfactory tumble with a lorry driver in his cab on the way back from a Garry Glitter concert.

Jamie was bright and cocky. The uniformed boys would slip him a fag while he was in the cells, and have a chat with him. They talked about cars and football, man to man, and invited him to the youth club for a game. He said he'd come, but he never did. Table tennis and five-a-side can't compete with handbrake turns and police chases. Milky coffee doesn't give you the same buzz as Evostick.

I hated him. Dave and the others saw the victims as they sat in their homes, shell-shocked, and asked: "Why?" Why was he so mindlessly destructive? Why did he have to torch their car? Why did magistrates allow him out on the streets to commit offence upon offence? It was nothing for Jamie to be arrested while on bail, while on probation, while awaiting to appear before the youth court, for a string of separate offences. More than once his hearing had ground to a halt because the prosecution thought they were in court for a stolen car, the defence were all wound up about a burglary and the child psychiatrist had spent most of her weekend analysing why a fourteen-year-old brought up by his grandma would steal her pension book. We had a computer programme dedicated solely to sorting his progress through the system because it was too complicated for the human mind. He was on first-name terms with all the duty solicitors and they loved him.

I didn't. He made a mockery of my overtime budgets, ruined my clear-up statistics and wasted resources that could have been used to solve proper crime. Or what I thought of as proper crime. I hated him, but not for that. Not for any of that. I had other reasons to hate him.

"Fancy going for a pint tonight?" Dave was asking.

"Oh, er, yeah. Good idea," I replied. We went for a pint nearly every Wednesday night.

"We could go to the Spinners Arms," he suggested.

"That'll make a nice change," I said, because we always went to the Spinners Arms. "Ring Nigel and tell him we'll see him there," I added. Nigel Newley was one of my hot-shot proteges who'd recently moved on to HQ in the quest for fame and glory.

"I've tried, but he's on holiday. Shirley said she might come." Shirley was Dave's wife, who didn't usually come out with us but it was all right by me.

"OK," I said.

"And Sophie might, too."

"Good," I said, trying not to sound too pleased. Sophie was his daughter, my goddaughter, who I regard as my near-est family. She would be going to university in October and she is tall, graceful and beautiful. When God smiles on some people he really gives them the works. Sophie coming along was definitely all right by me, but I didn't let it show. Dads can be touchy about their daughters. I shuffled the remain-ing papers on my desk into a neat bundle and shoved them back into the in-tray. "Tell you what," I began, "let's do some proper policing for the rest of the day."

But I didn't get a chance. The phone rang and I spent the next hour talking to a Prosecution Service solicitor about some evidence we had on a serial thief who specialised in stealing underwear from washing lines. It doesn't sound great crime, but it unnerves the victims, and can lead to other things. We'd marked some stuff and left it hanging out in his usual area of operations and he'd risen to the bait. Trouble was, the underwear we used was bought from the back room at the Oxfam shop, and it was hot stuff. Open crotches, black and red frills, suspender belts. Phew! Now the CPS solicitor was saying that unnecessary temptation might be a good defence. He wasn't keen, but I persuaded him to let it run. We might not get a conviction, but we'd be sending out the right messages.

Five o'clock the War Cabinet was having a cup of proper coffee in the super's office when the phone rang. He listened, looked at me, said: "He's here," and grunted a few times. The word *ominous* flashed through my mind as he replaced the phone.

The War Cabinet comprises of Gilbert Wood, the superintendent and overall boss at Heckley nick; Gareth Adey, my uniformed counterpart; and me; plus any sergeant or other rank who didn't escape quickly enough at the end of his shift. We try to meet at the end of the day for a relaxing cuppa, a general chinwag and to discuss the state of play with the villains and population in general on our corner of God's Own Country. Today we discussed Jamie Walker, our one-small-person crime wave, and regretted not having the power to drive him to a remote corner of the country and push him out of the car. Cape Wrath would do nicely. Sometimes, in the absence of possible avenues of action, we descend to fantasy.

"Go on," I invited Gilbert. "Tell me the worst."

"Right up your street," he replied. "Chap rung in to say he's done a murder. They're making it easy for you, these days."

Gareth rose to his feet asking: "Is somebody on their way?"

"It's Marborough Close, on the West Woods," Gilbert told him, "and there's a car handy."

The West Wood estate was the first flush of post-war private housing to hit Heckley, back in the Sixties. They were mainly semis, bought by young couples who believed that marriage came before children, even though this was supposed to be the permissive age. The real revolution in morality came twenty years later, but nobody sang about it. They all had kids at the same time and for a while the place became one giant playground. But youngsters have this habit of growing into teenagers, and the West Woods featured more and more in our statistics, until they all eventually matured, like the leylandii trees in their gardens, moved on and had kids of their own. Things evened out, and now the estate is a pleasant backwater, with a good mix of ages and races.

"I'll go down to control," Gareth announced, finishing his coffee in a gulp and leaving us. He likes to create an aura of efficiency and bustle, but mostly he just makes splashes.

"Get the biscuits out, please, Gilbert," I said. "The chocolate digestives you keep in the bottom drawer. I've a feeling that I might not be eating for a while."

Eight minutes and four biscuits later the phone rang again. Gilbert listened for a while then told them that we were on our way. "It's genuine," he told me. "Grab your coat." Going down the stairs I learned that there was one dead male at the house on Marlborough Close, with another male, alive, sitting in a chair saying he did it.

We went in separate cars with me leading the way, and were there in less than fifteen minutes. One of our Escorts was parked outside number 15, the corner house at the end of a cul-de-sac with a PC standing in the gateway. He stepped forward and opened my door as I coasted to a standstill.

"Hi, Jim," I said, climbing out. "What've we got?"

"Hello, Mr Priest," he replied. "We've got a murder. One bloke dead, in the kitchen, and a guy in the front room saying he did it."

Gilbert had joined us. "Hello, er, John," he said. "What have we got?"

"Hello, Mr Wood," Jim said, and repeated what he'd told me.

"Let's go have a look then, shall we?" Gilbert suggested, moving towards the house. A woman was standing in next door's garden, watching us, and another woman from further along came out to join her.

"You're sure he's dead, Jim?" I asked.

"Yeah, they don't come any deader," he replied, "but not for very long."

"A wild guess at how long?" I invited.

"One or two hours. No rigor, and the blood's hardly dry."

"Great," I said to him. "It's nearly six o'clock. If this body lived here his family might be coming home any time now. Have a word with those two," I nodded towards the neighbours, "and see what you can find out."

"Right, Boss," he replied, then hesitated. "Er, how much can I tell them?" I'd known Jim a long time. First in Halifax, and now at Heckley. He had about twenty years in and was solid and dependable, but unimaginative. This wasn't the first dead body he'd attended.

"Say it's a suspicious death," I told him. "Find out who lives here, what they look like. Then radio in and see who's on the electoral roll for this address."

"Right," he repeated, and headed towards the women.

The house looked sad and seedy, with unwashed windows and weeds growing in the borders. The lawn had been mown recently, but the grass cuttings were still lying on it, as if the owner felt that clearing them up was a task too far. I wondered if mine looked like this to a casual visitor and vowed to have a crash clean-up, when I had the time. The two cars parked on the drive didn't look neglected. There was a Citroën Xantia tight up against the garage door and an Audi A8 behind it, at a slight angle, with the driver's door not fully closed. The front door of the house was wide open. I stepped over the threshold and that old feeling hit me, like the smell of a bacon sandwich on a frosty morning. Some primordial instinct was being tapped: the thrill of the chase, and all that. At times like these, when news of a murder is breaking, I wouldn't change my job for any in the world. At others, when there are names and faces to fill in the blank spaces, and I've lived with the grief that people cause each other, I could walk out of it at a moment's notice. Except that someone else would have to do it. There's always an *except that*.

I was in a hallway that faced straight on to a staircase, with a grubby biscuit-coloured carpet on the floor, nice but impractical, and Victorian bird prints on the walls. One of the first things I look at in someone else's home is their pictures. It's usually depressing and today was no exception.

Gilbert was in the front room, to my left, and I heard him say: "Do you live here, sir?" I peeked in and saw a man slumped in an easy chair, head down, his elbows on his knees. Gilbert was sitting facing him, his back to me, and another PC was standing nearby. The PC saw me and I winked at him. There was a glass door, slightly ajar, at the end of the hall. I placed the knuckle of my forefinger against it and eased it open.

I was in a kitchen of the type they grandly call a galley, which is probably one of the finer examples of the estate agent's art. Cooking might be the rock 'n' roll of the Nineties, but back when these houses were built they had the real thing and food was something you grabbed between living. Somebody had been preparing dinner. A pan was on the worktop, lid alongside it, and a spaghetti jar was standing nearby. One gas ring was burning at full blast, and it was hotter than Hades in there. The floor was done in brown and cream carpet tiles, and spread-eagled across them was the body of a man. A turkey carver was sticking out of his chest, in the approximate vicinity of the heart. That's the way to do it, I thought. He was wearing a white shirt, before someone ruined it, with the sleeves loosely rolled halfway up his forearms. That's how middle class people turn them up. Workers, proper workers, take them right over the elbow.

The man in the parlour, talking to Gilbert, was wearing a blue suit.

It looked to me as if the person lying dead on the kitchen floor had lived here, and the one in the other room with Gilbert was a visitor. It takes years of experience to make deductions like that.

The PC came to join me standing in the doorway to the kitchen. "Shall I take over outside, Mr Priest?" he asked.

"Oh, er, hello Martin," I replied. "Yes, if you will please. How much has laddo told you?" I took three careful steps across the kitchen and turned the gas off.

"Not a great deal. His opening words were: 'I killed him,' but since then he's clammed up, refused to answer any questions."

I backed out again, trying to place my feet on the same brown squares. "Right. I'll radio for the team if you'll take up station on the gate and log all visitors, please. There might be someone – family – coming home from work anytime, so watch out for them and don't let them in."

"So will you do a full enquiry?" he asked.

"We'll have to," I told him.

"What? SOCOs and all that?"

"You bet."

"Even though you know who did it?"

I tapped my nose with a finger and said: "Something's fishy."

"Blimey," he replied, and went outside.

When I stepped into the front room Gilbert looked up at me and shook his head. "This is Detective Inspector Priest," he said to the man, enunciating the words as if he were addressing a foreigner. "Perhaps you would like to talk to him."

It looked to me as if the chief suspect was playing dumb. "Maybe we should let Sam have a look at him," I suggested. Sam Evans is the police surgeon, and we needed him to certify the victim dead, but when a witness or suspect is in any sort of a state it's always useful to have a medical opinion, if only for self-defence at a later date.

"Good idea," Gilbert said, rising to his feet. "I'll send for him while you…" he gestured towards the man, "…try to have a word."

"I haven't sent for the team, yet," I said to his back.

"I'll do it," he replied.

The team was comprised of the collection of experts we had on duty round the clock, plus a few others that we always called in for a murder enquiry. They'd be at home now, tucking into their fish fingers and chips or playing with the kids, but they'd grab their jackets with unseemly haste and be out of the door before their wives could ask what time they'd be back. We needed SOCOs and a photographer to record the murder scene before anything was moved, exhibits and statements officers, and sundry door-knockers. Then there was the duty DCS at region, the coroner and the pathologist to inform. I dredged up the checklist from the recesses of my mind and ticked off the procedures.

The man was smartly dressed, with slip-on shoes that gleamed and a gaudy silk tie dangling between his knees. The top of his head was facing me and he was completely bald, his scalp as shiny as his shoes. I placed my hands on his lapels and eased him upright.

"Could you just sit up please," I said to him, "so I can see you."

He didn't resist, and flopped against the chair back. His eyes were red, as if he'd been crying, or rubbing his knuckles into them, and there was blood on his fingers.

"That's better," I said. There were stains on the front of his jacket, too, but I couldn't be sure what they were. "Like my superintendent told you," I began, "I'm DI Priest from Heckley CID. Now could you please tell me who you are?"

He didn't reply, and the corner of his mouth began to curl into the beginnings of a sneer. He shook his head, ever so slightly, and leaned back, staring up at the ceiling.

"Your name, sir," I tried. "Who are you?"

He mumbled something I couldn't catch.

"Could you repeat that?" I asked.

He looked at me and said: "It doesn't matter."

"What doesn't matter?"

"All of this. Who I am. It doesn't matter."

Before he could protest I reached forward, pulled his jacket open and whipped his wallet from his inside pocket. The secret is to make sure you go for the correct side. He made a half-hearted attempt to grab it back, then resumed his slumped position in the chair.

It was just a thin notecase, intended for credit cards and a few tenners for emergencies. I didn't count them but there looked to be about ten. I read the name on a Royal Bank of Scotland gold card and checked it against the others. They were all the same.

"Anthony Silkstone," I said. "Is that you?"

He didn't answer at first, just sat there, looking at me with a dazed, slightly contemptuous expression. I didn't read anything into it; I'm not sure what the correct expression is for when you've just impaled someone with the big one out of a set of chef's knives.

"I killed him," he mumbled.

Well that was easy, I thought. Let's just have it in writing and we can all go home. "You killed the man in the kitchen?" I asked him.

"Yes," he confirmed. "I told the others. How many times do I have to say it."

"Just once more, for the record. And your name is Anthony Silkstone?"

He gave a little nod of the head. I handed him his wallet back and said: "Stand up, Mr Silkstone. We're taking you down to the station." He placed it back in his pocket and rose shakily to his feet.

I held his arm and guided him down the driveway and out into the street. A small crowd had gathered but Martin was doing sterling work holding them back. I sat Silkstone in the back of the police car and gestured for Martin to join me.

"Anthony Silkstone," I began, "I am arresting you for the murder of a person so far unknown…" He sat expressionless through the caution and obligingly offered his wrists when I produced the handcuffs. "Take him in as soon as some help arrives," I told Martin. "I'll tell the custody sergeant to expect you."

At the station they'd read him his rights and find him a solicitor. Then they would take all his clothes and possessions and label them as evidence. Even his socks and underpants. Fingerprints and DNA samples would follow until the poor sod didn't know if he was a murder suspect or a rat in a laboratory experiment. He'd undress, sit down, stand up, say "Yes" at the appropriate times and meekly allow samples of his person to be taken. Then, dressed like a clown in a village play, he'd be locked in a cell for several hours while other people determined his fate and came to peep at him every fifteen minutes.

Gilbert and Jim joined me on the driveway. "You've arrested him," Gilbert commented.

"It's a start," I said, turning to Jim. "Any luck?"

"Yes, Boss," he replied. "A bloke called Peter Latham lives here. He's single, lives alone, and works as some sort insurance agent. Average height, thin build, dark hair. Sounds like the man on the floor."

"He does, doesn't he. Single. Thank God for that."

"Somebody'll love him," Gilbert reminded us as his mobile phone chirruped into life. He placed it to his ear and introduced himself. After a few seconds of subservience from the super I deduced that it was the coroner on the phone. Gilbert outlined what we'd found, told him I was on the job and nodded his agreement at whatever the coroner was saying. Probably something along the lines of: "Well for God's sake don't let Charlie touch anything." Gilbert closed his phone and told us: "We can move the body when we're ready."

"We haven't certified the poor bloke dead yet," I informed him.

"Well he'd just better be," he replied.

A white van swung into the street, at the head of a convoy. "Here come the cavalry," I said. "In the nick of time, as always."

As soon as Sam Evans, the doctor, confirmed that the man on the kitchen floor was indeed dead, and had been so for about an hour, we let the photographer and scene of crime loose in the place. They tut-tutted and shook their heads disapprovingly when I confessed to turning off the gas ring. Sam's opinion, only given when requested, was that death was possibly induced by the dagger sticking out of the deceased's heart. Police doctors and pathologists are not famed for their impetuous conclusions.

I asked Sam if he'd go to the station and give an opinion about the state of mind of Anthony Silkstone, the chief suspect, and he agreed to. The doc's an old pal of mine. I've plenty of old pals. In this job you gather them like burrs. Some stick, some irritate, most of them fall off after a while.

As we hadn't set up an incident room we had our initial team meeting with lowered voices in the late Mr Latham's back garden. I sent the enquiry team, all three of them, knocking on doors to find out what they could about the dead man. Except that they wouldn't have to knock on any doors because everybody was outside, standing around in curious groups, wondering if this was worth missing *Coronation Street* for or if it was too late to light the barbecue. We wanted to know if anybody had seen anything within the last three or four hours, the background of the deceased, and anything about his lifestyle. Visitors, girlfriends, boyfriends, that sort of thing. I was assuming that the dead man was the householder. As soon as someone emerged who was more than just a neighbour I'd ask them to identify the body.

We knew that Silkstone had the opportunity, now we

needed a motive and forensic evidence. He might retract his confession, say he called in to see an old friend and found him dead. Maybe he did, so if he wasn't the murderer we needed to know, fast. Gilbert went back to the station to set up all the control staff functions: property book, diary, statement reader, etcetera, plus vitally important stuff like overtime records, while I stayed on the scene to glean what I could about a man who aroused passions sufficiently to bring about his elimination.

The SOCO was doing an ESFLA scan on the kitchen floor, looking for latent footprints, so I had a look around the upstairs rooms. It was a disappointment. There was nothing to indicate that he was anything other than a normal, heterosexual bloke living on his own. No gay literature, no porn, no inflatable life-size replicas of Michelangelo's *David*. Except that the bed was made. His duvet was from Marks and Spencer and his wallpaper and curtains probably were too. It all looked depressingly familiar. I promised myself that from now on I'd lead a tidier life, just in case, and dispose of the three thousand back issues of *Big Wimmin* that were under my bed.

There were ten suits in his wardrobe. "That's nine more than in mine," I said to myself, slightly relieved to discover a discrepancy in our lifestyles. And he had more decent shirts than me. The loo could have been cleaner but wasn't too bad, and the toilet paper matched the tiles. He'd changed his underpants recently, because the old ones were lying on the bathroom floor, with a short-sleeved shirt. There was a sprinkling of water in the bottom of the bath, and the towel hanging over the cold radiator was damp. At a guess he'd showered and changed before meeting his maker, which would be a small comfort to his mother. In his bathroom cabinet I found Bonjela, Rennies and haemorrhoid cream. Poor sod didn't have much luck with his digestive tract, I thought.

I gravitated back into the master bedroom. That's where

the clues to Mr Peter Latham's way of living and dying lay, I
was sure. Find the lady, I was taught, and there were framed
photographs of two of them on a chest of drawers, opposite
the foot of the bed. I stood in the window and looked down
on the scene outside. Blue and white tape was now ringing
the garden and the street was blocked with haphazardly
parked vehicles. Neighbours coming home from work were
having to leave their cars in the next street and Jim, the PC,
was having words with a man carrying a briefcase who did-
n't think a mere death should come between him and his castle. I gave a little involuntary smile: he'd get no change out
of Jim.

The first photograph standing on the chest of drawers in
a gilt frame was one of those wedding pictures you drag out,
years afterwards, to amuse the kids. It was done by a so-
called professional, outside a church in fading colour. The
bride was taller than the groom, with her hair piled up to
accentuate the difference. She looked good, as all brides
should. This was her day. Wedding dresses don't date, but
men's suits do, which is what the kids find so funny. His was
grey, with black edging to the floppy lapels of his frock coat.
The photographer had asked him to turn in towards his new
wife, in a pose that nature never intended, and we could see
the flare of his trousers and the Cuban heels. Dark hair fell
over his collar in undulating cascades. He'd have got by in a
low budget production of *Pride and Prejudice*. It wouldn't
have stood as a positive ID but I was reasonably confident
that the groom and the man lying on the kitchen floor were
one and the same. So where was she, I wondered? The second picture was smaller, black and white, in a simple wood-
en frame. It showed a young girl in a pair of knickers and a
vest, taken at a school sports day. She'd be ten or twelve, at
a guess, but I'm a novice in that department. Some men
would find it sexy, I knew that much. Her knickers were
tight fitting and of a clingy material, with moderately high
cut legs; and a paper letter B pinned to her vest underlined

the beginnings of her breasts. It was innocent enough, I decided, but she'd be breaking hearts in four or five years, that was for sure. Maybe a niece or daughter. At either side of her you could just see the elbows and legs of two other girls, and I reckoned that she'd been cut from a group photograph. A relay team, perhaps. As with the other picture, I wondered if this young lady might come bounding up the garden path anytime now.

"Boss?"

I turned round to see the SOCO who was standing in the bedroom doorway, still dressed in his paper coveralls. I hadn't put mine on, because the case had looked cut and dried.

"Yes!" I replied, smartly.

"We've finished in the kitchen," he said. "We just need the knife retrieving."

"I'll have a look before anybody touches it," I told him.

"Oh. We, er, were hoping that you'd, er, do it."

"Do what?"

"Well, retrieve it."

"You mean...pull it out?"

"Mmm."

"That's the pathologist's job. He'll want to do it himself."

"Ah. We have a small problem there. He's on his way back from London and his relief is nowhere to be found, but he's spoken to Mr Wood and he's happy for you to do it if we take a full record of everything."

"I see. What does it look like for prints."

"At a guess, covered in 'em."

"Good. What do you make of those?" I asked, nodding towards the photographs.

"The pictures?" he asked.

"Yep."

"It looks like their wedding day."

"I'd gathered that. Do you think it's him?"

"Um, could be." He looked more closely, adding: "Yeah, I'd say it was."

"Good. What about the other?"

"The girl? Could be their daughter," he replied. "The hair colour's similar, and they both look tall and thin."

"Or the bride as a schoolgirl," I suggested.

The SOCO bent down to peer at the picture. After a few seconds he said: "I don't think so."

"Why not?"

"Because the timing's wrong."

"You've lost me," I told him.

"Can't be sure," he went on, "but they both look as if they were taken around the same time. About fifteen or twenty years ago, at a guess. Maybe a bit less for that one." He pointed towards the schoolgirl.

"How do you work that out," I asked, bemused.

"The knickers," he replied. "Long time ago they'd be cut straight across. Now they wear them cut higher. These are in-between."

"I take it you have daughters," I said.

"Yep. Two."

"Some men would find a picture like that provocative," I told him.

"I know," he replied. "And you can see why, can't you?"

I suppose that was as close as we'd ever get to admitting that it was a sexy image. "I don't find it sexy," we'd say, "but I can understand how some men might."

"Why," I asked him, "do the knicker manufacturers make them with high-cut legs when they know that they are intended for children who haven't reached puberty yet?"

"Because that's what the kids want. There's a demand for them."

"But why?"

"So they can be like their mothers."

"Oh."

All knowledge is useful. Knowledge catches crooks, I tell the troops. But there are vast landscapes, whole prairies and Mongolian plains, which are a foreign territory to me.

They're the bits surrounding families and children and relationships that have stood the test of time. My speciality, my chosen subject, is ones that have gone wrong. Never mind, I consoled myself; loving families don't usually murder each other.

We went downstairs into the kitchen. Peter Latham hadn't moved, but there was a thin coating of the fingerprint boys' ally powder over all his possessions. "We decided not to do the knife *in situ*," one of them told me.

"So you want me to pull it out?"

"Please."

"Great."

"But don't let your hands slip up the handle."

"Maybe we should use pliers," I suggested, but they just shrugged their shoulders and pulled faces.

"Have we got photos of it?" I asked. We had.

"And measurements?" We had.

"Right, let's have a look, then."

Sometimes, you just have to bite the bullet. Or knife, in this case. I stood astride the body and bent down towards the sightless face with its expression cut off at the height of its surprise, a snapshot of the moment of death. Early detectives believed that the eyes of the deceased would capture an image of the murderer, and all you had to do was find a way to develop it.

I felt for some blade, between the handle and the dead man's chest, and gripped it tightly with my thumb and forefinger. It didn't want to come, but I resisted the temptation to move it about and as I increased the pressure it moved, reluctantly at first, then half-heartedly, like the cork from a bottle of Frascati, until it slipped clear of the body. The SOCO held a plastic bag towards me and I placed the knife in it as if it were a holy relic.

"Phew!" I said, glad it was over. I could feel sweat on my spine.

"Well done," someone murmured.

My happy band of crime-fighters started to arrive, wearing the clothes they'd intended spending the rest of the evening in. Annette Brown was in jeans and a Harlequins rugby shirt, and my mouth filled with ashes when I saw her. She's been with us for about a year, and was now a valuable member of the team. For a long while she'd kept me at a distance, not sure how to behave, but lately we'd been rubbing along quite nicely. She was single, but I'd never taken her out alone, and as far as I knew nobody else had. Inevitably, there were rumours about her sexual inclination. She has wild auburn hair that she keeps under control with a variety of fastenings, and the freckles that often go with that colour. I looked at my watch, wondering if we'd have the opportunity to go for that drink later, and ran my tongue over my teeth. No chance, I thought, as I saw the time.

I sent Sparky and Annette to talk to the house-to-house boys, collating whatever they'd discovered, and asked Jeff Caton to do some checks on the car numbers and the two people in the house. At just before ten the undertaker's van collected the body. We secured the house, leaving a patrol car parked outside, and moved *en masse* to the incident room that Mr Wood had hopefully set up at the nick.

The coffee machine did roaring service. As soon as I'd managed to commandeer a cup I called them all to order. "Let's not mess about," I said. "With a bit of luck we'll still be able to hit our beds this side of midnight. First of all, thank you for your efforts. First indications are that the dead man might be called Peter Latham. What can anybody tell me about him?"

Annette rose to her feet. "Peter John Latham," she told us, "is the named householder for number 15, Marlborough Close, West Woods. He is also the registered keeper of the Citroën Xantia parked on the drive. Disqualified for OPL in 1984, otherwise clean. Latham's description tallies with that of the dead man, and a woman at number 13 has offered to identify the body. She's a divorcee, and says they were close."

"Do you mean he was doing a bit for her, Annette?" someone called out.

"No, close as in living in the adjoining semi," she responded, sitting down.

"Thanks Annette," I said, raising a hand to quieten the laughs. "It appears," I went on, "that Latham was killed with a single stab wound to the heart. We'll know for certain after the post-mortem."

"Arranged for eight in the morning," Mr Wood interrupted. He was on the phone in his office when I'd started the meeting, organising the PM, and I hadn't seen him sneak in.

"Thanks, Boss," I said. "It doesn't appear to have been a frenzied attack, but all will be revealed tomorrow. You OK for the PM, Annette?"

She looked up from the notes she was making and nodded.

"The man who claims to have done it," I continued, "is called Anthony Silkstone. What do we know about him?"

Jeff flipped his notebook open but spoke without consulting it. "Aged forty-four," he told us. "Married, comes from Heckley and has a string of driving convictions, but that's all. His address is The Garth, Mountain Meadows, wherever that is."

I knew where it was, but didn't admit it.

"Yuppy development near the canal, on the north side of town," Gareth Adey interrupted. "We've had a car there, but the house is in darkness and the door locked. Presumably the key is in Silkstone's property."

Jeff waited until he'd finished, then went on: "He shares the place with a woman called Margaret Silkstone, his wife, I imagine, and drives an Audi A8 with the same registration as the one parked outside the dead man's house."

"Nice car," someone murmured.

"What's it worth?" I asked.

"They start at about forty grand," we were informed.

"So he's not a police officer. OK. Number one priority is find Mrs Silkstone – we'd better get someone round to the house again, pronto – get the key from Silkstone's property. Then we need next of kin for the dead man."

"We're on it, Charlie," Gareth Adey said.

"Cheers, Gareth. And we need a simple statement for the press." He nodded to say he'd take that on, too.

The door opened and the afternoon shift custody sergeant came in, wearing no tie and a zipper jacket over his blue shirt to indicate that he was off duty and missing a well-earned pint.

"Just the man," I said. "Has our friend been through the sausage machine?"

"He's all yours, Mr Priest," he replied. "He's co-operating, and beginning to talk a bit. Dr Evans says there's no reason why he shouldn't be questioned, and he's not on any medication."

"We think there's a wife, somewhere. Has he asked for anybody to be informed?"

"No, Boss, just his solicitor. I've never heard of them, but apparently they're an international firm with a branch in Manchester, and someone's coming over."

"Tonight?"

"That's what they said."

"They must be able to smell a fat fee." I turned to the others. "Right, boys and girls," I said. "Anybody short of a job, see me. Otherwise, go home to bed and we'll meet again at eight in the morning. With a bit of luck we'll have this sewn up by lunchtime."

They drifted away or talked to the sergeants to clarify their tasks. Sparky found me and said: "Well that mucked up our nice quiet drink, didn't it?"

"And I could use one," I replied.

"If you get a move on we might manage a swift half over the road," he said.

"You go," I told him. "I'll hang about a bit in case anybody wants a word." I like to make myself available. They might be detectives, but some of them are not as forthcoming as others. There's always someone who seeks you out to discuss an idea or a problem, or to ask to be allocated to a certain task. This time it was Iqbal, who was on a fortnight's secondment with us from the Pakistan CID and who never stopped smiling. He was lodging with Jeff Caton, and apparently had come in with him.

"Where would you like me to go, Inspector Charlie?" he asked.

For over a week he'd followed me round like a bad cold, and I was tempted to tell him, but he outranked me and the big grin on his face made me think that his provocative phrasing was deliberate.

"Ah! Chief Inspector Iqbal," I said. "Just the man I'm looking for. Tomorrow you can help me with the submission to the CPS. That should be right up your street."

"The dreaded MG forms," he replied.

"Precisely."

Before I could continue Annette came by and said: "Goodnight, Boss. See you some time in the morning."

"Er, we were thinking of trying to grab a quick drink at the Bailiwick," I told her. "Fancy one? Dave's paying."

"Ooh," she replied, as if the thought appealed to her, then added: "I'd better not. I don't want to feel queasy at the PM. Thanks all the same."

"The PM!" I exclaimed, as enlightenment struck me. "What a good idea. How do you feel about taking Iqbal along with you?"

Whatever she felt, she declined from expressing it. I don't know how Iqbal felt about watching a body being cut open, but I suspected he'd rather eat a whole box of pork scratchings than be shown around by a woman. He tipped his head graciously and they arranged to meet at the General Hospital, early.

As they left us Sparky said: "Annette's a nice girl, isn't

she?"

"She is," I replied. "Very sensible. But she will insist on calling me Boss all the time."

He grinned and shook his head.

"What did I say?" I demanded.

"Nothing," he replied.

A couple of others came to clarify things with me and it was about ten to eleven as we walked along the corridor towards the front desk. Some of the team had already gone across to the pub. The duty constable was talking to a short man in a raincoat, and when he saw me he indicated to the man that I was the person he needed.

"This is Mr Prendergast, Mr Silkstone's solicitor," the constable told me, before introducing me as the Senior Investigating Officer. Prendergast didn't offer a handshake, which was OK by me. I'm not a great shaker of hands.

He didn't waste time with unnecessary preliminaries or pleasantries. "Have you charged my client?" he asked.

"No," I replied. "We haven't even interviewed him, yet."

"So he is under arrest and the clock is running?"

"Yes."

"Since when?"

"Since about six forty-five this evening. The precise time will be on the custody sheet." He was a keen bugger, no doubt about it. I mentally slipped into a higher gear, because he'd know every dodge in the book and screw us if we made the slightest mistake.

"And when do you propose to interview him?" he demanded.

"In the morning," I replied. "We normally allow the prisoner to sleep at night. He's been offered food and drink, and given the opportunity to inform another person of his arrest, but he has declined to do so."

"Yes, Yes," Prendergast said, swapping his briefcase from his left hand to his right. "I'm sure you know the rules, Inspector, but I would prefer it if you interviewed him tonight, then perhaps we can explain away this entire sorry event."

"I think that's unlikely, but I'm happy to interview him if he's willing." I turned to Sparky who was hovering nearby, and said: "Looks like we're in for a late night, Sunshine. You'd better ring home."

"Right," he replied, grimly. Anybody who keeps Sparky away from that desperately needed pint is walking near the edge. We took the brief through into the custody suite to have words with the sergeant, then locked him in the cell with his client, so they could get their story straight. After ten minutes we knocked on the door, but he asked for another ten minutes. We didn't wait idly while they were conferring. Phone calls to friends in the business told us that Prendergast specialised in criminal law for a big firm of solicitors based in Luxembourg who worked for several large companies with tendencies to sail close to the wind. It was nearly midnight when Sparky pressed the red button on the NEAL interview recorder and I made the introductions.

Tony Silkstone, as he called himself, was of barely average height but built like a welterweight. I could imagine him working out at some expensive health club, wearing all the right gear. The stuff with the labels on the outside. His pate still glistened, so I decided he was a natural slaphead and not one from choice. He had a suntan and his fingernails were clean, even and neatly cut. Apart from that, his paper coverall was pale blue and a trifle short in the arms.

"Today," I began, after the formalities had been committed to tape, "at about five p.m., police officers were called to number 15, Marlborough Close, Heckley. Did you make that call, Mr Silkstone?"

"Yes," he replied in a firm voice, and Predergast nodded his approval.

"When they arrived there," I continued, "they found the body of a man believed to be one Peter Latham. He was lying dead in the kitchen. Did you kill Mr Latham?"

That threw them into a tizzy, but I wasn't in a mood for tip-toeing round the issue. I wanted it sewn up, so I could go home. Silkstone had been offered a meal; Prendergast had probably dined lavishly on smoked salmon and seasonal vegetables, washed down by a crisp Chardonnay; I'd had a Cornish pasty twelve hours ago. And, I remembered, four chocolate digestives in Gilbert's office. Prendergast grabbed his client's arm and told him not to answer, as I'd expected.

"That's a rather leading question, Inspector," he said.

"And I'd like a leading answer," I replied.

"I think I'd like to confer with my client."

"Mr Prendergast," I said. "It is after midnight and I am tired. Your client has had a stressful day and is probably tired, too. Do you not think it would be in his interest to conduct this interview in the morning, when we all have clear heads? If you are constantly asking for adjournments we could be here until the day after tomorrow."

Except, of course, that there would be other places where Prendergast would prefer to be tomorrow. Like the golf course, or entertaining one of his corporate clients who was having alimony problems. Silkstone himself came to the rescue. He ran his hand over the top of his head and massaged his scalp with his fingers, before saying: "It's all right, Mr Prendergast. I'd like to answer the inspector's questions."

"In which case," I stated, "I would like it on record that this interview is continuing at your insistence and not under any duress from me."

Prendergast put the top on his fountain pen and sat back in his plastic chair.

"Why did you make that phone call, Mr Silkstone," I asked.

"Because Peter was dead."

"You knew he was dead?"

"I was fairly certain."

"You didn't send for an ambulance?"

"There was nothing anybody could do for him."

"Who killed him?"

"I did."

Prendergast sat forward in an involuntary reaction, then relaxed again.

"Tell me about it."

"I followed him home. We had words and I pulled a knife out of the set of carvers that just happened to be on the worktop. I stabbed him with it, in the chest, and he fell down. He moved about for a bit, then lay still. I could tell he was dead."

"What did you do then?" I asked.

"I sat in the other room for a while. Driving there I'd been seeing red. Literally. I always thought it was just an expression, but it isn't. I'd been mad, raging mad, but suddenly I was calm again. I could see what I'd done. After about ten minutes I rang the police."

"So you are confessing to killing Peter Latham, by stabbing him in the chest?"

"Yes. I did it."

"And the man is indeed Peter Latham?"

"Yes, it's Peter."

"You knew him well?"

"Yes."

"So why did you kill him?"

Silkstone put his face in his hands and leaned forward until his forehead rested on the little table that separated us.

I said: "Why did you follow him home and stab him?" and he mumbled something through his fingers.

"I'm sorry…?" I said.

He sat up, his eyes ringed with red. "He killed her," he told us.

So that was it, I thought. Some old score settled. Some grudge over an old sweetheart, real or imagined, that had festered away for years until it could be contained no longer. I'd seen it all before. I even held one myself. "Who did he kill?" I demanded.

"My wife. He killed my wife."

I leaned forward until my elbows were on the table. "When was this?" I asked. "When are we talking about?"

"Today. This afternoon. He…he…he raped her. Then he strangled her."

There was a "clump" as the front legs of Sparky's chair made contact with tiled floor, and Prendergast's eyes nearly popped out. I interlaced my fingers and leaned further forward.

"You're saying that Latham killed your wife this afternoon, Mr Silkstone?" I said, softly.

He looked up to see if there was a clock on the wall, but it was behind him. "Yes," he replied.

"Where exactly did this take place?"

"At my house. I came home early and saw him leaving. She…Margaret…she was upstairs, on the bed. He'd…he'd done things to her. So I followed him home and killed him."

I looked across at Sparky. "Sheest!" he mumbled.

"Interview terminated while further investigations are made," I said, reading off the time and nodding for him to stop the tape. I rose to my feet and glanced at the hotshot lawyer who looked as if he was trying to run uphill with his shoelaces tied together. "I think it's safe to say we'll be holding your client for a while, Mr Prendergast," I told him.

"I'm not surprised, Inspector," he responded, shaking his head.

Chapter Four

The estate agent's advert had said that Mountain Meadows was a pleasant development on a flat strip of land alongside the canal. There were only seven houses, all detached and with decent gardens. Sparky and myself went to investigate, in my car, after ringing Mr Wood with the latest bombshell. The roads were empty and I drove fast. Soon we were clear of the streetlamps, tearing along through the night.

"You seem to know where you're going," Dave observed.

"I came to look at them, once," I replied.

"What? You were thinking of moving?"

"Mmm."

"You kept that quiet."

"I don't tell you everything."

A cat darted halfway across the road, then stopped and stared into my headlights. I hit the brakes and the front of the car dipped and pulled to the right as a wheel locked. The moggie regained the power of movement and leapt to safety.

After a silence Dave said: "You and Annabelle?"

"Yeah. We could have afforded one reasonably comfortably if we'd pooled our resources."

Annabelle was my last long-term relationship. We were together for about five years, which was a personal best for me, but she decided the grass was greener when seen through the windscreen of a Mercedes. I live in the house I inherited from my parents, and she owned an old vicarage. When things were good between us we'd done the tour of a few places, including Mountain Meadows. On paper it had looked ideal, but a quick visit one summer's evening destroyed the dream. The smoke from all the barbecues and the incessant drinky-poos with the neighbours would have ruined our lungs and livers. Then she left me, so it was just as well that we hadn't moved.

Except, maybe, if we had... Ah well, we'd never know.

"So what do you think," Dave asked, changing the subject.

"We'll soon find out," I replied. "This is it."

I turned off the lane and slowed down for the speed humps, hardly recognising the place. The darkness was almost absolute, broken only by an occasional lighted window, and all the twigs with garden centre labels on them that had dotted the open plan gardens were now luxuriant shrubs and trees. As my headlights swung around, probing the shadows, we saw that the conservatory salesman had done a roaring trade, and since my last visit the registration letters on the cars parked outside every house had progressed two places along the alphabet. Two houses, next to each other, had speedboats. Tony Silkstone had told us that his house, The Garth, was the last one on the right. "The one with the converted gas lamps along the drive," he'd added. Somebody's million-watt security light flicked on behind us, turning night into day.

The panda sent by Inspector Adey was parked outside The Garth. We'd radioed instructions for them to guard and contain the property until we arrived. I freewheeled to a standstill behind it, yanked the brake on and killed the lights as the two occupants opened their doors and stretched upright. "Got the key?" I asked the driver.

"Right here, Boss," he replied.

"Thanks. Hang around, we might need you."

The converted gas lamps were not switched on and a Suzuki Vitara stood on the drive, nose against the garage door. The house was in total darkness, although all the curtains were pulled back. Dave put the key in the Yale latch, turned it and pushed the door open. When Silkstone dashed out he hadn't locked the door deliberately; he'd just pulled it shut, or it had slammed behind him. Mr Yale had done the rest. So far, so good.

As we stepped inside a wind chime broke into song above our heads. "I could do without that," I hissed.

The feeble illumination from a digital clock was enough to tell us that we were in a kitchen, and it was a good deal larger than the last one we'd stood in. Edges of implements and utensils in chrome and stainless steel reflected its glow. Unblinking green and red pilot lights watched us, like animals in the jungle, wondering who the intruders were, and a refrigerator added a background hum.

I found a light switch and clicked it on. The shapes became Neff appliances and the jungle animals lost their menace. Dave handed me a rolled-up coverall and I started to pull it over my feet. I wasn't sure if it was necessary, but I was playing safe. Sometimes I cut corners, occasionally I'm reckless, but never where forensics are concerned. Hunches are no good in this game. A hunch never swayed a jury or earned the sympathy of a judge. Motive, opportunity, witnesses, forensic. They're what convict criminals, with the emphasis on the forensic. You can fudge the other three, but not the forensic. That's what I'd always believed, and, so far, it had done well for me. That was the received wisdom, as taught at Staff College.

We had a lot to learn.

"Close the door," I said, and Dave pushed it shut with an elbow. We pulled latex gloves on to our hands and eased our feet into over-socks. We didn't bother to pull the hoods over our heads. My mouth was dry and I could feel my heart banging against my ribs. The thrill of the chase had long since degenerated into the drudgery of killing, the sordidness of death. It always does. Apart from the occasional gangland shooting there's no such thing as a good murder. This wasn't a straightforward, cut-and-dried jealous husband killing any more; it was something squalid. A clock was ticking somewhere in the room, measuring each second with well-oiled precision.

"OK?"

"OK."

"C'mon, then."

The interior door opened on to a hallway. I wasn't there to admire the furnishings and look at the pictures – that would come later – but I couldn't help doing it. I switched the light on and absorbed the scene.

The Axminster carpet was covered in swirly patterns and felt as heavy as leaf mould under the feet. Facing us was an oil painting of a vaguely European city scene on a rainy day, churned out on a production line in Taiwan, hanging over an antique captain's desk that I'd have accepted as a week's salary anytime. The wallpaper was red, cream and gold stripes and a grandfather clock modelled on Westminster stood in a corner. Here, I thought, lived a man who knew what he liked. I found another switch and illuminated the staircase.

It's the boss's prerogative to lead the way. I climbed the stairs slowly, keeping well over to the left in case we needed to do a footprint check on them, and Dave followed. "Silkstone said first door on the right," he reminded me.

The door was open, and we could already see what we'd expected by the glow from the landing lights. I reached around the doorframe and found the bedroom switch, just to do the job properly.

She was lying face down on the bed and appeared to be naked below the waist. I stepped forward into the room and stooped beside her, looking into my second dead face that night. There was a pair of tights knotted round her neck, and the bulging eyes and pig's liver of a tongue lolling from her mouth confirmed that she'd died by throttling. I'd have preferred the knife in the heart, anytime. I scanned her body feeling like the worst sort of voyeur and noticed that she was, in fact, wearing a short skirt that had been pulled up around her waist. My eyes went into the routine, as they had done too many times in the past, and the questions popped up one by one like the indicators on an old-fashioned cash register: Signs of a struggle? Anything under the fingernails? Bruising or bleeding? Is this where the attack took place?

Dave was standing just outside the room, to one side, and I rejoined him. "Seen enough?" I asked, and he nodded. We stepped carefully down the stairs and retraced our path back out to my car. I rang Gilbert and told him the news. He'd contact the coroner and the pathologist and off we'd go again. We decided to get the SOCOs on the job immediately and leave everything else until after the morning meeting. Which was, I noticed, looking at the car clock, just six hours away.

"You didn't really want to live here, did you?" Dave asked as we sat waiting.

"It was just a thought," I replied.

"You wouldn't have been happy."

"I'm not happy now."

"Unhappy with money in the bank is better than unhappy skint," he replied.

"I suppose so."

"This'll bring the property prices down," he added, looking out of the window.

"That's a consolation."

The SOCO's white van came swaying round the corner, bouncing over the speed humps and triggering the big security light. "Looks like Michael Schumacher's on duty tonight," Dave observed as we opened our doors. I pointed to a spot behind me and the SOCO parked there and doused his lights.

He's young, fresh faced, and can still boogie 'til dawn then appear in court bright as a squirrel. "Hi, Mr Priest," he said, slamming the van door. "What's going on? Is it two-for-the-price-of-one night, or something?"

"First of all, it's Charlie," I told him. "Secondly, there are people in bed and I'd prefer them to stay there, and thirdly, don't be so bloody cheerful at this time in the morning." We told him what we'd found, and a few minutes later another patrol car came into the estate, followed by the other SOCO and the photographer. Bedroom lights came on in the neighbouring houses and curtains twitched. We were having an operational meeting, in hushed voices, when we heard a police siren in the distance, gradually growing louder. A minute later a traffic car, diverted off the motorway, careered round the corner and nearly took off over the humps. Somebody had dialled 999. I had words with the driver, persuaded him to turn his blue lights off, and sent him back to cruising the M62. A man from one of the houses joined us, saying he was chairman of the local Neighbourhood Watch, demanding to know what was going on. He wore a flying-officer moustache and a dressing gown over pyjamas. I ushered him to one side and asked him – "just between the two of us" – what he knew about the people who lived at The Garth, adding that I'd be very grateful if he could put it all in writing for me, before nine o'clock in the morning. He wandered off composing a hatchet job on the neighbour with the ghastly street lamps in his garden.

That was all we could do. Priorities were identification of the bodies and times and causes of death. These would be checked against Silkstone's story and we'd see if anything else we discovered supported or disputed the facts. If he were telling the truth the Crown Prosecution solicitors would decide the level of the charge against him; if he were lying I had a job on my hands.

We left the experts doing their stuff, with the uniformed boys outside to keep the ghouls at bay, and went home. Come daylight, we'd be back in force.

While I was addressing the troops about the killing of Peter Latham, young Jamie Walker was practising the new scam he'd learned at the detention centre. He'd strolled into a pub in the town centre, one he knew the layout of because they had no scruples about serving juveniles, and sidled his way towards the toilets, carefully avoiding being seen by the bar staff. When nobody was looking he'd slipped upstairs to the landlord's living quarters and rifled them. Pub landladies collect gold jewellery like some of us collect warm memories, and he made quite a haul. He escaped in a Mini taken from the car-park and celebrated by driving it through the town centre flat out. The traffic car that came to Silkstone's house had earlier chased young Jamie for a while, but he escaped by driving along the towpath. Two of our pandas spent the rest of the night driving from one reported sighting to another, without success. We know it was Jamie because he left fingerprints in the pub and in the mini, which he had to abandon before he could torch it.

I found all this out much later. When I arrived home I took off all my clothes, found a fresh set for next day and cleaned my teeth. I slipped under the duvet and closed my eyes.

The house Annabelle and I nearly bought was two along from Silkstone's, backing on to a rocky field that the estate agent called a paddock. It had a double garage that dominated the front aspect, with an archway over the path and a wrought iron gate. Inside were four bedrooms, two with *en suite* bathrooms, and a study. The downstairs rooms had dado rails and patio doors, and the next door neighbours were members of the National Trust. They introduced themselves, saying we'd be very happy there, and gave us some membership forms. Annabelle said they were sussing us out.

We could have been happy there. The house was warm and dry and airy, with decent views over the fells; and pissing-off the neighbours would have been no problem. We could have locked the doors and closed the curtains, and played her Mozart and my Dylan to our hearts' content. I'm sure we'd have been very happy there if we both hadn't been such bloody reverse snobs.

Today – no, yesterday – I pulled a carving knife out of a dead body, standing astride it as if I were harvesting carrots. Play the film in reverse and you'd see the knife going in, feeling its way between rib and cartilage, following the line of least resistance as it severed vein, nerve and muscle. A dagger in the heart doesn't kill you. It's not like an electrical short circuit that immediately blows a fuse and cuts off the power. Blood stops flowing, or pumps out into the body's cavities instead of following its normal well-ordered path, and the brain dies of starvation.

Today it was strangulation. A pair of tights knotted around the neck, stopping the flow of air and blood until, again, the brain dies. A pair of tights: aid to beauty; method of concealing identity favoured by blaggers; murder weapon. She had black hair and white skin, and may have been attractive, once. Before fear twisted her features and the ligature tightened, building up the pressure in her skull until her eyeballs and tongue tried to escape from it.

Murder doesn't come stalking its victim at night, skulking from shadow to shadow, whispering unheard threats. It comes in the afternoon, with the sun casting shadows on the wall and the curtains blowing in the breeze. It comes from familiar hands, that once were loving.

The collared doves that live in next door's apple tree were tuning up like a couple of novice viola players, and my blackbird was doing his scales prior to the morning concert. I got out of bed and staggered to the bathroom for a shower. I put on the clean clothes, brushed my hair and opened the curtains.

The sky was light, with Venus the palest speck on the horizon, not quite drained of its glow by the advancing sun. Above it was the disc of the moon, a duller blue than the sky, one edge dipped in cream. They hovered there like the last two reluctant guests to leave a party. I picked up the alarm clock and went downstairs to grab an hour's rest on the settee.

The night tec' was sitting at my desk when I arrived in the office, reading the morning paper. "Hi, Rodge, anything in about us?" I asked, slipping my jacket off.

"Morning, Charlie. No, not yet," he replied, moving out of my chair.

"Pity. I was hoping they'd have it sorted for us."

"You've had a busy night."

"Oh, just two murders," I replied. "Nothing special. And you?"

"Sex or money?"

"Sex. Sex all the way."

We only have one detective on duty through the night, in case the uniformed boys come across anything that requires a CID presence. He slid a typed report across to me, saying: "Jamie Walker. He was out causing grief again but we've got some dabs – I had to borrow a SOCO from City because ours were otherwise engaged. Hopefully, we'll pick him up today."

"And as soon as we put him in front of the mags they'll give him bail," I said. "God, I could do without him."

I told him to carry on looking after the stuff outside the murder enquiries, adding that we'd have them sorted as soon as the PM results came through to confirm what we already knew. He went home to breakfast with his wife, a nightshift staff nurse at the General, and I read his report. "Jamie Walker, aged fourteen, why do I hate you?" I said to myself as I slid it into the *Pending* tray.

The team, plus a few reinforcements from HQ CID, reassembled at eight in the small conference room and there were gasps of disbelief when Mr Wood told them about the developments. After his pep talk I split them into two groups and appointed two sets of control staff, as if the murders were separate enquiries, and sent the troops back out on to the streets. Priorities were the backgrounds of the three leading players and their relationships with each other. The neighbours would be given their opportunity to dish the dirt, so that might throw up something, and we needed the post-mortem results desperately. I told the Latham team to reconvene at three and the Silkstone team at four.

We could hold him in custody without charging him for twenty-four hours, and then ask for extensions, but we're supposed to charge a prisoner as soon as is practicable. We decided to do him for a Section 18 assault, that's GBH with intent, purely as a holding charge, and let the CPS lawyers decide at their leisure whether to go for murder or manslaughter. He appeared in front of a magistrate that morning and our man explained the seriousness of the offence. It's not necessary to present any evidence at this stage. The magistrate obligingly remanded Silkstone into our custody for seven days while we completed our enquiries. After that period he would appear again and hope-fully be committed to appear before the crown court at sometime in the remote future. We booked his solicitor, Prendergast, for eleven a.m., when the fun would begin.

Dave and I made a return visit to Silkstone's house at Mountain Meadows. The sun was shining after a shower as we turned into the development, and it looked good. Several of the gardens had weird trees with twisted branches and dangling fronds, like you see in Japanese watercolours, and pampas-grass was popular. There were two panda cars out-side The Garth and blue "keep out" tape stretched across the driveway.

The PC in charge showed me the visitors' book and entered our names in it. I saw that the undertakers had called at six a.m. to take the body away, and a reporter from the *Gazette* had been tipped off by a friendly neighbour. We stepped over the tape and walked down the drive.

It looked different in the daylight. Allowing for the Silkstones' crap taste, it looked highly desirable. Everything they had was expensive, top of the range, and they had everything. We stood in the kitchen, where we'd stood with such different feelings a few hours earlier, and took it all in. The wind chime gave a single, hollow, *boing* but I reached up and disabled it before it could run through its repertoire. There were Toulouse-Lautrec prints on the walls and a rope of garlic hanging behind the door.

"Not bad," Dave admitted. From him, that's an Oscar.

I sniffed the garlic, then felt it. "Plastic," I said. "No won-der it didn't work."

"Work?"

"It's supposed to keep evil at bay."

He looked at me without turning his head, and said: "Er, listen, Charlie. I wouldn't put that in your report if I were you. One or two people have been saying things about you, recently…"

The sitting room was a surprise. With its two leather chesterfields and dark wood it looked more like a gentlemen's club than a room in a suburban house. The fireplace was polished stone, complete with horse brasses, and a photograph of the householder took pride of place above it. A beaming Silkstone was standing next to a much taller and slightly embarrassed man who looked remarkably like Nigel Mansell, former World Formula 1 champion.

"He moves in fast company," I remarked.

"Golf tournament," Dave said, which was fairly obvious from the single gloves, silly trousers and the clubs they were leaning on. "Probably a charity do, or something."

"Right. What do you think of the room?" The carpet was plain blue and vertical blinds covered the windows. There were no flowers or frills, no Capo di Monte shepherd boys – *Alleluia* for that small mercy – and not a single pot plant. The wallpaper was blue and cream stripes, edged in gold, on all four walls.

"It's a bit austere," Dave remarked, turning round in a circle. He paused, then said: "The wife wanted me to put one of them up."

"One of what?"

He pointed. "A dildo rail."

I said: "It's called a dado rail," not sure if I'd fallen into a trap.

"Is it? I'm sure she said dildo."

"Maybe you misunderstood."

"Sounds like it."

"C'mon," I told him. "Let's go upstairs. That's where the story of Tony and Margaret begins and ends."

The path we'd pioneered the night before was designated with blue tape so we stayed with it, although it wasn't necessary. In the bedroom little adhesive squares with green arrows on them indicated items of interest that were invisible to my eyes. They were scattered randomly over the carpet near the bed, and concentrated around the disturbed surface of the duvet. Dave bent down and examined the area.

"Doesn't look like blood," he announced, straightening up.

"Other bodily fluids," I suggested. The SOCO had probably found spots and splashes by using an ultra violet lamp or Luminol spray.

Next door was the woman's room, all done in pink and lace, with a dressing table crowded with the things some ladies need to apply before they can face the world. She wore Obsession perfume and Janet Reger undies. A wedding photograph, similar in style to the one in Latham's room, stood on the dressing table but pushed to the back, behind all the jars and bottles and aerosols. It was lightly covered with powder either from her compact or left by the fingerprint experts. In it, Silkstone was wearing a morning suit and his wife a traditional white dress. They were a handsome couple and it was impossible to date this one, unlike Mr and Mrs Latham's.

The husband had his own room. It was furnished in a mock tartan material that looked pretty good and the bookcase was filled with coffee-table manuals about cars. We had classic cars, the world's fastest cars, the most expensive cars, Ferraris, Porsches, and so on. There were yearbooks about the Grands Prix going back about ten years and a collection of Pirelli and Michelin calendars for a similar period. They were all big glossy books, heavy on pictures, light on words.

I found his reading books on the bottom shelf. They were by people like Dale Carnegie and Mark McCormack, and had titles such as *How To Sell Crap To People Who Didn't Know They Needed It*; and *What To Do With That Second*

Million. When this is over, I thought, I could do worse than read one or two of these. Or perhaps even write one.

There was a framed photograph of Silkstone on the wall behind the bed, and another of Nigel Mansell, autographed, on the facing wall. Silkstone was posing beside a Mark II Jaguar and looked about twenty. It was a snapshot, blown up to poster size, and was badly focused, but the numberplate was legible. He had a faint blond fuzz on his head, like a peach, which for a young bloke was seriously bald. Dave joined me as I was staring at it.

"Not as nice as your Jag," he said.

"It's not, is it."

"Ever regret selling it?"

"Mmm, now and again." I turned to face the other picture. "What do you reckon to that one?" I asked.

"It's great. Our Daniel would love it." Daniel was his son, a couple of years younger than daughter Sophie.

"Why Mansell? He's not a gay icon, is he?"

"No, of course not. He's a happily married man."

"He has the moustache."

"So has Saddam Hussein."

"He *is* gay."

"Yeah, as gay as a tree full of parrots. Listen," Dave said. "Mansell was the greatest driver of his day, and lots of other days, because he was such a fierce competitor. He liked to win. At everything. That's why people like Silkstone look up to him. He's a winners' icon, not a gay one."

"Mmm, makes sense," I agreed.

Dave looked at his watch, saying: "It's time we were off."

The friendly neighbourhood spy had informed his contact at the *Gazette* that I was on the scene, and a reporter was waiting for us as we emerged from The Garth. She had spiky red hair, a ring through her nose and a bullish manner.

"Are you the investigating officer?" she demanded.

"Yes," I told her, resigning myself to making some sort of statement. "And just who are you?"

She rattled off one of those names that rhymes with itself, like Fay Day or Carrol Barrel, as if it were self-evident who she was and only a parochial fool like myself wouldn't know. This woman was ambitious, going places, and a small-town murder meant nothing more to her than a by-line. Next week she'd either be applying for Kate Adie's job or back on hospital radio. "And is the raid on this house related to the murder last evening at West Woods?" she asked.

News travels fast, I thought. I drew a big breath and launched myself into it: "We are investigating a suspicious death at a residence in the West Woods estate," I told her, "and have arrested a person. Our enquiries have brought us here, where we have found the body of a woman. At this point in the investigation we are not looking for anybody else. Our press office will release further information as and when it becomes available." I can reel out the cop-speak with the best of them, when I don't want to say what I'm thinking.

She couldn't believe her luck. "You mean there's still a body in there?" she demanded, her eyes gleaming.

"No," I said. "It was removed earlier this morning, for post-mortem examination. Now if you'll excuse me."

She produced a mobile phone – it was hanging on a thong around her neck – and called for a photographer, *House of Death* headlines buzzing through her head.

The PC on duty asked if I wanted the integrity of the scene maintaining and I said I did. We had a quick word with the house-to-house people, but they had no great revelations for us, and drove back to the nick.

On the way Dave said: "You're not happy with this, are you?"

"Just playing safe, Dave," I replied.

"What's the problem?"

"No problem. According to Silkstone, Latham killed his wife so he killed Latham. Motive – revenge. Taking into consideration the balance of his mind, and all that, he'd be done for manslaughter and could be free in a year."

"That's true," Dave said. "And if he was on remand for a year he could be released straight after the trial."

"But what if," I continued, "they were both in on it? What if they were both there when Mrs Silkstone died? That could mean a life sentence. This way, he's put all the blame on Latham, who is in no position to defend himself."

Dave thought about it, before saying: "You mean, they were having some sort of three-in-a-bed sex romp, and it all went wrong?"

I glanced sideways at him. "Do people do such things in Heckley?" I asked.

"Not to my knowledge," he replied.

"Maybe they were over enthusiastic," I suggested, "and she died. They invented some sort of story but Silkstone thought of a better one. He killed Latham and came to us."

"It's a possibility," Dave agreed.

"Alternatively," I began, exploring the possibilities, "perhaps Silkstone did them both, all alone and by himself. It'd be cheaper than a divorce."

"And tidier," Dave added.

"And possibly even profitable," I suggested. "That's something to look at."

"We're getting ahead of ourselves," Dave cautioned. "Let's wait for the DNA results." He was silent for the rest of the way. As we turned into the car-park he said: "The bloke's lost his wife, Charlie. Don't forget that."

"I know," I replied, adding: "I think I'll ask the professor to look at the crime scene, see what he thinks." The professor is the pathologist at Heckley General Hospital, and at that very moment he was turning his blade towards the fair skin of Mrs Margaret Silkstone, subject of our debate. I locked the car doors and we headed for the entrance.

There was a message from Annette waiting for me at the front desk. A neighbour had positively identified Peter Latham, who had died from a single knife wound to the heart. Time of death between three and six o'clock,

Wednesday afternoon. I passed it to Dave and asked if Prendergast had arrived yet. He was locked in the cell with his client, I learned, discussing strategies, defences and tactics. The truth was outside his remit.

"'Ello, Mr Priest," a squeaky voice said, behind me. I spun round and faced two traffic cops straight in the eye. They were wearing standard-issue Velcro moustaches and don't-do-that expressions, but neither had a ventriloquist's dummy sitting on his arm. I tilted my gaze downwards forty-five degrees and met that of a grubby angel standing between them.

"Jamie!" I exclaimed, treading an uneasy path between disapproval and surprise. "What are you doing here?"

"Bin invited in to 'elp you wiv enquiries, 'aven't I?" he replied.

"And can you 'elp – help – us?"

"Nah. Don't know nowt about it, do I?"

"Well do your best." I turned back to the desk, but he said: "'Ere, Mr Priest. Is it right you used to 'ave a knee-type Jag?"

"That's right," I told him. "A red one."

"Cor!" he replied. "Best car on t'road."

They took him away to feed him on bacon sandwiches while he fed them a pack of lies, and we arranged to interview Silkstone in ten minutes. I went to the bog and washed my face. There was a mounting pile of reports on my desk, but they'd have to wait. I always read them all, but on every murder enquiry we have a dedicated report reader who siphons off the important stuff. I like to read all the irrelevant details, too: the minutiae of the lives of the people who pass through our hands. Sometimes, they tell me things. As Confucius say, wisdom comes through knowledge.

Prendergast was wearing a blue suit and maroon tie, and could have been about to deliver a budget speech. He didn't. He launched straight into the attack by complaining about our treatment of his client, who was, he reminded us, traumatised by the sudden and violent death of the woman he loved.

I apologised if we had appeared insensitive, but reminded them that Mr Silkstone had, by his own admission, killed a man and we were conducting a murder enquiry. We'd collect some of his own clothes for him, I promised, as soon as the crime scene was released, and I told him that his wife's body had been taken to the mortuary. We needed Silkstone to formally identify the body later, and he agreed.

"Will he be taken there in handcuffs, Inspector?" Prendergast asked.

"As Mr Silkstone surrendered himself voluntarily I don't think that will be necessary," I conceded. I must be getting soft.

The preliminary fencing over, we started asking questions. Silkstone stuck to his story, saying that he'd come home to see Latham leaving his house. Inside, he'd found Margaret lying on the bed with a ligature around her neck. He'd attempted to remove it, but quickly realised that she was dead. The rest was a bit vague, he claimed. It always is. He agreed that he must have followed Latham home and gone in the house after him. He suddenly found himself standing in the kitchen, with Latham's body lying on the floor, between his feet. There was a knife sticking out of Latham's chest, and on the worktop there was one of those wooden blocks with several other knives lodged in it. He did not dispute that he stabbed Latham, but claimed to have no memory of the actual deed.

When he realised the enormity of what he'd done he sat in the front room for a while – about ten minutes, he thought – then dialled 999. Prendergast made sympathetic noises about the state of his client's mind and suggested that Unlawful Killing might be an appropriate charge.

"Do you think there was any sort of relationship between your wife and Latham?" I asked, and Silkstone's shrug suggested that it was a possibility. The tape doesn't pick up shrugs, but I let it go. "Could you explain, please," I asked.

He stubbed his cigarette in the tin ashtray and left the butt there with the other three he'd had. Only prisoners are allowed to smoke in the nick. "I wondered if they were having an affair," he said. He thought about his words for a while, then added: "Or perhaps Peter – Latham – wanted to start one, and Margaret didn't. Last week, last Wednesday, I went home early and he was there, talking to her. He said he'd just called in for a coffee, and she said the same. But there was a strained air, if you follow me. They seemed embarrassed that I caught them together. Maybe, you know, he was trying it on."

"How well did Margaret know him?" I asked, adding: "Officially, so to speak."

"Quite well," he replied. "We – that's Peter and I – married two sisters, back in 1975, and he came to work for me. Neither marriage lasted long, but we stayed friends."

"What line of work are you in?"

"I'm Northern Manager of Trans Global Finance, and Peter is – was – one of my sales executives."

"Wasn't he working yesterday?"

"No. He often sees clients at weekends, when it's convenient for them, and takes a day off through the week."

"Is it usually Wednesday?"

"Yes, it is."

"And Margaret? Did she work?"

"For me. TGF is heavily into e-commerce, and Margaret acted as my secretary, working from home."

"E-commerce?" I queried, vaguely knowing what he meant.

"Electronic commerce."

"In other words, your company doesn't have a huge office block somewhere."

"That's right, Inspector. We have very small premises, just an office and a typist, in Halifax and various other towns. Our HQ is in Docklands, but that's quite modest. Our parent company resides in Geneva."

I exhaled, puffing my cheeks out, and tapped the desk with my pencil. Dave took it as his cue and came in with: "Mr Silkstone, you said that Latham was at your house the previous Wednesday, when you arrived home early."

"Yes." He reached into his pocket and removed a Benson and Hedges packet.

"What time was that?" Dave asked.

"About four o'clock. Perhaps a few minutes earlier."

"Was it unusual for you to come home at that time?"

"Yes. Very unusual."

"So Latham could have been there the week before, and the week before that, and you wouldn't have known."

He lit a cigarette with a gold lighter borrowed from his brief and took a deep draw on it. "Yes," he mumbled, exhaling down his nose. There were four of us in the tiny interview room and three of us were passively smoking the equivalent of twenty a day, thanks to Silkstone. The atmosphere in there would have given a Greenpeace activist apoplexy. Carcinogenic condensates were coagulating on the walls, evil little particulates furring-up the light fittings. What they were doing to our tubes I preferred not to imagine but I vowed to sue him if I contracted anything.

"But yesterday you came home early again," Dave stated.

Good on yer, mate, I thought, as our prisoner sucked his cheeks in and felt round the inside of his mouth with his tongue.

"That's true," Silkstone admitted.

"Twice in eight days. Very unusual, wouldn't you say?"

"Gentlemen," Prendergast interrupted. "My client is senior management with an international company. His hours are flexible, not governed by the necessity to watch a clock. He works a sixty-hour week and takes time off when he can. I'm sure you can imagine the routine."

"But still unusual," Dave insisted.

"He's right," Silkstone agreed, talking to his lawyer. Turning to Dave he added: "Last week I wasn't feeling very well, so I skipped my last appointment and came home early. It wasn't business, just calling on one of my staff for a pep talk. Yesterday –" he shrugged his shoulders. "I finished early and went home. That's all."

Dave stroked his chin for a few seconds before asking: "Are you sure that's all?"

Prendergast jumped in again, saying this speculation was leading nowhere, like any good lawyer would have done. What he meant was that if his client went home early because he thought he might catch his wife in bed with her lover, we could tell the court that his actions were premeditated. And that meant murder.

Silkstone moved as if to stub the cigarette out, realised it was only half smoked and took another drag on it. "I don't know," he replied, ignoring his brief's protestations. "I've been wondering that myself. Did I expect to find them together again? Is that why I left the afternoon free? You know, subconsciously. I don't think I did. I loved my wife, trusted her, and she loved me. If I'd really expected to catch them together I'd have returned home even earlier, wouldn't I?" He took another long draw on the cigarette while we pondered on his question. "Truth is," he continued, "I've been worrying about the old ticker a bit, lately. Decided to cut my workload. That's why I came home early."

Which, I thought, was a good point. I quizzed him about how he'd felt as he drove to Latham's house; how he gained entry; about the knife and any conversation he had with Latham. It was a waste of time. Everything was obscured by the thick red mist of convenient memory loss. There's a lot more of it about than you'd ever believe, especially among murder suspects. "Interview terminated," I said, looking up at the clock and reading off the time. Dave reached out and stopped the tape.

"Your case papers will be sent to the crown prosecutors," I told Silkstone, "who will determine the level of charge against you. Assuming the results of the forensic tests validate what you say they may decide to go for a charge of manslaughter. If not, I shall be pressing for a murder charge. You will be committed for trial at crown court and we shall be applying for you to be remanded in custody until then. Is there anything you wish to ask me?"

Silkstone shook his head. Prendergast said: "I have explained the procedure to my client, Inspector. We will be making our own clinical and psychiatric reports and demand full access to any forensic procedures that are being undertaken. It goes without saying that we will be applying for bail."

"You do that," I replied, sliding my chair back and standing up.

We grabbed a bacon sandwich in the canteen and drove to Latham's house on the West Wood estate. There are no trees at the West Woods, because the landscape around Heckley does not suit them. The ground is rocky, the winters harsh and the sheep omnivorous. Archaeologists following the builders' excavators found remnants of a forest in the patch of peat bog they were building on, and an imaginative sales person did the rest. There is no North, South or East Wood.

We wandered around his home from room to room, looking in drawers, feeling through the pockets of his suits, like a couple of vultures picking over a carcass. Wilbur Smith's *Elephant Song* was lying on a shelf within reach of his easy chair, with a bookmark at about the halfway point. In the smallest bedroom, filled with junk, there was a big bag of fishing rods and a box of tackle. I hadn't marked him as a fisherman.

On his fridge-freezer door, held in place by a magnetic Bart Simpson, was a postcard showing a painting that I recognised. I eased it off and looked at the back, but it was blank. "Gauguin," I said, flapping the card towards Dave.

"You'd know," he replied.

I replaced it exactly where I'd found it and opened the

fridge door. He ate ready meals from the supermarket, supplemented with oven chips, and was seriously deficient in vegetables.

"He didn't eat properly," I said.

"You'd know," Dave repeated.

I was drawn, as always, to the bedroom. I was sitting on the edge of the bed, looking at the two photographs, when Dave joined me.

"Who do you reckon she is?" I asked.

He looked at the picture of the young girl without handling it. "Mmm, interesting," he mused. "Taken a while ago. Could be his wife, assuming that's them in the other picture. Is it, er, a bit on the salacious side, or is that just me?"

"It's just you," I told him, untruthfully.

"I don't think it's a daughter or niece," he continued.

"Why not?"

"Well, I wouldn't frame a similar picture of our Sophie and have it on display, and she'd certainly have something to say about it if I did. I reckon it's his wife, when she was at school. They keep it there for a laugh, or a bit of extra stimulation. I don't know, you're the one with all the experience. I'm just a happily married man."

"The SOCO reckons it was taken about the same time as the wedding photo," I said, "which means it's not the wife."

"Fair enough," he replied, adding: "Maybe all will be revealed at the meeting, when we learn something about his background."

"Let's hope so," I said. We left, locking the door behind us, and told the PC on duty that we still wanted the crime scene maintaining.

In the car Dave said: "That photo."

"Mmm."

"Of the young girl."

"Mmm."

"Maybe it's just a curio type of thing. The sort of picture you might pick up at a car boot sale, or something. Know what I mean?"

"I think so," I said. "A collector's item. Like some dirty old Victorian might have drooled over."

"Yeah. Voluptuous innocence and all that crap."

"Lewis Carroll and Alice," I suggested.

"Exactly. He used to photograph children in the nude, you know."

"Crikey," I said. "So where did he keep his spare films?"

We'd told the Latham team to assemble at three, but the Mrs Silkstone investigators were there too, keen to learn the big picture. Annette and Iqbar were sitting in the front row, and she passed me a foolscap sheet of the PM findings. That was what I'd wanted most of all. I perused it as everybody found seats and joshed with each other. The small conference room doubles as a lecture theatre, and is equipped with all the usual paraphernalia like overhead projectors and CCTV. At one minute to three I picked up the wooden pointing stick and rattled it against the floor, calling out: "OK, boys and girls, let's have some order."

As the hubbub died down Mr Wood entered the room. "Keeping them entertained, Charlie?" he said.

"Just doing a few quick impressions, Boss," I replied.

"I see. Any chance of you impersonating a police officer for the rest of the day?" He has a vicious tongue, at times.

Gilbert told the troops that HQ had sanctioned their overtime payments, which is what they wanted to hear, and thanked them for their efforts before handing over to me. I started by adding my appreciation for their work. A murder enquiry is always disruptive to the private lives of the investigators, as well as the principal characters. "This is a double murder enquiry," I told them, "and the eyes of the world are upon us, so it's important that we show them what we can do. As always, you have responded to the challenge, and we are grateful." I outlined the bare bones of the case, and then asked about the identity of the first body.

Inspector Adey said: "First body confirmed to be that of Peter John Latham. We contacted his ex-wife – he's a divorcee – who lives in Pontefract. She was reluctant to come over to ID him because she has young children, and showed little interest in knowing when the funeral might be. Eventually we asked a neighbour, Mrs Watson, who was friendly with him, and she positively identified him."

"Any other next of kin?" I asked.

"His mother in Chippenham, if she's still alive. She vacated her last known address to move into a nursing home, but we're trying to find her."

"Thanks Gareth. We might as well do the other one now," I said. "Any volunteers?"

A uniformed constable raised his hand and uncoiled from his chair. He'd taken Mr Silkstone to the mortuary at the General Hospital, he told us, where Silkstone had positively identified the body of a woman as being that of his wife, Margaret. I thanked him and he sat down.

"Was he suitably grief stricken?" I asked him.

"Yes sir."

Gareth Adey rose to his feet, saying: "Point of order, Mr Priest."

I was expecting it. Asking a murderer to identify an associated body was a trifle unusual, if not bizarre. "Yes, Gareth," I said.

"Do you not think, Mr Priest," he waffled, "that we might be leaving ourselves open to criticism by inviting the accused to ID a body allegedly murdered by the victim of his revenge killing?"

"Good point, Gareth," I told him. "We need a second opinion. Could I leave that with you, and I'd be grateful if you'd do the usual with next of kin."

He smiled contentedly and sat down.

"Cause of death," I said, pointing to Annette.

She was wearing jeans and a white blouse, her jacket draped over the back of the chair. She stood up, unsmiling, and brushed her hair off her face. "Peter Latham was killed by a single knife-wound to the heart," she told us. "The knife found in him would be identical to the one missing from the set in his kitchen. The blade entered his chest between the fifth and sixth ribs on an upward trajectory, puncturing the left ventricle. This indicates an underhand blow from someone of approximately the same height. Latham was only a hundred and sixty-eight centimetres tall. That's five feet six inches. The blade missed the ribs and unusual force would not be required."

"Time of death?" I asked.

"Between three and six p.m.," Annette replied.

"We can narrow that down," I declared. "Silkstone rang nine-double-nine at seventeen ten hours, saying he'd done it. Let's call it between three and five." Doc Evans had said between four and five, I remembered, and he was on the scene quite quickly. The professor was working from a cold cadaver, sixteen hours after the event. "On second thoughts, make it between four and five," I told them. Sometimes, knowing the precise time of death can be crucial.

Annette had taken her seat again, but I said: "Go on, Annette, you might as well tell us about the other one."

She rose, brushing the offending hair aside, and launched straight into it. She was a young attractive woman, one of only four in a room with thirty men, and I wondered if I'd been fair, sending her to the post-mortems. She said: "Margaret Silkstone died as a result of strangulation. There was a pair of tights knotted around her throat but there was also bruising caused by manual strangulation, apparently from behind. She'd recently had anal and vaginal intercourse, and semen samples have been recovered and sent for analysis."

"How recently," I asked.

"At about the time of death," she replied. "The professor's preliminary conclusions are that vaginal intercourse took place before death, and anal possibly after, but he wants to do a more considered examination."

"And when was the time of death?"

"Between two and six p.m."

"Right. Thanks for doing the gory stuff, Annette," I told her. "I appreciate it."

She gave me the briefest of smiles and sat down. After that I invited the team to let us know what they had discovered about the background of the deceased.

They all came from Gloucestershire. Silkstone had been a big wheel in a company based in Burdon Manor, variously known as Burdon Home Improvements, Burdon Engineering and Burdon Developments; and Latham was one of his salesmen. Back in 1975 they'd married two sisters but neither marriage had lasted. When the receiver finally pulled the plug on Burdons, Silkstone went to work for the now-defunct Oriental Bank of Commerce, or OBC, a name that sent a chill up the spine of every financial manager in the world. Now he was Northern big-cheese for a company called Trans Global Finance, and had been married to the late Margaret for ten years. Silkstone had five speeding convictions and two for careless driving. Latham had one for OPL and Margaret was clean.

"So now," I told the throng of eager, upturned faces, "you know all about them. Any questions?"

"Yes Sir," someone said. "Will you have the DNA results tomorrow?"

"No. Saturday," I replied.

There was nothing else, so I terminated the meeting. Someone brewed up in the big office and I carried a mug of tea into my little den in the corner. I opened an A2 drawing pad and divided the sheet into several boxes. Dave came in, followed by Annette. In Box 1 I wrote:

Silkstone telling truth. Latham killed Margaret,
then Silkstone killed Latham, in a rage.

"What next?" I asked.

"Three in a bed romp," Dave suggested. In Box 2 I wrote:

Sex game gone wrong. Latham and Silkstone killed
Margaret. Silkstone killed Latham to cover his tracks.

"Hmm, that's interesting," Annette said.

"Charlie's idea," Dave told her. "I don't know about such things. What next?"

In Box 3 I wrote:

Margaret and Latham having an affair.
Silkstone killed them both in a jealous rage.

Dave said: "I reckon that's the obvious explanation."

"It's the favourite," I agreed, "but how about this?" I wrote:

All a plot by Silkstone

and numbered it Box 4.

"What, like, cold blooded?" Dave asked. "You think he planned it all?"

"I don't think that. We just have to consider it. What if Silkstone killed Margaret for personal reasons and threw the blame on Latham? The whole thing might be a pack of lies. We need to know if he gains financially in any way." I turned to Annette. "That's a little job for you, Annette. Find out if he had her insured. How much do they owe on the house and will the insurance company pay out for her death, if you follow me?"

"You mean, if they had a joint life policy," she replied.

"Do I?"

"She's a clever girl," Dave said.

Annette picked up her still steaming mug of tea and walked out. I gazed at the door she'd closed behind her and said to it: "I didn't mean right now!"

I wrote M, O and F in each box, meaning motive, opportunity and forensic, and ticked them where appropriate. I didn't bother with W for witnesses, because the only one we had was Silkstone himself. "That's as far as we can go, Sunshine," I declared, "until we get some results from the lab and find out who spread his seed all over the crime scene." The phone rang before I could put cornices on all the capital letters and generally titivate the chart. It was the professor, replying to the message I'd left for him earlier in the day.

"It's The Garth, Mountain Meadows," I told him.

"What, no number?"

"No, but there's only seven houses."

"Pretentious twats. I'll see you there at five. You can have half an hour."

"Great, Prof. I appreciate it."

Annette came in as I was replacing the phone. I looked at her, bemused by the rapid departure and return. She said: "Silkstone paid nearly two hundred thousand for the house, and still owes over a hundred and fifty K on it. And yes, the mortgage is insured joint life, first death, so if he didn't kill Margaret himself they'll have to pay out."

It took me a few seconds to speak. Eventually I asked: "How did you find all this so quickly?"

"I went down and asked him," she replied, smiling. "Took him a cup of tea. It's not secret information. As he said, joint life is fairly standard practice, not necessarily sinister, but yes, he does come in for a handy payout."

"Told you she was a clever girl," Dave declared. He drained his mug, adding: "I'll leave you to it; there's work to be done."

When he'd gone Annette said: "And I've had a word with the Met. Asked them to contact the head office of Trans Global Finance just to confirm things."

"Brilliant, we'll make a detective of you yet." I told her about the call from the prof., and as Dave had vanished I suggested she come along with me to hear what he had to say. She seemed pleased to be asked, and went off to do her paperwork.

At twenty to five I gathered up a set of photographs of the Mountain Meadows crime scene, plus my new chart of possible scenarios, and let Annette drive us there in her yellow Fiat. The professor arrived at about five past. He greeted

Annette like a long-lost relative, then said: "Right, let's get on with it."

I laid out a set of photographs on the worktop in the kitchen, telling him what we'd found but not passing any opinions nor making any speculations. The professor nodded and sniffed a few times, peering at the photos through his half-spectacles, and asked to be shown the bedroom.

The bed was made up with a duvet in a floral pattern, but still bore the impression of the action that had taken place there, highlighted by the SOCO's little arrows. In the twenty-four hours since the killing the smell of neglect had pervaded the room. The cocktail of perfumes: her make-up, somebody's sweat and other fluids, flowed uneasily through the nostrils. I breathed through my mouth to avoid it. We had a preliminary report from the scientific boys, saying what had been found where, but no definitive DNA evidence to say from whom it all came. The professor examined the sites marked by the arrows, checking with the report after each one.

"We'll leave you to it," I said, and led Annette downstairs. It was the first time she'd been in the house and her eyes scanned everything, sweeping over the furniture, pausing to examine the decorations more closely. Partly, I supposed, from the professional point of view, partly as a woman in another woman's house. "Have a good look round," I invited, seating myself on a leather settee that was as hard as a park bench.

A coffee table book about Jaguar cars was propped in an alcove adjoining the fireplace. I reached for it and flipped through until I found the E-type. They'd photographed a red one, same as mine, from low down at the front. I'm not a car person, but the E-type was special and I felt a pang of regret for selling it.

"I had one like that," I said to Annette as she returned, holding the double-page spread open for her to see.

"What? An E-type?" she exclaimed, smiling wider than

I'd ever seen her.

"Mmm."

"Cor! I wish I'd known you then."

"Everybody said it was a good bird-puller."

"And was it?"

I smiled at the memories. "I suppose so. My dad bought it as a pile of scrap and restored it. When he died it came to me."

"I'm sorry," Annette said, sitting in an easy chair.

"Sorry?"

"About your dad. He was a policeman, wasn't he?"

"That's right. A sergeant at Heckley. He was a nice man."

"Yes, I can imagine." She stood up abruptly and walked over to the window. I watched her, wanting to join her there. It would have been the most natural thing in the world to slip my hand around her waist and stand with her, looking out over the garden. It might also have earned me a knee in the groin. Her hair was tied in a wild bundle behind her head. Difficult to manage, I thought, and smiled. "What's the verdict on the house?" I asked.

Annette turned to face me. Her cheeks were pink. "This house?"

"Mmm."

"The house is OK. Not sure about the occupants."

"I really meant the occupants."

"Right. The place speaks volumes about them. I'd say they were well off, but lacking in taste. He's a control freak, hasn't grown up yet. What sort of man…"

The professor was clomping down the stairs and Annette stopped speaking. He came into the room with a worried expression on his face, which meant nothing because his features were set that way. Anybody's would be, with his job. He pulled his spectacles off, wiped his eyes with a big white handkerchief, and flopped onto the other Chesterfield. It flinched slightly and creaked under his weight.

"Fancy a coffee, Prof.?" I asked.

Annette said: "I'll make us…"

"No, no," the professor insisted, flapping a hand. "Kind of you, but I'd rather not. Too busy."

"Right. So what can you tell us?"

"Not a great deal," he began. "Without the DNA results we're barking into the dark somewhat. She was killed on the bed, either during or just after sexual intercourse; and that's about it. You can definitely rule out her being killed elsewhere."

"One man or two?"

"Dunno. The lab should be able to tell us, though."

"Up to the point of death, was she a willing participant?"

"Good question. Apparently so, or to put it another way, she wasn't dragged kicking and screaming into the room. That doesn't mean that there wasn't some duress applied."

"Like, at knifepoint, for example?"

"Yes. Precisely."

I turned to my new partner. She was definitely more attractive than Sparky, but I didn't know how she'd be in a fistfight. "Anything, Annette?" I asked.

"Yes," she began. "From your earlier examinations, Professor, and what you've seen here, could you say if any violence was used during the acts of intercourse?"

"The actual penetration, you mean?"

"Er, yes."

"Difficult to interpret. Yes, entry was quite violent, but one man's – or woman's – violence is another's big turn-on. It was rough intercourse, but I cannot interpret the victim's feelings about that."

"How rough?" I asked.

"Some damage to the mucous membranes, but not excessively so."

"Both ends?"

"More so in the anus, but that's quite usual."

I spread my chart on the arm of the settee and explained it to the professor. We all agreed that what he had determined at the house fitted perfectly with Silkstone's story but I argued that it could also support the sex romp theory.

"Did you find any other supportive evidence?" the professor asked.

"Such as?"

"Well, for instance, did you find any pornography? Sex aids? Bondage paraphernalia? That sort of thing."

"No," I reluctantly admitted.

"Then I'd say it was unlikely."

My pet theory had just prised the bars open and escaped. "Unless the DNA tests show that they were both there," I argued.

"I suppose so," the professor said, in a tone that suggested I shouldn't hold my breath.

"How about Silkstone killing them both in a jealous rage?" I suggested, tapping Box 3 with the blunt end of my pen. "That's probably what we would have concluded had it not been for his admissions."

"Ye-es, I'd wondered about that," the professor replied, "but I'm not sure that what I've seen validates it. Force was undoubtedly used against Mrs Silkstone, but she wasn't knocked about and there are few signs of a struggle. There's no bruising to her face, but her arms bear evidence of being tightly gripped. It was a controlled force, in my opinion, by someone who knew exactly what he was doing."

"Was she a willing partner, in the sex?"

"Willing? Probably not. Reluctant, I'd say. She certainly didn't fight for her life until she had no chance."

"Are you suggesting that the motive for the assault was rape, pure and simple," I asked, "and killing her was an afterthought?"

"It's a possibility," he agreed, "although I'm not sure about the pure and simple. Assaults of this nature are not necessarily for sexual gratification – they're about inflicting humiliation on the victim. Which, I suppose, when you think about it, enhances the gratification. He's a control freak, likes to dominate – that's what stimulates him. I'm rambling a bit, Charlie. That side of it is not my field, thank goodness, I'm just the plumber."

I pointed to the fourth box on my chart. "And then there's the possibility that Silkstone orchestrated the whole thing," I said. "He killed them both but put the blame for Margaret on to Latham. That way he comes out of it with a fairly hefty financial gain."

The professor pursed his lips, deep in thought. He has a face like a dessicated cowpat, but always looks as fresh and clean as a newly bathed baby. His talcum smelled of roses or some other garden flowers. "It'd be a bugger to prove, Charlie," he concluded. "Let's wait and see what the DNA says, eh?"

We thanked the prof. and drove away in silence. I wasn't equipped to have a meaningful conversation with an attractive woman about the merits of rough sex, so I kept my thoughts to myself, but Annette had no such inhibitions. "Why do men – some men – want to do that?" she asked.

"Um, do what?" I enquired.

"Inflict humiliation. Why isn't the sex act enough in itself?"

"Good question," I said, stalling for time. "It's probably something deep in our psyche, in our genes."

"You mean all men are like that?"

"Well, um, I wouldn't say all men. I don't know, perhaps we are. At a very subconscious level. Most of us have never recognised it in ourselves, but it's probably in there, somewhere."

"Really?" She twisted in her seat to face me and nearly drove into the kerb.

"Put it like this," I said, checking my seatbelt. "Most men, I'm sure you know, find a woman in her underwear sexier than a woman in a bikini. Why do you think that is?"

"No idea. It's a mystery to me."

"Well, most men wouldn't know, either, if you asked

them. But it could be because a woman in her underwear is at a disadvantage. You've caught her partially dressed. However, the same woman in a bikini is fully dressed and completely in charge of the situation."

"Gosh! I'd never have thought of that."

"Whereas most men," I pronounced, holding my hands aloft, "rarely think of anything else."

There was a pub called the Anglers Rest about half a mile down the road, with an A-board outside saying that they did two-for-the-price-of-one meals before six o' clock. We'd missed that, but it reminded me that I was starving.

"Are you hungry?" I asked.

"Ravishing," Annette replied, and giggled.

"I can see that," I told her. "I asked if you were hungry."

"Mmm. Quite."

"Fancy a Chinese?"

She looked across at me. "Yes. That sounds like a good idea." Her cheeks were pink again.

"Take us to the Bamboo Curtain then, please," I suggested, and settled back into the seat feeling uncommonly content. Things were moving along quite nicely, and the enquiry wasn't going too badly, either.

I ate with chopsticks, to show how sophisticated I am, and we drank Czech beer, which I insisted in pouring into glasses. A glass is essential if you want to experience the full flavour of the drink. Itsy-bitsy sips from the bottle are a waste of time. I insisted on Annette doing several comparisons, and she politely conceded that I might have had a point. Drinking from the bottle, I told her, is an affectation encouraged by the brewing industry to save them the trouble and expense of washing glasses, that's all. Apart from that, the bottles have been stored for months outside some warehouse, and the security man's dog probably cocked its leg over them several times each night as they did their rounds. She smiled and humoured me.

Women in the police have a hard time. Be one of the lads

and you get a reputation as a slapper; stay aloof from all that and you're a lesbian. Times are changing and a new breed of intelligent, confident women are coming into the service, but old attitudes take a long time to be pensioned off. I like working with women, and they make good detectives. Traditionally we've always given them the jobs with an emotional content – child abuse, rape, that sort of thing – but they can be surprisingly hard at times. Harder than a man. Stereotypes and prejudices, I thought. The more you work at them, the deeper the hole you dig for yourself.

As far as anyone knew Annette had never been out with another copper, so the inevitable whispers had gone round the locker room. I'm as guilty as all the rest, and wouldn't have been surprised to learn they were true. Disappointed, but not surprised. We talked about the case, the job and the E-type, but steered clear of personal chat. We'd both considered teaching when we were younger. I had a degree in Art and she had one in Physics.

"A proper degree," I declared, sharing out the last of the beer.

"That's right," she agreed across the top of her glass, holding my gaze.

Mr Ho, the proprietor, brought me the customary pot of green tea, on the house, and I asked him for the bill. Annette produced a tenner and slid it across to me.

"Is that enough?" she asked.

"It's OK," I said. "I'll get these."

"No, I'd rather pay my way," she insisted. Men handle these things much better than women. Any of the male DCs would have said: "Cheers, I'll get them next time," but they wouldn't have spent all evening analysing my every word, waiting for the boss to proposition them.

"I'll arm wrestle you for it," I said.

"Please?"

"If you insist." I reached for the note and put another with it. "That's a one pound sixty tip," I said. "Alright with you?"

"Yes."

"Good."

It was a short drive back to the station, where my car was parked. No opportunity for an invitation in for coffee there. She parked the Fiat behind my Ford, without stopping the engine. Eyes would be upon us from within the building.

"That was very pleasant, Annette," I told her, opening the door.

"Yes, it was. Thank you," she replied.

They say the moon was formed when another planet strayed close to the fledgling Earth and its gravity tore a great chunk from us. I know the feeling. The car door was open, beckoning, and this beautiful lady was eighteen inches away, her face turned to me, her perfume playing havoc with my senses. I felt lost, pulled apart. Salome was dancing, but was it for me or was I in for the chop?

Just a kiss. That's all I wanted. Just a kiss. A simple token of affection after a harrowing day. No harm in that, is there? The scientists don't know it, but there's one force out there in the universe far more powerful than gravity. It's called rejection. I wrenched myself away, saying: "See you in the morning."

"Yes," she replied. "See you in the morning. Boss."

Chapter Five

It was no big deal. I drove home and collected the mail from behind the door. Six items, all junk. I put the kettle on and hung my jacket in the hallway. It wasn't nine o' clock yet but I was tired and felt like going to bed. There'd be no red faces in the office tomorrow, no mumbled apologies as we crossed paths in the corridor. We'd be able to continue working together as a team, and that was a big consolation.

I had loosely promised myself to clean the microwave oven tonight, but it could wait. There'd been a slight accident with an exploding chicken Kiev at the weekend, and the kitchen stunk of garlic, but I couldn't face pulling on another pair of rubber gloves and setting to work with the aerosol of nitric acid, or whatever it was I'd bought for the job. I was sure it said *self-cleaning* when I bought the oven, but it isn't. You just can't believe anything these days.

I made a pot of tea – more tea – and settled down with Dylan on the turntable, unaware of the fiasco being enacted in the town centre. *Last night I danced with a stranger, but she just reminded me you are the one.* Spot on, Bob. Spot on.

Dick Lane stretches down to the canal in a part of the town that has been heavily redeveloped. Legend has it that the street gets its name from a worker in the woollen industry who could carry bigger bales of wool than anybody else. Twenty-five stones, or some other mind-boggling figure. More mischievous sources say the name is derived from the row of cast-iron posts that runs across the end of the street. A now defunct Methodist church stands on the corner, and the posts were possibly placed there to deter the carters from taking a short cut to the loading wharves. They were erected by the minister of the day, and it is hard to believe that the foundry that moulded them was not having a joke at his expense, for the posts look remarkably like huge, rampant male members. The developers wanted to remove them, but the council, in its wisdom, slapped a preservation order on them. Dick Lane still has its dicks.

More important than all that is the fact that the posts are exactly sixty-four inches apart. There's no known reason, practical or mystical, for this. Nobody has come up with the theory that it's the distance between the Sphinx's eyes, or the exact width of the Mark IV Blenkinsop loom. It probably just looked about right to the bloke who installed them, nearly two hundred years ago.

At about half past eight young Jamie Walker, now on the run, stole a Ford Fiesta; his favourite car. The owner saw him drive off in it and phoned the police. He was a known drugs user and pedlar on the Sylvan Fields estate and demanded to know what we were doing about the theft of his only means of continuing in business. Control circulated the description, filed a report and went back to the *Sun* crossword. Ten minutes later one of the patrol cars, conveniently parked in the town centre where they could ogle the talent making its way to the various pubs, saw a green Fiesta with a white bonnet and red passenger door tearing the wrong way through the pedestrian precinct. It was Jamie. They did a seven-point turn and gave chase.

The rules of engagement say follow the target vehicle until the driver is well aware that you require him to stop. Then, if he continues to flee, drop back but try to remain in visual contact until assistance can be organised. The patrol car, siren and lights a-go-go, positively identified the registration number and was backing off when Jamie turned into Dick Lane.

"Gorrim!" declared the driver of the patrol car.

Jamie's Ford Fiesta was sixty-three inches wide, which gave him a clearance of half an inch each side as he slotted it neatly between the posts at the bottom of Dick Lane. That's an ample margin when you are escaping arrest, in somebody else's vehicle. He wiped the wing mirrors off, but he never used them anyway. The pursuing officers saw the Fiesta slow to a crawl and make a right turn on to the towpath, towards freedom.

What was actually said between the driver and his observer is open to speculation, as their stories conflicted at the resulting enquiry. What is known is that: a) They decided to continue the chase; and b) A Ford Escort of the type they were driving is sixty-six inches wide. The iron posts neatly redesigned the front wings of the police car, in a process known to engineers as extrusion, and then held it fast. Alpha Foxtrot Zero Three juddered to a standstill with the posts jammed solid halfway along its front doors.

The advent of closed circuit television has been, it is generally agreed, a wondrous breakthrough in the policing of town centres. Tonight it was to prove a curse. Two very large police officers trying to extricate themselves through the rear doors of a fairly small car makes very good television. The CCTV cameras recorded the build-up and several local yuppies with palm-sized Sonys committed the rest of the story to magnetic tape in much greater detail, negotiating contracts with Reuters and Associated Press via their mobile phones even as they filmed.

After doing some much-needed tidying in the kitchen I made myself a peanut butter, honey and banana sandwich and ate it in the bath, accompanied by Rachmaninov's *Piano Concerto number 2* played very loud on the CD. It's not one of my favourites, but it includes the *Brief Encounter* music, which amused me. I dried myself and fell into bed feeling reasonably wound down considering the day I'd had, totally oblivious of Jamie's latest exploits.

"Boss wants you. *Now*," I was told as I passed the front desk early Friday morning.

"What's he doing in at this time?"

"Don't ask."

I ran straight up the stairs to Mr Wood's office on the top

floor. First thought in my head was that Silkstone had topped himself in the cells.

"Morning, Gilbert," I said, after knocking and walking in. "You're in early."

"You haven't seen it then?" he asked without returning my greeting.

"Seen what?"

"Breakfast TV."

"I'd rather fart drawing pins. What's happened?"

"Watch this."

He went over to the monitor on another desk and pressed a few buttons. After a snowstorm of blank tape a well-polished couple with colour-coordinated hair flickered into view. I stayed silent, not knowing what to expect, but it was looking like a Martian invasion at the very least. The Chosen Two shared a joke which we couldn't hear because the sound was off and the picture changed to black and white.

"That's Heckley," I said, recognising the scene. "Down near the canal."

"Dick Lane," Gilbert stated.

"That's right."

A car jerked towards the camera in ten yard steps, like an early movie. The clock in the bottom right-hand corner said 2123.

"Driven by Jamie Walker," Gilbert informed me.

"Oh," I replied. "Last night?"

"Mmm."

There were some posts across the end of the street. The car – it looked like a Fiesta – was stopped by the camera as it reached them and in the next frame it was through and bits were flying off it. It exited to the left, narrowly avoiding falling into the canal, and another car jumped into the top of the picture.

"Watch," Gilbert ordered.

"One of ours?"

"Alpha Foxtrot Zero Three."

"Who up?"

"Lockwood and Stiles."

Jim Lockwood and Martin Stiles were first on the scene when we arrested Tony Silkstone. I felt uneasy, expecting their car to go into the water and drown them both, or roll over and burst into flames. All it did was get stuck between the posts. The coloured picture came back on, with the Golden Couple laughing just enough not to ruffle their coiffures or flake their make-up. I tried to stifle a giggle, but failed.

"You've got to laugh, Gilbert," I chuckled.

"What's so funny about it?" he demanded.

"It just is."

"We're a bloody laughing stock! It won't be funny when the Chief Constable sees it, I'll tell you that."

"Yeah, you're right," I admitted. "Nobody was hurt, that's the main thing. I was expecting to see someone hurt. What's happening?"

"I'm having them in at nine o'clock. I'll have to ground them, Charlie. And the car's probably a write-off. Jamie-fucking-Walker! I'd like to take the little scrote and...and ...oh, what's the point?"

"Who's investigating it?" I asked. He told me the name of a chief inspector from HQ who I hardly knew.

The super was right: it wasn't funny. Wrecking a police car is a serious matter. Lockwood and Stiles would be taken off driving while a senior officer made preliminary enquiries. It was back to the beat for them. If he'd committed a prosecutable offence it could be the end of the driver's career. "Were this a member of the public would further action be taken?" was the question that the investigating officer would be asking. Meanwhile, we'd lost the use of two men and a car.

"The point is, Charlie," Gilbert said, "we need young Jamie in custody. Number one priority, everybody on it.

Right?"

"I *am* conducting a double murder enquiry," I reminded him.

"Forget it. Get Jamie. Anyhow, it's all sewn up, isn't it?"

"Everybody seems to think so except me. I've got my doubts."

"Here we go again!" he complained, putting his hands on his head. "Listen, Charlie: Silkstone's confessed; Latham did the other. It all makes sense, no loose ends. Put it to bed, for God's sake, and concentrate on getting Jamie. We're going to be asked some searching questions about that young man before this is over, mark my words, so let's have him in. Understood?"

"If you say so."

"I do."

I said: "Fourteen years old, top of our Most Wanted list. Not bad, eh? He'll be dining out on that for the rest of his life, if anybody tells him."

"He'll be dining out in Bentley Prison maximum security unit for the rest of his life if I can help it," Gilbert responded. "Just...*find him*."

We had an informal meeting in the office and I wound down the murder enquiry until Monday. Even the smallest investigation soon develops branches until it looks like some ancient tree, every fork representing a Yes and a No answer to a simple question. "Did you know your wife was having an affair, Sir?" Go left for Yes, right for No. This one was no exception, but we'd have the DNA results in the morning and that would enable us to do some drastic pruning. Then, hopefully, we'd be able to file the whole thing until the wheels of justice came to rest against the double yellow lines of Her Majesty's Crown Court, or something. I handed the Jamie Walker case over to Jeff Caton, one of my DSs, and gave him full control of all the troops. What more could be done?

Annette went off to find Jamie's mother. I was hoping to have a quick word with Annette when nobody else was around, just: "Hello, how's things?" to maintain the momentum, but it didn't work out. She was wearing jeans with a scarlet blouse and looked breathtaking. Sparky came in as I eyed the pile of paper in my in-tray.

"I'm off looking for Jamie's mates," he said. "Anything you want to know before I go?"

"No, I don't think so," I replied. "I'll have a go at this lot and then start on a submission to the CPS."

"What are you doing over the weekend?"

"Housework, and coming here in the morning. Why?"

"I just wondered. You're not…you know…?"

"I'm not what?" I demanded.

"You're not, you know, taking Annette out?"

"No, I'm not. Whatever gave you that idea?"

"Nothing. I just thought you might be."

"Is that why you rather pointedly left us alone together yesterday?"

"Just trying to help an old mate."

"Well don't bother, thank you. Never get involved with a colleague, Dave. That's my motto."

"She's an attractive woman."

"Yes, I had noticed."

"And she obviously fancies you like mad."

"Does she? That's news to me."

"Because you're blind. So you're free on Saturday night?"

"Sadly, as a bird."

"Right," he said. "Sophie finished her A-levels yesterday, and says she's happy with the way they went, so we're taking her for a celebratory steak. And, of course, they say it wouldn't be the same without you. Can't think why."

"Oh, that's brilliant," I declared. "Well done Sophie. Is she in? I'll give her a ring."

"No, she's gone into Leeds with her mum. I heard Harvey Nicks mentioned, so it could cost me. All she has to do now is get the grades, then it's Cambridge, here we come. The kid's worked hard, Charlie. Harder than I ever have."

"I know. And think of the pressure, too."

"Well, we've never pressurised her. Encouraged her, but win or lose, we don't mind as long as she's happy. So shall I put you down for a T-bone?"

"You bet."

"And, er, will you be bringing a friend?"

"A friend? No, I don't think so," I replied.

"But you'll come?"

"Try stopping me."

"Why don't you ask Annette? You might be surprised."

"Wouldn't that make Sophie jealous?" I joked. She had a crush on me when she was younger, but I imagined she was long grown out of it. Now she'd see me for the old fogey I really was.

"No, not really. I told her about your prostate problems and she went off you. Oh, and I told her that you bought your clothes at Greenwoods. That clinched it."

"Thanks. Greenwoods do some very nice jackets."

"So will it be steak for one or two?"

"One please."

"Go on, ask her."

"I'll see."

"OK."

He went off to find his villains and I thought about Sophie. My previous girlfriend was called Annabelle, and she and Sophie became good friends. Sophie copied her style and mannerisms, even to the point of calling me by my Sunday name, Charles. I smiled at the memories. And soon she'd be off to Cambridge.

The internal phone rang. "Priest," I said into it.

"Just letting you know that the Deputy Chief Constable has arrived, Charlie," the desk sergeant informed me in a stage whisper.

"Thanks," I said. "In that case, I'm off."

I went down the back stairs and into the main office. Every major crime has an appointed exhibits officer and a connected property store, which in this case was a drawer in a filing cabinet. It's essential that a log is kept of every piece of evidence, accounting for all its movements and recording the names of everyone who has had access to it. There's no point in telling the court that a knife had fingerprints on it if the defence can suggest – just suggest – that the defendant may have handled it after he was arrested. I didn't want the knife, just the keys to Silkstone's house. I said a silent apology to Gilbert for leaving him in the clutches of the DCC and drove back to Mountain Meadows.

The panda cars and the blue tape had gone and the street had resumed its air of respectability. The Yellow Pages delivery man had done his rounds and the latest edition was sitting on the front step of several houses, neatly defining who was at home and who wasn't. I'd had Silkstone's Audi taken from Latham's house to our garage for forensic examination, so there was plenty of room for me to park on the drive alongside the Suzuki. I picked up the directory and let myself in.

First job was a coffee. They drank Kenco instant, although there was a selection of beans from Columbia and Kenya. I watched the kettle as it boiled and carried my drink – weak, black and unsweetened – through into the lounge. I sat on the chesterfield and imagined I was at home.

It was a difficult exercise. This was the most uncomfortable room I'd ever been in, outside the legal system. The furnishings were good quality, expensive, but everything was hard-edged and solid. No cushions or fabrics to soften things. Focal point of the room was a Sony widescreen television set big enough to depict some of TV's smaller performers almost life-size. I shuddered at the thought. After about ten minutes the wallpaper started dancing and weaving before my eyes, like a Bridget Riley painting. I stood up and went exploring.

There was a toilet downstairs, a bathroom upstairs with a bath shower and rowing machine, and one *en suite* with the room where we'd found Mrs Silkstone. A room under the stairs with a sloping ceiling was their office, where a Viglen computer and seventeen-inch monitor stood on an L-shaped desk. I sat in the leather executive chair and opened the first drawer.

An hour later I was in the kitchen again. I examined all the messages on the pin board and made a note of several phone numbers. The cupboard under the sink was a surprise: there was still some room in it. I spread a newspaper – the *Express* – on the floor, emptied their swing bin on to it and poked around in the tea bags and muesli shrapnel like I'd seen TV cops do. Then I went outside, dragged the dustbin into the garage and did it again, big time.

I washed my hands and had another coffee, sitting in the captain's chair at the head of their dining room table. It was all mahogany in there, with more striped wallpaper. The only picture on the walls was a limited edition signed print of Damon Hill winning the British Grand Prix. Number fifty-six of eight million. His room again, I thought.

I had a pee in the downstairs loo. It was the standard type, like the one in my 1960s house. I pulled the lever and watched the water splash about and subside. I'd have thought that a house as modern as this one would have had those low-level ones, where you watch everything swirling around, convinced it will never all go down that little hole. Personal preference, I supposed. I might even have chosen the same ones myself. I went upstairs into the master bed-room and, lo and behold, the *en suite* bog was the modern type, in coral pink. I did a comparison flush and decided that maybe these were better after all, but it wasn't a convincing victory. Just for the record I looked in the main bathroom. Old type, in stark white. Flushed first time, like the others. I didn't write any of this in my notebook.

I sat in one of the hard leather chairs for half an hour,

thinking about things. I enjoy being alone with my thoughts, and the seat was more comfortable than I expected. You had to sit well back and upright, but it wasn't too bad. Probably good for the posture, I thought. Next time I saw Silkstone I'd check his posture. A brandy and a cigar would have gone down well, or perhaps a decent port.

Jim Lockwood and Martin Stiles were coming out of the front door as I arrived back at the nick. Jim was wearing a suit and tie, Martin a short-sleeved shirt and jeans. They looked worried men.

"How'd it go?" I asked.

"He's sacked us," Martin blurted out.

"We're suspended," Jim explained.

"He can't sack you," I replied.

"He wants us sacked," Martin declared.

I looked at Jim. "Yeah," he confirmed. "He made that clear. Mr Wood tried to stand up for us, but the DCC went 'airless. Said we'd made a mock'ry of the force, and all that. It was on TV again this morning, apparently."

"Well he can't sack you," I repeated. "You know that. And next time you're in for an interview make sure you have the Federation rep with you. Don't let them two-one you."

"Right, Mr Priest," Martin replied.

"Meanwhile," I flapped a hand at the sky, "make the best of the decent weather. Paint the outside of the house, or something. It'll be a nine-day wonder, you'll see."

"Thanks, Boss," Jim said, and they skulked away like two schoolboys caught peeing off the bike shed roof.

I made a pot of tea – all that coffee makes you thirsty – and ate the M & S cheese and pickle sandwich I'd bought on the way back. The lab at Wetherton confirmed that I'd have the DNA results tomorrow, but otherwise they had nothing to tell me. I rang the CPS and agreed to a meeting with them on Monday afternoon.

The hooligans down in the briefing room had a recording of the Dick Lane Massacre and were delighted to show it to me. It was worse than I expected. Some local chancer had recorded the whole thing on his camcorder and networked it. He took up the story as Jim and Martin were trying to extricate themselves from the jammed car. Unable to climb into the back, they eventually reclined their seats and crawled out of the rear doors on hands and knees. It wasn't a picture of noble policemen fighting crime against impossible odds with courage and dignity. It was a fourteen-year-old twocker making two fully-grown cops look complete pillocks. The only good thing was that Jamie wasn't named. That would have made a folk-hero of him. Jim and Martin's so-called colleagues jeered and catcalled throughout the showing, relieved they weren't the subjects of such ridicule.

"If the car had caught fire and they'd been burnt to cinders, we'd be saying they were heroes," I said. I stomped back upstairs, wondering if that was the reason why I hated Jamie Walker.

The troops filtered back, empty handed. Dave called into my office and asked if I'd had a report on the DNA.

"Tomorrow," I replied. "You know they said tomorrow."

"Just thought you might have rung them and asked."

"I did. They still said tomorrow. What about you? Find anything?"

"Nah. Waste of time. His mates think he might be in Manchester, but the little toe-rag's screwing a bird from the Sylvan Fields, so they say he won't stay away long."

"Video games and sex," I said. "Kids today have it all."

"What did we have?" Dave asked. "Train spotting and snowball fights. Makes yer fink, do'n it?"

"Do'n it just."

"I called at this house in the Sylvan Fields estate," he said, "and there was this great big Alsatian in the garden, barking an' slavering. A woman was leaning out of an upstairs window and she shouted: 'It won't hurt you, love. Just kick its balls for it.' So I went in and kicked it in the balls and it ran away yelping and the woman shouted down: 'No, not them!

Its rubber balls that it plays with.'"

I laughed, against my wishes, and said: "You'd think they'd learn, wouldn't you?"

Annette knocked and came in, just as Dave said: "Well, I'd better report to Jeff. Hi, Annette."

"Hello Dave," she replied, holding the door for him. "Find anything?"

"Mmm. Ronald Biggs did the Great Train Robbery. Nothing on Jamie, though."

"Perhaps he's hiding in Brazil," she said.

"Could be. See you."

Dave went and I waved towards the spare chair. She sat in it and crossed her ankles. Her jacket was tweed, what might have been called a sports coat or hacking jacket a few years ago, and her blouse spilled from the sleeves and unbuttoned front in splashes of colour. She looked carelessly dishy, with extra mayonnaise.

"Hard day?" I asked.

"Waste of time," she replied. "Running about after a will o' the wisp. Word is that he's gone to Manchester. When he was in care his best pal was a youth from there called Bernie, so all we have to do is track down all the Bernards who were in care at the same time as our Jamie. Methinks he'll resurface long before then."

"Methinks you're right," I agreed. She was wearing a ring on the third finger of her right hand. A delicate gold one with a tiny diamond. Wrong hand, I thought.

"So," Annette began, "I was just wondering if anything had come through from Wetherton about the samples?"

"No, they said tomorrow," I told her.

"Oh. I thought you might not be able to resist giving them a ring and asking if they'd found anything."

"I couldn't," I admitted, "but they haven't. We should have the full report at about ten in the morning."

"Right."

She uncrossed her ankles, as if to stand up and leave. I

said: "Thanks for coming with me last night, Annette. It was nice to have some company for a change."

"I enjoyed it," she replied. "Thanks for inviting me." She smiled one of her little ones, barely a movement of the corners of her mouth, but her cheeks flushed slightly.

"As a matter of fact," I went on, "tomorrow night I'm going to the Steakhouse with Dave and his family. It's a bit of a celebration. If you're not doing anything I'd love for you to come along."

"Saturday?" she asked.

"Mmm."

"No, I'm sorry, I can't make it."

"Oh, never mind. His daughter has just finished her A-levels, and she's been accepted for Cambridge if she gets the grades, so we're taking her out. They do good steaks there. That's the Steakhouse, not Cambridge. I think she needs two As and a B. Sophie's my goddaughter. And other stuff, if you're not a steak eater." I waffled away. See if I care.

"Sophie?" Annette asked. "Dave's daughter Sophie?"

"Yes. Have you met her?"

"Of course I have. She used to come on the walks."

"That's right, she did. You'd just joined us. I used to wonder what you kept in that great big rucksack you carried."

"Did you?"

"Yes."

She stood up, saying: "Remember me to Sophie, please, Boss, and give her my congratulations."

I pulled a pained face and said: "Annette. Could you please call me Charlie once in a while? Everybody else does. I shan't read anything into it, honestly. It just helps maintain the team spirit. That's all."

She sat down again, and this time the smile was fulsome. "Sorry," she said. "Charlie."

"That's better. I hope you have a good weekend. If you ring me I'll tell you the results of the tests."

"Oh, I'll come here first, in the morning," she asserted.

"You've no need to, if you're going away. Anywhere special?"

"Um, York, to a friend's, that's all. I'll come here first, for the results."

"If you say so."

She went off to report to Jeff about Jamie's movements, leaving a faint, tantalising reminder of her presence in my office. Annabelle came on some of the walks we'd organised, and the two of them had surely met. Annabelle – Annette, I thought, Annette – Annabelle. A man would have to be careful with two names like that, in a passionate situation. Not that one was ever likely to arise. I wondered about the mystery friend in York and growled at the next person to come into the office.

The forecast for the weekend was good so I told the troops that we'd have a meeting about the murders on Monday. Most of them said they'd pop in Saturday morning, for the results. I still do a few paintings, when the mood takes me or someone commissions one. I only charge for materials. Mr Ho at the Bamboo Curtain had asked for one, for on his staircase, so I decided to make a start on it. It was going to be six feet by four feet six inches, abstract but with a Chinese theme. On the way home I called in the library and borrowed a book on Chinese art.

I had a trout for tea, with microwave oven chips and peas. Not bad. Chinese art is big on impossible cliffs and bonsai trees. I hinted at a few terracotta warriors and coolie hats, for the human touch, and a couple of tanks to show where the power lay. By midnight I'd done the underpainting and it was looking good. What a way to spend Friday night, but better than cleaning the oven. The next part, laying on the colour straight out of the tubes, was the best bit. Therapeutic. I had a shower and went to bed.

I couldn't sleep. Maybe it was the trout, maybe it was the enquiry. If the DNA results were as expected we'd have that

sewn up tomorrow, so no problem there. Maybe I was thinking about the sad life I was drifting into. Maybe I was thinking about a woman. Maybe I should set it to music.

I listened to the World Service for a while, then switched
to the local station. There'd been a bad accident on the
Heckley bypass, something about a jack-knifed lorry, and
traffic disruption was expected to last into the morning. Six
o'clock I went downstairs and made some tea.

I was lying on the settee using the remote control to pick
out my favourite tracks on *The Bootleg Series* when the
phone rang, right in the middle of *Blind Willie McTell*.
Anybody who interrupts *Blind Willie* had better have a good
reason.

It was the night tec'. "Sorry to ring you at this time,
Charlie," he began.

"No problem, Rodger." He doesn't telephone me lightly
and his voice was strained. "What've you got?"

"There's been a bad RTA on the bypass."

"I know. I'm up and heard it on the radio. What happened?"

"Head on, between a Mini and a milk tanker. The Mini's
jammed underneath."

"God, that sounds nasty." I visualised the carnage. "How
many in the Mini?"

"Just one, as far as we can tell. I'm pretty sure it's Jamie
Walker."

I didn't speak for a while. "You still there, Charlie?"
Rodger asked.

"Yeah, I'm still here," I replied. "Dead, I assume?"

"Instantly."

"Was he being chased?"

"No. We didn't even know he was in the area."

"Thank God for that. You got some help?"

"Everybody and his dog's here. Just thought you'd like to
know."

"Right. Thanks for ringing, Rodge, and stay with it, please."

Jamie Walker, aged fourteen, wouldn't be stealing any more cars, and our figures would resume their steady downward path after the recent hiatus. Jamie Walker, who I hated, was eliminated from the equation. I had cornflakes and toast for breakfast and went into the garage to look at the painting. It looked as good as I remembered. At seven, because I couldn't think of anything else to do, I drove to the nick.

By the time the troops arrived at our office on the first floor they'd all heard about Jamie. It was mainly smiles all round, because Jamie had killed himself. All too often it's someone completely innocent who pays the price. Rodger came in, looking completely shagged out, and told us the details. Jamie had come round a bend on the wrong side of the road and hit the tanker at a combined speed of about a hundred and ten. The tanker driver was unhurt but in hospital under sedation.

"He'd stolen the Mini from the bloke who lives next door to where he was staying," Rodger told us. "This bloke works for a security firm, on about eighty quid a week. He has two daughters who are asthmatic, and he runs the car so he can take them to the coast every weekend. Someone told him sea air would do them good. Don't ask me to weep for Jamie Walker, because I can't. Good riddance to the little bastard, I say."

"Go home, Rodger," I said. "You've had a tough night. Take whatever it is that makes you sleep and snuggle up to your Rosie." But I doubted if there'd be any sleep for him today, or tomorrow, or even the next day. He walked away, jacket slung over his shoulder, and we looked at our watches, waiting for the mail to arrive.

Gilbert rang from home, asking for news, and I promised to let him know as soon as we had anything. Annette came in, wearing a shortish skirt and high heels, which was unusual. Her working clothes are practical, and she only wears a skirt for court appearances. I gave her a wink and was rewarded with a smile. At five past ten a traffic car arrived, with the report. I opened the envelope and read the resume that preceded the detailed stuff.

"What does it say?" someone asked.

"Wait," I told them, reading.

"They close at four," someone complained.

"Shurrup!"

"Sorry."

"That's all right. OK, it's as we expected." I handed the report to Annette, who was sitting directly in front of me. "The semen samples are all from Peter Latham. Hairs were found in the bed from all three of them."

"Which isn't surprising, as it was Silkstone's bed," Dave told us.

"Pubic hair, in this case, I presume," someone added.

"Yes," I agreed, "It does say that." They started chattering between themselves, so I hushed them, saying: "There is just one more thing." When they were silent I told them: "According to the lab, traces of a spermicidal lubricant, as used on condoms, were also found in Mrs Silkstone. That's something for us to think about."

"In where? Does it say?" someone asked.

"Not sure," I replied, looking at Annette. She thumbed through the pages, there were about ten, scanning each briefly as she shook her hair away from her face.

"Can you find it?"

"Yes, it's here. It says: 'Traces of a spermicidal lubricant, of a type commonly used on condoms, were found in the anus and rectum.'"

"Does it say if any was found on Latham's dick?"

Annette turned the pages back, looking for the information.

"Is it there?"

"Yes, I think this is it." She studied the report for a few seconds then read out aloud: "A spermicidal lubricant of a similar type as that found in the female body was found on the subject's penis."

I thanked her, saying to the rest of them: "If any of you has a theory about how all this came about, I'll treat the information in the strictest confidence. Meanwhile, we'll prepare a condensed version and do the necessary. Any questions that won't wait until Monday?"

Nobody had one, so I thanked them for coming in and telephoned Gilbert.

"So Silkstone's story holds water," he concluded, when I finished.

"It looks like it," I admitted.

"Good. Let's have it sewn up, then. And young Walker won't be causing us any more trouble, I hear."

"Unless his mother sues us for not arresting him."

"Bah! Bloody likely, too. But we'll cross that bridge when we come to it. Meanwhile, I'm off for an hour's fishing. Fancy coming, Charlie? Do you good."

"No thanks, Gilbert. Sticking a hook through a small creature's nose is not my idea of entertainment."

"You wouldn't catch anything!" Gilbert retorted. "What makes you think you'd catch anything?"

"I meant the maggots," I replied. "Maggots have feelings, too."

I would have fallen hopelessly, crazily, desperately in love with Sophie as soon as I saw her, except that I already was. She was wearing a blue silk dress and her hair was piled up in a sophisticated style that I'd never seen her wear before. "You look sensational," I said, pecking her on the cheek. "Cambridge won't know what's hit them."

"She's gonna be a spy," her younger brother, Daniel, informed me. "That's where they train them all."

"Well that's better than being a traitor," she retorted, referring to Danny's ambition to play football for Manchester United and not Halifax Town.

We went in my car. I'd have to drive home afterwards, so this meant that Dave could have a few drinks. His wife,

Shirley, said: "Hey, this is all right, being chauffeured about by the boss."

"Let's get one thing clear," I told her as we set off. "Tonight I am taking my favourite goddaughter out for a meal. You three are just hangers-on."

"I'm your only goddaughter, Uncle Charles," Sophie reminded me, and her brother jumped straight in with: "You don't think you'd be his favourite if there was another, do you?"

"It's going to be one of those evenings," Shirley remarked.

I'd made a bit of an effort with my appearance, for once, and was glad I had. Blue jacket with a black check, black trousers, blue shirt and contrasting tie. Dark clothes suit me and add to that air of mystery. I'd even put some aftershave on.

"You look handsome tonight," Shirley had told me when I arrived. "Dave said you might bring a friend."

"He speak with forked tongue," I'd replied.

"Annette Brown. He reckons she has the hots for you. She's a lovely girl."

"Tomorrow, he die." I explained that she wasn't my type; I didn't want to be involved with another officer and as far as I knew she was already in a perfectly happy relationship.

"So you asked her."

"I didn't say that!"

Four of us had fillet steak and Dave had the speciality mixed grill, which includes a steak and just about every other bovine organ known to science. Two bottles of a Banrock Shiraz helped it down quite nicely. We talked about Jamie Walker and the Silkstone case, without being too explicit, and I had my favourite apple pie for pudding. I asked Sophie why she'd chosen Cambridge and not Oxford, and she said: "Everybody goes to Oxford."

We had more coffee back at their house and sat talking until midnight, when the kids went to bed. Dave fell asleep on the settee, snoring with his mouth wide open, which I took as a good time to leave. It was a warm evening, and Shirley walked out to the car with me.

"Thanks for inviting me, Shirley," I said. "It was considerate of you."

"You're part of the family, Charlie," she replied. "You were married to Dave before I was."

"Well, I wouldn't have put it quite like that, but I appreciate it."

At the gate I said: "He was quiet tonight. Not his usual self."

"No," she replied, "he wasn't, was he?"

"Has the Jamie Walker business upset him?"

"A little, perhaps. Daniel was that age not too long ago, but I think it's mainly because of Sophie."

"Sophie?"

"Mmm. Going to university, leaving the nest and all that. If it's not Cambridge it will be somewhere else. She's just finished with her first boyfriend, but there'll be more. Danny was always my son, but Sophie is Dave's daughter, and he's losing her. It hurts. You worry about them, Charlie. The temptations, the pressures, the mistakes they'll make. You want to live their lives for them, but you can't. You have to step back and let them do it their way, and sometimes it's painful."

"It's called love," I told her.

"Yes, it is."

We kissed cheeks and said goodnight.

At home I cleaned my teeth and hung up my clothes. I poured a glass of the plonk that was open, to catch up with the others, put Vaughan Williams on the CD and went to bed with the curtains open, so I could watch the clouds drifting past the window, like the backdrop of a silent movie. There was a new moon, and it and Thomas Tallis gave magic to the night. The wine and my thoughts probably helped.

But there's a dark side to the moon, and clouds are fickle.

New faces came to me, pushing aside the ones I cherished. Young Jamie Walker was dead, and I didn't care. His death had lifted a weight off me, eased the tourniquet that tightened around my spleen whenever I'd heard his name. Monday morning someone would come out with a Jamie Walker joke – "What does Jamie Walker have on his cornflakes?" – and I'd laugh with the rest of them. I didn't hate him for being a thief. I didn't hate him for the grief and misery he caused people who were as poorly off as he was. I didn't give a shit about our crime figures. I hated him for making me not care about his death. For doing that to me, I could never forgive him.

Sunday I gave the microwave a wash and brush-up. The fine spell was holding and the weather forecasters were predicting a good summer because the swallows were flying high and the grasshoppers were wearing Ray-Bans. I went to the garden centre to buy some new blades for the hover mower and had to park in the next field. Forget banks, knock-off a garden centre.

In the evening I watched a video about the space race that Daniel had loaned me. Apparently the USA bagged Mars first, so Russia decided to concentrate on Venus. They didn't know until they sent the first probe there that the atmosphere was comprised largely of sulphuric acid. As my mother used to say; "There's always someone worse off than yourself." Danny is envious that his dad's generation witnessed the moon landings, as they happened. To him it's just another event in history, like World War II or the Battle of Hastings. I'm eternally grateful to the Americans for taking a television camera on the trip. OK, they did it for self-publicity, because they needed public approval for all that expenditure, but it was a brave thing to do. It could have all gone dreadfully wrong.

I have a photograph of Daniel and Sophie, standing alongside my old E-type. It was taken at Heckley Gala a couple of summers ago, after we'd taken part in the grand cavalcade, and published in the *Heckley Gazette*. I knew roughly where it was and soon found it. Sophie was all legs, posing elegantly with one hand on the car door, and Danny was wearing his trade-mark grin. The photo was in black and white, ten by eight, and slightly over-exposed. I turned it over and looked at the *Gazette's* rubber stamp mark on the back. The copyright was theirs and a serial number was written in ink in the appropriate box. The date space was empty. I propped it against the clock and wondered about framing it.

Margaret Silkstone had consenting sex with Peter Latham on her marital bed. He wore a condom initially but removed it later. A disagreement arose between them and he strangled her. That was about as much as we could be sure of.

"Maybe she objected to him removing the condom," Gilbert suggested.

"Or to his, er, sexual proclivities," the CPS lawyer said, adding, "putting it another way, she didn't want it up her bum."

"Why does other people's love-making always sound so bloody sordid?" I asked.

"Because you're not getting any," Gilbert stated.

"*Putting it another way!* I like that," the lawyer chuckled. He was young and bulky, in a charcoal suit that bulged and gaped like the wrapping of a badly made, slightly leaky, parcel. Prendergast would eat him for breakfast, but he was the best we had. I looked at him and wondered who the anonymous genius was who coined the phrase *big girl's blouse*.

"Whichever it was," Gilbert stated, "we'll never know. But it does look as if Peter Latham murdered Margaret Silkstone. All agreed?"

"Yes, I think we can be certain about that," the lawyer replied.

Gilbert was looking at me over his spectacles, defying me to launch into a conspiracy theory. "Yep, the evidence points that way," I concurred.

"Good. Now what about Tony Silkstone?"

"We have one witness, namely Silkstone himself, and some forensic," the lawyer told us, "and all the forensic indicates that he is telling the truth. Have you anything to the contrary, Mr Priest?"

I shook my head. "Nope."

"So we go for manslaughter."

"Except I don't believe it," I said.

"What you believe, Charlie," Gilbert snapped, "is neither here nor there. It's evidence that sways a court."

"Evidence," I repeated. "*Evidence*. I wish I'd known that. I'd have brought some along."

"What makes you think it's murder?" the lawyer asked.

For murder we needed to prove a degree of premeditation, or an intention to kill. Silkstone had almost admitted that he thought his wife might be having an affair, during that first interview when he was trying to show us what a forthright fellow he was, but his brief would have soon made him aware of that folly. I thought about him, images from the little I knew about the man lining up for inspection and moving on as the next one popped up. All that surfaced was that he had a photograph of Nigel Mansell on his wall. Hardly damning. "Nothing," I replied. "Let's go for manslaughter."

"Oppose bail?" the lawyer asked.

"Definitely," I insisted, as if the alternative were unthinkable.

"On what grounds?"

Bail is rarely granted in murder cases, but is fairly common for manslaughter. The accused has to show the court that he is unlikely to abscond, interfere with the course of justice or commit another crime. As Silkstone had a clean record up to now, was in gainful employment and could reside in the area once we had deemed his house no longer a crime scene, he'd probably be granted it.

"Psychiatric reports," I said. "He's pleading some sort of

mental aberration, red mist and all that rubbish. Of a temporary nature, of course, from which he has now miraculously recovered. We need to show that either he never had it or it's still there. I don't mind which."

"Our expert witness will be a registrar from the General on a flat fee," the lawyer told me. "His will be a whiz kid from Harley Street who lights his cigars with ten-pound notes." His tie had little Mickey Mouses on it, and a faded patch where he'd removed a stain.

"But Silkstone has killed someone," I said. "Sticking a knife in somebody's heart takes a lot of explaining away. They'll let him out eventually, but let's hold him for as long as we can."

The lawyer agreed and said he'd do his best. I felt sorry for him, but not as sorry as I felt for Margaret Silkstone.

"So?" Dave asked when I arrived back in the office.

"Manslaughter," I told him. "As we expected."

"Fair enough," he replied.

"It's not fair enough if he planned the whole thing," I retorted. "Involuntary manslaughter and he could be out in a year. He might not even go to jail at all."

"But Latham was shagging his wife," Dave stated.

"Oh, so that makes it OK, does it? What law's this, Sparkington's law?"

"You know what I mean."

"No I don't."

"Mc-whatsit made the laws. What does he say about it?"

"The McNaughton Rules? He says that to establish a defence against murder they have to prove that the defendant was off his trolley, which they probably can do. He came home and found his wife dead in bed, murdered and raped by one of his employees. It's strong stuff, if that's what happened. I think we'd best resign ourselves to calling this a double clean-up and get on with keeping the streets safe."

"Everybody else is happy with that, Charlie. You're the one wanting to make a meal of it."

"Yeah, well," I said.

I went downstairs to find the custody officer. He was in the briefing room, listening to one of the other sergeants, a new guy, regaling the troops with stories from his holiday in Florida. He had a suntan and a big mouth, and was thrust upon us by HQ for reasons we knew not.

"And this hostess was coming down the aisle," he was telling them. "Typical American – all tits and teeth. 'Would you like some TWA coffee, sir?' she asked. 'No,' I told her, ' – *but I wouldn't mind some TWA tea!*'"

They laughed as only a captive audience can. I caught the custody sergeant's gaze and he followed me into his purpose-designed domain.

"He's in fine form," I said.

"Isn't he just."

"Have a brotherly word with him, Bill, or I might have to."

"Right."

"We've decided to do Silkstone for manslaughter."

"Good," he replied, opening a drawer in one of his filing cabinets. "In that case we'd better ring his brief and get on with the paperwork."

Something was troubling me. Nothing I could name or explain or put in a report to show what a clever boy I was at a later date. There was a loose end – less than that, more like a draught around the edge of a closed window – that was making me feel uneasy. I collected the keys from the connected property store and drove to number 15, Marlborough Close, home of the late Peter Latham.

The spaghetti jar still stood on his worktop, next to the pan lid, as if the cook had been interrupted by the ringing of the telephone, and a carton of milk was making unhealthy smells. I took it outside and dropped it in his dustbin. The woman next door peered at me shamelessly, but didn't come to investigate. The pile of mail behind the door looked depressingly familiar, with not a single hand-written envelope amongst it all. I toyed with the idea of writing: *Dead, return to sender* on everything, but resisted the temptation. They'd probably all send it back asking for it to go to the next of kin.

The bird prints on his walls were Audubons, and good quality. Maybe I'd underestimated Peter Latham. I climbed the stairs slowly, listening for creaks, wondering if he'd ever led Mrs Silkstone up them, tugging at her hand. If walls could speak, what would they tell us? The door to his bedroom was ajar. I pushed it open and went in.

The sun cast a big geometric patch of light across the bed and wall, showing off the room as if in an advertising brochure. There's something inviting and evocative about sunlight spilling across a made-up bed. Three tiny Zebra spiders scurried across the windowsill, alarmed by my intrusion, but a dead or sleeping wasp ignored me. The photograph of the young girl was still there, smiling shyly, self-consciously, as she had done for God-knew how many years, and the new Mrs Latham was still gazing down into his eyes. But it was the girl I was interested in.

I sat on the bed and removed a pair of latex gloves and my Swiss Army knife from a jacket pocket. The room was chilly but the sunlight warmed my legs. I wriggled my fingers into the gloves and tried to open the big blade of the knife. Couldn't do it. My thumbnail wouldn't engage with the little groove. I removed one glove, opened the knife and replaced the glove. You live and learn.

Carefully, I eased back the metal sprigs that held the photo in the frame. There was a stiff backing card, a sheet of acid-free paper to stop the picture discolouring, and then the photo itself. Something about it had reminded me of the one I owned with Sophie and Daniel on. Both pictures were black and white, and exposed to the same degree. Mine was taken and printed by the *Heckley Gazette*.

This one had a similar stamp on the back. Both sides were trimmed to isolate this girl only, and one edge of the stamp had gone, but it told me that the photographer had worked for the *Burdon and Frome Exp*...and the serial number was 2452...? We were in business.

Five minutes later I was on Latham's phone, dialling a Somerset number. A small intuitive leap had told me that the picture came from the *Burdon and Frome Express* and I was right first time. Sometimes, you have to trust your instincts.

"Gillian McLaughlin," a voice said, after I'd asked to be put through to the editor in charge. I introduced myself and asked if she were the editor.

"Deputy editor," she stated. "Mr Binks is not in at the moment. How can I help you?"

"In the course of an enquiry," I began, "we have come across a photograph which apparently comes from your paper." I explained what it was and told her the number on the back.

"Shouldn't be a problem, Inspector," she replied, and went on to tell me that the number was the edition number and only the digits which identified the actual page and photograph were missing. They were now up to edition 3,582.

"So this picture was taken just over a thousand editions ago," I stated.

"Um, yes, which is about, um..."

"Are you a weekly?"

"Yes, we are."

"About twenty years, then."

"Um, yes. Twenty years," she agreed.

She also agreed to extricate the full article from the archives and fax me a copy. I told her that we were trying to track down a dead person's relatives, and we suspected this girl might be one of them. If there was a story in it, I assured her, she'd be the first to know.

Nothing was spoiling back at the nick so I went home.

My house wasn't as tidy as Latham's, I decided, so I made the bed, just in case, and washed and dried a two-day pile of crockery. When you live alone you don't notice how the sloppy habits slowly overtake you. The decay starts in the unseen corners, then spreads like mould on a bowl of fruit. For tea I had boil-in-the-bag cod with pasta. If you put the pasta in the same pan as the cod it saves on washing up. The telly cooks never tell you useful stuff like that.

Big Jim Lockwood was leaving the car-park as I arrived on Tuesday morning, wheeling an upright bicycle that was last used when *Whitehall one-two one-two* was the number you dialled after the villains had said: "It's a fair cop, Guv." I wound the window down and spoke to him.

"Back with us, eh, Jim?"

"Looks like it, Mr Priest," he replied, "but we're still grounded."

"Have they said how long for?"

"Indefinitely. Calling it a new initiative. Bobbies in the community and all that. It'll get me fit, lose some weight."

"That's one way of looking at it." I drove into my space, shaking my head at the stupidity of it.

Gillian McLaughlin's fax was waiting for me when I came out of the morning prayer meeting. "Come and dig this," I said to all and sundry as I bore it into the office. They gathered round and peered at it. There were four girls on the photo, all carrying the letter B on their chests. They were, the text told us, the victorious Under 13s relay team at the recent Burdon schools sports day, and the girl second from the left was called Caroline Poole.

"Caroline Poole," I heard Annette whisper. "Where are you now?"

"With looks like that," someone said, "I'm surprised she's not on t'telly. I bet she grew up into a right cracker."

"She's certainly a bonny 'un," another agreed.

"Let's find her, then," I suggested. "And the others.

Should be easy enough. They'll be in their early thirties, now." I turned to Annette. "Can I leave that with you, Ms Brown?"

She smiled, saying: "No problem, Boss."

"No hurry," I told her. "There's nothing in it for us, more than likely. She's probably a relative of Latham's, that's all."

Four of us, including Annette, went down to the canteen for bacon sandwiches. "Mr Wood's sent Jim Lockwood and Martin Stiles out on the beat, on bikes," Jeff Caton stated.

"It wasn't Mr Wood," I disclosed. "The order came down from above."

"What, God?"

"His deputy."

"Bloody crackers, if you ask me."

"It's a new initiative. Get the bobby back on the beat."

"On a 1930s bike that weighs half a ton and has rotting tyres. They'll be laughing stocks."

"They became that when they got the car stuck."

We chuckled at the memory. "You've got to admit it was bloody funny," Jeff said.

Annette and Dave came back from the counter carrying the teas. Annette placed a mug in front of me, saying: "No milk or sugar for you, Charlie."

"Wait a minute. Wait a minute," Jeff demanded. "How come you know that the boss doesn't take milk or sugar?"

"The same way as you know," she told him, without hesitation.

"Oh. And did you know he liked his belly rubbed with baby oil?"

"Cut it out," I said. "You might not be embarrassing Annette but you're embarrassing me. I don't want everybody in the station knowing my little foibles."

I was sitting with my back to the canteen counter, and a phone started ringing behind me. I raised a finger in a *listen* gesture, and after a few seconds was rewarded with a call of: "Mr Priest, it's for you," from the office manageress.

The other three stirred, with mumbles of "I'll get it," but I beat them to it.

"Priest here," I said.

"Detective Inspector Priest?" The voice was new to me.

"That's right. How can I help you?"

"This is George Binks, editor of the *Burdon and Frome Express*. I've just discovered that my deputy has faxed you a photograph that you were interested in."

"Hello, George. That's right. Ms McLaughlin found what I wanted. Pass on my thanks to her, please."

He said he would, and asked me why I was interested. I gave him the sanitised version, without mentioning dead bodies, and then he explained why he'd rung. I was sprawling across the canteen counter, leaning on my elbows because the phone cord wasn't long enough. "Wait a second," I told him, putting the phone down and going behind the counter. I picked it up again, found a seat and said: "Go on."

Annette had said something funny and they all laughed out loud as I approached the table. They quietened as they saw me and Jeff pushed a chair towards me with his feet.

"Are you all right, Chas?" Dave asked. "You look as if you've seen a ghost."

I shook my head and sat down.

"What is it, Charlie, bad news?" Annette added, concerned.

"That was the editor of the *Burdon and Frome Express*," I told them. "He's just seen a copy of the fax on his desk. Apparently, the girl in the photograph…Caroline Poole…four years later, in 1984, when she was sixteen…she was raped and strangled. Nobody was ever done for it."

Annette said: "Oh God no!" and her hand reached out and covered mine. She pulled it back as I said: "I'm afraid so. We'd better take another long hard look at Peter John Latham."

Chapter Six

I rang my opposite number in Somerset. His euphoria evaporated when I told him that Latham was dead, so there was little point in coming to Yorkshire to interview him. However, we did have the man who killed Latham in our cells, and the two of them went back a long time. Maybe he could throw some candle power on Latham's movements at the time of Caroline's death. It had been a big hunt. Caroline had grown into a beauty, as predicted, and her face had captured the public's imagination. We all remembered her when we saw the later picture that they'd used during the search.

Two detectives from Somerset said they would drive up and interview Silkstone some time on Wednesday. Wednesday morning they rang to say that they'd been delayed and they'd now be with us on Thursday. They confirmed that Latham did not appear to be related to Caroline in any way. Late Wednesday afternoon they said they were on their way and could we have Silkstone and his brief primed for a ten a.m. interview. They sounded keen.

Trouble was, Thursday morning I'd been requested to attend a high-power committee meeting, about catching murderers, chaired by the Deputy Chief Constable. I insisted that someone from Heckley sit-in on the Silkstone interview, and nominated Dave Sparkington.

The DCC considers himself an expert at murder enquiries. Early in his career he arrested a drunken husband who'd stabbed his wife to death in the middle of a bus queue, and that became the launch pad for his rise to fame. Fact is, the best collar he's felt in the last twenty-five years is on his dinner jacket. He'd resigned himself to never having the top job, so he wanted to make his mark by creating the definitive programme for a murder enquiry. Something that would bear his name and be used by police forces world-wide as a template – his word – in their quests to solve the most dastardly crimes of all. His name – Pritchard – would be in all the text-books, alongside those of Bertillon, Jeffreys and Kojak. And he wanted me to help put it there.

They'd been meeting for months, unknown to me, and had commissioned a video showing how to examine the crime scene during those first, crucial minutes. It was good, which wasn't surprising considering that the combined salaries of those involved would have paid for a battleship. They'd watched a lot of television, and remembered or made notes on how it was done. I couldn't fault it.

"You all know Charlie," the DCC told them. "Charlie has caught more murderers than anyone in the division, and I'm sure you'll all be interested to know what he thinks of our lit-tle enterprise. Over to you, Charlie. What have we forgotten?"

I stood up, mumbling something, and told them how impressed I was with the film. As Mr Pritchard had said, those first few minutes were crucial and recording evidence without destroying other evidence was the essence of the early enquiry. "I thought the way the film demonstrated the importance of reading the complete crime scene, the overall picture, was particularly well demonstrated," I told them, and the collective glow they radiated nearly ignited my shirt. "However," I continued, "perhaps there is one small point that you've overlooked," and they shuffled in their seats. All I needed now was to think of one.

I wasn't knocking them. Some of us like to be out on the streets, some of us are more suited to administrative jobs. He couldn't have done mine as effectively as I do, and I couldn't have done his. Put me in charge of discipline and complaints and anarchy would reign. Give me the budget and we'd be bankrupt in a month.

"Context," I said.

"Context?" the DCC murmured, his head tipped to one side, one finger pressed to his chin.

"Mmm, context," I repeated. While we were watching their film I'd been thinking about the space video young

Daniel had loaned me, and it had come to my rescue. "The first men on the moon," I began, "stuffed their pockets with the first rocks they found and brought them home. Frankly, they were a bit of a disappointment. On the last expedition, Apollo 17, they sent a geologist. He looked for rocks that were out of context, and found some interesting stuff. If you are looking for meteorites, here on earth, you don't look on a beach. You'd never recognise them amongst all those different stones. You go to one of the big deserts, or better still, Antarctica, and set up your stall there. If you find a rock in the middle of an ice field it is out of context, and chances are it came from outer space." I swept my gaze across them, one by one. Eye contact, that's what it's all about. They were all listening.

"In a murder enquiry," I continued, "we do something similar. We look for the unusual, the everyday item that is in the wrong place. If you look in the dead man's shoe cupboard – or the accused's shoe cupboard – and find shoes, no problem. If you look in his shirt cupboard, and there's a pair of shoes tucked under there, start asking questions. One of the suspects in the case I'm on at the moment is as bald as a coot. If I'd found a comb in his pocket I'd have wanted to know about it."

"For his eyebrows?" someone suggested and everybody roared with laughter.

"I'd've accepted that," I replied, nodding, and they laughed even more.

It was the buzzword they were looking for. "Context," they mumbled as we gathered our papers and prepared to leave. "Context," "Context," "Context."

Bollocks, I thought.

"Charlie."

It was the DCC. "Yes, Boss," I replied.

"Any chance of you giving me a lift to Heckley? My car's in for a service."

"Sure, no problem. What have we done to deserve a

visit?" As if I didn't know.

"I'm wearing my D and C hat, seeing those two prats who got the car stuck between the bollards. Lockwood and Smiles, isn't it? He won't be smiling when I've finished with him, I'll tell you that much."

"Stiles," I told him. "Lockwood and Stiles."

"Is it? Oh."

I opened his door but didn't wait to close it behind him, and threw my briefcase on the back seat. On the bypass a speed limit sign went by at well over the stated figure and I eased off the accelerator. If you think being followed by a police car is bad, you should try having the Deputy Chief Constable sitting in your passenger seat with his discipline and complaints hat on. I said: "Bit over the top, isn't it, Sir, suspending them and you handling it personally?"

"High profile, Charlie," he explained. "The media are involved. Made a laughing stock of the whole force. I'm seeing them at two."

"Right," I said, nodding in slow motion to indicate how I understood his position.

To change the subject I told him about the Latham case and how young Caroline Poole had suddenly come into the picture, complicating things. He saw it as two clear-ups, with a possible third. We're very extravagant with our clear-up figures. Jamie Walker's death would allow us to put every stolen car for the period he was out of detention down to him, and therefore solved. We'd just have to be careful not to have him doing two at the same time, in different parts of town. Perhaps we'd be able to put Caroline's murder down to Latham. Somerset would close the file, issue a statement saying that they were not looking for anybody else. There might even be a crumb of comfort in it for her parents.

After a silence Pritchard said: "Never took you for an astronomer, Charlie. Interested in that *Star Trek* stuff, are you?"

"No, that's fantasy," I replied. "I'm more interested in the real thing. Science in general, I suppose. Sometimes it comes in useful, like today."

"I'm sure you're right, I'm sure you're right. And it's good to have an outside interest. Too much work, and all that."

"Yep. That's what I think."

Another long silence, then I decided to give him the works. I said: "Back in the early Seventies, when the space race was in full flow, the Americans sent an unmanned craft to Mars and took a few photographs so the Russians, determined to match or outdo the Yanks, decided to send one to Venus. Unfortunately for them the atmosphere was so hot that the lens cap melted on the front of the camera, and they didn't get any pictures."

"Ah! Serves the buggers right," he commented.

"Being Russians," I continued, "they announced it as a glorious triumph for the Soviet people and vowed to continue the exploration of space on their behalf. The scientists involved were invited to sit on Lenin's tomb for the next May Day parade. The following year they sent another probe up, at a cost of a few more zillion roubles, but this time with a high melting-point lens cap on the camera. It also carried a device to scoop up some soil from the surface of Venus and analyse it."

"Clever stuff," the DCC said. "Marvellous what they can do, these days."

"It is, isn't it. And this time, everything worked perfectly. The lens cap flew off and the camera took a photo of Venus's soil, which looked very much like any other soil. Then the arm stretched out and the scoop picked up a sample and brought it back on board for analysis." I paused to let the pictures form in his mind, then went on: "Trouble was, the scoop had picked up the lens cap. They spent all that money, travelled a hundred million miles, to analyse something they took with them."

He looked across at me. "You're kidding!" he scoffed.

"According to the telly," I replied.

"The daft buggers."

"It was hailed as another Soviet success story," I told him, "and the scientists were awarded the Order of Lenin and given free holidays on the Black Sea." We'd arrived at the nick. I freewheeled into my space and yanked the handbrake on.

"Ha ha," he chuckled. "That's a good story, Charlie. A good story. With a moral in it, too. Learn from other people's mistakes, eh."

"That's right, Mr Pritchard," I said, adding: "And you've got to admit, it makes writing-off a Ford Escort sound small beer, don't you think?"

He called me a devious sod, but he was grinning as he said it. I hoped I'd done Big Jim and Martin a favour, but I wasn't sure.

Dave and the two tec's from Somerset were in Gilbert's office, waiting for me. They were a DI and a DS, and were a little taken aback when I introduced Pritchard to them. He'd insisted on being present and they weren't used to their top brass being so accessible. After handshakes all round and mugs of tea for me and the DCC, Gilbert said: "Apparently, Charlie, Latham is totally unrelated to Caroline Poole and there is no obvious reason why he should have that photograph of her."

Dave said: "The picture came from the *Burdon and Frome Express*, as we know, but they have no record of the buyer. If it was paid for in cash, in advance, and collected in person, they wouldn't have."

"Or he could have used a false name," the DCC suggested, eager to help, but failing.

"So what does Silkstone have to say?" I asked.

The DI was a huge man in a light grey suit, with a clipped moustache and nicotine-stained fingers. He said: "We'll start before that, if you don't mind. The reason that we decided not to come up yesterday morning was because we'd done some preliminary investigations in the Caroline Poole files. Or, to be more precise, Bob here had."

Bob, the DS, nodded.

"Bob discovered that the names Latham and Silkstone were in there, would you believe."

"Go on," I invited. It had been a big case, and probably every male in Somerset was in there.

"A car was seen in the vicinity of the last sighting of Caroline. A dark one, British Leyland, possibly a Maestro. In the next three months the owners of eighteen thousand dark Maestros were interviewed, without any success. Two of them belonged to Latham and Silkstone. Or, to be more accurate, to the company they worked for: Burdon Home Improvements."

When we talk to people in large numbers like that, there's not a great deal you can ask. "Where were you on…" is about it. We insist on an answer, and then ask if anyone was with them, to confirm the story. If there was, and they do, that person is eliminated from enquiries, as we professionals say.

"This is where it gets interesting," the DI was saying.

"Just one thing," the DCC interrupted, to prove he was awake, and interested, and really on top of things. "Are the files computerised?"

"After a fashion," Bob replied. "It's an ancient system, from before the mouse was invented, but it works, once you find someone who knows about these things. At the moment, because it was an unsolved case, it's all being updated to the latest HOLMES standard."

"Good, good. Sorry to chip in."

"That's OK, Sir. Like I was saying, this is where it gets interesting. Caroline was last seen walking home from a school play, at about nine fifteen. Latham said he was in a pub at the time in question, twenty miles away. He gives one Tony Silkstone as his alibi, plus two women they just happened to talk to. When Silkstone was interviewed he gave

Latham's name, plus the two women."

"Were the women traced?" I asked.

"Yep. It's all here." He rattled his knuckles against the file on the desk.

"But you won't have had time to find them again?"

The DI shook his head but didn't speak.

"Right. So what does Silkstone say *now*?"

"Silkstone says," he began, "that he was out with his current girlfriend at the time in question, a lady called Margaret Bates. He was a married man, and this was an illicit affair. He later left his wife and married Margaret. She became the late Mrs Silkstone."

"*Cherchez la femme*," the DCC mumbled, nodding as if everything was suddenly clear. I was beginning to wish I hadn't brought him. Gilbert caught my eye and winked.

"Meanwhile Latham, we are informed, was playing fast and loose with another woman, called Michelle Webster, who was a friend of Margaret Bates. According to Silkstone he was terrified that his wife would find out, but Michelle was his only alibi for the night Caroline disappeared. He asked Silkstone to say that he was with him, and that they just happened to meet two women in a pub outside Frome, The Lord Nelson. Silkstone agreed, he says, and persuaded the two women to say that they'd all met, briefly, at the pub."

Dave said: "They were married to two sisters, weren't they?"

"Yes," the DI confirmed.

"And then they were knocking off two mates?"

"That's right."

"It all sounds a bit cosy."

"It does, doesn't it? But the important thing is that Silkstone's story tallies with what's in the files. He was with Latham, Latham was with him, in the Lord Nelson. The two women confirmed seeing them there. Bingo – eliminated from enquiries, even though it's a pack of lies."

"Margaret Silkstone's dead," I said. "What about the other one?"

"Michelle Webster?" Bob replied. "We haven't found her yet, but she's our next priority."

"It'll be interesting to hear what she has to say," I stated.

"Ye-es, very interesting," the DCC agreed.

It was Iqbal's last day with us, Allah be praised, and Annette came to tell me that the troops were meeting in the Bailiwick at home time, to give him a send-off. I told her to make two coffees for us, and bring herself back to my office. Maybe she'd appreciate the assertive approach.

When she was seated opposite me I told her all about the Silkstone interview. She listened gravely, and offered the opinion that lack of alibi and possession of a photograph was hardly enough to convict a man for murder.

"Except that he went on to kill again," I said.

"That's not evidence," she stated.

"No," I agreed, "but the Somerset boys can go back and look at the case again, with Latham in mind. We haven't seen the file. There might be a load of stuff in there that will all fall into place, now."

Annette was right, though. We have to be careful. You can't arrest a man because he has a scar on his cheek, and then announce to the court that he has a scar on his cheek, just like the witness said. Latham was only in the frame for Caroline because he possessed her photograph. We couldn't then use that piece of non-evidence to clinch his guilt. I heaved a big sigh and took a bite of chocolate biscuit.

"You look tired, Charlie," she observed.

"Yeah, a bit."

"So where does all this leave us?"

"Us?" I queried.

"I meant the Latham case. Our Latham case."

"Everybody agrees that it's sewn up," I told her. "Latham killed Mrs S. Mr S came home and found her, then he killed Latham. Balance of mind, manslaughter, three years top whack, free in one."

"I thought you weren't happy about it."

"I'm happy," I protested. "The evidence is good. Why does everybody want me to be out of line?"

Her face lit up in a smile. "Because that's where you belong," she said.

We sipped our coffee in silence for a few moments, her left hand absentmindedly straightening the papers near the corner of my desk until they were exactly parallel to the edges. "Do you think of Georgina Dewhurst very often?" she asked.

I wasn't expecting it, and it took me a few moments to reply. Georgina was a little girl, murdered by her stepfather. "Yes," I admitted. "Probably more often than is healthy."

"I was a WPC on that case," Annette told me.

"I know. You were with the Child Protection Unit."

"Good grief!" she exclaimed. "I'm amazed you noticed."

I grinned, saying: "As SIO, it was part of my remit to keep a fatherly eye on all the young WPCs."

Her smile was warm and comfortable, the best I'd ever seen her give. "That's when I decided I wanted to be a detective," she said. "Not just be a detective, I wanted…well…oh, never mind."

"Wanted what?"

Her smile was still there, fighting to be seen through the blush that crept over her face like a desert sunset. "Oh, nothing," she said.

I didn't insist on an answer. People with red hair and freckles blush easily, but it was strange that she never did when answering questions about our clients that some people would find embarrassing. Then, she was totally professional. It was only when…Ah, well, it was something for me to ponder over.

"Tonight," I began, "after we've given Iqbal a send-off. We could go for a Chinese again, if you've nothing on. Or a curry. I'm just as well-known in the Last Viceroy as I am in the Bamboo Curtain. You missed a good steak on Saturday, by the way."

She nodded and said: "Right. See you in the pub."

I did paperwork and made phone calls until after half-past six, then walked over the road to the Bailiwick. The lab had done a micro-analysis of various samples taken from the Silkstone bedroom and their report was in the post. Expecting me to wait for it was like asking a child to wait until Easter for his Christmas presents. I asked for a condensed version over the phone.

They'd found skin flakes from all three involved, but not too many from Tony Silkstone. The sheet and duvet cover were probably clean on that day, which had made things easier. The footprint scans were relatively straightforward, too, as the whole house had been thoroughly vacuumed. All three of the protagonists had climbed up and down the stairs a couple of times, and last one down was Silkstone himself. No signs of a struggle, no tracks left by trailing heels. All good stuff, which led us nowhere. Mrs Silkstone liked a tidy house and clean sheets for when her lover called, and that was about it. The jammy sod, I thought. Pity about the dagger in the heart.

Jeff and Iqbal were sitting in a corner, behind half-empty glasses, the barman was reading the *Mirror* and the cat was asleep on the jukebox. All-day opening has closed more pubs than any temperance society ever did.

"Ah, Inspector Charlie!" Iqbal exclaimed as I entered. "What can I purchase for you?"

"Oh, a pint of lager would go down nicely, please," I replied, and Iqbal went over to the bar.

"Where is everybody?" I whispered to Jeff.

"Dunno. Playing hard to get, by the look of it."

"Annette said she'd be here."

"I saw her leave, in her car."

"Oh." I tried not to sound disappointed.

Iqbal returned with my drink. He placed it carefully in

front of me, saying: "Jeffrey was just explaining how the legal system in your country, and therefore in mine also, dates back to the twelfth century, and that there are still several anomalies in the statutes book that have no relevance to the modern world."

"So they say, Iqbal," I replied, adding: "Cheers," and taking a long sip of Holland's major contribution to international goodwill. It was an old chestnut that poor Jeff had dug up to keep the conversation flowing.

"For instance," he continued, "Jeffrey tells me that it is still permissible, due to an oversight or perhaps lack of time in Parliament, for the driver of a vehicle who is taken short to urinate against the front offside wheel of the aforementioned vehicle. Is that really so?"

"Not quite," I told him. "It's the front *nearside* wheel."

"Offside," Jeff asserted.

"Nearside," I argued.

"Offside."

"Uh-uh. Nearside."

"It's the offside. I looked it up."

"Are you sure?"

"Positive."

"Oh heck. No wonder I got some funny looks in the High Street this morning." One or two of the others arrived, so Iqbal's send-off wasn't a complete disaster. I was just starting my third pint, which is about double my normal intake, these days, when Annette arrived. She was wearing a blue pinstripe suit with a shortish skirt and high heels. I smiled at her and moved along to make some room, but didn't speak. I wasn't sure I could control what might come out if I tried to talk. Someone fetched her an orange juice.

At half past eight people started to make excuses and drift away. We all shook hands with Iqbal, telling him what a delight his stay with us had been, wishing him well for the future. I pointedly asked Annette if she'd like a Chinese, and she said: "What a good idea."

I opened the invitation to the others but they all politely declined. Dave had eaten, he said; some had meals waiting for them, and Jeff had defrosted a vegetarian lasagne for himself and Iqbal. "Just us, then," I told Annette, and our ears were burning like stubble fires as we walked away from them all.

"Your reputation is now in tatters, you know," I said as I fastened my seatbelt in her Fiat.

"That's what reputations are for," she replied, clunking the car into first gear.

We went through the menu and had fun. I introduced Annette to wontons and Mr Ho introduced both of us to various other delicacies he kept bringing from the kitchen. "Umm, delicious, what is it?" Annette would giggle, and he would reply in Chinese.

"What's that in English?" she'd demand.

"You no rike if I tell you in Engrish," he'd laugh.

I grabbed the bill when it came. "This was my idea, and I earn more than you," I told her, not allowing her the chance to object.

"Oh, er, right, thanks," she said.

"My pleasure. Any chance of a lift home?"

She wouldn't come in for coffee. We were sitting outside my house with the car's headlights still on and the engine running. Switching off, stopping the engine, would have been a statement of intent. It didn't come.

"At the risk of being politically incorrect," I began, "you look stunning, Annette."

"Oh, I can take political incorrectness like that," she replied with a smile.

"Good. I've enjoyed tonight."

"Mmm, me too."

After a silence I said: "Are you going away this week-end?"

The smile slipped away and she fiddled with a button on the front of her jacket. "Yes," she replied, very softly.

One of the neighbours came walking down the pavement with his little dog on a lead, returning from its evening crap at the other end of the street. I have very considerate neighbours. "Is he a good bloke?" I asked.

Annette turned to face me. "How do you know it's a bloke?" she asked.

I shook my head. "I don't, but it usually is."

"Normally. You mean normally."

"Usually, normally. They're just words."

"I'm the station dyke, Charlie," she replied. "Surely you know that."

"You're a great police officer and I'm very fond of you. That's all I know."

"Would it bother you if I were?"

"What? Gay?"

"Mmm."

"No."

"Why not?"

I was tired. I hadn't thought out my arguments. Or my feelings. "I don't know. It just wouldn't," was the best I could manage.

The button came off in her fingers and she gave a tiny snort of dismay. "They don't make them like they used to," I said.

"It's been loose all night," she replied.

"You could've had that coffee, and I could've sewn it back on for you."

The smile came back. "Role reversal," she said. "I'm all in favour of that."

"They teach you to sew buttons on in the SAS," I told her.

"Were you in the SAS?"

"Mmm. Under twelve's branch. They threw me out because I wouldn't wear the oblong sunglasses."

She laughed, just a little, and called me a fool. And Charlie. "You are a fool, Charlie" she said, in the nicest possible way.

"Thank you for a pleasant evening, ma'am," I said, opening the door. "Don't be late, in the morning."

"What time do you want picking up?" she asked.

"God!" I exclaimed, pulling the door closed again. "My car's still outside the nick, isn't it. Um, in that case, whenever."

"About twenty to eight?"

"Yeah, that's fine. If I can get up. I think I'm slightly pissed."

I opened the door just enough for the interior light to come on. Annette said: "For the record, yes, he is a good bloke."

"Your friend in York?"

"Mmm."

"Does he deserve you?"

"I think so. He's a schoolteacher, and has two daughters, seven and nine."

"Divorced?"

"Widower."

"Rich?"

"He's a schoolteacher."

"Right," I said. "Right." I felt hollow inside. A schoolteacher I could deal with. I'd ask the local boys to waste him and arrange for the coastguard to drop his weighted body off the edge of the continental shelf. Not the girls, though. I couldn't be that much of a bastard.

"Annette…" I began.

"Mmm."

"Would you be willing to…you know…make allowances for my intoxicated state if I…sort of…transgressed, type of thing?"

"I'm not sure," she replied, warily. "What do you have in mind?"

"Um, well, I was just wondering, er, if there was any chance of, um, a goodnight kiss?"

She leaned over and gave me a loud peck on the cheek,

completely catching me off guard. It wasn't quite what I had in mind, but it was a start. "There," she said.

"Thank you," I told her, pushing the door wide.

"Charlie…"

I twisted back to face her. "Mmm."

"You should get pissed more often."

Friday morning I put eggs, bacon and tomatoes from the fridge out on the worktop, together with corn flakes, bread, marmalade, a tub of Thank Christ It's Not Butter, the frying pan and the toaster. It was my attempt at humour, but Annette waited in the car for me. I finished my coffee and went out.

"Another day, another collar," I said, winding myself into the Fiat's passenger seat. Italian cars make no concessions towards the different body shapes of their European neighbours. Short legs and long arms – take it or leave it. "Thank you, Ms Brown. The office, please."

But there were no collars to feel, that day. Some of the team were out looking at burglary scenes, others, me included, caught up with paperwork and reading. Dave went out for sandwiches at lunchtime, and brought me hot pork in an oven bottom cake, with stuffing. They don't do them like that in M & S. And at a fraction of their price.

In the afternoon the remains of Jamie Walker, loosely arranged in some sort of order, were buried with full Christian pomp. His mother prostrated herself on the coffin, for the *Gazette*'s photographer, then repeated the scene, with sound effects, when local TV arrived. Practice makes perfect. He was a good son, she told them: everybody loved him and his mischievous ways. This wouldn't have happened if the police had been more firm with him, and she was considering taking legal action against them. Nobody from the job went to the funeral, under orders, but we all caught it on TV later that evening.

Last phone call before I left work was from Bob, the

Somerset DS. "We've traced Michelle Webster," he told me. "She married and changed her name, but she's now divorced and has reverted back to her maiden name."

You can't revert forward, I thought. "Have you spoken to her?" I asked.

"No, Mr Priest. She's living in Blackpool, would you believe. Our chief super's making noises about expenses and thinks there's no need for us to see her ourselves. He said to let someone local interview her. He wants to wait until after the inquests then issue a statement saying that we are not looking for anybody else, and that would be the Caroline Poole case cleared up."

"Which would please the relatives, I suppose."

"That's what he said."

"How would you feel if someone from here nipped across and had a word with Michelle?"

"No problem, Mr Priest. That's partly why I'm ringing you. You're a couple of hundred miles nearer to her than we are."

"Call me Charlie, Bob. Everybody else does."

"Oh, right."

"Give me the address. I'll try to send someone next week, and let you know the outcome."

"We'd appreciate that, Charlie. Thanks for your help."

"My pleasure."

And it would be, too. Blackpool might be the last resort, but a day there with Annette sounded a good way of adding the finishing touches to the Latham case. I straightened my blotter, washed my mug and went home.

Jamie's funeral, on TV, made me angry. "You should get pissed more often," Annette had told me. No way. I'd staggered down that road a long time ago, and didn't like the scenery. My Sony rasta-blaster holds three CDs. I chose carefully, then carried it into the garage where the unfinished painting leaned against the wall. I laid the tubes of colour out in the same order I always use and screwed the caps off. Yellow ochre, to start with, I decided. I squeezed a six-inch worm of it onto the palette and dipped a number twelve filbert into the glistening pigment.

The knock on the garage door came about halfway through the second playing of Mahler's *Symphony No. 5.* The neighbour was standing there with his little dog. I stared at him, brush in one hand, palette knife in the other.

"Um, er, your radio's on a bit loud, Mr Priest, if you don't mind me saying so."

It was. That's how you listen to Mahler. "I'm sorry," I said. "I didn't know you could hear it outside."

"Well you can, and it's keeping Elsie awake."

"I really am sorry," I repeated, because I was. I like to consider myself the invisible neighbour. "I was painting. What time is it"

"About ten to one."

"What!" I exclaimed. "I didn't realise it was so late."

"She's been in bed since just after the play ended. It's her waterworks, you know."

"Really. Well it won't happen again." I moved back into the garage and switched off the CD. He stepped into the vacant space in the doorway and his gaze settled on the nearly-finished picture. "It's supposed to represent China," I explained, as I wiped away the blob of cerulean blue that I'd accidentally dabbed on the Sony.

"China?" he repeated.

"Mmm."

"China China?"

"That's right." As opposed to cup-and-saucer china, I think he meant. "That's the Great Wall, and that's a panda." I pointed to the images, some strong, some barely hinted at, and read them off. "The Long March, Tiananmen Square, coolie hats, bonsai, typical scenery, Chairman Mao."

"I don't like this modern stuff," he declared.

"This is hardly modern," I told him. "I don't like much of

the really modern stuff." I manoeuvred him outside and walked him towards the gate. "And apologise to your wife about the noise, please. It won't happen again."

"The wife? She's stone deaf, like me. Neither of us ever hears a thing once we switch off."

"Oh. You said, er, Elsie."

"Elsie." He tugged the dog's lead. "This is Elsie."

"Right. Er, right."

Next morning at ten a.m. I rang Michelle Webster, provider of alibi for a child murderer, and arranged to see her in the afternoon. Don't ask me why, but sometimes I feel more at ease when dealing with the criminally insane.

The rain started as soon as I passed over the tops and began the long descent into Lancashire. Having Annette with me would have been pleasant, but she was in York with her friend, and the thrill of the chase was more than I could resist. I was quite pleased about the rain – maybe it would keep the traffic down. It didn't, and we had the usual stop-go on the M6. There's this crackpot idea that the more roads you build, the more traffic you create. It all started after they opened the M25. Two million Londoners apparently said: "Ooh, good, they've built a new road. Let's dash out and buy a car." It's now used as an argument for not making new roads or widening existing ones, and the M6 is doomed to permanent gridlock.

Michelle Webster had given me extremely detailed directions, which I hadn't listened to, and sounded determined that I shouldn't get lost. All I recorded was that she was on the south side, but not quite St Anne's. There's posh, I thought, as I looked at the map: they've retained the apostrophe.

When I was in the general vicinity I asked, and soon was creeping along a street of respectable, if slightly dilapidated, pre-war semis. They had shingled bay windows and mature trees in the gardens. I saw the number and parked between an ageing Range Rover and a Toyota Celica with a dented corner. Michelle Webster opened her front door before my finger was off the button, halfway through the second bar of *Strangers in the Night*.

She looked sixty, pushing nine. Little girls like to dress up in their mother's clothes, I'm told. This was serious role reversal. She was wearing a pink micro skirt, black silk blouse, black tights and black suede boots that would have come well above her knees had not the tops been turned down, cavalier fashion. I remembered the joke about the woman who went to the doctors complaining of thrush. He gave her a prescription to take to the cobblers, to have two inches taken off the top of her boots.

"Mrs Michelle Webster?" I asked. I'd done a calculation on the way over and reckoned she'd be in her mid forties.

"It's *Miss* Webster," came the reply, as she stood to one side to let me through with hardly a glance at my ID. A little dog came yapping towards me out of the gloom of the hallway. Michelle said: "Hush, Trixie," and picked it up. It had lots of hair, and looked as if it had just escaped from a serious accident with a tumble drier. "There-there darling, it's only a nice policeman come to see Mummy," she told it, planting a kiss into the middle of the ball of fur, and for a moment their hair merged like two clouds of noxious gasses after a chemical spillage.

"So what's he done now?" Michelle asked with a touch of glee in her voice, when we were seated in her front room, which I suspected was called the parlour. She'd moved a menagerie of fluffy toys to make room for me, and straightened the antimacassars on the chair arms. There were pictures on the walls of various stars of stage and screen, with autographs scrawled across them by a girl with a rubber stamp in an office in Basingstoke.

"Who?" I asked.

"Greg, my ex. It's about him. Isn't it?"

It wasn't, but I did some gentle probing. Greg was part owner of a club in town, and into all sorts of wheeling and dealing. She could tell me stuff that would make my hair curl. Mafia? Don't talk to her about the Mafia.

So I didn't. "You were in showbusiness?" I asked, flapping a hand towards the photos and recognising Roy Orbison in a central position amongst all the bouffant hair and gleaming teeth of the ones who didn't make it to his level.

"Not on the performing side." She smiled and crossed her legs, which was difficult with the footwear she had on. "Not enough talent, unfortunately," she explained with a modest shrug. "No, Greg and I were more into management and promotions."

"You were evidently successful at it." The house was probably hers, and prices in Blackpool are no doubt above average.

"Oh, we were, we were. They were great days. And then the shit ran off with a dancer from the Tower whose cup size was as far as she ever made it through the alphabet. The fat little cow."

"I haven't come to talk about Greg," I told her, anxious to steer the conversation back on course. "I want to talk to you about people you knew when you lived in Burdon, back in the Eighties."

"Burdon? That was a long time ago."

"1984, to be precise. Did you know a man called Peter Latham?"

She pretended she wasn't sure – "There were so many, Inspector" – until she realised that I wasn't going to be more forthcoming. Then she remembered him. I told her that he was dead, as was her friend Margaret Silkstone, nee Bates, under suspicious circumstances, and we'd be very grateful for any help she could give. After a little weep it all came out.

They were a foursome: she and Peter Latham; Margaret and Tony Silkstone. They met three nights a week at a pub near Frome – the Nelson – where there was music and dancing, and paired off when the alcohol and hormones started to work. Peter, she said, was kind and relaxed. Unlike Silkstone, who was a show-off, always wanting to have more, do better than anyone else. They were married to two sisters, which was why they knew each other. Peter's wife, Michelle said, was a "hatchet-faced cow, and frigid with it." I remembered the wedding photo I'd seen, of a tall brittle blonde who towered over him, and decided that the description could be accurate.

The affair came to an end when Latham was breathalysed and banned from driving. They struggled to meet for a while, playing gooseberry with Silkstone and Margaret, but Michelle came to Blackpool for a holiday and met Greg. End of a beautiful friendship.

"He was a lovely man," she sobbed, for the tears had started again. "He knew the names of things. Birds and flowers an' stuff like that. And poetry. He knew whole poems. Not the ones you did at school. Daft ones, that you can understand, by him from Liverpool. Paul McCartney's brother."

And had a penchant for sex with young girls, I thought.

"Not like Tony," she continued. "All he knew was the price of cars." She sniffed and dabbed her nose with a tissue. "I married Greg because he was a bit in-between, if you follow me. Except with him it was show-biz."

I wasn't sure I did follow, but I skipped asking for an explanation. "You were obviously fond of him," I said. "I'm sorry I had to bring you bad news." But now for the *bad* news. I said: "Do you remember when a girl called Caroline Poole went missing?"

She did. Nobody who lived in Burdon would ever forget it. "It was the biggest manhunt ever held in Somerset," I told her. "Everybody was questioned, including Tony and Peter. According to the records they said they were with you and Margaret that night. Do you remember?"

She pursed her lips and shrugged, warily, and I imagined her growing pale under the makeup. Lipstick was beginning to bleed away from the corners of her mouth like aerial views of the Nile delta. "I never asked you if you'd like a drink!" she exclaimed, pulling herself to her feet. "What must you think of me?" Trixie, who was curled up on her lap, fell to the floor.

There was a bar in the corner of the room, behind me, with a quilted façade and optics on the mirrored wall. A personal replica of the real thing for those times when you can't face the world. I twisted in my seat as she poured clear liquid from a decanter. "What would you like, Chief Inspector?" she asked.

There was no coffee percolator quietly gurgling on the counter. "Not for me, thank you," I said. Glass clinked against glass, suede swish-swashed against suede and she resumed her seat, slowly easing herself down into it like a forklift truck lowering a crate of eggs. If it was gin she now held in her hand she'd be talking in hieroglyphics before she was halfway through it. "Whose idea was it to lie?" I asked, getting straight to the point.

She took a long drink, slurped, gurgled and coughed. "I don't know." The end of Trixie that didn't have a curly tail looked up at her, then decided not to bother. The dog sloped off and crashed out on a folded sheepskin rug near the fireplace.

"Did Peter ask you?"

"Ask me what?"

"Did he ask you to say he was with you?"

"No. I don't think so. I'd stopped seeing him by then."

"By when?"

"By when the police were asking questions. It was months after the girl was murdered."

"Was it Silkstone, then?"

"I don't know. It was a long time ago. I used to drink a lot…" She downed half of the tumbler to demonstrate how it was done and re-crossed her legs.

"Was it Margaret's idea. Did she persuade you to say that

you saw Peter and Tony in the Lord Nelson, that night?"

"I was never very good at times, and days of the week."

"Was it Margaret's idea?"

"I think so."

"What did she say?"

She downed the last of whatever it was and stared gloomily at the empty glass. Her legs uncrossed themselves, as if she were about to go for another, but she decided not to and sank back in the chair. There'd be plenty of time for that when the nice policeman had gone.

"She said that Peter was scared stiff that his wife would find out about, you know, me an' 'im. We used to go to the Nelson to hear this group. They were called the Donimoes…the Dominoes. Gerry and the Donimoes. They did all Roy's stuff. When Gerry sang 'In Dreams' they used to dim all the lights, an' the group, they used to turn their backs to the audience, as if to say that this was 'is spot. All 'is." She closed her eyes and the savage lips melted into a smile.

"*In dreams I walk with you,*" she sang, very softly, her head weaving gently from side to side. "*In dreams I talk to yo-ou.*"

"It's a lovely song," I said.

"Do you like it?"

"Mmm. You were telling me what Margaret said to you?"

She looked at the glass, realised it was still empty and leaned forward to place it on the coffee table. Her fingers fumbled, lost their grip, and it rolled on to the floor. It was a heavy tumbler, cut glass, and the rug was luxurious, so it didn't break. I picked it up and placed it just out of her reach.

"What did she say?"

"She shaid…she said…that Peter had told Tony that he didn't 'ave a…a…a nalibi for the night that little girl went missing. He was wiv me, she shaid, she…said, bur 'e couldn't tell the police that, cos 'is wife would find out."

"What did she tell you to do?"

"Just that we saw 'em in the pub. The Nelson. I was wiv Margaret, an' we saw these two blokes, called Peter and Tony. They dint buy us a drink or anything, but we spoke to them. If the police came and asked where I was on that Wednesday night, I'd to say I was in the Nelson, wiv 'er."

"And did they?"

"Did what?"

"Did the police ask you where you were?"

"Yes, but ages after. I could 'ardly remember."

"And was Peter with you, that Wednesday night?"

"That's the funny fing. I didn't realise until I fought about it. We went to the Nelson free times a week, when the Donimoes…the Dominoes…were playing. But they were on a Sunday and on a Tuesday and on Thursday nights. Not We'nsdays. We never went on We'nsdays. It was old time dancing on We'nsdays."

I made her a black coffee, but I couldn't do much about the brewery in the corner. Leaving her alone with her real or imagined memories, a CD of Roy Orbison's greatest breakdowns and a gallon of spirits was like playing Russian Roulette with her, but I didn't see what else I could do. Hopefully she'd collapse and sleep it off. She must have been half cut when I arrived, so she knew the score.

The rain drove all the day-trippers away early, so it was a twenty-minute crawl to reach the motorway. I stopped at the Birch services for a meal but changed my mind when I saw the prices. I always do. Instead it was a trout from Sainsbury's, with Kenyan green beans and new potatoes, followed by half a pint of strawberry Angel Delight. I did the trout under the grill, with lashings of butter, and it was delicious.

I hadn't lied to Michelle. I saw Roy Orbison, once, at Batley Variety Club, and he was brilliant. I took Vanessa, my wife, soon to be ex-wife. He sounded exactly the same live as he did on record, which is more than you can say for most of them. I went upstairs to the spare bedroom, humming *Pretty*

Woman, and logged on to the computer that lives in there.

"Michelle Webster admitted that she lied when asked by the investigating officer if Peter Latham was with her on the night Caroline Poole disappeared," I typed. I expanded the story, with all the dates and legal-speak to make it sound professional. As an afterthought, I added that she was totally kettled when I interviewed her, and was an unreliable witness, open to manipulation. When it was finished I ran off two copies and deleted the file.

Monday morning I'd post it to Somerset, augmented with a phone call. They'd use the information to pin a sixteen-year-old girl's murder on Latham, and close the case. It wasn't much, but he had, after all, gone on to commit another murder up in Yorkshire, hadn't he?

Meanwhile, we'd reinforce our case against the man by regarding him as someone who had killed before, down in Somerset. It wasn't what might be called a Catch 22, but there ought to be a name for it. Ah well, I thought, the coroners will have to sort that one out.

Latham did leave his sperm all over Margaret Silkstone's thighs, I remembered as I logged off, and felt happier. Were he still alive he'd be having difficulties arguing that small fact away. Thank God for sperm samples – where would we all be without them? Jeff Caton had loaned me the video of Ridley Scott's *Blade Runner*, with Harrison Ford, and I watched it while sipping lager I'd brought from the supermarket. It was the later version, the director's cut, with the voice-over removed. Sorry, Mr Scott, but you ruined it. Sometimes, the man in charge just doesn't know best. You can be so close to something that you don't see the wet fish coming until it slaps you in the chops.

Monday morning I followed a double-decker bus all the way into town. Since the buses were regulated – or was it de-regulated? – they've started painting them in fancy colours and allowing different companies to sponsor individual buses.

Sometimes you don't know if it's the one you want coming down the road or a bunch of New Age travellers. On the back of most of them, covering the panel that conceals the engine, it states: *Bus advertising works. You're reading this, aren't you?*

Dave's and Annette's cars were already in their places when I swung into the station yard. Latham's ex-wife, who lives in Pontefract, started work at the local hospital at ten a.m., and they'd arranged to drive over and catch her early. I filled them in with my weekend discoveries but suggested they concentrate initially on our enquiry, not Somerset's. The Caroline Poole case was muddying the waters, and it wasn't fair to Latham to use it to pre-judge him.

Dave said: "Where's our rock, then?" to change the subject. What he meant was don't tell your grandma how to suck eggs.

"What rock?"

"Our Blackpool rock. You had a day at the seaside and you didn't bring us any rock back?"

"It was raining. I didn't hang about."

He turned to Annette. "Shows how much he thinks of us."

Annette looked thoughtful. She said: "So Latham didn't have an alibi for the Caroline Poole job."

"No, he didn't."

"Which means, of course, that Silkstone probably didn't have one, either."

"Yes, Annette," I agreed. "That thought had occurred to me, too."

"Unless he was alone with Margaret at the time," Dave suggested.

"But she's dead," Annette and I replied, simultaneously.

They went off to Pontefract and I went upstairs for the morning prayer meeting. Gilbert huffed and puffed and thought I was wasting time on details when the big picture was as plain as a gravy stain. The Caroline Poole case wasn't ours. End of story. Latham killed Margaret. Silkstone killed Latham. End of story.

"But we don't know that Silkstone wasn't involved with Margaret's death," I argued.

"Well if he was he's got away with it. Good luck to the bloke, we can't win 'em all, Charlie."

Gareth Adey offered his considered opinion, which agreed with Gilbert's. It always does. "I think Mr Wood is right, Charlie," he told me. "Good grief, two murders cleared up is pretty good going by anybody's standards. Well done, I say, and I bet the Chief Constable is thinking the same way. Now, can we talk about the new CCTV in the market place?"

So we did. Three minutes about two murders, half an hour about his poxy TV cameras. "Well done, Charlie. Two murders cleared up. Maybe you'll get a commendation." And what about frigging justice, I thought?

I rang Michelle Webster when I was back in my office, to satisfy myself that she was OK. "I was worried about you," I told her, after the formalities. "That was rather a large G and T you made yourself." She giggled, saying that there was no T in it, and hoped that she had behaved herself. We chatted for a while, had a laugh and said goodbye. She never asked about Latham or his funeral, never mentioned the man who killed him, never asked how her friend Margaret had died. I replaced the phone and wondered why I'd bothered.

Somerset were more interested, when I rang them, and thanked me for my efforts. As Gilbert said, they were regarding it as a clear-up. In the middle of our conversation someone in the big office held up a phone and mouthed: "For you," at me, through the glass. I shook my head and waved the one I was holding.

He took a message then came to deliver it, leaning in the doorway of my little office until I'd finished. "That was the Jeff from the court," he said. "The magistrate has remanded Silkstone in custody and he's been taken to Bentley. His solicitor has intimated that they'll be pleading guilty to manslaughter, with provocation and lashings of mitigating circumstances."

"Hey, that's good news," I said. "I expected him to be let loose. Good for the CPS, for once."

"A short, sharp shock," he replied. "Teach him what he's in for. They'll free him next time."

"Yep," I agreed.

We had a loose-ends meeting at four o'clock. Annette placed a huge bag of Pontefract cakes and one of all-sorts on the table in front of me. "Where did you get these?" I asked.

"Pontefract."

"They do sell them in the supermarket," I argued.

"Not fresh ones, straight from the oven."

I found a coconut mushroom and popped it into my mouth, saying: "Dese are by faborites," as I passed the bag across the table.

"There's a castle there," Dave said.

"Where Richard the Second was murdered," Annette added.

"It's an interesting place."

"And stinks of liquorice."

"But it's quite a pleasant smell, really."

"And every other building is a pub."

"OK, OK, spare me the travelogue," I protested as I sucked a piece of coconut from between my teeth. "Next weekend we'll all have a day out in Pontefract. Now can we talk about you-know-what, please."

Other information had come in and been collated. Most significant were the facts that Silkstone and his wife had blazing rows and were in severe financial difficulties. The car was leased and he'd slipped behind a couple of times with his mortgage payments. His salary, we discovered, was quite modest, and the hefty commissions that he was used to weren't coming his way. Margaret's death had given him a timely leg-up out of the shit creek.

Neighbours confirmed that Latham was a regular Wednesday afternoon visitor. No bedroom curtains were pulled across after he arrived, but it wasn't possible for anyone to see into the room.

"Actually," Dave confided, "between us and these four walls, it's quite pleasant in the afternoon, with the curtains open."

"Put that in your report," I told him. The phone in my office rang and I went to answer it. It was the CPS solicitor to ask if I'd received the news about Silkstone. I said I had and congratulated him on a minor victory. I suspected that was what he wanted to hear. When I went back into the main office Dave was in full swing.

"...and my dad told me to keep a big sweet jar under the bed," he was saying, "and to put a dried pea in it every time we made love. And then, after I was forty, to take one out every time we made love. He said that nobody ever emptied the jar."

"Subject normal," Annette explained as I resumed my seat.

"And have you emptied it?" somebody asked.

"Not yet," I interrupted, "but I'm helping him. Where were we?"

Latham's wife had married, and divorced, for a second time. Silkstone had given her husband a job as a salesman, first in double glazing, then in the financial sector, but he did it very reluctantly. It just wasn't his scene, she'd said, but the money was good. Apparently his affable manner took punters by surprise, and they trusted him, so he did reasonably well without trying too hard. Silkstone came north because of the job, and Latham followed him, but his marriage failed soon after.

"What went wrong?" I asked.

"Partly boredom, partly the affair," Annette replied. "She was attracted to him because of his laid back approach to life, but it quickly paled. At first she couldn't believe that he'd had enough go in him to have an affair. Coming up here was a fresh start, but it didn't work out."

"And what about Caroline Poole? Did you get round to her?"

"Yes, Boss. She remembered, with a bit of prompting, that Peter's car was the same type that we were looking for. She thinks she mentioned it to him and he just shrugged it off. They never discussed it again."

"But Latham wasn't at home with her on the night in question?"

"She doesn't think so, and he didn't ask her for an alibi. It was all a non-event as far as she was concerned."

"Anything else?"

"Yes. She doesn't believe that he killed Margaret. He was the least-violent person imaginable, she said."

"She couldn't believe he was having an affair, either," I pointed out.

"I know," Annette agreed, with a shrug.

Dave said: "I reckon that's about as far as we can go with this, Chas. We've done our bit."

"Yep," I replied, "that just about sews it up. Now answer me this. If bus advertising works, why do they have to advertise it on the backs of all the buses?"

Dave said: "Eh?" and Annette's expression implied something similar.

"Why," I repeated, "do they have to advertise bus advertising? It obviously doesn't work, otherwise they'd advertise something that pays them, like Coca-Cola or Fenning's Fever Cure, wouldn't they?"

"Is that what you've been thinking about all day?" Dave grumbled.

"It was just a thought, troubling my enquiring mind," I replied, but neither of them looked convinced. "OK," I continued, clapping my hands briskly, "reports on my desk by nine in the morning, please. Then we can concentrate on keeping the streets of Heckley safe for the good burghers of this town. Mr Wood wants us to restore the times when you could drop your wage packet on the pavement and it would still be there when you went back for it."

"It would now," Dave said. "Lost in all the rubbish. And nobody would recognise a wage packet, these days."

"What's Fenning's Fever Cure?" Annette asked.

Chapter Seven

A couple of years ago Annabelle and I had a lightning drive down to London to see an exhibition of Pissarro's work at the Barbican. I like him, the reviews were good, and it was an excuse for a day out. On the way home, late that night, Annabelle was making conversation to keep me awake. "If you could have one painting," she began, "just one, to hang above your fireplace, which would it be?"

"Of Pissarro's?" I asked.

"No. Anybody's."

"Oh, in that case, a Picasso. Any Picasso."

"Except him." She knew I was a Picasso freak.

"Right." I gave it a long thought. We were approaching Leicester Forest services and I asked if she wanted to stop. She didn't. "I think it would be a Gauguin," I told her.

"A Gauguin? I've never heard you championing him before."

"Oh, I'm very fond of him," I said, "but there's one in particular that gets me." I thumped my chest for emphasis, saying: "Right here."

"I know!" she exclaimed. "One with lots of nubile South Sea Islanders showing their breasts."

"Where do you get these ideas about me?" I protested. "Actually, it's a self portrait. Gauguin is just coming home from a walk, and his landlady is greeting him at the garden gate. It's called *Bonjour, Monsieur Gauguin*. He captures the moment beautifully. Haven't you ever seen it?"

"No, I don't think I have."

"You'll like it. The colours glow like a stained glass window. I have it in a book somewhere."

The conversation was preserved in my mind with almost every other word that passed between us, but I hadn't expected it to be recalled in this way. The Bart Simpson fridge magnet was drawing my thoughts back to Peter Latham's house, or, more precisely, to the postcard that it pinned against the cold metal. It was the same picture as I'd told Annabelle I'd like to have on my wall, before all others: Gauguin's self portrait, *Bonjour, Monsieur Gauguin*.

There was no message written on the back, no pinhole through it. It was as blank as a juror's expression. Cards like that are only available in galleries. Had Latham bought it for himself, because he liked it above all the other offerings on show? That was something for me to ponder over.

Tuesday morning we hit the headlines. The *UK News*, Britain's foremost tabloid, written for Britons by Britons, with lots of white British bosoms for red-blooded British men, carried yet another world exclusive. Yesterday it had been the convent schoolgirl with the fifty-two inch bust – *Only another seven days to her sweet sixteenth, then all will be revealed!* – today it was: *Why is this man in jail?* above a near life-size photograph of a tearful Tony Silkstone.

Silkstone, we were told when we turned to page five, was living in a prison hell because he had rid the world of a scumbag. Latham was a child killer and rapist who had gone on to kill Silkstone's wife. Cue blurred holiday snap of Margaret, wearing a bikini. Silkstone had done what any good citizen would have done – what the courts should have done years ago – and made sure Latham wouldn't be raping or murdering anybody else. Good riddance to him, but meanwhile poor Silkstone had to wait in an overcrowded prison, three to a cell, while the geriatric legal system, aided and abetted by a police force only interested in statistics, argued what to do with him. *Give him a medal, says the* UK News! On the next page was a picture of Caroline Poole – not the sports day one, thank God – and all the gory details of how her violated young body was found, back in 1984.

Prendergast! I thought. Bloody Prendergast! The courts are supposed to be isolated from public opinion, but if you believe that you probably still think that Christmas is the time of goodwill to all men. And why shouldn't the public have their say, you may argue: it's the public's law, after all. And while we are at it, let's bring back lynching.

Wednesday I went to the Spinners with Dave and we had a good chinwag. We've lapsed a few times, lately. Thursday night I ate at home, alone. I didn't have the opportunity to ask Annette if she fancied a Chinese, and I didn't go looking for her. No point in appearing eager.

Summer fell on the third of July. Otherwise, it slipped by in the usual mixture of showers and mild days. As the saying goes: If you don't like the English weather, just wait ten minutes. I did some walking, finished the painting and one Saturday, in an unprecedented burst of enthusiasm, dug all the shrubs out of the garden. They weren't as labour-saving as I'd planned, so I decided to sow annuals from now on.

It was the silly season. A family in Kent – Mum, Dad and two kids – changed their names so that their initials matched the numberplate on their Mitsubishi Shogun. It was easier and cheaper than doing things the other way round. Heckley's first space probe exploded on the launch pad up on the moors, and a man was drowned trying to sail across the Channel in a shopping trolley.

In the job, we had the opportunity to catch up with burglaries and muggings, and made a few good arrests. A female drug dealer whose home we were raiding one morning drove over Dave's foot while trying to escape. There were all the usual "hopping mad" jokes, and for a few days he came to work with it heavily bandaged, minus shoe. I appointed him office boy, and the troops started calling him Big Foot behind his back. The new CCTV cameras were installed in the market place and soon earned their keep, and the chief constable's daughter was fined and banned for driving while pissed. That cheered everybody up.

Annette took two weeks' leave. I didn't ask her if she was going away, but a card from the Dordogne appeared on the office notice board. The day she was due back I booked into my favourite boarding house in the Lakes. The weather stayed fine, sharpened by the first suggestions of an early autumn, and I bagged a few good peaks.

"Nice holiday?" I asked, when I saw her again.

"Mmm," she nodded, without too much enthusiasm. Ah well, I thought, she has been back at work for a whole week. "And you?" she asked.

"Mmm," I echoed, adding: "You caught the sun." Her freckles were in full flush against a background hue several shades deeper than usual.

She blushed, adding to the rainbow effect. "I try to stay out of it," she said, "but you caught it, too."

"The weather," I explained. "I caught the weather."

On August 19th Sophie learned that she'd earned three straight As, and the following day a magistrate allowed Tony Silkstone out on bail. Swings and roundabouts. We knew he was likely to be released but we'd opposed it, and I'd gone to court in case the magistrates had any questions. They didn't. Silkstone was unlikely to abscond as he'd phoned the police himself to confess, and psychiatric reports were available which said that he was sane and unlikely to offend again. Coming home twice to find your wife murdered and raped by your best friend would be downright bad luck. What probably clinched it was the fact that he had a job to go to. Heckley magistrates' court hadn't tried anyone with a job for nearly two years. Silkstone had been inside on remand for eight weeks, which would be deducted from any sentence he was given, and there were conditions to his bail. He had to surrender his passport, reside at The Garth, Mountain Meadows, and report to Heckley nick twice per week. We wouldn't be inviting him to stay for tea and biscuits.

While I was slogging up Dollywagon Pike, sweating off a hangover, the troops had collared a burglar who put his hand up to just about every outstanding blag on our books. I saw it as making the citizens of Heckley safer in their beds at night, to Gilbert it was an opportunity to make our clear-up figures look better than Olga Korbut's on a good day. Dave and Annette sat him in the front seat of Dave's car and took him for a ride. He took pride in his work, liked to show off about his nefarious deeds. Put him in the company of an attractive lady and he sang like the Newport Male Voice Choir the time they beat the All Blacks. I didn't like using Annette that way, didn't like the thought of his hungry eyes dragging over her contours, stripping her naked, but sometimes I have to act like a grown-up. It's not easy for me.

"A hundred and nineteen," she sighed, five fifteen Thursday evening, as she flopped into the spare chair in my office.

"That'll do," I told her. "No more days out for Laddo with my glamorous assistant. Do they all check out?"

"The ones we've looked at do. He remembers how he got in, what he took, the make of everything and how much he sold it for. A hundred and nineteen householders are going to find out that their burglary – *their* burglary – has been taken into consideration. All that grief, and he walks. He doesn't give a toss about any of them. It doesn't seem fair, Boss."

She was right. He'd stand trial for the one we caught him for and, if found guilty, the judge would be informed of the other offences. The TICs. They'd make a marginal difference to his sentence, his slate would be wiped clean and our figures would look good. Everybody happy except the victims. But villains don't commit crimes against individuals, they commit them against society. It might be your house that is burgled, your car that is stolen and torched, but the crime is against the state, so tough luck.

"It's not fair," I agreed, "but that's the law, and our job ends when we nab him and gather the evidence. Don't worry about it, Annette. If he gets a light sentence and never does another crime, then the system has worked. If he keeps on blagging, we'll keep on catching him. His cards are well-marked."

"I suppose so. Sorry to be a moan, Boss."

"No problem."

She bent forward, as if to rise from the chair, then stopped. "Um, it's Thursday, today," she said, looking me straight in the face.

"Yep, I had noticed."

"Well, after four days of him I don't feel like going home and cooking. Fancy a Chinese? I owe you one."

I pursed my lips, sucked in my cheeks. Anything to look noncommittal. I failed, miserably. "Um, yeah," I said. "Smashing."

"What time?" she asked, rising to her feet.

"Er, now?" I wondered, following her up.

She wanted to go home and change, and it wasn't a bad idea for me to do the same. At seven thirty, clean shaven and crisply attired, I parked outside her downstairs flat on the edge of the town. Annette saw me arrive and came out, wearing jeans and a Berghaus fleece over a T-shirt. Her hair was tied back, where it exploded from out of a black band in an untamed riot. I wanted to sit there and tell her how good she looked, but I didn't.

I settled for: "Hi Kid, still Chinese?"

"Yes, please."

"We could have a change, if you'd prefer it."

"No, Chinese is fine."

"OK." I put the car in first gear and eased away from the kerb. "If I remember rightly," I told her, "it's my turn to get you drunk."

Mr Ho wasn't there, so we didn't have a cabaret or free tea, but it gave us a chance to talk. The holiday had been good but I gained the distinct impression that something about it wasn't too brilliant. The company, perhaps? They'd canoed down the river for four days, staying at campsites and imbibing copious amounts of local produce. It sounded heaven to me. She didn't want to talk about it, and her friend was never mentioned by name. When I ventured to ask if the two girls had enjoyed themselves the first flicker of enthusiasm came into her eyes and she said they had. Inevitably, the conversation found its way back to the job.

"I saw Silkstone this morning," Annette said, "when he came to sign the bail book. He was larger than life and twice as cheerful."

"Cocky little sod," I replied. "I haven't seen him since he was given bail. Anybody would think he'd won the welterweight championship, the way he was jumping up and down, shaking hands with his brief."

"He wants to change his day next week, because he's talking at a sales conference."

"Has his solicitor applied to the court?"

"Yes. He was asking if we'd had notification."

"Did they let him?"

"I imagine so."

"Well they shouldn't have." I adopted my stern expression and growled.

"You think he's got away with it, don't you, Charlie?"

"I don't know, Annette. I really don't know."

"The famous intuition?"

I shook my head. "No, definitely not. I have no sense of intuition. I study the picture, weigh the facts. All the facts, including the seemingly irrelevant."

She tipped her head to one side and rested it against her fist. "Such as what?" she asked.

The waiter brought the portion of toffee bananas we'd decided to share and I spooned a helping on to my side plate. "These are delicious," I told her, passing the remainder across the table.

"Mmm!" she agreed after the first mouthful.

"What do you do with junk mail?" I asked.

"Throw it away, usually," she replied.

"No. In detail, please. Step by step."

"Step by step? Well, I look at the envelopes, then usually

put it all to one side."

"So you don't throw it straight in the bin?"

"Um, no."

"Go on."

"It stays on the hall table until I have an idle moment. Then I open it, read it a bit…and…that's when I chuck it in the bin!"

"What about charity stuff?"

"Charity stuff? That hangs about a bit longer. I usually save it until I have a clear out, then it goes the way of the rest, I'm afraid."

"Do you reply to any?"

"Not as much as I should. Mum has bad arthritis, and I'm scared of it, so I usually send them something. And children's charities. One or two others, perhaps, but not very often."

"I'd say you were a generous, caring person," I told her. "You probably feel uncomfortable about not helping more, but sometimes resent being blackmailed by the more emotional appeals."

"Yes, I think I do."

"There were four items of junk mail in Latham's dustbin, two of them from charities. He'd opened them all and the return envelope and payment slip from one of the charities – the World Wildlife Fund – was pinned on his kitchen noticeboard. Silkstone, on the other hand, handled things more efficiently. There were two items in his bin, both of them unopened. One of them, from ActionAid, was postmarked the day before the killings, so it had probably only arrived that morning." I grinned, saying: "Of the two of them, I'd rather pin it on Silkstone. Wouldn't you?"

She smiled and carefully lifted a spoonful of toffee banana towards her mouth. I watched her lips engulf it and the spoon slide out from between them. "So…" she mumbled, chewing and swallowing, "So…if you were a psychiatrist, doing a profile of whoever had killed Mrs Silkstone, you'd go for the person who dumped his junk mail, unopened."

"Every time."

"What about the evidence?"

"We're just talking profiles. You used the word, I try to avoid it."

"Why?"

"Because most of it is common sense. I don't need a psychiatrist on seventy grand to pinpoint crime scenes on a map for me and say: 'He lives somewhere there.'"

"It might be common sense to you, Charlie. It's mumbo-jumbo to most of us."

"It'll come. There's no substitute for experience."

"So how did Latham's semen get to be all over Mrs Silkstone?" Annette asked.

I shrugged and flapped a hand. I suspect I blushed, too. "In the usual manner?" I suggested.

"So he was there when she died?"

"It looks like it."

"But you think Silkstone was with him?"

"I don't know, Annette," I sighed. "What do some people get up to behind their curtains? It's all a mystery to me. Profiling isn't evidence. It should be used to indicate a line of enquiry, and you should always bear in mind that it might be the wrong line. When you do it backwards, like we've done, it's next to worthless."

She smiled, saying: "That was interesting. Thank you."

"You're welcome, ma'am." A waiter placed the bill in front of me but Annette's arm reached out like a striking rattlesnake and grabbed it.

"My treat," she said.

Light rain was falling when we hit the street, and I guided Annette under the shelter of the shop canopies, my hand in the small of her back. "Shall we have a drink somewhere?" I asked.

"Mmm. Where?"

"Dunno." I was out of touch with the town-centre pubs. Most of them were good, once, but *yoof* culture had taken them over and the music made thinking, never mind conversation, impossible. Annette might not mind that, I thought, and something gurgled in the pit of my stomach. I didn't have a calculator in my pocket, but elementary mental arithmetic said she was nineteen years younger than me. Nowhere would that gap be more evident than in a town-centre pub.

Across the road there blinked the neon sign of the Aspidistra Lounge, Heckley's major nightspot. Formerly the Copper Banana, formerly Luigi's Nite Scene, formerly Mad John's Fashion Emporium, formerly the Regal Kinema. The later two of these enterprises were run by Georgie Casanove, formerly George Hardwick. Georgie was our town's answer to Pete Stringfellow, but without the finesse.

"We could try there," I said, nodding towards the lights.

"The Aspidistra Lounge?"

"Mmm. We could call it work, claim on our expenses. Georgie, the proprietor, isn't exactly a Mr Big, but I think he could finger a few people for us, if he were so inclined. Let's put some pressure on him."

"Right!" she said. "I'm game."

We dashed across the road, avoiding the puddles, and stepped through the open doorway of the disco. A bouncer with a shaven head and Buddy Holly spectacles was leaning on the front desk, chatting to the gum-chewing ticket girl. He straightened up and stepped to one side, taken off-guard by the sudden rush of customers, and tried to look menacing. I've seen more menace on the back of a cornflakes box.

"Two, please," I said to the girl, not sure whether to speak under, over or through the armoured glass that surrounded her. We could have flashed our IDs like TV cops would have done, and they would have let us in, but I preferred it this way.

The words: "Ladies are free before ten," came out of her

mouth in a haze of peppermint that evaporated in the air somewhere between her and the bouncer, who she was gazing towards.

"Oh, I'll take three, then," I answered.

"That'll be seven pounds fifty."

I pushed a tenner towards her and she slid my change and two cloakroom tickets under the window. "Thank you." The bouncer strode over to a door and yanked it open. I ushered Annette forward and said: "Cheers," to him. We were in.

I know one tune that's been written in the last ten years by any of the so-called Brit-Pop stars I see on the front pages of the tabloids, and the DJ was playing it.

I leaned towards Annette and said: "Verve," into her ear. She stared at me, her eyes wide. "Bitter Sweet Symphony," I added, determined to exploit my sole opportunity to swank. It's a simple catchy rhythm, repeated *ad nauseum*. I nodded my head in time with it: *Dum-dum-dum, dum-dum-dum, dum-dum-dum-dum, dum-dum-dum*. Once heard, it's ringing through your brain for days, a bit like *Canon in D*.

"I'm amazed!" she gasped, and I rewarded her with a wink.

Our brains slowly modified our senses to accommodate the sudden change in environment. Irises widened to dispel the jungle gloom and nerves in our ears adjusted their sensitivity to just below the pain barrier. Noses twitched, seeking out pheromones from anyone of the opposite sex who was ripe for mating. Four million years of evolution, and this was what it was all leading to.

"It's a bit quiet," I shouted above the battery of chords bouncing through my body.

"It's early," Annette yelled back at me, in explanation.

It was the same as every other disco I remembered from my younger days. A bright, small dance floor; bored DJ sorting records behind a console straight from NASA; pulsating lights and lots of red velvet. OK, so we didn't have lasers and dry ice then, but they're no big deal. Still permeating everything was that same old feeling of despair. These places always look a dump when you see them with the house lights up. This looked a dump in semi-darkness. When I was a kid we called it the Bug Hutch, and came every Saturday to catch up with Flash Gordon's latest adventures.

Georgie himself was behind the bar, attired like a cross between Bette Davis on a bad night and Conan the Barbarian. "It wouldn't cost much to convert this back to a cinema, George," I told him, flapping a hand in the direction of the auditorium.

"Hello, Mr Priest," he growled, managing to sound threatening and limp simultaneously. "Not expecting any trouble, are we?"

"Who could cause trouble in an empty house?"

"It's early. We'll fill up, soon as the pubs close."

"Two beers, please." The locks on his head were platinum blond, but those cascading through the slashed front of his satin shirt were grey.

"What sort?"

I looked at Annette and she leaned over the bar, examining the wares. "Foster's Ice, please," she said.

"Two," I repeated.

He popped the caps and placed the bottles on the counter. "That'll be four pounds fifty," he told me.

I passed him another tenner, asking: "How much is there back on the bottles?"

"Isn't he a caution," he said to Annette as he handed me my change.

We walked uphill, away from the bar and the speakers, feeling our way between the empty tables to where the rear stalls once were. It was much quieter back there, and a few other people were sitting in scattered groups, arranged according to some logic based on personal territory. As the place filled territories would shrink and a pecking order emerge. There were two couples, three men presumably from out of town, and a group of girls. We looked for a table equidistant from the girls and the couples, but before we could sit down one of the girls waved to me.

It was Sophie, with three of her friends. I nudged Annette and gestured for her to follow. The girls moved their chairs to make room for us, removing sports bags from the vacant ones.

"It's Charles, he's my uncle," Sophie told her friends, a big smile illuminating her face.

"Hello, Uncle Charles," they chorused.

I introduced Annette to them, and Sophie rattled off three names that I promptly forgot. She and Sophie renewed their acquaintance.

"You don't do this for amusement, do you?" I asked, looking around at the decor.

"We've been playing badminton at the leisure centre," someone informed me.

"We just come in for a quick drink and a dance," another added.

"It's free before ten," Sophie said.

"Right," I nodded. Apart from the price of the drinks, it sounded a reasonable arrangement. I gritted my teeth and asked them what they'd have.

"Thanks, Uncle Charles," they all said when I returned, six bottles dangling from between my fingers. One of the girls, dark-haired, petite and vivacious, said: "Can I call you Charlie, Uncle Charles? I already have an Uncle Charles."

"I'd prefer it if you all called me Charlie. Uncle Charles makes me feel old."

"How old are you?"

"Twenty-eight," I lied, glancing up at the ceiling.

"Gosh, that is old."

They were in high spirits, the adrenaline still pumping after a couple of hours on court, and I began to wonder if joining them had been such a good idea. Four confident young women at the crossroads: left for marriage and a family; right for a career in whatever they chose; straight on for both. I didn't feel old – I felt fossilised.

The music paused, the DJ spoke for the first time, and when it started again the four of them jumped to their feet, prompted by some secret signal.

"We dance to this."

"Come on, Annette. Can you dance, Charlie?"

"Can I dance? Can I dance? *Watch my hips.*"

I had a quick sip of lager, for sustenance, and followed them on to the floor. The difference in rhythm or melody was invisible to me, but this was evidently danceable, what had gone before wasn't. I joined the circle of ladies, swivelled on one leg and wondered about joint replacements.

The style of dancing hadn't changed, so I didn't make a complete fool of myself. The girls put on a show, swaying and gyrating, lissom as snakes, but I gave them a step or two. Fifteen minutes later the DJ slowed it down and the floor emptied again, faster than a golf course in a thunderstorm.

We finished our tasteless beer and left. There was a street vendor outside, selling hot dogs. The girls' ritual was to have one each then make their ways home. I couldn't have eaten one if Delia Smith herself was standing behind the counter in her wimple. Just the smell of them made me want to dash off and bite a postman's leg. We stood talking as they wolfed them down. Young appetites, young tastes, young digestive systems. Here we go again, I thought.

Annette shared my views on hot dogs, and declined one. When we'd established that nobody needed a lift we left. "That was fun," Annette said as we drove off.

"It was, wasn't it."

"Sophie's grown up."

"I had noticed."

"The little dark one – Shani – took a shine to you."

"Understandably."

"And not a size ten between them," she sighed.

I freewheeled to a standstill outside her flat, dropping on to sidelights but leaving the engine running. "Thanks for the meal, Ms Brown," I said.

"You're welcome, Mr Priest," she replied. "I've enjoyed myself."

"Good. That's the intention."

"Well it worked."

After a moment's uncomfortable silence I asked: "Are you…are you going away, this weekend."

"Yes," she mumbled.

"Right."

She pulled the catch and pushed the door open. "Charlie…" she began, half turning back towards me.

"Mmm?"

"Oh just, you know…thanks for…for being, you know…a pal. A friend."

"A gentleman. You mean a gentleman."

"Yes, I suppose I do."

"Just as long as you understand one thing."

She looked puzzled, worried. "What's that?"

"That it's bloody difficult for me."

"Is it?"

"Yes."

Her smile made me want to plunder a convent. "Goodnight, Charlie," she said.

"Goodnight, Annette."

The house was in darkness, blind and forlorn. The outside light is supposed to turn itself on at dusk, but it looked as if the bulb had blown again. The streetlights illuminate the front, but the side door is in shadow. I avoided the milk bottle standing on the step and felt for the keyhole with a finger, like drunks do, before inserting the key. It was cold inside, because a front had swept in from Labrador and the central heating was way down low. I turned the thermostat to thirty and the timer to constant. That'd soon warm things up. I made some tea and lit the gas fire. I was too alert to sleep, too many thoughts and rhythms tumbling around in my head. The big CD player was filled with Dylan, but that wasn't what I needed:

I know that I could find you, in somebody's room.
It's a price I have to pay: you're a big girl all the way.

Not tonight, Bob, thank you. I flicked through the titles until one flashed a light in my brain. Gorecki's third; a good choice. Sometimes, the best way to deal with a hurt, real or imaginary, is to overwhelm it with somebody else's sadness. I slipped the gleaming disc from its cover and placed it on the turntable.

"What do some people get up to, behind the curtains?" I'd asked Annette. "Profiling isn't evidence," I'd said. They get up to everything you could imagine, and plenty of things you couldn't, and that's the truth. Read the personal column in your newspaper; look at the magazines on the top shelf in any newsagents; explore the internet; look at the small ads in the tabloids. That's the visible bit.

We don't stop when we prove that someone committed a murder. We carry on until we prove that everybody else involved didn't commit it. Sometimes, with some juries, nothing less will do.

If it wasn't for the evidence, we'd have arrested Silkstone for the murder of his wife. Everything pointed to him, except the evidence. That's a big except. The evidence, and the witness, pointed to Latham. That witness, of course, was Silkstone, and Latham was in no position to defend himself. The obvious solution was that Silkstone killed them both after discovering that they were lovers, but that's not what he said happened, and he was the only witness. Next favourite, for me, was that Silkstone killed Latham out of self-preservation, because they were both there when Margaret died, but, like the professor said, it would be a bug-ger to prove. Perhaps they did the Somerset job together, too. Sadistic murdering couples were usually a male and a female, with the male the dominant partner, but there were exceptions. Some people think the Yorkshire Ripper didn't always act alone, and the Railway Rapist almost certainly had an accomplice. And even if they're wrong, there's got to be a first time. There's always got to be a first time.

My job is to catch murderers. It's a dirty job, and dirt rubs off. Like the men who empty my dustbin, I come home with the smell of it following me. To catch a jackal you must first study its ways. Before you can look a rat in the eyes it is necessary to get down on your belly and roll in the dirt. Silkstone and Latham had known each other for a long time; married two sisters; committed adultery with two women who were friends. No doubt they'd shared a few adventures. Had they shared their women, too?

How does it start? A casual boast, man to man, after a few pints? A giggled comment between the wives after one too many glasses of wine? Expressions of admiration, followed by a tentative suggestion? Jaded senses find new life, curiosity is aroused, objections dismissed. "If we all agree, nobody gets hurt, do they?" Next thing you know, you're alone with your best friend's partner, undoing those buttons that you've looked at so often across the table, revealing the mysteries that they conceal.

Is that what happens? Don't ask me. I thought Fellatio was a character in *Romeo and Juliet* until I was thirty-two. I awoke to Dawn Upshaw in full voice, and on that pleasant note crawled up the stairs to bed.

Monday morning I rang the clerk to the court who had granted Silkstone a variation to his bail conditions. "I believe he's supposed to be speaking at a sales conference," I said.

"That's what his solicitor told us in the application, Mr Priest."

"Did he say what time?"

"Yes, I have the letter here. He's speaking at two p.m., for half an hour, but he asked if he could spend the full day at the conference. We saw no reason to object and we've told him to report tomorrow, instead. It's not our intention to interfere with his employment."

"No, that's fair enough. And where is this conference, exactly?"

"Um, here we are: the Leeds Winchester Hotel."

"Good. Thanks for your help."

"Is there a problem, Mr Priest? Would you have preferred it if we'd contacted you earlier?"

"No, no problem at all. I was just thinking that I might go along and listen to him."

The troops had plenty to catch up on, and the super was more interested in his monthly fly-fishing magazine, so I didn't tell him my intentions. Just before one I walked out of the office and drove to Leeds.

The Winchester Hotel is part of the revitalised riverside area, to the south of town, near the new Royal Armouries. Leeds has an inner ring road, which is only half a ring, and something called the Loop, which doesn't join up with it. I missed the hotel, drove into the city centre and came out again following the M1 signs, except that the M1 is now called the M621 and the new M1 is not what I wanted. I drove back into the city centre and tried again.

This time I found it. The Winchester chain of hotels caters for business trade working to a budget. It's room-only accommodation, without the frills. No Corby trouser press, no complimentary shower cap. If you want to eat, there's a restaurant on the ground floor. I pushed my way through the door at a few seconds before two, just as the tail end of a group of people disappeared into the lift. The doors closed, leaving me stranded. I looked around for a sign saying where the conference was being held, but there wasn't one. Presumably it wasn't necessary. Ah well, I'm not a detective for nothing. The illuminated indicator above the lift door had flicked through the lower numbers and was now stationary at number five. That must be it, I thought, pressing the button.

There was a movement beside me and I turned to see a

little man standing there, his face moist with perspiration. The indicator over the lift door to my left stopped at G, something pinged and the door opened. I gestured for the man to enter first. You never know, maybe there'd been a failure of electronics and the lift wasn't really there. He didn't fall to his death so I followed him in.

"Five?" I asked.

"Yes please." He was seriously overweight and appeared to be wearing a skirt over his blue-check trousers. A name badge declared that he was called Gerald Vole.

"Er, napkin," I whispered, nodding towards his nether regions.

"Oh God!" he exclaimed, snatching it from his belt. He managed a nervous smile, saying: "The service was terrible in the restaurant," by way of explanation.

"It always is," I confirmed, airily.

The door pinged and opened, and I gestured him forward. "Enjoying the conference?" I asked.

"Yes, very much. There's so much to learn, though. Are you with the company?"

"Yes, for my sins," I lied.

"Sales?"

"Head office," I told him, adding: "Personnel," because it felt good.

"Gosh!" he replied, impressed.

"Charlie Priest," I said, offering him my hand.

"Gerry Vole," he squeaked as I crushed his clammy fingers. "Pleased to meet you."

"Welcome to TGF, Gerry," I said.

The door we entered through was at the back of the room, fortunately. The conference facilities consisted of one side of the whole fifth floor being left empty, the space divided into three by sliding partitions. Trans Global Finance had booked the lot, so all the partitions were retracted. The place was nearly full, but we found chairs on the end of the back row and sat down. Gerry produced a typist's pad from a pocket and rested it on his knee. I stared at row after row of shaven necks poking from blue suit collars. It could have been a Mormon revivalist meeting. Gerry's checks and my sports jacket were the only discordant notes. Gerry would have to learn to conform; I make a speciality of not doing so.

The door behind me closed with a bang and I took a sly peep back. A man and woman who would have looked completely at home on local-network breakfast TV were standing there, and he'd pulled the door shut. She had nice knees, and I'd seen her type a hundred times before. Sometimes she, or her sister, was in the precinct, handing out freebies for the local newspaper; other times she was there in her clingy T-shirt and Wonder Bra extolling the virtues of holidays in Cornwall or Tenerife. A promotions girl. Anxious to shake the dust of Heckley from her stilettos but not good looking enough to be a model, not bright enough to be a holiday rep. Promises of riches galore had brought her into the finance industry, and today she was a cheerleader.

"Welcome back!" a voice boomed from the front. The owner had oddly luxuriant grey hair and could easily have done Billy Graham on *Stars in Their Eyes*. "And now for the session you're all waiting for," he proclaimed. "It's my proud duty to introduce the man we all think of as the Prince of Closing. The man who can, literally, walk on water…"

Boy, this I've got to see, I thought. Gerry Vole beside me was wriggling in his seat, trying to make himself taller.

"Ladies and gentlemen…"

"No! No! No!" Silkstone was there, waving his arms as he dashed on to the stage to interrupt the eulogy, but just too late, of course, and the rest of it was drowned by the applause. It started behind me in a burst of small explosions and rattled through the audience like machine gun fire. "Good afternoon!" Silkstone shouted.

"Good afternoon," we yelled back.

"I didn't hear you! GOOD AFTERNOON!"

"GOOD AFTERNOON!" This time they heard us in Barnsley.

"Right on!" I added as the reverberations faded away, and nudged Gerry with my elbow.

"Yeah!" he shouted, recovering his balance and punching the air with a podgy fist.

"What is that magical quality that converts a lead into a sale?" Silkstone demanded of us.

"Closing!" The word jumped around the auditorium like a firecracker.

"What are the three golden bullets in the salesman's armoury?"

"Closing, closing, closing."

"You don't seem sure!" he shouted. "So I'll tell you!" There was a table and chair on the low stage, with a glass and water jug on the table. Silkstone leapt up on to the chair and shouted: "Number one – closing!" Long pause for effect as he made eye contact with the front rows. "Number two – closing!" Another leap took him on to the table. "Number three – CLOSING!"

Gerry, beside me and beside himself, was busy scribbling. He'd written: *3 golden bullets: 1 – closing, 2 – closing, 3 – closing!!!*

Silkstone, still up on the table, was launching into an anecdote about how Bill Gates got to be the world's richest man. Presumably, I thought, because gates are good at closing. After five minutes I'd had enough. I reached out and took Gerry's pad from him. On it I wrote: *4 – treat every client as if he might be an eccentric millionaire* and winked as I passed it back. "I'm off," I said, rising to my feet. "Good luck." He read what I'd written and stared at me, eyes wide, mouth open, as if I'd just given him the co-ordinates of the Holy Grail.

I yanked the door open and took a last look at Silkstone. He had one foot on the floor, one on the chair when the movement at the back of the room caught his eye. He froze in mid-stride and fell silent as he recognised me. Other heads turned my way. I stepped out through the opening and closed the door behind me. "That'll give him something to think about," I mumbled to myself as I headed towards the lift.

Gwen Rhodes played netball for England and hockey for Kent. I had trials with Halifax Town as a goalkeeper, but wasn't signed up. I considered myself a sportsman, years ago, although I never reached the heights that Gwen did. We sit on a committee together, and have talked about the value of sport over a cup of coffee in the canteen. These days, the only place you can regularly see honesty, courage, passion is on the playing field. Out there, with the sting of sweat in your eyes and the taste of blood in your mouth, where you come from and who you know is of no help at all.

So when I saw the note on my desk saying that she wanted me to ring her I didn't wait. "The Governor, please," I said, when the switchboard at Bentley Prison answered.

"Who wants her, please?"

"Detective Inspector Priest, Heckley CID."

"One moment."

I waited for the music, wondering what might be appropriate – *Unchained Melody? Please release me, let me go?* – but none came. "Hello, Charlie. Thanks for ringing," Gwen's plummy voice boomed in my ear.

"My pleasure, Gwen. Long time no see. Shouldn't we be having a meeting soon, or did you ring to tell me I'd missed it?"

"Between you and me, Charlie, I think that committee has probably quietly faded away. We didn't achieve much, did we?"

"Lip service, Gwen, that's what it's all about. Make it look as if you are doing something. So what can I do for you? I'm available, Saturday morning, if you need a goalie."

"Oh, those were the days. I may have some information for you, Charlie, but first of all, an apology."

"Go on."

"You know that we monitor inmates' calls, tape-record them for transcription at a later date."

"Mmm."

"Well, we've rather fallen behind lately, so this weekend I put one of my officers on to them, and he's come up with something that might be of interest to you."

"I'm all ears, Gwen."

"Does the name Chiller mean anything?"

"Chiller?"

"Yes."

"No."

"You disappoint me."

"I'm sorry."

"He's supposed to be the most wanted man in Britain, according to the tabloids."

"Chiller?"

"That's his nickname, a contraction."

I repeated the name softly, to myself: "Chiller-Chiller-Chiller," until it hit me. "Chilcott!" I pronounced. "Kevin Chilcott!"

"That's the man."

"He's a cop killer," I said, suddenly alert. "What can you tell me?"

"Just that one of our inmates, a hard case called Paul Mann, telephoned a London number, four weeks ago, asking for a message to be sent to someone called Chiller about 'a job'. Since then there has been a quantity of rather enigmatic traffic, but the name was never mentioned again. Sums were quoted. There's lots of other stuff which may or may not be related."

"Chilcott's a hitman," I said. "Maybe someone's putting some work his way."

"That's what my man thought. He's ex-Pentonville, and was there at the same time as Kevin Chilcott. He said everybody called him Chiller, and he rejoiced in the name."

"When can I come over and see this stuff?"

"I should be free about four-thirty," she replied.

"Right, put the kettle on. Will you make it right for me at the gate, please?" Getting into prisons is harder than getting out of them.

"It's a long time since you were here" she observed. "I'm over the road, now. Just ask and they'll point you in the right direction."

I did some thinking before I went down to Control to find someone authorised to interrogate the computer systems. The CRO would tell us Chilcott's record, the PNC would have other stuff about him. Confidential stuff. Trouble was, his name would be tagged in some way, and any enquiry we made would be relayed straight to Special Branch and NCIS. They were on our side, I decided, so I did it anyway.

The print-outs didn't make pleasant reading. Chilcott started young, served the usual apprenticeship. He had a full house of cautions, followed by probation and youth custody. As an adult he'd served two years for robbery and eight for armed robbery. After that, it was all hearsay. A series of building society raids were put down to him, as was a bank heist that netted over half a million and left a security guard shot dead. I was wrong about one thing – he wasn't a cop killer. A uniformed PC, under-experienced and over-diligent, walked into a stake-out that nobody had told him about and was shot for his troubles. He didn't die, but in his shoes I'd have preferred it. The bullet fractured his spine, high up, and left him a quadriplegic. Chilcott escaped and fled the country. Nothing had been heard of him since 1992, but rumour linked him with a string of gangland killings. Maybe the money was running out, I thought.

Her Majesty's Prison Bentley sits four-square on a hill just outside Halifax. It's a Victorian-Gothic pile, complete with battlements, crenellated turrets and fake arrow-slits, but with the proportions of a warthog. The architect was probably warned about the gales that howl down from the north, so he built it squat and solid. It strikes terror in my heart every time I visit the place. I swung into the car-park, mercifully empty because we were outside visiting hours, and gazed up at the gaunt stone walls, wondering if Mad King Ludwig ever had a skinhead brother.

Gwen had told the gatehouse to expect me, but they put a show on before accompanying me to her office. Double-check my ID, a quick frisk and then through the metal detector. She runs a tight ship. She has to; Bentley houses some of the most dangerous men in the country, as well as remand prisoners.

I'd forgotten how handsome she is, in a Bloomsbury-ish sort of way. Strong features, hair pinned back, long elegant fingers. No faded delicacy with Gwen, though. At a shade under six feet tall she'd be a formidable opponent, tearing towards you brandishing a hockey stick. We shook hands and pretended to kiss cheeks, and I flopped into the leather chair she indicated.

I told her she looked well and she said I looked tired. That made it twice, recently. One of her officers, male, approaching retirement age, knocked and poked his head round the door to ask if I preferred tea or coffee. Gwen thanked him, calling him Thomas. He called her ma'am.

"These are the transcripts," she said, reaching across the polished top of her desk to pull a sheaf of loose sheets towards us. She'd joined me at the wrong side of it, where you stood to receive her wrath; or words of encouragement; or the news that your wife and the bloke you didn't grass on had run away to Spain with all the money. "I've highlighted the relevant bits," she added, pulling her chair closer to mine, so we could both read them. I detected the merest hint of her perfume, which was heavy and musky and put me off balance for a moment or two.

I studied the lists, then said: "I never realised just how much work was entailed with these, Gwen." Someone had to obtain a printout of all the calls, with times and numbers, and then transfer that information to a transcript of all the tape-recorded conversations that somebody else had prepared.

"It's a bind, Charlie. And all for so little return."

"Now and again you come up with gold," I said. "Maybe this is one of those times. How do you know who made the calls?"

"The hard way. An inmate has to ask to use the phone, and we keep a book."

"Which wing is whatsisname on?"

"Paul Mann? A-wing."

Maximum security, for long term prisoners in the early years of their sentences, and the nutcases. "What'd he do?"

"Poured paraffin over his girlfriend and ignited it. It burns deeper than petrol, apparently."

"She died?"

"Eventually."

"Mr Nice Guy." I read the scraps of conversation from the sheet, next to the London number he'd dialled:

V1: Billy?
V2: Yeah.
V1: S'me. Can't talk for long. Only got one f———- card. Tell Davy I need a job doing, don't I. [Indecipherable] S'important.
V2: A job? What sort of f——— job.
V1: Never you f——— mind. Just tell him I know someone who wants to buy a Roller.
V2: A f——— Roller? What you on about?
V1: Listen, c—-. Ask Davy to have a word with Chiller about it. And don't ask no f——— questions.
V2: Oh, right.
V1: I'll ring you Tuesday.
V2: OK. S'long.
V1: S'long.

Tuesday's conversation was even less fulsome:

V1: Billy?
V2: Yeah.
V1: You talk to Davy?
V2: Yeah.
V1: What's he say?
V1: He says a decent f——— Roller is hard to come by these days. Could be f——— expensive. Cost your friend a packet.
V1: How expensive?
V2: Fifty big ones, plus expenses. Number f——— plates, an' all.
V1: [Indecipherable]
V2: You what?
V1: I said tell him I'll f——— think about it.

Two days later we had:

V1; That you, Billy?
V2: Yeah. Listen. Davy can do your friend the Roller, at the price agreed, including all expenses, if you can arrange accommodation. No f——— problem. And he wants to know when he'd like to take delivery. He says sooner the f——— better.
V1: Right. Right. Tell him we might have a f——— deal.

Thomas came in with the teas, on a tray with china cups and a plate of biscuits. We both thanked him and Gwen poured the tea. I reached for a bourbon, saying: "Whoever transcribed this cares about your sensibilities."

She beamed at me. "Sweet, isn't he?"

"What's Mann's tarrif?" I asked.

"Thirty years," she replied, easing an over-filled cup in my direction.

"So ordering a Rolls Royce would seem a little premature?"

"I'd say so."

"And would you say that fifty thousand pounds was a reasonable price for killing a man?"

The cup was halfway to her lip. She paused and lowered it back to its saucer. "Mann killed his girlfriend because the baby was crying," she told me.

I bit half off the biscuit and slowly chewed it. When my mouth was empty I asked: "What did he do with the baby?"

"The baby? Oh, the room was on fire, so he tried to save the baby. He threw her out of the window. Says he forgot they were on the seventh floor."

"Jee-sus," I sighed.

Chapter Eight

The prisons have a dilemma. It doesn't take long for a hierarchy to form, with men like Mann and Chiller as the kingpins. They build up a coterie of acolytes and prey on the weaker inmates. Contrary to popular opinion, for most prisoners once is enough. All they want to do is put their heads down, serve their time and never come back. Faced with someone like Mann, they back down, accept the bottom bunk, hand over their phone cards and cigarettes. The men at the top never want for drugs, booze, cigarettes or sex. They still run their outside empires through a network of contacts, and anyone who steps out of line gets hurt. The occasional broken leg, slashed face or crushed hand is amazingly good for business

So the prison governors move them. They allow the hard men to become established and then transfer them to the other end of the country, with maximum inconvenience. It's called ghosting. He eats his breakfast in Brixton, full of the joys of life, and at lunchtime finds himself hobbling out of the van in Armley, squinting up at the coils of razor wire above the walls, wondering who the top cat is. On any Monday morning prison vans, usually accompanied by the local police, are criss-crossing the country like worker bees seeking out new feeding grounds.

There is a down-side, of course. The constant exchange of prisoners creates an unofficial inter-jail communications network that cannot be improved upon. When the inmates of Hull decide to have a dirty protest, or to hurl tiles down from the roof, it's no coincidence that the prisoners in Strangeways, Bentley and Parkhurst choose exactly the same time to do exactly the same thing. The great revolution of the late twentieth century has been in communications, and the prison population is leading the field.

Some of it is high-tech, some of it lower than you'd

believe people could go. Phone cards, not snout, are the new currency, but the big porcelain phone in the corner is available to everyone with a strong stomach. The days of slopping out are over because most cells now have a toilet. The prisoners are not as overjoyed about this as you might expect. Once they had a room, now they have a shithole in the corner of the cell, behind an aluminium sink unit to give a modicum of privacy when you're sitting there. What no one envisaged was the communications opportunities this created. What no one realised was the ingenuity of caged men.

All the toilets lead down to a common drain. Take a small receptacle – your cellmate's drinking cup will do fine – and drain all the water out of the toilet u-bend. Pour it down the sink. You are now connected to the drain. If somebody else does the same thing elsewhere in the prison, even in another wing, you can now have a conversation without raising your voice above a whisper. There may be interruptions of a nature that BT users never experience, but you'll never be left hanging on through three movements of the *Four Seasons*. To break the line, terminate the call, you simply flush the toilet.

I didn't feel hungry. I'd had no lunch but the thought of having a long and meaningful conversation with your head down the pan, listening to all the extraneous noises, savouring the odours, is a wonderful appetite suppressant. Perhaps I could sell the concept to Weight Watchers and never have to work again. I won twenty-five thousand pounds in a quiz programme on television, then had a long hot soak in the bath. Freshly scrubbed, I managed a tin of chicken soup, with some decent bread, followed by a few custard creams. In deference to all the people who think I looked tired I went to bed early and, unusual for me, slept like a little dormouse.

"Where were you, yesterday?" Gilbert asked at the morning prayer meeting.

"Bentley prison," I replied, sliding a chair across and placing my mug of tea on a beer mat on his desk. "I left word." There were only the two of us, because Gareth Aidey had a court appointment and was polishing the buttons on his best tunic.

"So you really went to Bentley?"

"Of course I did. Where did you think I was – having a round of golf?"

"I don't know what you get up to. I'm only the super. Regional Crime Squad were after you, said that Special Branch had tipped them off that you were on to something."

"Christ, that was quick."

"Nobody had a clue what it was all about. I felt a right wally."

"Sorry, Gilbert, but I didn't know myself until after five o'clock. I was at Bentley until nearly seven."

"So what was it about?"

I found the transcripts in my briefcase and laid them on his desk. "It looks as if someone in Bentley prison is trying to organise a hitman to do a job, and the hitman is a certain Kevin Chilcott. Remember him?"

"Kevin Chilcott? He killed a police officer, didn't he, ten or twelve years ago?"

"As good as. I consulted the PNC about him and SB must have picked it up."

"Humph!" he snorted. "Makes you wonder what else they pick up. So what have you got?" Gilbert read the excerpts, running his finger along the lines like a schoolchild. He mumbled to himself and turned the page over.

"That's just the usual stuff," I told him.

"What do you call the usual stuff?"

"Oh, you know…" – I adopted a whining voice – "*That you Sharron? Yeah. I love you. I love you. How's your mum. She's all right. Tell her I love her. She sez she love's you. How's your Tracy? She's all right. Tell her I love her. She's pregnant. Is she? Yeah. Whose is it? Dunno. When's it due? January. It can't be mine, then.*"

Gilbert said: "OK, OK, I get the message. So this stuff stands out, then."

"Like a first-timer at a nudist colony."

"You'd better let RCS know."

"I'll do it now."

Gilbert stood up and retrieved his jacket from behind the door. "I'm off to headquarters," he told me. "Monthly meeting. You're in charge. What can I report about the Margaret Silkstone case?"

"Solved," I replied.

"Good. And the Peter Latham job?"

"Solved."

"Good. As long as you remember you said it. Do you want me to tell them about this?" He waved a hand towards the papers on his desk.

"Might as well," I replied. "Give you something to talk about."

Special Branch are not a band of super-cops, based in London. Every Force has an SB department, quietly beavering away at god-knows what. They have offices at all the airports and other points of entry, and keep an eye on who comes in and goes out of the country. Anti-terrorism is their speciality, but they keep a weather-eye open for big-league criminals on the move. If you don't mind unsociable hours and have a high boredom threshold it could be the career for you. Special Branch don't feel collars, they gather information. The Regional Crime Squads specialise in heavy stuff like organised crime, the syndicates and major criminals. They are experts at covert surveillance, tailing people and using informers. They move about, keep a low profile, infiltrate gangs. Dangerous stuff.

"So where is he?" I asked an RCS DI in London when I finally found myself talking to someone with an interest in the case.

"Wish we knew," he confessed. "Over the last five years

we've had sightings in Spain, Amsterdam and Puerto Rico. He moves around. What we do know, though, is that the money must have run out by now, even if he's living very modestly. Half a million sounds a lot, but when someone charges you thirty per cent for converting it to used notes or a foreign currency, and someone else charges you for their silence, and so on, it soon depletes."

"In the transcripts he says make it quick," I told him.

"Sounds like he's getting desperate, then. We'll dig out a new description of him and circulate it to all points of entry. After that, we can only hope that someone spots him. Which district are you?"

"Number three."

"So that will be our Leeds office?"

"That's right."

"Any chance of you getting the transcripts over there? If the conversations took place a month ago we might be too late already."

"'Fraid not. I'll address them to you and leave them behind the front desk." It was their baby, so they could do the running around.

"OK. I'll arrange for them to be collected, and thanks for the information."

"My pleasure." I asked him to keep us informed and replaced the receiver. Another satisfied customer, I thought, as I delved into Gilbert's filing cabinet where he keeps his chocolate digestives.

After two of them I rang Gwen Rhodes at HMP Bentley and told her that the hard men were now on the Chiller case and that they had promised to keep us informed, but don't hold your breath. People say they will, then don't bother. It's a mistake. I always make a point of saying my thank-yous, letting people know what happened. They remember, and next time you want something from them you get it with a cherry on the top.

Gwen said: "So the message was definitely for Chilcott,

was it?"

"They think so, Gwen. Apparently his money should have run out by now, and they're expecting him to make a move. This might be it."

"Good," she said. "Good. Glad we could be of assistance."

"Listen, Gwen," I said. "While you're on the line, there's something else I'd like to ask you."

"Ye-es, Charlie," she replied, in a tone that might have been cautious, may even have been expectant. What was I going to ask her? How about dinner sometime? The theatre?

"A few weeks ago you had a remand prisoner of mine called Anthony Silkstone," I said. "I was wondering how he took to life on the inside."

"Silkstone," she repeated, downbeat. "Tony Silkstone?"

"That's the man."

"Killed his wife's murderer?"

"That's him. Anything to report about his behaviour?"

"I read about him in the papers but I didn't realise he was one of yours, Charlie. Knew we had him, and he certainly didn't cause any problems. Let's see what the oracle says…" I heard the patter of keys as she consulted the computer terminal that sat on her desk, followed by a soft: "Here we are," to herself, and a long silence.

"Gosh," she said when she came back on the line. "You can send us as many like him as you can find, Charlie. A golden prisoner by any standards."

"Oh," I said. "What did he do?"

"It's all here. First of all the other inmates, the remandees that is, regarded him as some sort of folk hero. It explains that the person Silkstone killed had murdered his – Silkstone's – wife and was also a sex offender. Is that true? Was he a sex offender?"

"Um, it looks like it."

"So that gave him a big pile of kudos, in their eyes. You

know what they all think of nonces. It goes on to say that Silkstone took an active part in the retraining programme we're conducting, and became a popular lecturer in salesmanship. He even promised one or two of them an interview with his company, when they were all released. We need more like him, Charlie. Send us more, please."

"That sounds like my man. He's a little treasure, no mistake."

"He certainly is. Anything else you'd like to ask?"

Dinner? The theatre? "No, Gwen," I replied, "but thanks a lot."

Wednesday morning Sophie Sparkington received a letter from the admissions tutor at St John's College, Cambridge, where she would be reading history, and I received one from the matron of the Pentland Court Retirement Home, Chipping Sodbury.

Mine was handwritten on headed paper, and was addressed to the senior detective at Heckley Police Station. It said:

> Dear Sir
> One of our clients, Mrs Grace Latham, who is elderly and frail, dictated this letter to me and asked for it to be forwarded to you. If you have any queries please do not hesitate to contact me.
> Yours faithfully
> Jean Hullah (Mrs) (Matron)

Stapled behind it was another sheet of the same paper, with the same handwriting. This one read:

> Dear Sir,
> My name is Grace Latham and I am the mother of Peter John Latham who was murdered. Now that he is dead the papers are saying terrible things about him.

These are not true but he cannot defend himself. Peter was a good son and I know he could not have done these terrible things. He was kind and gentle, and wouldn't hurt a fly, and was always good to me. Please catch the proper murderer and prove that my son, Peter, did not do it.

Yours faithfully
Jean Hullah (Mrs) (Matron)
p.p. Grace Latham

Dave came in and I handed him the letters. He read them in silence and shrugged his shoulders.

"Mothers," I said.

"Yeah," he replied.

"Which would you rather be: the murderer's parent or the victim's parent?"

"Don't ask me. I wonder if Hitler's mother said that she always knew he'd turn out to be a bastard, or if she loved him right to the end. What do you want to do with it?"

"Drop her a reply, please. Not the card. Make it a letter, in my name. Then show it to Annette and stick it in the file."

"OK. Nigel rang," Dave said. "Wants to know if we're going to the Spinners tonight. He says long-time-no-see."

"What did you tell him?"

"Eight thirty."

"Looks like we are, then."

"Oh, and he says not to laugh, but he's grown a moustache."

"A moustache?"

"That's what he says."

"Nigel?"

"Mmm."

"This I've got to see."

But I didn't, because he never came. We've developed a new routine for our Wednesdays out. The Spinners is about two miles from each of our houses, so we walk there. It's a half-hour power walk and that first pint slides down like snow off a roof when you stroll into the pub and lean on the bar. Towards closing time Dave's wife, Shirley, comes in the car for an orange juice and takes us home.

Dave had arrived first and was sitting in our usual corner. I collected the pint he'd paid for and joined him.

"Sophie heard from Cambridge this morning," he told me before I was seated. "We're going down at the weekend to look at her accommodation."

"Fantastic. I'll have to buy her a present. Don't suppose there's any point in asking you what she might want."

He looked glum. "Just about everything. Pots, pans, microwave. You name it, she needs it. Then there's a small matter of books, tuition fees, meals, rent. It's never-ending."

"That's the price of having brainy kids," I said.

"Brainy *kid*. Daniel wants to be a footballer or snooker star."

"He could be in for a rude awakening," I warned.

"He'll take it in his stride. We did."

"That's true." We were both failed footballers. Dave had his trial with Halifax Town the same time as me, with a similar result: don't call us, we'll call you.

"This beer's on form," I said, enjoying a long sip.

"It is, isn't it."

"So where's Golden Balls with this flippin' moustache?"

But at that very moment Detective Sergeant Nigel Newley's full attention was elsewhere. He was gazing into the green eyes of Marie-Claire Hollingbrook, her face framed by the riot of golden hair heaped upon her pillow, her full lips parted and her naked body languidly spread-eagled across the bed. They were the first green eyes Nigel had ever seen, and he was stunned by their beauty. They were unable to return his gaze, because Marie-Claire had been strangled, several hours earlier.

"Do you ever regret not making it as a footballer?" Dave asked me.

"Nah," I replied. "This is a lot better. Do you? They'd have taken you on if you hadn't fluffed that goal."

"No, I don't think so. Can't imagine how I missed it though. An open goalmouth in front of me, and I kicked it over the bar."

"As I remember it, you kicked it over the grandstand."

"It was a wormcast. The ball hit a wormcast and bobbed up, just as I toe-ended it. The rest, as they say, is history."

"Sentenced to a lifetime of ignominy by a wormcast." I said.

"I know," he replied, glumly raising his glass and draining ·it.

"Just think," I continued. "Of all the millions of worms in the world, if that one particular specimen hadn't crapped on that one particular square centimetre of grass on that one particular day, you might have married one of the Beverly sisters."

"Blimey. Frightenin', innit?" he replied.

"Innit just. Same again?"

"Please."

"Pork scratchings?"

"Cheese and onion crisps."

I went to the bar to fetch them.

The phone call we were hoping for but not expecting came next morning, just as I was having my elevenses. I went downstairs to control, to catch the action. Arthur, a wily old sergeant, was in the hot seat. He slid a filled-in message form towards me as I moved a spare chair alongside him.

"Anything come in about the dead girl in Halifax?" I asked. There'd been a report about it on the local news.

"Just the bare details, pulled off the computer. We haven't been asked to assist, yet."

"Our young Mr Newley will be up to his neck in that one," I said, secretly wishing that I was there, too.

"Ah! Nigel'll find 'em."

"So what have we here?"

"From the Met Regional Crime Squad," he said as I read. "One of their men thinks he's seen Kevin Chilcott at the Portsmouth ferry terminal. He rang in from a phone box and is now trying to follow him. Last report came from the arrivals concourse at 10:37 hours."

"So what do they expect us to do?" I asked.

"Be alert, that's all. He could be going anywhere."

I explained to Arthur that we were responsible for raising the APW on Chilcott, because of the messages from Bentley prison, but the phonecalls were to London, and that was probably where he was heading. "Stay with it," I told him, "and keep me informed. I'll be in the office."

I went back upstairs and finished my coffee. One by one, for no reason that I could think of, I rang Dave, Annette, Jeff and three others on their mobiles and told them what was happening. "Keep in touch," I told them, "he might be coming this way."

The super was unimpressed when I told him. "He'll be heading for London," he declared, dismissively.

"Yeah, you're probably right," I agreed.

But he wasn't. Arthur rang me on the internal at 14:20 hours, saying that Chilcott, with the RCS chief inspector tagging along behind him, had boarded the 13:30 express from Kings Cross to Leeds. I went downstairs again and spoke directly to the RCS control, in London. Their man, I was told, was starting his holiday, but had found his way into the arrivals section hoping to meet his parents, who were coming home. He'd seen Chilcott come off the boat and followed him. They caught the train to Waterloo and transferred to Kings Cross, where Chilcott had purchased a single to Leeds. The DCI was unable to communicate from the Portsmouth train, but he could from this one. He was, they said, wearing holiday clothes, which made him somewhat conspicuous.

Our own Regional Crime Squad, based in Leeds, went on

to full alert, borrowing our ARVs and booking the chopper for the rest of the day. They made arrangements to evacuate the station minutes before the London train arrived and dressed several officers in natty Railtrack uniforms. Marksmen were positioned around the adjacent platforms and steps taken to block-off all the exits and roads. ETA was 16:01, and Chilcott's feet wouldn't touch the ground.

At 15:06 the express stopped at Doncaster and Chilcott left it. The RCS detective got off, too, but had to hide behind a wall until Chilcott boarded the 15:40 to Manchester. That arrived at 17:00 hours and Chilcott and his faithful shadow then boarded the 17:12, Manchester Piccadilly to Newcastle.

"Could be Leeds, after all," the super stated. He'd joined me in control when he realised that this one wasn't going away. Dave wandered in and I told him to collect as many bodies as he could, urgently.

"No, Boss," I told Mr Wood. "If there's one place he isn't going, it's Leeds. He could have stayed on the Kings Cross train if he was going to Leeds."

The Met's RCS control room had managed to find someone in the railway business with the authority to spend some time talking to them, and were now being relayed times and destinations. "That train stops at Heckley," I told my contact. "Where else does it stop?"

I wrote them down as he read them off. Oldfield, Huddersfield, then Heckley, Leeds, York and Newcastle.

"What time at Heckley?"

"17:54."

"Six minutes to six. Struth, any chance of delaying it? I think he could be coming here and we're a bit depleted."

They said they'd do what they could.

I sent someone to Heckley station to arrange things there. We needed parking spaces and easy access. Mr Wood rang the Assistant Chief Constable to organise the issuing of weapons. Our ARVs were in Leeds, so we improvised, borrowing two off-duty officers from the tactical firearms unit who'd missed the shout to dash to Leeds, in their own cars.

"Just the man," I said when Jeff Caton wandered in. "Did I see your crash helmet in the office, this morning?"

"I've come on the bike, if that's what you mean," he replied.

"Good." I turned to Mr Wood. "Can we have a word, Boss?" I asked. He adopted his worried look and the three of us moved outside, into the corridor.

"So far," I said, "all we are concentrating on is lifting Chilcott. What I'd really like to know is: what is he doing over here? If he's up to something on my patch, I want to know what it is."

"What are you suggesting, Charlie?" Mr Wood demanded wearily.

"Just that we don't arrest him straight away. I think we should follow him for a bit longer, find out who he's working for."

"No," Mr Wood stated. "Definitely not."

"He's been tailed for three hundred miles. Another twenty won't hurt."

"I said no."

I turned to DS Caton. "What do you think, Jeff?"

He shrugged, embarrassed by the position I'd placed him in. "Mr Wood's the boss," he said.

"But could you do it, on the bike, working with someone in a car?"

"Yeah, no problem."

"No, Charlie," Mr Wood said. "If he gets off at Heckley, you arrest him. And that's my last word."

"It seems a shame, though, doesn't it?"

Gilbert heaved a sigh that would have blown a small galleon off the rocks. "Just…just make it look good," he said.

"Right," I replied. "Right." I looked at my watch. It was

17:33. Twenty-one minutes to go.

We had a lightning rehearsal in the briefing room, with me drawing a plan of the station and slashing arrows across it. I designated who would ride with whom and appointed Annette as my driver.

"Code names?" someone asked.

"They're Batman and Robin," I replied.

"Da-da da-da, da-da da-da," they all chanted.

"Who's who?"

"Chilcott's Robin. Put my phone number in your memories, but we'll use the radio when the action starts, switched to talk-through but no chit-chat. OK?"

"OK," they replied.

"And no heroics. He's dangerous, so don't forget it. There's enough widows in Heckley already."

They strode out, talking too loudly and fooling around, but I hung back as Jeff zipped up his leather jacket and pulled his helmet on. Two others joined us and then Annette came over. "What do you think, Jeff?" I asked.

"Always obey the last order, that's my motto," he replied.

"And you two?"

"We're game," one of them replied.

"OK," I said. "Nothing's decided, yet. We'll play it by ear if he gets off the train. Just listen for my instructions."

"Of course," one of them said, "there's always the possibility that he has already jumped off, or he stays on it, isn't there."

"He'll get off," Jeff stated, his voice muffled by the gaudy helmet. "I can feel it in my water."

"What was all that about?" Annette asked as she jerked my car seat forward. The clock on the dashboard said 17:41.

I told her briefly what I had in mind.

"Does Mr Wood know?" she asked.

"Um, partly."

"And he agrees?"

"Yes. Well, no, not really."

"Oh, Charlie!"

I rang the RCS control on my mobile and gave them my number. Batman had commandeered a phone from a fellow passenger and was in regular communication with them. All along the line itchy-fingered policemen were assembling outside the railway stations, wondering if the nation's most wanted criminal was going to grace their gunsights with his presence. The possible receptions varied. In some places he would be discreetly followed, in others shot on sight. We, I hoped, were doing it properly. As the train left each station Batman would pass a message back to the RCS and they would alert whoever was in charge at the next one down the line. At Heckley, that was me.

The train station is just down the road from the nick, so we made it with minutes to spare. A uniformed PC was at the coned-off entrance to the car-park, supervising a man in overalls who was working on the barrier. I thanked them both and told them to go for a cup of tea. We spread ourselves out, enjoying the luxury of all those parking places. Other cars, frustrated by having to drive round the block, started to fill the remainder.

"Presumably," Annette said, "if he is getting off here somebody will be meeting him. Taking a taxi would be risky."

"Good point," I agreed. We sat in silence for a few seconds, until I asked her if she was going away for the weekend. My mobile rang before she could reply, but her expression and the hesitation told me the answer. "Heckley," I said into the phone.

"Leaving Huddersfield," the RCS controller told me. "Still on-board."

"Understood. Out."

I turned to Annette. "They've left Huddersfield. We're next." I clicked the transmit button on the radio I was holding in the other hand and said a terse: "Stand by, we're next," into it. You can never be too sure who's listening to radio traffic.

"There's an interesting BMW just pulled in," Annette told me.

"Where?"

"Behind us."

I adjusted the wing mirror with the remote control, so I could see it without turning my head. It was R registered, silver, with four headlights. "Looks expensive," I remarked as I made a note of the number.

"Series seven," Annette stated. It sounded about right to me but cars aren't my strong point. She produced a tube of mints and offered me one. I shook my head. The clock changed from 17:50 to 17:51.

"Let's have some music," she said, pushing the radio power button. A politician was sounding off about something or other. He used the expressions *spin doctor* and *mind set* in the same sentence, and would probably have slipped in a *sea change* had Annette not hit a station button. Two more tries and she was rewarded with Scott Walker's warm tones. "That's better," she said.

"We haven't been for a meal for a while," I remarked.

"No," she agreed.

"It's Thursday."

"So it is."

"If Chilcott's not on this train we could go for one."

"A girl's got to eat," she declared, throwing me a big grin.

I smiled at her and started to say: "You should laugh more often. It suits you," but the phone started warbling somewhere in the middle of it.

"Heckley," I said.

"He's on his feet, heading for the door. Looks like this is it."

"Understood. Out."

I needed a pee. It's always the same: the least bit of excitement and I remember that I haven't been to the loo for four hours. "This could be it," I told her, and clicked the send button on the RT. "Charlie to the Young Turks," I said into it, "it's looking good for us." Three cars down in the facing row Dave raised a finger off the steering wheel in acknowledgement, and a face in a window to my left raised an eyebrow. I *wish* I could do that. Smoke puffed from the exhaust of the car in front as he started the engine. I reached forward to kill Scott Walker and we both pulled our seatbelts on.

It all went off like a dream, exactly as planned, but you'd never have believed it. The Regional Crime Squad DCI was called Barry Moynihan, and he was one of the grumpiest little piggies I've ever come across. Now he was slumped in a chair in the corner of Mr Wood's office, elbows on his knees, face in his hands. He'd ranted and raved all the way to the station and plenty more when he was inside, but it's hard to take a bollocking from somebody wearing three-quarter length Burberry check shorts and a Desperate Dan T-shirt. Gilbert was lounging back in his executive chair, staring at the blank wall opposite. I was on a hard seat, left ankle on right knee, wondering if breaking the silence would be polite. I picked up my coffee cup and took a long loud slurp. Gilbert glared eloquently at me, but didn't attempt to put his feelings into words. I shrank into my jacket and placed my mug back on his desk as if it might explode.

Moynihan leapt to his feet and paced across the office. "She might be in Le Havre now, for all I know," he declared. He thrust his hands into the pockets of his shorts, then took them out again. "God knows where she and the kids are."

"Try ringing her again," Gilbert suggested.

"How can I?" he snapped. "How can I? The daft cow's got the friggin' mobile switched off." He was back at his chair. He spun it round and crashed down on it, back to front, resting his chin on his forearms. "She's never driven the Frontera before," he informed us.

"You should be able to join her tomorrow," Gilbert ventured.

"Where?" he demanded. "Portsmouth? France? I only popped across to arrivals to see if my parents were there." He banged a palm against the side of his head, saying: "And my friggin' passport's in the glove box."

I had to admit it; he was in a predicament. No money, no credit cards, stranded in Yorkshire without a passport, in clothes like that. I must have smirked or sniggered, because suddenly he was on his feet again, pointing at me. "You're history," he snarled. "You're fuckin' history."

"That's enough," Gilbert told him. "I'll not have you talk to one of my senior officers like that."

"He deliberately didn't arrest him," Moynihan ranted. "A target criminal, and he let him go."

"He had his reasons," Gilbert said.

"He deliberately disobeyed instructions."

"Listen," I said, looking at Moynihan. "We had less than forty minutes notice that he was on a train that stopped at Heckley. Two minutes notice that he was getting off. RCS had taken all our firepower. We'd had no time to evacuate the station and I wasn't going to risk the lives of my officers and any civilians on your say-so. We contained the situation and have isolated the target. We have also identified his accomplices. I'd call that good work."

"God!" Moynihan cursed, "What a friggin' hole."

There was a knock at the door and Mr Wood snapped: "Come in!" so loudly my ankle slipped off my knee and my foot slammed down. The door opened and DS Jeff Caton emerged, leather jacket flapping, hair plastered down with sweat, grinning like a new dawn. He had a red line over his bloodshot eyes and down his cheeks, where the helmet had pressed.

"Good," Mr Wood said. "So what's the position, Jeff?"

"Pretty hunky-dory," he replied, flexing the fingers of his right hand. "We followed him over the tops and he turned off on to the old Oldfield Road, then down a narrow lane that goes right over towards Dolly Foss, past the dam. You know where I mean, Boss?" he asked, turning to me.

"I think so," I replied.

"By the way, this is DCI Moynihan from the Met RCS," Gilbert told Jeff.

"Pleased to meet you," Jeff said, extending a hand. Moynihan ignored it and Jeff said: "Suit yourself."

Gilbert had acquired the appropriate OS map and we leaned over his desk as Jeff traced the route they'd taken. "That's the house," Jeff said, laying a finger on the map. "It looks to have a name."

"Ne'er Do Well Farm," Gilbert read out, because the map was the right way up for him.

"Ne'er Do Well?"

"That's what it says."

"Sounds appropriate."

"What's the layout like," Gilbert asked.

"Couldn't be better, I'd say," he replied. "It's an old farmhouse, with signs of some restoration work, so it's in reasonable condition. There's a dry gill behind it and about five hundred yards away, on the other side of the gill, there's a rock outcrop, not far from a track. It's a perfect place for an OP."

"We won't need an observation post," Moynihan asserted. "As soon as we've enough bodies we're lifting him. Where can I use a phone?"

He spent half an hour on the telephone in the secretary's office and Gilbert used the time to ring the Deputy Chief Constable. His advice was to let them get on with it. Give any assistance they might ask for, but otherwise leave it to them. Jeff told us about tailing Chilcott and I made some more coffee. He'd alternated with the Fiesta, hanging about a quarter of a mile behind, and was certain they hadn't been spotted.

"You did well," I told him.

"*He* did bloody well," Gilbert told us, nodding towards the adjoining office where Moynihan was brewing something. "All that way, without being rumbled."

"Dressed like that," I added.

Moynihan came back in and we fell silent. "Right," he said. "From now on it's an RCS shout. A team from the Met are coming up to lift him, probably on Saturday morning. In the meantime – tonight and tomorrow – number three district RCS will keep an eye on the farm. Thank you for your help, gentlemen, but we won't require any more assistance from you. If you don't like it, contact Chief Superintendent Matlock."

With them it's personal. Chilcott was as good as a cop killer, one of their target criminals, and someone at the Met wanted the pleasure of feeling his collar. It would look bad if a bunch of hicks from Heckley did the job for them.

"Good," Gilbert said. "Good. That takes the pressure off us. All the same, we will keep a weather eye on things, if you don't mind. Just in case. We do like to know exactly what's going off in our little neck of the woods."

Annette had vanished but didn't answer the phone when I rang her flat. I'd stayed behind to brief our local RCS boys, and it must have been after eight when I left the station. I drove straight to a pub up on the moors and had the landlady's steak and kidney pie. Friday morning I apologised to Annette and said I'd tried to ring her.

"I thought you'd be here until late," she replied, "so I went to the Curtain."

"Aw, I am sorry. I wish I'd known. Did Mr Ho entertain you?"

"Yes. He was sweet. I said you might be along later, and when you didn't turn up he was all apologetic and filled with concern. He said you must have had a good reason for not being there."

"Mmm, stupidity," I replied.

I told her all about the RCS take-over and she said she'd enjoyed the shout. Her adrenaline was high and it had kept her awake all night.

"Maybe that was the monosodium glutamate," I suggested.

"Yes, perhaps it was," she agreed, but there was just a tinge of pink on her cheeks as she said it.

"This weekend…" I began. "Are you going away?"

"Yes, unless…"

"Unless?"

"Unless you want me to work."

"Er, no. No, I don't think that will be necessary."

"Right. Thanks"

I spent the rest of the morning on the word processor, typing a full account of the Heckley station caper in graphic detail. I even slipped in a few semi-colons, because I suspected it would be read in high places. I laid it on thick, saying that I thought it unsafe to approach Chilcott, a suspected killer, in a public place when we were ill-prepared. In fact, I made such a good job of it I decided that any other course of action would have been downright irresponsible. Ah, the power of the pen.

It gave me a headache. I found some aspirin in my drawers and washed a couple down with cold tea. I was rubbing my eyes with my forefingers when there was a knock at the door and it opened. I blinked and looked at my visitor. It was Nigel Newley, my one-time whizz-kid protégé.

"Hiya, Nigel," I gushed. "Sit down. Do you want a tea?"

"No thanks, Charlie. I was in the building, so I thought I'd call in."

"You did right. So where's the famous moustache?"

"Ah." He rubbed his top lip. "You heard about that, did you? I decided it wasn't quite the part. Looked too frivolous."

"For a detective on a murder case? Sounds a nasty job. How are you getting on with it?"

"Pretty good. We found semen samples on her, so we're going straight for mass testing, no messing about. That's why I'm here."

"Nothing on the data base?"

"No, unfortunately. She was gorgeous, Charlie. Beautiful and intelligent. I wouldn't be surprised if somebody wasn't stalking her, but we haven't turned anything up yet."

"Boyfriend? Ex-boyfriends?"

"Married last Easter to a childhood sweetheart who has a cast-iron alibi. He was building a bridge in Sunderland at the time. We haven't cleared him with the DNA yet, but we will."

"And what does Les say about it all?" Les Isles was Nigel's new superintendent, and an old pal of mine.

"Oh, he's OK. A bit different from you, but he's OK. He wants to go ahead with the mass testing, soon as possible. Says there's no point in hanging about."

"That sounds like Les." I moved the computer mouse to cancel the screen saver, and clicked the save icon. I was playing for time, organising my thoughts. "Tell me this," I said. "This girl…"

"Marie-Claire Hollingbrook."

"…Marie-Claire. The reports say she was sexually assaulted. What exactly did that mean?"

"She was raped. Strangled and raped."

"Post-mortem?"

"Possibly."

"Was she assaulted anally?"

"Why?"

"Because I want to know."

"You want to know if there's any comparison with your case. Margaret Silkstone."

"Yes."

"I thought that was cleared up."

"It is, but maybe this is a copycat."

"Mr Isles has considered that. Yes, she was raped vaginally and anally, but I didn't tell you. We're not releasing that information."

"We didn't release it for Mrs Silkstone, but the *UK News* got hold of it."

"Maybe they were kite flying."

"No, they knew about it. Someone spoke out of turn."

"So," he said, pointing to the little bottle on my desk and changing the subject. "What's with the pills."

I picked it up and placed it back in the drawer. "It's nothing," I said. "I've just been staring at that thing for two hours. It's a bit bright for me. Do you know how to change it?"

"Just alter the contrast," Nigel replied.

"How?"

"With the contrast control."

I looked at the blank strip of plastic under the screen. "There isn't a contrast control."

"It's on the keyboard. You alter it on the keyboard."

"There's nothing wrong with the contrast on the keyboard," I argued. "It's the display that's too bright. It's giving me spots before my eyes."

"What sort of spots?"

"Just, little spots."

"Do they go away when you stop looking at the monitor?"

"I don't know. I can't see them all the time."

Nigel said: "Turn towards the window and close your eyes." I did as I was told. "Can you see them now?" He asked.

"Yes."

"Right. Cover one eye with your hand." I did. "Can you see them now?"

"I can just see two of the little buggers, close together near the middle."

"Do they move when you look up?"

"Um, yes. Not straight away. They follow, quite slowly."

"OK. Now the other eye."

I swapped hands and the two spots vanished, but now I

could see three others, spread about. "I can see three now," I told him.

"They're floaters," Nigel informed me.

"Floaters? What are they?"

"Dead cells, floating about in the fluid of your eyeball."

"Oh. What causes them?"

"Age. It's your age."

"Well how come I have three in one eye and only two in the other? They're both the same age."

"It's not that specific."

The door burst open and Dave Sparkington was standing there. "What do you want?" he demanded, looking at Nigel.

Nigel faced up to him, saying: "I came to have a conversation with the *Big Issue* seller, not his mongrel."

"We were talking about floaters," I said to Dave.

"Floaters?" he queried.

"Yeah. Do you ever get them?"

"Floaters?"

"Mmm."

"Well, now and again. Especially if I've been eating chicken chow mein."

We agreed to meet on Wednesday evening and Nigel drifted off to organise a caravan in the market place where all the males of the town would have six hairs plucked from their heads, or would donate some other body sample, if they so preferred. It would be voluntary, but a close eye would be kept on those who didn't attend. Superintendent Isles would have prepared a list of the usual suspects, and they'd be encouraged along. I told Dave what Nigel was doing.

He said: "Les Isles will have his balls for a paperweight if he finds out that Nigel's been talking to you about it."

I said: "There are certain similarities with our Mrs Silkstone job."

"Copycat," he replied. "All the gory details were in the paper."

"That's what I said."

In the afternoon a superintendent from the Met RCS came in and introduced himself. He was obviously on a damage limitation exercise, shaking my hand, calling me Charlie, saying what a good job we'd done. I showed him Ne'er Do Well Farm on the map, then took him there, via the lane at the other side of the gill where the rock outcrop was.

Barry Moynihan was in charge, wearing a shell suit that somebody two sizes smaller had loaned him, with a decent growth of stubble on his face. Three others, from number three district, were also there; two of them permanently watching the farm. I had a look through their binoculars, but the place was as still and silent as a fog-bound airport.

Two more arrived, bringing flasks of soup, blankets and waterproofs. As they lifted them from their boot I glimpsed the dull metal of a Heckler and Koch rifle barrel. I had no doubt they had a whole armoury of weapons in their cars: H & K A2s for general purpose killing; Glock PT17s for close range killing; and perhaps a Heckler 93 sniper rifle, for long-range killing. I had an uneasy feeling that Kevin Chilcott would not be walking away from this one.

They were reluctant to discuss tactics in front of me and I began to feel like a rogue sausage roll at a bar mitzvah, so I glanced at my watch and said I'd better be off. It was just after half-past four when I left, and ten to five when I walked into the office, quietly whistling to myself: *The hills are alive, with the sound of gunfire.* At twenty-six minutes past five the phone rang. It was Superintendent Cox, the RCS super that I'd just taken up on to the moors.

"Did a motorcycle pass you, Charlie, on the way back to Heckley?" he asked.

"A motorbike? Not that I remember," I replied.

"Shit! A bike left the house, about one minute after you. We clocked him heading that way, but lost him soon afterwards. He was probably in front of you."

"You think it was Chilcott?"

"Yeah, didn't you know? A bike's his chosen mode of transport when he's on a job. He can handle one. Used to race at Brands Hatch in his younger days."

"No, I didn't know that."

"Christ, Charlie, I hope this is a dummy run and not the real thing. If it is the shit'll hit the fan."

And I bet I knew who'd catch it all. "Do you have a number for the bike?" I asked.

"No. Just those of ones stolen locally in the last couple of weeks."

"You have done your homework. What make did he race?"

"What did he race? No idea, why?"

"Because bikers are often loyal to one make, that's why."

"Christ, that's a thought, Charlie. That'd narrow it down. Well done."

He was telling me that they'd asked traffic to look out for him when someone at that end attracted his attention. "Wait a minute, Charlie," he said. "Wait a minute…he's back. Thank fuck for that. We can see him, riding towards the house."

I hung about for another hour, but no reports of gunshots or dead bodies came in, so it must have been a training spin. Cox didn't bother to ring me back so I went home via Sainsbury's and did a major shop. My favourite check-out girl wasn't on duty, which meant that the ciabatta bread and feta cheese were pointless purchases.

I had them for supper, toasted under the grill with lots of Branston pickle until they were bubbling. Welsh rarebit, Italian style, but it wasn't a good idea. I lay awake for most of the night, thinking about a man who was loose in society with the intention of killing someone. Thinking about Annette. Thinking about her friend.

What if…what if…what if Chilcott shot his target, who, by the type of coincidence that you only find in cheap fiction, just happened to be Annette's friend? Would I be

pleased? Would she turn to me for consolation? Yeah, probably, I thought, to both of them. That's when I dropped off,
just before the cold breath of a new day stirred the curtains
and the bloke in the next street who owns half of the market and drives a diesel Transit set off for work.

Saturday is his busiest day, and I had a feeling that this
one might be mine too. I had a shower and dressed in old
Wranglers, cord shirt and leather jacket. I put my Blacks
trainers on my feet, designed for glissading down scree
slopes. You never know when you might need to.

According to the electoral role, the tenants of Ne'er Do
Well Farm were Carl and Deborah Faulkner. According to
the DVLA, the series seven BMW that picked Chilcott up at
the station belonged to Carl Faulkner. According to our
CRO, Carl Faulkner had a string of convictions long enough
to knit a mailbag and Deborah had a few of her own. His
were for stealing cars, bikes, household items and bundles of
bank notes, plus GBH and extortion. Hers were for receiving, causing an affray, and a very early one for soliciting. The
one thing that they certainly weren't was farmers.

"Nice couple, aren't they?" Dave said as I returned the
printout to him. He sat in the spare chair and placed his coffee on my desk.

"He saved her from a life on the streets," I commented,
sliding a beer mat towards him.

"Blimey, you're in a good mood," he said.

"And why not? It's a new day, the weekend."

"Chilcott might be the Met's," he responded, "but these
two are ours."

"They haven't done anything."

"Well that'll make it harder, won't it," he declared. He had
a sip of coffee and continued: "There's harbouring a fugitive,
for a start. And conspiracy. And probably stealing a bike.
And I bet they don't have a TV licence."

"First time they poke their heads above a windowsill
they'll probably have them blown off," I said.

"Yeah, that's a strong possibility," he agreed.

Word came through that strange policemen were congregating in our canteen and eating all the bacon sandwiches. They were the Met's Regional Crime Squad. At nine o'clock Mr Cox came in to my office on a courtesy call, to tell me that they were having a meeting in the conference room and they'd be very grateful if I could make myself available to answer any questions that might arise about local conditions, whatever they were. He looked as if he'd spent the night on a bare mountain, which he had. I said: "No problem," and followed him downstairs.

They were an ugly-looking bunch, chosen for their belligerence in a tight situation and not their party manners. Any of them could have moonlighted as a night-club bouncer or a cruiserweight. A couple wore suits and ties, some wore anoraks and jeans, others were in part police uniform, bulging with body armour. I gave them a *good morning* when I was introduced and settled down to listen.

It was the usual stuff: isolate; control; maximum show of power, minimum violence. There was only one road going past the farm, with junctions about half a mile away to one side and two miles away at the other. A bridlepath crossed one of the roads. I told them that it was not negotiable by a car but a Land Rover or a trail bike might do it.

They would set up roadblocks on the lane, either side of the farm, and the local force would create an outer ring of roadblocks, just in case. This last comment raised a few sniggers, because they all knew it to be superfluous. Nobody would get past them. Mr Cox asked the various teams to acknowledge that they were clear about their duties and said: "OK, gentlemen, let's bring him in."

I was guest of honour, invited to ride with him. Our car-park was filled with their vehicles, haphazardly blocking the regulars in or out, and others were parked outside, straddling the yellow lines and pavement. We slowly disentangled ourselves and moved in a convoy out of town, towards the moors. I suspected that some of them had never seen a land-scape devoid of houses, billboards and takeaways.

A steady drizzle was percolating through the atmosphere as we crossed the five hundred foot contour, blurring the colours slipping by our windows to a dirty khaki. Just how I like it. Superintendent Cox turned his collar up in an involuntary action and switched the windscreen wipers on.

"That's the lane to the other side of the farm," I told him. He slowed and jabbed his arm several times through his open window. I swivelled round in my seat and counted five vehicles turn in that direction. Two miles further I said: "And this is our lane to the farm." He turned off the main road and set his trip odometer to zero.

"I reckon we make the block in about one point three miles," he stated, slowing to a crawl. Three minutes later, with the farm still not in sight, he stopped and switched the engine off. "This'll do," he said.

Three vehicles from our side and two from the other were going to approach the farm and make the arrests. The others would act as roadblocks in case someone made a run for it. Our three moved ahead and parked in single file. Doors swung open and black looks were cast at the sky. Stooped figures opened boots, lifting out pieces of equipment: water-proofs; body armour; weapons. They donned hats and base-ball caps, or pulled hoods over their heads. I stepped out and felt the cool rain on my face. Beautiful.

Cox was on the radio, calling up the observation post. I heard them report that the farm was as quiet as a grave. About half an hour earlier the curtains in an upstairs room had opened, and that was the only activity they'd seen. He made contact with the other section of our small army, code name T2, but they hadn't turned into the lane yet. The chopper was standing by, he informed us.

T1 was us, or more precisely the three cars that would do the job. When the snatch teams were kitted up they squashed themselves into the cars and waited, steam and smoke rising from the open windows as they waited for the call. Every couple of minutes a cigarette end would come curling from one of the windows to *sizz* out in the wet grass. Our remaining three cars arranged themselves at angles across the narrow lane, completely blocking it.

"The trap is set," Cox told me with a satisfied grin. He produced a half-empty hip flask of Famous Grouse from the depths of a pocket and took a long swig. I shook my head when he offered it to me, so he had mine, too.

He was on the radio again, chasing up T2 when there was a crackle of interference and a voice shouted: "They're moving, they're moving!"

"Quiet please! Come in OP," Cox said.

"Activity at the farm, Skipper," came the reply. "Three figures have dashed out of the house. In a hurry. I reckon they've rumbled us."

"T2, acknowledge."

"T2 receiving."

"Are you at the lane end yet?"

"We're at a lane end, Skip, but it's only a dirt road." "That's the bridle path. The lane you want is about half a mile further on. For fuck's sake get there, now! OP, come in."

"OP receiving."

"What's happening?"

"They're in the garage, I think. Yes, the big door's opening and a motorbike's coming out."

"My team, T1, did you hear that?"

"Yes, Skip."

"He's making a run for it. Stand by." Car doors opened and they tumbled out, brandishing their Heckler and Kochs.

"OP, OP, which way'd he go?"

"He's not reappeared yet from behind the house. A Land Rover and the BMW have also just come out of the garage and gone round the house. I can see the bike now. He's turned left, heading east."

"That's towards us. Good."

"And the other two are heading west."

"Right. Did you clock that, T2?"

"Yes, Skip."

"Are you at the lane end yet?"

"Not sure, Skip. There's a dam and a reservoir with a lane…"

"That's the wrong way!" I yelled at Cox. "They've turned the wrong friggin' way!"

"You've turned the wrong way," Cox told them, trying to read the map that was draped over his steering wheel. "You need to be about three miles the other way, and get a move on." He turned to me, saying: "Fortunately Chilcott's coming towards us." I rang Heckley control and told them to let our boys know that he'd made a run for it. It looked as if we might have to do the job for them after all.

The road ahead undulated like the spine of the Loch Ness monster and bent to the left. I climbed out of the car and peered at the furthest crest in the road. After a few seconds the bike appeared, rising into view then falling out of sight as it sank into a hollow. Then it appeared again, nearer and bigger, travelling quite cautiously, and dropped out of sight. In front of me the RCS crew spread out across the road and adopted kneeling positions, firearms at the ready. The bike rose into view again and fell away. One more brow left. We could hear it now. They pressed rifle butts against shoulders and peered down sights.

The rider's head appeared, then shoulders, windscreen, wheels: a splash of colour – red, white and fluorescent green – in the murky landscape.

"Here he comes," a voice said at my elbow. It was Cox, his eyes bright with excitement. In the next few minutes he'd be reciting the caution to the most wanted man in Britain or zipping him into a body bag. Either would do. The bike stopped, a hundred and fifty yards down the road. I could sense the fingers tightening on triggers, and I desperately needed a pee.

"Easy boys, he's not going anywhere," Cox shouted.

The biker tried to do a U-turn, but the road was too narrow. He paddled the bike backwards a few feet and completed the manoeuvre, driving off back towards the farm with a new urgency. The engine note rose and fell as he went up through the gears, the bike and rider bright as a tropical fish as it crested the brows.

"T1 to T2," Cox yelled into the radio. "He's coming back your way. Where are you?"

"T2 receiving, at the lane end," I heard them confirm. "Forming roadblock now."

"Have you seen the other two vehicles?"

"Negative, Skip."

"He'll be with you in about two minutes."

The same thing happened at their end. The biker stopped, turned round, and headed back this way.

"OK, let's tighten the net," Cox ordered. We climbed back into our seats and moved half a mile down the road, until the farm was clearly in view. We'd just reassembled into a roadblock when the biker came burbling round the corner, the rider sitting up, only one hand on the handlebars.

"He's a cool customer," I said.

"Bravado," Cox explained. "He knows the show's over."

The biker turned round, went back, saw the others blocking his flight and turned towards us yet again. He accelerated, front wheel lifting off the road, as if about to do an Evel Knievel over our heads, then slowed to a crawl. Cox was right: he could handle a bike. T2 moved forward, shrinking his playground.

There was a gate in the wall about a hundred yards in front of us, marking the beginning of the bridle path. The rider stopped, leaned the bike on its side stand and made a dash at the gate. Cars from both sides accelerated towards him, tyres spinning on the wet road. We held back, maintaining the roadblock. He pushed the gate open and leapt back onto the bike, gunning it towards the gap as the car from our side swerved to a standstill feet from him.

I'd started to say that he wouldn't get far on a bike like that when events made my words redundant. The motorcycle bucked, a leg tried to steady it but the bike spun sideways and shot from under its rider. Policemen were running towards him, guns pointing, shouting orders across each other.

The leather clad figure rolled over onto his back, one leg smeared with mud.

"Stay still!" Someone shouted.

He stayed still. In seconds he was surrounded by enough guns to blow a battleship out of the water, except we're taught that you can never have enough. And I'd proved it to be true, once, a long time ago.

"Don't move." Hands reached down, pressed against him, passed over his limbs and torso, feeling for hard objects.

"Now, sit up, slowly."

The figure sat up, very slowly.

"Now, very slowly, remove your helmet."

A gloved hand moved deliberately towards the chinstrap and fumbled with the fastening. Then the other hand came up and started to ease the helmet over the rider's head, twisting it from side to side, forcing it upwards over flattened ears. A chin emerged, then a nose and eyes as it lifted clear. The rider's hair was still inside the helmet. When it was high enough the hair fell down, a cascade of shoulder-length peroxide-blonde locks that would have looked good on any Page Three girl. "Was that slowly enough?" she asked with a smile.

"Oh fuck!" Cox exclaimed. I couldn't have put it any better myself.

I phoned the nick and told them what had happened. T2 stopped the BMW, driven by Carl Faulkner, which meant that Chilcott was in the Land Rover and had probably fled cross-country, bypassing our roadblocks. Deborah Faulkner, the motorcyclist, was handcuffed and taken to Leeds, her husband to a different nick in that city, but they both played dumb, refusing to answer questions. The helicopter came thumping over the hill, somewhere up in the clouds, and made a wide banking turn before heading back towards the valley and civilisation.

Cox liaised with our control, with number three district RCS and with the Met RCS before admitting: "That's it. It's out of our hands, now."

"I'm going to the house," I said, walking in that direction. I'd almost reached it when the depleted convoy overtook me.

Barry Moynihan and the rest of the observation team had already arrived, walking across the moor from their overnight position. He'd borrowed a waterproof coat and leggings, but was still wearing the sandals with the rugged soles and more buckles and straps than an S & M salesman's sample case. His colleagues were brandishing guns as if they were no more lethal than walking sticks, and the whole scene could have been newsreel footage from the latest East European war zone.

"We've swept the house, Mr Cox," a tall guy with a bristly moustache and a military bearing said as he came out of the front door, "and it's clean." He was carrying a Remington pump action shotgun, probably loaded with CS gas cartridges.

"Thanks, Bruce," Cox replied. "Let's see what we can find, then."

"Gentlemen," I called, raising my voice above the hubbub. They all turned to me. "Can I remind you that this is a crime scene," I continued, "and ought to be inspected with that in mind, by the appropriate people."

"Don't worry, Charlie," Cox said. "We'll be careful." He wandered inside followed by his acolytes, and after a few gestures of helplessness I followed. They moved through the kitchen and into the living rooms. I headed for the fire burning in the iron range and stood with my back to it. They could trample on as much evidence as they wanted, but this was as far as I was going. The house had triple glazing, but any attempts at modernisation ended with that. The kitchen floor was stone-flagged, and ashes from the fire had spread away from the hearth, crunching under your feet as you moved around. All the furniture was bare wood, working class antique, and the sink was a deep stone set-pot.

Barry Moynihan came in and looked around. "They're all through there," I told him.

He joined me by the fire, saying: "I'm perished," as he balanced on one leg and tried to dry a soaking foot against the flames.

Suspended from the ceiling by a system of strings and pulleys was a rack filled with clean washing, hung up to dry. I pulled a wooden chair from beneath the table and stood on it. The washing was dry. I removed a threadbare towel and a pair of hiking socks from the rack and handed them to Moynihan. "Put them on," I told him, "or you'll catch pneumonia."

He took them from me and sat on another chair, drying his feet. When he'd finished he stood up, stomped around a few steps, then pronounced: "That's better. Thanks."

"We got off to a bad start," I said.

"Yeah, well."

"Have you contacted your wife?"

"Yeah. She went home. At first it sounded a daft thing to do, but I suppose it was for the best. I've spoken to her a couple of times and she's calmed down. Now I'm hoping the firm will recompense me."

"They ought to," I told him.

There was a shout from the next room that sounded like my name. We stood there waiting for it again, until Cox appeared in the doorway and said: "We've identified

Chilcott's target, Charlie. Come and look at this."

We followed him through into what was the living room. It was gloomy, even with all the lights on, furnished with overstuffed easy chairs and flowery standard lamps. Centrepiece of the room was a highly polished table that was no-doubt worth a bob or two, and spread over it was a series of black and white photographs.

"We found them in this," Cox said, showing me a cardboard folder. "What do you think?"

The cops around the table parted to make room for me. There were six pictures, arranged in a big square. Top left was simply the frontage of a house, such as an estate agent might produce. Next one, a male figure was emerging from the door at the side of the house. After that it was his car, focusing on the numberplate. Then the man himself, stooping to unlock the car, followed by two more of him behind the wheel.

I picked up the last print and held it towards the light. It was taken through the side window of the car, and the driver was completely unaware of it. Next time, it might be a gun, blowing his brains out. Somebody coughed.

"It's me," I said, looking at Cox. He didn't reply. Everyone was silent, empty expressions on their faces. "It's me," I repeated. I placed the photo back on the table, carefully aligning it with its fellows. "Why would anyone want to kill me?" I wondered out loud, and I swear they all shrank back a step.

Chapter Nine

Four days is the magic figure. The chopper clocked the Land Rover entering the multi-storey car-park in Heckley and that was as much as they could do. It was later found neatly parked on the next-to-top floor, with the doors unlocked. It had, needless to say, been stolen two weeks earlier. From the car-park there are covered walkways leading to the shopping mall and the old town area, and other exits at street level. He could have taken any one of them. Within minutes the place was flooded with Heckley's finest, all twelve of them, but Mr Chilcott had vanished. We suspect he had a safe house somewhere, and was holed-up in that.

Back at the farm I'd requested assistance from Heckley nick, which didn't come because they were busy, and from the scenes of crime people, who never have anything better to do on a Saturday lunchtime. Having a *fatwa* on me earned a certain amount of respect from the RCS team, so when I ordered them all out of the farmhouse they did as they were told. They piled into their vehicles and hot-footed it to Heckley, desperate to salvage some credibility. I stayed behind and they kindly left a car and three men with me, just in case. We stoked the fire and made coffee.

Four days is the time a terrorist on the run is trained to stay concealed. The police employ psychologists who have worked out that a fugitive would stay underground for three days before making his bid for freedom. After that time, we assume we've lost him. So the terrorists enlist more expensive psychologists who tell them to hide for four days before legging it. Fortunately our anti-terrorist people have become wise to this, and they brought it to our attention. OK, Chilcott wasn't a terrorist, but they all download the same manuals.

Nigel extended his hands towards me so that I could extricate my new pint from between his fingertips. He placed another in front of Dave and an orange juice and soda on his own beer mat.

"Cheers," we said.

"Cheers," he replied, taking a sip. As Chilcott was still on the run and appeared to have a reasonable working knowledge of my movements, we had forsaken the Spinners and were having our Wednesday night meeting in the Bailiwick. "So what time were you there until?" Nigel asked.

"Seven o'clock." I said. "We were stuck at Ne'er Do Well Farm until after seven. The SOCOs had left about four."

"We were running about like blue-arsed flies," Dave said.

"Flashing blue-arsed flies?" I suggested.

"And them."

"Do you think he's still in Heckley?"

"God knows."

"It's four days today. SB said he'd lie low for four days."

"Don't remind us."

I took a sip of beer and said: "Well it proves one thing."

"What's that?" they asked.

"That I'm not paranoid."

"Just because someone *is* trying to kill you doesn't mean you're not paranoid," Dave argued.

"Of course it does."

"No it doesn't. He's only one man. It's not a conspiracy."

"Of course it's a conspiracy."

"No, it's not. He was doing it for money. It's not personal."

"What difference does that make? The whole thing is one big conspiracy."

"Against you? One big conspiracy against you?"

"Against everyone."

"So someone's out to kill Nigel, too. And me. Is that what you're saying?"

"I might be."

"You definitely are paranoid."

"Is that what you think? Is that what you really think?"

"Yes."

"Right," I said. "Right. Let me tell you something. You see this place?" I gestured towards the ceiling and they nodded. "Good. And you see the names on all those labels behind the bar?" I read them off: "Tetley's, Black Sheep, Bell's, Guinness, Foster's, and so on, and so on?"

"Ye-es," they agreed.

"OK. Now let's look at what's outside. There's the Halifax opposite, and Barclays, and the NatWest. Further down there's Burger King and Pizza Hut. There are jewellers, clothes shops galore, snack bars and…oh, you name it and there's one out there."

"So what's the point of all this?" Dave asked. Nigel grinned and took another sip of orange juice.

"The point is," I told him, "that it's all a big conspiracy. Why do all these companies exist? Go on, tell me that."

"To do what they do," he replied. "To make beer or whatever, to provide a service, to employ people and to make a profit for their shareholders."

"No they don't."

"Well go on, then, clever clogs. You tell us why they exist."

"They exist, every one of them, for one sole purpose."

"Which is…?"

"Which is…to convert my money into their money. That's what it's all about."

"So that's why you're so reluctant to go to the bar," Nigel commented.

"Cheeky sod!" I retorted.

"You are paranoid," Dave concluded.

Shirley came to take us home and Dave bought her a tonic water. We were finishing our drinks when a familiar warbling tone came from somewhere on Nigel's person. "Oooh, oooh," we groaned, expressing our disapproval. Mobile phones are *verboten* on walks and in the pub. Nigel blushed and retrieved it from his pocket.

"Nigel Newley," he said. I drained my glass and Dave did

the same. "Hello, Les." Sounded like it was Les Isles, his boss. "Hey! That's brilliant!" Good news. Lucky for some. "Where does he live?" Sounded like Nigel had some work to do. "Right. In the morning? Right. See you then. Thanks for ringing." It would be an early alarm call for someone. He closed the phone and replaced it in his pocket, his face pink with enthusiasm.

"Guess what?" he said, "We've had a match. One of the donated samples matches the DNA in the semen we found on Marie-Claire Hollingbrook. We're bringing him in first thing."

"That was quick," Dave said.

"It was, wasn't it."

"So, er, where does he live?" I asked.

"Um, Heckley. He lives in Heckley."

"Really? In that case he's one of ours, isn't he?"

"Oh no he isn't," Nigel assured me. "Oh no he isn't."

I had a bodyguard, of course. It was all over the papers that we'd let Chilcott, Enemy Number One, slip through our fingers; if he still managed to complete his mission we'd really have egg on our faces. Well, they would; I'd have something else on mine. The two of them, Tweedle Dee and Tweedle Dum, sat patiently in the pub, backs to the wall, sipping soft drinks, while we tried to ignore them. I didn't like it, but knew better than to object. Shirley took me home first and they followed. I handed my keys over and one of them entered the house, casually, without making a drama out of it. "You know where everything is," I said when I was allowed in, waving towards the coffee ingredients, videos and sleeping bags that had accumulated in my front room. "Make yourselves at home, gentlemen, I'm off to bed."

"I've brought *Terminator Two*," one of them told me as he filled the kettle.

"Seen it," I lied. "Early night for me. Keep it low."

"Right. Tea?"

"Yes please. Will you bring it up?"

"No chance, you can wait."

I felt like a guest in my own home. An unwelcome one at that. I took the mug of tea and trudged up the stairs to bed. Drinking doesn't suit me, and lately it had been creeping up a bit. I'd been thinking a lot, also, and the conclusions weren't good. I was at a funny age. From now on, it wasn't going to get much better. The good years, or what should have been the good years, were all in the past. Friday teatime Chilcott had gone on a dummy run, Superintendent Cox had said. I disagreed. I'd been up on the moors, watching the farm. Chilcott had come to Heckley looking for me, and he could have been out of the country again by the morning. Detectives are supposed to work regular hours, and on a Friday the whole world tries to get off home on time. It was his first opportunity to do the job, but my car hadn't been outside the nick, so he'd had to abort. A bullet through the brain, while I was sitting at the traffic lights; or here at home, sleeping, didn't sound too bad. I could live with that. It's all the alternatives that terrify me.

Annette took it badly. She'd sat there, white faced, when I'd announced that I was Chilcott's intended target. Afterwards she came into my office and asked what I was going to do. She thought I'd move away, stay in the country until things blew over, but I explained that it wasn't necessary. I had my minders, and Chilcott's number one priority, now, was making his escape. Even if he'd been paid in advance, nailing me would be off his agenda. I tried to sound as if I knew what I was talking about, as if the inner workings of an assassin's mind were my workaday fodder, but I don't think she believed me. I played safe and didn't suggest we go for a meal, that week.

Nigel and Les Isles arrested Jason Lee Gelder and charged him with the murder of Marie-Claire Hollingbrook. He'd walked into the caravan in Heckley market place, large as life, and donated six hairs and his name and address. Science did the rest. An arcane test, discovered by a professor at Leicester university as recently as 1984, reduced the DNA in Gelder's hair roots to a pattern of parallel lines on a piece of film that exactly matched the lines produced from the semen left on Marie-Claire's thighs. It was his, as sure as hedgehogs haven't grasped the Green Cross Code. It made the local news on Thursday evening and the nationals the next day. The people of the East Pennine division probably slept a little more contentedly in their beds, that weekend, knowing that a sex killer was safely behind bars.

"That was quick," I said, when I spoke to Superintendent Isles on the telephone.

"I think he wanted catching," he admitted. "He was hanging around as they set-up the caravan. He went for a burger then came back and made a donation. Wanted to know what it was all about. It was only about the fifteenth they'd taken at that point."

Sometimes they do it to taunt the police, or to make the stakes higher. Ted Bundy killed more than thirty women across the USA. He moved to Florida because they had the death penalty. Trying to figure out why is like asking why a flock of birds turned left at that particular place in the sky, and not right. Nobody knows. Maybe tomorrow they'll go straight ahead. We do tests to see if these people are sane: ask them questions; show them pictures; gauge their reactions. A man kills thirty women and they show him inkblots to decide if he's sane. Someone needs their head examining.

"So he's coughing, is he?" I asked.

"Oh no, he's not making it that easy for us," Les replied. "Say's he didn't do it; was nowhere near where she lived and has never been there."

"Alibi?"

"Watching videos. He's classic material, Charlie, believe me. We're waiting for the lab to do another test, the full DNA fingerprint job, but I haven't cancelled my holiday."

"I'd like a word with him, Les," I said.

"I thought you might. Why?"

"To see if there's anything to be learned about the way we handled the Margaret Silkstone case."

"You mean, is this a copycat?"

"Something like that."

"Has young Newley been talking to you? If he has, I'll have his bollocks for a door knocker."

"So when can I see him?" I asked. Not: "Can I see him?" but: "When can I see him?" It's what salesmen call closing. When I went to that sales conference I'd really listened.

"Give us two or three days for the reports," Les said, "then you can have a go at him."

"Thanks. And he's called Gelder?"

"That's right. Jason Lee Gelder."

"In olden times a gelder was a person who earned a living by cutting horse's testicles off," I told him.

"Yeah, I know. It's a pity someone didn't cut his off."

If you really want to ingratiate yourself with someone, you let them get the punch line in. I put the phone down and wondered what to have for tea.

The Regional Crime Squad paid renewed interest in the tapes Bentley prison had recorded of the conversations that led, we believed, to Chilcott being hired. Someone was willing to pay £50,000 to have me bumped off and they wanted to know who. We had the name of the people on both ends of the line, but it wasn't a big help. They were real nasties: professionals who'd tell you less than the Chancellor does on the eve of the budget. Except they'd do it belligerently, in language politicians only use when it slips out.

I had a passing interest myself in who was behind it all, so I made my own enquiries. I started by telephoning Gwen Rhodes, Governor of HMP Bentley. It took me all day to track her down, but she was duly shocked when she learned what it was about, and gave me the freedom of her computer terminal, plus a crash course in using it.

On the morning I was there they turned the key on eight hundred and two inmates. That's screw-speak for the number of prisoners they had. In addition, a further one hundred and sixty-eight had passed through in the period I was interested in. Some had been released, some moved to less secure units, one or two possibly found not guilty. I printed out lists of their names and highlighted the ones that I thought I knew. One in particular leapt straight off the page at me.

"When you had Tony Silkstone," I began, on one of the occasions when Gwen came back into the office, "I don't suppose he could have had any contact with Paul Mann, could he?" It was Mann's phone calls that started the whole thing.

"Not at all," Gwen assured me. "Silkstone was on remand, Mann in A-wing, and never the twain shall meet. However," she continued, "you know how it is in places like this. Jungle drums, telepathy, call it what you will, but word gets around."

"Who would Silkstone meet during association?"

"Fellow remandees. That's all."

"What about the rehabilitation classes that Silkstone took? Who might he meet there?"

"Ah," she sighed, and I swear she blushed slightly.

"Go on," I said.

"Mainly cat C, with a few cat B. The ones making good progress, who we felt would benefit."

"Is there always a warder present?"

"Yes. Always."

"But he might have the opportunity to talk with them."

"I doubt it, Charlie, but what might happen is this: he discusses his case with a fellow remandee, one who is about to go for trial and knows he'll be coming back. He leaves D-wing in the morning to go to court, but has a good idea that he'll be back in A- or B-wing by the evening. He could offer to have a word with someone he knows in there."

I said: "Not to put too fine a point on it, Gwen, the system's leaky."

"Leaky!" she snorted. "Of course it's leaky. We can't prevent them from talking amongst themselves. What sort of a place do you think this is?"

"It wasn't meant to be a criticism," I replied.

I'd underlined four names, and we printed hard copies of their notes. Gwen showed me another file which showed who Silkstone had shared a cell with, and I printed their names and files, too.

Two of them were still there. Gwen used her authority and they both found they had a surprise visitor that afternoon. It cost me the price of four teas and four KitKats from the WVS stall to learn that Silkstone was a twat who never stopped complaining. He'd "done over" a nonce, they said, and that made him all right, but half the time they hadn't known what he was talking about. He had big ideas and never stopped bragging about what he'd do when he was freed. They were both looking at a long time inside, and soon tired of him. I thanked Gwen for her assistance and went home.

One of the other names was Vince Halliwell, who I'd put in the dock eight years ago. According to Gwen's computer he'd attended the same rehabilitation classes as Silkstone and had recently been transferred to Eboracum open prison, near York. He was nearing the end of his sentence, and considered a low risk, even though he was doing time for aggravated burglary. Halliwell was a hard case, but I remembered that there was something about him that I'd almost admired. He was tall, with wide bony shoulders and high cheeks, and blond hair swept back into a ponytail. I think it was the ponytail I envied. He had problems. All his life he'd lived in some sort of institution, and he had a record of binge drinking, paid for by thieving. The aggravated burglary – armed with a weapon – that we did him for was an escalation in his MO.

At first I hadn't considered talking to him, but that evening I started to change my mind. He'd refused to co-operate when he was arrested, but became garrulous when interviewed for psychiatric, social enquiry and pre-sentencing reports. They made sad reading, and he had a chip the size and shape of a policeman on his shoulder. It was hard to blame him. I rang Gwen at home and asked her to oil the wheels for me at HMP Eboracum. Next morning she rang me and said the Governor there was willing to play ball.

It was the probation officer I spoke to. She wasn't too keen on the idea, but the Governor was the boss...I assured her that Halliwell was a model prisoner, unlikely to blot his record at this late stage in his sentence, and I'd take responsibility if it all went pear-shaped. We settled for Friday morning.

When long-stay inmates are nearing the end of their sentences the prison authorities like to gradually re-introduce them to life on the outside; to give them a taste of freedom, in small doses. One way is by home visits, another is by what are called town visits. Vince Halliwell had no home to go to, so it would have to be a town visit. I knew he wouldn't talk to me in jail – somebody always knows it's a cop who's called to see you – but he might if I met him on neutral territory, away from screws and inmates and the gossip of a closed community.

The probation officer gave him strict instructions and a ten-pound note. It was a tough test. He had to catch the ten o'clock bus from the prison gates into York, walk to the Tesco supermarket, buy himself a pair of socks there, have a cup of coffee in the restaurant and catch the next bus back to the jail. He'd have to walk past all those pubs, all those shelves stocked with whisky and rum and beer from places he'd never heard of, with money jangling in his pockets. Anything less than superhuman effort and he'd be back at Bentley, category A again. At eight thirty, nice and early, I started the car engine and headed towards the Minster City.

I arrived with enough time to do my shopping, which was intentional, and to have a quick breakfast in the restaurant before he arrived, which was an afterthought. Their curries were a pound cheaper than Heckley Sainsbury's. At ten thirty I walked across the car-park towards the road he would come down.

It was a warm morning, with people strolling about in their shirt sleeves and summer dresses. Four-wheel drive vehicles with tyre treads like Centurion tanks slowly circulated, following sleek Toyota sports cars and chunky Saabs, all looking for a space near the entrance. In the afternoon they'd do the same outside the health club. The indicators flashed on a BMW like the one that met Chilcott at the station, and an elderly couple in front of me steered their trolley towards its boot. A few minutes later, out on the main road, they drove past me. The driver's window was down and I could hear the sound of Pavarotti coming from inside it. BMW spend countless millions of pounds and thousands of hours on wind tunnel tests. They install the finest music system money can buy, with more speakers than an Academy Awards ceremony. They design a climate control – that's air conditioning to the rest of us – better than in the finest operating theatre in the world, and what happens? People drive around with the window down; that's what.

I hardly recognised him. Some thrive in prison, put weight on; others are consumed by it. Halliwell's time inside had reduced him to a shambling shell. Always a gaunt figure, he was now stooped and hollow and looked well into his fifties, although he was only about thirty-six. He crossed the road at the lights, waiting until they were red and then checking that the traffic had stopped, glancing first this way, then the other, but still not moving until everybody else did. He was wearing grey trousers that had been machine-washed until they were shapeless, a blue regulation shirt that was almost fashionable, and cheap trainers. His jacket was gripped in one hand. I stood in the queue for the park-and-ride bus until he'd passed, then fell in behind him.

There were supermarkets before he went inside, but a man forgets, and the rest of us take progress, if that's what it is, for granted. He stopped to examine the rows of parked trolleys as if they were an outlandish life-form engaged in group sex, and stared at the big revolving doors as they gobbled up and regurgitated a steady stream of shoppers. Slowly, nervously, he made his way into the store.

The security cameras were probably focused on this suspicious, shabbily dressed character who wandered about aimlessly, occasionally changing direction for no reason at all, picking up packets and jars at random only to replace them after reading the labels, but nobody challenged me. How Barry Moynihan had followed Chilcott for eight or nine hours dressed like he was, without being spotted, I couldn't imagine. After a good look up and down the rows Halliwell selected a pair of socks and took them to the checkout. I replaced the jar of Chicken Tonight I was studying – 0.4g of protein, 7.7g of fat – and headed for the restaurant.

It was a serve-yourself coffee machine with scant instructions. Halliwell watched a couple of people use it before having a hesitant attempt himself. His first try dumped a shot of coffee essence and hot water through the grill, then a woman took over and showed him how to do it. He smiled and made an "I'm only a useless man" gesture and allowed her to pass him in the queue at the till. For a few seconds I was afraid they would sit down together, but she had two cups on her tray and joined a waiting friend at one of the tables. Halliwell headed for an empty table in a corner. I collected a tea and joined him.

"It's Vince, isn't it?" I said, sitting down.

He looked at me, speechless, for a long time. His eyes were frosty blue, and the ponytail had given way to a regulation crop that still, annoyingly, looked good on him. He could have been a jazz musician on his way home from a gig, or a dissolute character actor researching a part. He had, I decided, that elusive quality known as sex appeal. His jacket was draped across his knees. He fumbled in the pockets until he found a tobacco pouch, and in a few seconds he was puffing on a roll-up.

"What you want?" he asked, eventually, as a cloud of smoke bridged the gap between us. A woman who was about to sit at the next table saw it and moved away.

"I was just passing," I lied.

"Like 'ell you were. It's Priest, innit? Mr Priest?"

"Charlie when I'm off duty."

"You still with the job, then?"

"'Fraid so."

"So this is all part of it, is it?"

"Part of what?"

"The test. This is all part of the test?"

"Oh yes," I agreed. "This is all part of it. All over York there are people from your past who are going to pop out in front of you, confront you with situations to see how you react. Then there are the markers. Women with clip boards and coloured pens, following you, giving you marks for style, difficulty and performance. So far you're doing well."

He grinned, saying: "They always said you were a bit of a card. Did you set all this up? If you did, you're wasting your time."

He stood up to leave, but I said: "Sit down, Vince, and hear what I have to say." He sat down again. That's what eight years inside does to a man.

The roll-up was down to his fingertips. He nipped it and looked for an ashtray but there wasn't one, so he put the debris back in the pouch and made another.

"Could you eat a breakfast?" I asked.

"Not at your prices," he replied.

"No charge. My treat."

"No, thanks all the same."

"It comes on a real plate, made of porcelain, with a knife

that cuts."

"I'll do without."

I said: "Listen, Vince. It's not going to be easy for you. You'll need all the help you can get, so if someone offers you a free breakfast, take it. That's my advice."

"You weren't so generous with your 'elp and advice eight years ago," he reminded me. "You knew…well, what's the point." He left the statement hanging there, dangling like the rope from a swinging tree.

"I knew it wasn't your gun. Is that what you were going to say?"

"And the rest." He twisted around in his chair until he was half-facing away from me.

"It wasn't my job to tell the court it wasn't your gun," I said. "It was your brief's. It was yours. You could have said whose it was."

"And a fat lot of good it would 'ave done me."

"It'd have got you five years instead of ten. Aggravated burglary's a serious offence."

"You knew it wasn't mine. I've never carried a shooter, and you knew it."

"There's always a first time, Vince. I wanted you to get fifteen years; keep you out of my hair for as long as possible. Now you're doing full term because you've refused to admit it was your gun. It's your choice all along, Vince. Take responsibility for your actions. Now, tell me this: How do you like your sausages?"

A youth in a white shirt was hovering near us. I looked up at him and he said: "I'm sorry, Sir, but this is the no-smoking area." Halliwell looked annoyed but nipped the tip of his cigarette.

I said to him: "Go sit over there. I'll fetch you a break-fast," and he carried his coffee to a table with an ashtray on it.

I kept a weather eye on him as I stood in the queue, but he sat patiently waiting, occasionally sipping the coffee, his glance following the succession of people who moved away from the pay point carrying trays and leading toddlers. I placed the plate of food in front of him and walked off towards the cigarette kiosk without waiting for a thank you. When I flipped the packet of Benson and Hedges on to the table, saying: "If you must poison me, do it with something reasonable," he grinned and said: "Right. Cheers."

I sipped the fresh tea I'd brought myself as he ate the first food he'd had in eight years that he could be sure nobody had dipped their dick in. When he'd half-cleared the plate he said: "You not eating, then?"

"I had mine before you came," I replied.

He manoeuvred a piece of egg white on to a corner of toast and bit it off. "So this is all a fit-up, eh? You arranged the whole thing," he mumbled.

"I thought you'd appreciate a day out," I replied.

"You're wasting your time."

I shrugged. "It's a day out for me, too."

"I'm sticking to my story."

"That you didn't know the name of the bloke with you. You planned a burglary with him, did the job together, and never asked each other's names."

He took a cigarette from the packet and lit it. "Yeah, well," he said, exhaling. "That's how it was."

"And you don't grass each other."

"That's right."

"He'd have grassed you. They always do."

"Not always."

"You were a fool, Vince. A twenty-four carat mug, believe me."

"Yeah, well, I can sleep at nights."

I changed the subject. "How does Eboracum compare with Bentley?" I asked.

"It's OK," he replied.

"Only OK? I'd have thought it would be a big improvement."

"Oh, it is. It's just that, at Bentley, you knew where you stood, what the rules were, if you follow me. At this place, you're never sure. Some of the screws say one thing, then another will say summat different. 'Ere, what time is it? I'd better be getting back."

"That's OK," I told him. "They know you're with me."

"You sure?"

"I'm sure." I decided to speed things up. "Did you meet Tony Silkstone while you were in there?" I asked. "He's one of mine, on remand."

He grinned and said: "Silko the Salesman? Yeah, I met him."

"How come?" I asked. "I thought you'd be on separate wings."

"We were, but we had association. Well, not proper association, but we had these classes. Silko took one of them, sometimes, and we all joined. Well, it was an hour out of your room wasn't it? He couldn't 'alf talk, about, you know, motivation an' plannin' an' all that. We could all be million-aires, 'e told us, without breaking the law. Mind you, 'e did wink when 'e said that last bit."

"That sounds like Tony," I remarked.

"Yeah, well. He killed a nonce, didn't 'e? Good riddance, we all said. Come to think of it, we talked about you, once."

"About me?"

"Yeah. We were in the classroom, me, 'im and this screw, waiting for the others to arrive. I used to get the room ready, clean the blackboard an' tidy up. I'd just finished when they walked in. 'E was grumbling to the screw, saying that 'e'd be out, now, if it wasn't for this cop who was 'ounding 'im. This cop called Inspector Priest. I said that it was you that 'ad done me. That you'd…well, you know."

"That I'd fitted you up?"

"Yeah, well, summat like that."

"So what did he say?"

"The screw laughed. He said that you'd just done someone

you were chasing for twenty-odd years. It was in the papers, he said. Summat about a fire."

"There was a fire in Leeds," I explained. "Back in 1975. Three women and five children were burnt to death. We just found out who started it."

"Blimey," he said, quietly. "You got the bastards?"

"We got them. So what happened next?"

"Yeah, well, like I was saying. The screw thought it was a right giggle. 'E said that if 'e'd done summat wrong the last person 'e'd want on the case was you. 'E said that you never forgot, an' that 'e 'oped Silkstone was telling the truth, for 'is sake, 'cos 'e'd never be able to sleep at night if 'e wasn't."

"Right," I said. "Right." My tea was finished and Halliwell was chewing his last piece of toast. "So did Silkstone have anything else to say?" I asked.

"No," he replied. "The others came in, then, an' we started. Come to think of it, though, he wasn't as chipper as 'e usually was, that lesson."

I lifted my jacket off the back of the chair and poked an arm down a sleeve. "Do you want a lift back?" I asked.

"No thanks, Mr Priest," he replied. "I 'ave to be careful what company I keep."

"Scared of being seen associating with the enemy?"

"Summat like that."

"I take it you are going back?"

"Dunno." A little smile played around his mouth, the wrinkles joining up into laughter lines. "Would it get you into trouble if I didn't?" he asked.

"No," I lied. "Nothing to do with me."

"Then I might as well go back." He stood up, uncurling from the chair and stretching to his full height with a display of effort. "Thanks for the breakfast, an' the fags. Sorry you 'ad a wasted journey."

"I'll give you a lift, if you want one."

"No, Mr Priest," he said. "I want to walk down that road like all these other people. Past the shops, an' all. Enjoy my freedom while I can. It's been a long wait."

"I hope it works out for you, Vince," I told him. "I really do."

We walked across the car-park together. As we emerged on to the pavement I said: "Vince." He turned to face me, his face etched with worry, scared I was about to spring something on him. He'd already had enough excitement for this day.

"Tony Silkstone took out a contract on me," I told him. "He offered someone fifty thousand to kill me. Did you hear anything about it?"

"To…to kill you?" he stuttered. "Fifty thousand to kill you?"

"That's right. Who did he talk to?"

"Dunno, Mr Priest. First I've 'eard of it."

"He hired a man called Chilcott. You ever heard of him?"

"Chiller? Yeah, I 'eard of 'im, but 'e wasn't in Bentley."

"I know. He was abroad. You didn't hear any talk?"

"No, Mr Priest, not a word. Honest."

"If you remember anything, get in touch."

"Yeah, right."

"OK. Thanks anyway. Mind the road."

I began to turn away but I heard him say: "'Ere, Mr Priest."

"Mmm?"

"Is this what it was all about, an' not the other job?"

"That's right, Vince. The other job's history, as far as I'm concerned. We knew who was with you, just couldn't prove it."

"So I told you what you wanted to know?"

"You gave me the reason that Silkstone had for wanting me dead. Yes."

"You devious bastard."

"I'm a cop," I said, as if that was a full explanation.

"Fifty Gs, did you say?"

"That's right. Would you have taken the contract, if you'd

known?"

"No," he replied. "Not my scene. But I'd 'ave chipped in."

He had the grace to smile as he said it. I flapped a hand at him and we walked our separate ways. Me back to the car and Heckley, him to his room in jail and the calendar on the wall that said that in two years he'd be let loose, with nobody to order him around, nobody to feed and clothe him.

The sun was in my eyes on the way back. I drove with the visor down, listening to a tape I'd compiled of Mark Knopfler and Pat Metheny. There'd been a shower and the roads were wet, so every lorry I passed turned the wind-screen into a glaring mixture of splatters and streaks. I stayed in the slow and middle lanes, driving steadily, doing some thinking, my fingers on the wheel tapping in time with 'Local Hero' and 'The Truth Will Always Be'. These days, in this job, you rarely have time to think. Something happens and you react. Time to reflect on the best way to tackle the situation is a luxury.

Halliwell said he would have contributed towards the fifty thousand if he'd known about it. If he'd guessed the truth he'd have donated the full sum. We knew who his accomplice was because we'd arrested him the day before, and he'd turned informer, gushing like a Dales stream about the Big Job he was doing the following night. Halliwell was set up by the man he refused to grass on, and we were wait-ing for him. The gun was a bonus; we hadn't expected that. It was found afterwards, thrown behind a dustbin on the route Halliwell had taken as he tried to flee the scene. He denied it was his, and we admitted in court that we hadn't found his fingerprints on it. Because he wouldn't say who his accomplice was the judge credited him with the weapon and gave him ten years.

I'd give my right arm to be able to make music like that. Not to have to deal with all this shit. Nobody asked us about the bullets. The gun had been wiped clean but we found a fingerprint on one of the bullets. It belonged to the accomplice, who just happened to slip through our fingers. This was eight years ago, before the law changed, and like I said: nobody asked.

Gilbert had some good news for me. A British couple starting their annual holiday had been held up at gunpoint outside Calais and their car stolen. The hijacker answered Chilcott's description. As I had grumbled to him every day about my bodyguard Gilbert reluctantly agreed that Chilcott was probably making his way across France and Tweedle Dee and Tweedle Dum could safely return to their normal duties. I didn't point out that it would also help his staff deployment problems and overtime budget, but I did tell him about my confrontation with Vince Halliwell. Gilbert gave one of his sighs and peered at me over his half-moon spectacles. "You're saying that Silkstone took the contract out on you because he wanted you off his case. You have a reputation for never forgetting, and he wanted to be able to sleep at nights. Is that it?"

"In a coconut shell," I replied.

"Why?"

"Why what?"

"Why does he want you off the case? He's admitted killing Latham."

"Because he's a worried man. He has something to hide. Everybody else is saying: 'Well done, Tony. You rid the world of a scumbag.' I'm the only one saying: 'Whoa up a minute! Maybe he was there with Latham when Margaret died.'"

"You know what the papers are saying, don't you."

"That he's a hero. Yes."

"And that we're hounding him unnecessarily."

"I haven't started hounding him yet."

"You really think he was there, when she died?"

"Yes, Gilbert. I do."

"OK, but play it carefully. Let Jeff take over the everyday stuff, and you spend what time you need on this. And for God's sake try to keep off the front page of the *UK News*."

Gilbert's a toff. He listens to what I have to say and then lets me have my way. If I were too outlandish, way off the mark, he'd step in and keep me on track, but it doesn't happen very often. He protects me from interference by the brass hats at HQ; I protect him from criticism by giving him our best clear-up rate. If you want to commit a murder, don't do it in Heckley. Don't do it on my patch. I searched in my drawer for an old diary. I needed some information, the sort they don't print in text books, and I knew just the person to ask.

Peter Drago lives in Penrith now, but he was born in Halifax and was in the same intake as me. We attended training school together and got drunk a few times. He made sergeant when I did and inspector shortly after me, but he also made some enemies. With sexual predilections like his, that was a dangerous thing to do. He was eventually caught, *in flagrante*, by the husband of the bubbly WPC he was making love to in the back of her car, and they had a fist fight.

Next day Drago was busted back to PC and posted to Settle and the WPC told to report to Hooton Pagnell. That's how things worked in those days. Step out of line and you were immediately transferred to the furthermost corner of the region. It changed when the good citizens of these far-flung outposts discovered that the handsome and attractive police officers with the city accents that kept arriving on their doorsteps were all the adulterers and philanderers that the force had to offer. I found his home number and dialled it.

"Fancy doing Great Gable tomorrow?" I asked without ceremony, when he answered.

After a hesitation he said: "That you, Charlie?" No insults, no sparkling repartee, just: "That you, Charlie?"

"The one and only," I replied. "How are you?"

"Oh, not too bad, you know. And you?"

"The same. So how about it?"

"Great Gable? I'd love to, Charlie, but I'm afraid I won't be climbing the Gable again for a long time."

"Why? What's happened?" This wasn't the Dragon of old, by a long way. His motto was: if it moved, shag it; if it didn't, climb it.

"I've just come out of hospital. Triple bypass, three weeks ago."

"Oh, I am sorry, Pete. Which organ?"

"My heart, pillock," he chuckled.

"What happened? Did you have an attack?"

"Yeah. Collapsed at work, woke up in the cardiac unit with all these masked figures bending over me. Thought I'd been abducted by aliens."

"I am sorry," I repeated. "And was it a success? Are you feeling OK now?"

"I'm a bit sore, but otherwise I feel grand. *Right champion*, in fact."

"OK," I said. "We'll take a rain check on the Gable, but only for six months. Next Easter we're going up there, you and me, so you'd better get some training in. Understood?"

After a silence he said: "You know, Charlie, that's the best tonic I've had. Next Easter, and sod what the doctors say. It's a date."

We chatted for a while, reminiscing about walks we'd done, scrapes we'd shared when we were PCs together. He asked about Dave and his family, and I told him that his daughter Sophie was about to start at Cambridge. Eventually he asked why I'd rung.

"Oh, it doesn't matter," I replied. "It was a bit personal, and I don't want to excite you."

"Now you do have to tell me," he insisted.

"Well," I said, "it really *is* a bit personal. Are you able to, you know, talk?"

"Yeah, she's gone for her hair doing. Tell me all about it."

I didn't ask who *she* was; Pete's love life has more dead ends and branch lines than the London Underground. "Well, it's like this," I began. "There's this bloke, and he's having an affair with a married woman."

"He's shagging her?"

"Er, yes."

"I just wanted to clarify the situation. Sorry, carry on."

"That's all right. He sees her every Wednesday afternoon, at her house, while her husband is at work."

"Presumably this is a purely hypothetical case," Pete interjected.

"Oh, definitely. Definitely."

"Right. Go on."

"Thanks. Now, this woman is in her early forties, and she isn't on the Pill, so her lover has to take precautions."

"As a matter of interest, is her lover married?"

"Er, no. As a matter of interest, he isn't."

"Has he ever been?"

"Um, yes, as a matter of interest, he has."

"I think I'm getting the picture. Carry on, please."

I carried on, loosely describing what we'd found at Mrs Silkstone's house, speculating how things may have happened. I think – I hope – that he eventually realised that I wasn't one of the protagonists in the whole squalid episode. He gave me the benefit of his experience in these matters, and I was grateful.

It was a long phone call. As we went through the ritual of ending it he said: "Did you ever hear what John Betjemen is supposed to have said on his death bed, Charlie?"

"Something about wishing he'd had more sex, wasn't it?"

"That's right, and I agree with him. Get it while you can, Charlie, you're a long time dead."

I reminded him about Easter and put the phone down, reflecting on the Pete Drago philosophy: get it while you can. He was a good bloke: intelligent, fair and generous; but something drove him, far harder than it drives most of us.

And, God knows, that's hard enough. Bob Dylan included
rakes in 'Chimes of Freedom', his personal version of the
Beatitudes: *tolling for the rebel, tolling for the rake*. I'd never
understood why, until now. Maybe he had it right.

We had a killing through the week. A youth was stabbed to
death in the town centre, and my heart sank when I learned
that he was from the Asian community. I breathed again
when it was revealed that his attacker was his brother-in-law,
and it was all about family honour. I'm only interested in
guilty or not guilty, and was relieved not to have a race war
on my hands. Family feuds I can deal with. Saturday
lunchtime I tidied my desk and fled, rejoicing at my new-
found freedom, eager to be out in the fresh air. I drove to
Burnsall, one of the most attractive Dales villages, and
donned my boots. The route I took was loop-shaped,
through Thorpe and Linton to Bow Bridge, then following
the Wharfe back to the village. It's a beautiful river, sometimes rushing over boulders, sometimes carving deep lan-
guid pools and sandbanks. Dippers used to be common-
place, not very long ago, and I've seen the kingfisher there.
The morning showers had passed over, and the afternoon
sun made the meadows steam.

There were lots of people about. It's a popular place, and
the last flush of summer always brings us out, determined to
stock up on the beneficial rays before the dark nights close
in. A group of people were vacating some rocks at the side
of the water, packing their picnic remnants into Tupperware
boxes and rucksacks. It was a good spot, in a patch of sunshine, with trees on the opposite side and the river gabbling
noisily. Very therapeutic. I moved in after them, heading for
a seat on a dry boulder, and as I sat down a dead twig, brittle as egg shells, snapped under my feet.

I'd called in Marks and Spencer's when I left the office,
for a prawn sandwich and a packet of Eccles cakes. I wolfed
them down with a can of flavoured mineral water, sitting

there watching the stream go by. Swallows were skimming the surface, stocking up on flies before their long journey south, and a fish made ripples, out in the middle where it flowed more slowly.

There weren't many places that I would rather have been, but there's more to happiness than that. I wondered if Annette were doing something similar, picnicking with another man and his children as a different river slid past them. I leaned forward and picked up a piece of the branch I'd stepped on. It was about four inches long, dead as last week's scandal and encrusted with lichen. I tossed it, underhand, out into the stream.

It hardly made a splash and bobbed up and down, buoyant as a cork, until the current took hold and pushed it into the flow, heading towards a cleft between two rocks. I watched it accelerate towards them, turning as opposing forces caught and juggled with it. It entered the chute between the rocks, one end riding high, and plunged over the mini-waterfall.

The pressure held it down and the undertow pulled it back. There was a wrestling match between the flow of water and the buoyancy of the twig, but there could only be one result. After a few seconds it broke free of the water's grip and burst to the surface. I watched it rotate in the current like an ice skater taking a bow and nod away towards the North Sea, eighty miles down river.

I couldn't do it again. I broke another piece off the branch and threw it into the stream, but it was swept straight through the rocks and away. I tried bigger pieces and smaller ones, with variable quantities of lichen, but it didn't work. It was the balance that was important. Big twigs were more buoyant, but the water had more to press down on. On the other hand, the lichen provided drag, which should have helped the water. I tossed another piece into the stream and watched it slide away.

"My, that looks good fun," a voice said, behind me.

I turned, squinting into the sun, and saw an elderly couple standing there. They were wearing lime green and blue anoraks, and had two pale Labradors on extending leads, which they'd thoughtfully reeled in as they'd approached me.

"Hello," I said. "I didn't hear you. Isn't it a nice day."

"Wonderful," the man said. "So what is it? Pooh sticks?"

"You need a bridge for that," I told him. "No, I was just doing some experiments, studying elementary hydraulics."

"Elementary hydraulics, eh. And I thought it was at least Life, Death and the Universe."

"No, not quite. Are you going far?"

"Only to the footbridge and back. And you?"

"I walked up to Bow Bridge, and I'm heading back to Burnsall. Far enough for this afternoon."

"Well enjoy your experiments," he said. "Hope we didn't disturb you."

"Not at all. Enjoy your walk." His wife gave me a special smile. She was attractive, had once been beautiful. Probably still was, when you knew her. I watched them stroll away, the dogs leaping about on long leads now, biting each other's necks. It was easy to forgive them their matching anoraks.

No, I thought, as I hooked my rucksack over my shoulder. Not Life, Death and the Universe. Just Life, Death and Elementary Hydraulics.

Chapter Ten

Monday morning Superintendent Isles gave me permission to interview Jason Lee Gelder at HQ, where he was being held. I cleared my diary and reallocated a few tasks to accommodate him. Dave had driven to Cambridge over the weekend, to look at Sophie's room in the students' quarters. He was a lot happier now that he knew where she'd be staying, and told us all what a smashing place it was. Expecting displays of enthusiasm from him is normally like expecting impartial advice from your bank manager, but today he was full of it. I decided to attempt to harness the quality.

"And I've a special little job for you, Sunshine," I told him.

"Like what?" he asked. From him, that's eager.

"One I wouldn't trust to anybody else."

"I'll think about it."

"Good. I want you to go to Boots and buy one hundred condoms."

"A hundred condoms!"

"That's right. You can put them on your expenses."

"You want me to buy a hundred French letters and put them on my expenses?"

"That's what I said."

"You can cocoa!"

"I'm serious."

"So am I! Go buy them yourself."

I found a notebook with empty pages and put it in my pocket with a couple of fibre-tipped pens. "You just can't get the staff," I said standing up and sliding my chair under the desk.

Sparky had his cheeky grin on. "So, er, things are looking up, are they?" he asked.

"No, they're not," I snapped, adding: "If you want a job doing properly, do it yourself."

"Why a hundred?" he asked. "With your luck a packet of

three would last you until the use-before date."

"You can be very hurtful," I told him, opening the door and switching the light off.

"Yeah, it was a bit. Sorry."

"That's OK. How much are they, these days?"

"Johnnies? A pound for two from the machine in the Spinners' bog."

"Is that plain or flavoured?"

"Plain. The flavoured are two quid for three."

"You seem to know all about them."

"I read the machine while I'm having a pee. What do you do?"

"Try to drown a fly. That'd be fifty quid, and I'd have to go to the bank for coins. And then the machine would run out and I'd have to ask the barman for my money back. It'll have to be a chemist's."

"Are you serious?" he demanded.

"Never more. Want to change your mind?"

"No."

"Fair enough, but I'll have to put it on your record. I'm off to HQ, to talk to young Mr Gelder. Try not to breach too many guidelines while I'm gone."

I parked in town and went to Boots. The condoms were on the self-service shelves but there was a small queue at the pay counter, so I wandered around for a few minutes until it had gone. Fetherlites came in packs of a dozen, costing £8.85, so I'd have to buy...I did the mental arithmetic...six twelves are seventy-two, seven twelves are eighty-four, eight twelves are ninety-six...nine, I'd have to buy nine packs, which would leave eight condoms over. Ah well, they might come in handy, some day.

The queue had gone so I gathered up a handful of pack-ets. Dammit! There were only eight on display. Ninety-six. That meant I needed two packets of three to make up the shortfall. I added them to my collection and headed towards the counter.

A woman got there before me, but that was OK. I fell in behind her, my purchases clutched to my body, as she handed over a brown bottle of tablets and a ten pound note. The grey-haired assistant looked at the bottle and turned towards the glassed-off enclave where the pharmacist was busy counting pills.

"Paracetamol!" she shouted, and he raised his head and nodded his consent to the sale.

A wave of panic swept through me. Was she about to yell "Condoms!" to all and sundry when she saw what I was buying? "You know that they contain paracetamol, don't you?" she told the customer, who said that she did. Personally, I'd have thought that that was why she was buying them. And as it said *Paracetamol* in large letters across the label, it seemed not unreasonable to assume that she knew the chief ingredient.

"Can I, er, take those, please," I mumbled, when it was my turn, half expecting her to warn me that I'd never make a baby if I wore one of these, on the off-chance that I was a lapsing Catholic. I passed the bundle two-handed across the glass-topped counter, followed by my credit card. She was counting them when the phone rang. "Excuse me," she said, placing my goods in a neat pile and turning to answer it. Unfortunately Durex packs are shiny and rounded, and don't stack up well. They slid over and spread-eagled themselves across the counter, fanning out like a hand of cards. I turned and smiled guiltily at the baby in the arms of the young girl who headed the queue that was forming behind me. The girl smiled back at me.

Seventy-six flippin' quid they cost. And thirty pence. I grabbed the bag that the assistant handed over and turned to flee, only glancing at the five women and two men in the queue behind me enough to notice that the last man looked suspiciously like my window cleaner. As I passed him he touched my sleeve. I turned to say hello, but he just said "Receipt."

"Pardon?"

"You forgot your receipt."

"Oh, thanks." I went back to the counter and the grey-haired assistant passed it to me. I felt as if I ought to make a witty remark, but she was already listening to her next customer.

Jason Lee Gelder wasn't what I'd expected. I try not to be fooled by first impressions, but he took me for a ride. I shook hands with his brief, the duty solicitor, when he introduced himself, although we meet nearly as often as the swing doors down at the Job Centre, and sat down opposite them.

"Is it Jason or Lee?" I asked.

"Er, Jason," he replied. He had the palest blue eyes I'd ever seen, short fair hair in a sensible style, a high forehead and a full mouth and jaw-line. When it came to looks, he was a heart-breaker, and I could imagine the girls falling for him like lemmings off a cliff. But nature gives with one hand and takes away with the other.

"Right, Jason," I began. "Are they looking after you well?"

"Er, yeah."

"I see they've given you your own clothes back."

"Er, yeah."

"We were allowed to collect some from his home," the solicitor explained, "but most of his clothes are with your forensic people."

"For tests," I told Jason. "We do tests on them." Before either of them could speak again I said: "This is an informal interview, to clear up a few things about this and another case. We are not recording or taking notes, but I have to tell you, Jason, that you are still under caution and anything you say may be taken down and used in evidence. Do you understand?"

"Yeah," he said, which meant that he was probably the only one of us who did.

"Which newspapers do you read, Jason?" I asked.

He shuffled uncomfortably in his seat and stared down at somewhere near his navel.

"*The Sun*?" I suggested. "Or the *Sunday Sport*?"

He shook his head and curled up even more.

"If I may," the solicitor interrupted. "Jason has reading difficulties. He doesn't buy a newspaper."

"Oh, I'm sorry," I said, taken aback for a moment. Then I remembered the magazines that were found in his room. "You like pictures, though, don't you?" I asked. "Which paper has the best girls in it? Tell me that, Jason."

"Dunno," he mumbled.

"But you look at them?"

"I suppose so."

"Which ones?"

"Dunno."

"Where do you see them?"

"All over."

"Such as?"

"Anywhere."

"Tell me, Jason. I'm trying to help you."

He shrugged his shoulders and looked towards his brief for help. The solicitor waved a palm towards me in a gesture that said: "For God's sake tell the man."

"In the pub," he replied.

"What?" I began. "You mean, people leave them in the pub and you collect them?"

"I don't collect them. I just 'ave a look."

"Where else?"

"Mates' 'ouses. All over."

"Which papers do you like best?"

"I dunno. They're all the same."

"*The Sport*?"

"Sometimes."

"The *UK News*? Do you like the *UK News*, Jason?"

"Dunno if I do or not."

"Where do you get your magazines from?"

"From mates."

"Do you buy them?"

"No. We just swap them."

It always looks good in the report of a trial: *Police found a number of pornographic magazines in the accused's house.* Of course we did, because they're all over the place. There isn't an establishment in the country that employs a majority of males where you couldn't find some sort of unofficial library of top-shelf literature, and that includes most police stations. Jason would have been more interesting to the psychiatric profession if we *hadn't* found any sex books at his home.

"Tell me about your girlfriends," I suggested.

"'Aven't got one," he replied.

"But you've had one, haven't you?"

"I suppose so."

"Good looking lad like you," I said. "With a little car. Wouldn't have thought you'd have any problem pulling the birds. Am I right?"

"Sometimes."

"Who was your last girlfriend?"

"Can't remember."

"Can't or won't? How long since you last had a girl in the car, Jason?"

He thought about it, his brow a rubbing-board of furrows. "'Bout three weeks," he eventually volunteered. "Maybe a bit longer."

"So that would be before Marie-Claire Hollingbrook was murdered," I said.

"Yeah. 'Bout a week before."

"How did you learn about her murder?"

"In the pub. They were talking about it in the pub."

"Did you know her?"

"No."

"Did you ever see her?"

"No."

"So you didn't recognise her from her picture in the papers?"

"No."

The solicitor leaned forward and said: "Inspector, could you possibly explain where this line of enquiry is leading? My client has strenuously denied any knowledge of Miss Hollingbrook or any involvement in her death. There are several hours of taped interviews in which he answers all questions fully and satisfactorily."

"There is some rather heavy evidence against your client," I pointed out.

"Which is being contested," he rejoined. "There are precedents, Inspector, in which DNA evidence has been discredited. We are currently investigating the whole procedure for taking and examining samples from both the crime scene and witnesses."

Here we go, I thought. O.J. Simpson all over again. O.J. bloody Simpson. It wasn't my job to give him lines of defence, so I just accepted what he said. I turned back to Jason and asked: "What was this girl called that you last went out with?"

"Dunno," he replied.

"You don't know? Didn't you ask?"

"Yeah, but I've forgotten."

"Well try to remember. It could be important."

"I've forgotten."

"OK. Let's go through it. Where did you meet her?"

"At that club in Heckley with the daft name."

"The Aspidistra Lounge."

"Yeah, that's it."

"Go there a lot, do you?"

"Yeah, I suppose so."

"What nights?"

"Sometimes Thursdays, and most Fridays."

"And what night did you meet this girl?"

"Not sure. Think it was Friday."

"So what did you do?"

"What did we do?" he asked, looking even more bewildered.

"Did you dance?"

"Yeah, a bit."

"Buy her a drink?"

"Yeah."

"What did she drink?"

"Lager. And Blastaways."

"Blastaways. Right." I knew that was a sickly combination of cider and a ready-made cocktail called a Castaway. "And did you ask her name?"

"I suppose so."

"Which was?"

"Can't remember."

It's at times like this that I wished I smoked. I could take out the packet of Sobranies, flick one between my lips, light it with my gold-plated Zippo and inhale a long satisfying lungful of nicotine-laden smoke. All I'd have to worry about was an early grave from cancer, not trying to keep an uncommunicative twerp like Jason from spending the rest of his natural being used as a trampoline in an open prison.

"Did you take her home?" I asked.

"Yeah."

"Straight home?"

"Er, no."

"Where did you go?"

"To the brickyard."

Atkinson's brickyard was long gone, but the name lingered on. It was now a lawned-over picnic site, only the red shards poking through the grass indicating its industrial past. More people meet there after dark for sex than ever eat at the primitive tables during daylight hours.

"Did you have sex with her?"

"Yeah."

"In the back seat?"

"No, in the front."

"Really! Wouldn't you have found it more comfortable in the back?"

"Yeah, but…"

"But what?"

"We just started, you know, snogging, in the front, and that was it."

"You were carried away."

"Yeah. Well, she was. Dead eager for it, she was."

"She took the initiative?"

"Yeah."

I expected his brief to interrupt, but I think he was as fascinated as I was by the sexual mores of the young. I dragged the conversation back on course. "Was she on the Pill?" I asked.

"No."

"So what did you do? Risk it?"

"No."

"You'd gone prepared."

"Yeah."

"Very commendable. So did you arrange to see her again?"

"Not really. I said I might see 'er in the…the whatsit, the club."

"You don't sound as if you were keen. Why not?"

"Because she was a slag, that's why."

"But you must have asked her name."

"Yeah, I suppose so."

"Which was…?"

"Can't remember."

I turned to the brief and told him that we were going to have a five-minute break. I said I was trying to help his client and the name of the girl might be of use in my line of enquiries. Jason was in hot water about as deep as it gets, and anything he told me could only help his case. I suggested they did some serious thinking.

Les Isles wasn't in his office, and Nigel was nowhere to be found, either. Two DCs were busy in the main office, working at computer keyboards that were in danger of being engulfed by the paperwork heaped around them. Who invented the expression *paperless office*? Woody Allen?

"Where's the boss?" I asked the nearest DC.

"Mr Isles?"

"Mmm."

"Review meeting at Region. It's Mr Priest, isn't it?"

I didn't deny the fact and we shook hands. He'd attended one of my talks at the training college and said he enjoyed it. "I'm interviewing Jason Gelder downstairs," I told him, quickly adding: "with Mr Isles' permission. Nobody told me he was ESN."

"Who, Mr Isles?" he replied with a grin. "That explains a lot."

"I meant young Gelder."

"Sorry about that. Strictly speaking, and according to the experts, he's not. Put in layman's language, he's thick, but he's not slow."

"I see," I said, "or at least, I think I do. Where does he get his money from?"

"He works for a living, down at the abattoir. Spends his working day scraping flesh from animal skins. They pay him fairly well because nobody wants to do it, and he goes home stinking like an otter's arse."

"Right. Thanks for your help. *Thick but not slow*, I'll have to ponder on that one."

Down in the interview room Jason was slumped at the table and the brief was leaning on the wall, a polystyrene coffee cup in his hand. He shrugged his shoulders as I entered and resumed his seat.

"Where were we?" I asked, briskly, rubbing my hands together. "Didn't you want a coffee, Jason?" and was rewarded with a shake of the head.

"So what was this girl called?" I demanded.

"I don't know," he stated, staring straight at me. The brief must have given him a hard time because he looked as if he'd been crying.

"What did you talk about? If you did any talking?" I asked.

"Not much," he replied.

"How old was she? Did you ask her that?"

"No, I don't think I asked."

I wasn't surprised. What was that other one from Pete Drago's list of sexual aphorisms: *If they're big enough, they're old enough.* "How old did you think she was?"

"About eighteen. She was about eighteen."

"So she wasn't under age."

"No, definitely not. She'd left school."

"Did she work or go to college?"

"I don't know."

"So if she was over sixteen why won't you tell me her name."

"Because you won't listen," he sobbed. "I keep telling you, I don't remember."

"OK," I said. "Let's go through it again. You meet this girl at the Aspidistra Lounge, either on Thursday or Friday night…"

"Friday," He interrupted. "I think it was Friday."

"But you're not sure?"

"No."

"Right. You buy her a few drinks, have a dance and a smooch, and take her home. Did you stay right to the end?"

"No."

"What time?"

"Dunno."

"Before or after midnight?"

"About midnight."

"Then you went to the brickyard, had sex with this young lady in the front seat because you were both too desperate to climb into the back, and that was that. You had ten minutes of passion but didn't bother seeing her again. Why not?"

"Because she was a slag. I've told you once," he stated, almost shouting at me now. I decided to push him.

"A slag! Aren't all the girls you pick up slags?" I demanded.

"No. Not all of them."

"But this one was?"

"Yeah."

"Was Marie-Claire a slag, Jason. Was she another slag?"

"I don't know. I never met her." Tears were running down his cheeks and he turned to the brief for help. "Why won't they believe me?" he begged.

"Because you're not telling the truth, Jason." I stated. "This girl at the club; what was she called?"

"I don't know!"

"Why are you protecting her, if you think she was a slag?"

"Because you wouldn't believe me. You don't believe anything I say."

He was cracking. I'd closed on him. "What wouldn't I believe?" I asked.

"Anything."

"Tell me what I wouldn't believe, Jason."

"I can't."

"Why? Why can't you tell me?"

"Because!"

"Because what?"

"Just because."

He'd turned a ghostly white and was hyperventilating. The solicitor placed a hand on his arm, saying: "Jason, if there's something you have to say, I think you should tell Mr Priest. It can't do you any harm."

Jason stared at me, defiant, and I stared back at him. "Go on, Jason," I encouraged. "Who was she?"

"I don't know her name."

"You said we wouldn't believe you. What wouldn't we believe?"

"You'd 'old it against me. Gang up on me."

"Why would we do that?"

"Because it's what you do."

"Tell me what you know, Jason," I asked.

"Tell Mr Priest," the brief added.

Jason breathed deeply a few times, gathering his strength, then blurted the words out. "'Er dad's a copper," he informed us.

"A copper?" I echoed. "What sort of a copper?"

"A detective. He's a detective. At 'Eckley nick."

It wasn't what I expected, or what I wanted to hear. Images of him having it away with his kid sister, or his probation officer, or some other unlikely person, were swirling around in my mind, but not this. "Are you sure?" I asked, my voice a whisper.

"Yeah. She said 'er dad was a detective, in the CID at 'Eckley. I didn't ask 'er, she just told me."

"But…you can't remember her name?"

"No."

"Good," I mumbled. "Good. I think that will do for now."

Chapter Eleven

I went into a sandwich shop, but when I saw them all lying there like shrink-wrapped museum exhibits waiting to be catalogued I decided I wasn't hungry. I bought a bottle of flavoured water, that's all, and sipped at it sitting on a bench in the town centre, because I couldn't think of anywhere else to go. It must have been a cold day because people were hurrying about with their collars upturned and I had the seats all to myself. I don't feel the cold.

O.J. Simpson was found not guilty of murder because his legal team declared that the DNA evidence was flawed. The jury accepted their claim because the police were a bunch of racists, and it was a glitch in the procedures for processing the DNA evidence that gave them the excuse to do so.

Blood samples from accused and victims were taken to the same laboratory, and O.J.'s thousand-dollars-an-hour attorney convinced the court that DNA could have floated about in the atmosphere and transferred itself from one sample dish to another. It's not as crazy as it seems. They'd used something called PCR, or polymerase chain reaction, to amplify a tiny stretch of DNA, too small to be useful, into a big sample. It's a procedure that a California scientist called Kary Mullis thought of while driving his car through the desert at night. It's a magical experience for anyone, but Mullis wove some real magic that night, enough to win himself a share in the Nobel prize.

He knew that if you took one single shred of a DNA molecule and gently heated it in a test tube, with an exotic brew of the right proteins and enzymes, the two strands would untwine, and as you cooled it down again each would create a copy of the partner it had just lost. In other words, you would now have two pieces of the DNA. How you knew that there was only one molecule in the tube to start with, and how you kept track of it, wasn't explained in the book I read. The heating and cooling process only took a few minutes, so do it again and you'd now have four pieces of DNA. It's a fiendishly complicated process – this was strictly the Ladybird version, intended for under-sevens and police officers.

Mullis stopped the car and did some sums. He calculated that in twenty heating and cooling cycles, which would only take until coffee break, you'd have over a million copies of your original sample. Still not enough to be visible on the head of a pin, but you were getting there. Keep going, and by the end of the week you'd be bringing in the enzymes by specially laid road and rail connections, and moving the DNA out by the barge-load. In a month you could fill the Grand Canyon and make a start on the Marianas Trench.

You don't need that much in a criminal case. O.J.'s lawyers said that with all the DNA being made, who could say that a spare flake hadn't floated into the wrong test tube or Petri dish or whatever they use, and nobody had enough clout to argue with a thousand-dollars-an-hour attorney. This DNA swirling about in the atmosphere could just as easily have belonged to Thomas Jefferson or Christopher Columbus, but nobody mentioned it. As the newspapers put it: *money talked, O.J. walked*.

Black spots were breaking out on the pavement in front of my feet, like some deadly infection, and a raindrop scored a direct hit on my neck. Jason Lee Gelder's solicitor was on the basic rate for the job, we had enough semen to do all the tests we needed and different samples are always processed in different labs. There was no comfort for him there. I took a sip of water and looked at the pigeons that had joined me, expecting to catch a few crumbs. They were all exactly alike, each a replicant of some distant ancestor, their lives pre-programmed in the genetic code. I wish I'd been a scientist. I screwed the top back on the bottle and went to find the car.

A solitary detective, David Rose, was at work in the office when I arrived back. He was in his shirtsleeves, surrounded by paperwork as he peered at the VDU screen on his desk, pencil behind his ear. He turned as I closed the door and said: "Hi, Charlie."

"No." I replied.

"No what?"

"No, whatever it was."

I went straight into my little office and gathered up all the papers put there to attract my attention. They could wait. I picked up the phone, dialled the HQ number and put the phone down again. Scenes of crime would have gone over Jason's car with the proverbial, in the faint hope of finding evidence that Marie-Claire had been in it and was therefore known to him. They'd failed, I knew that, but they must have found some evidence, like fingerprints, of other people who'd ridden with him. Like the girl he took to the brickyard. The detective's daughter.

I drummed my fingers on the phone, indecisive. I needed to know who he'd been with, not sure if I could face the truth. There are sixteen detectives at Heckley, and I knew all their families, had visited all their houses. I brought out a staff list and took the top off my pen, with the intention of writing their kids' names in the margin. The pen hovered next to the first name but I couldn't do it. I couldn't sully them by giving substance to Gelder's accusations. There was only one name that fitted, and I felt ashamed at even considering what was going through my mind. I tore the list into shreds and dropped them in the bin. But, I argued, someone was with him, somebody's daughter, and these were promiscuous times. Or at least, we were constantly being told they were. Myself, I wasn't too sure. Times had changed, of course they had, but people, including kids, made their own moralities and sometimes they were surprisingly high. I stood up and strode over to the window. It only took two.

I'd beaten the rain back, but it was catching up. Rooftops were glistening across the road, but this side was still clear. Even as that fact registered the first flurry dashed against the window and the street lights flickered on. We were in for a downpour. Black clouds were banked like pit heaps behind St Mary's Church, at the other side of town, blotting out the hills. A straggle of people was going in when I'd driven past, for afternoon mass or, perhaps, an organ recital. They'd get wet when they came out, but I don't suppose they'd mind. Not the faithful ones.

A report on the news had said that church attendance on Sundays was down by seven percent over the last ten years. A couple of spokesmen, Bishop Inevitable and Archbishop Complacent, said that it wasn't all bad news because attendance through the week was on the increase. I wasn't sure if going in to listen to a Bach fugue or buy mince pies from the WI stall counted, but it was good for the statistics and the offering.

Trouble is, nobody has any faith anymore. I'd never had any. Doubt, not blind belief in something I couldn't comprehend, was always my driving force. I wish it were otherwise, but it isn't. I returned to my desk and picked the top document off the pile I'd made. Would I like to contribute to Mr Pritchard's leaving present? I fished a ten-pound note from my wallet, placed it in an envelope with the letter and sealed it.

It wasn't true, I told myself. I did have faith. It might not be in a god, but it was there. I believed in the people around me, colleagues and friends, like I'd believed in my parents. Had faith in them. "So prove it," I told myself, picking up the telephone and dialling the custody sergeant at HQ. "Sorry, Sophie," I whispered as I waited for him to answer. "Forgive me for doubting you."

"This is DI Priest at Heckley," I told him. "I came in this morning and interviewed Jason Gelder, and I'd like to talk to him again, as soon as possible. Will it be alright if I come over?"

"You'll be lucky, Mr Priest," he replied. "We've just sent him to Bentley. You'll find him in the remand wing."

"Damn," I said. "OK, thanks." It would have to be tomorrow.

Gwen Rhodes wasn't there, so I had to use the proper channels, just like everybody else. The visits office said they couldn't possibly accommodate me on Tuesday, but after a pathetic display of subservience and respect for their difficulties they agreed to squeeze me in on Friday. They like us to know that they can't be pushed around. I said: "Thank you, Friday will be fine."

Tuesday, I went to court instead. After hanging about for two hours and another half-hour talking to a magistrate, I came away with a warrant to search Silkstone's house and a special circumstance attached to his bail conditions. He had to stay out of the way while we did so.

I rang him on his mobile and told him to bring his brief with him when he came to sign the book on Thursday. I wanted to do a substantive interview, to clarify his exact movements on the day his wife died. I didn't mention the search warrant.

"What if I refuse to stay?" he ventured.

"Then I'll arrest you," I told him. The time had come to put pressure on Mr Silkstone. He'd had a long break, had probably grown complacent about his predicament. He was due for a wake-up call.

Wednesday I drove to the lab at Wetherton and had a long talk with one of the professors. He listened to what I had to say, sounded sceptical but agreed to loan me a scientist. At a price, of course. He followed me back to Heckley, where I held a briefing with Dave Sparkington, Jeff Caton and four members of the scenes of crime team. Compared to them, the professor had sounded jubilant and enthusiastic.

"So you were serious," Sparky declared.

"I'm always serious, Dave," I replied.

"What exactly are *we* looking for?" one of the SOCOs asked.

"You have the difficult bit," I told him. "Silkstone killed Peter John Latham with a kitchen knife, ostensibly belonging to Latham. It just happened to be available, on the worktop. If the murder was planned in advance Silkstone wouldn't have left anything to chance. What I want to know is whether Silkstone was aware that the block containing the knives would be there, or if he took it with him. Ideally, I'd like to link the knives with Silkstone. Had the block stood on his worktop before it went to Latham's house? We're talking micro-analysis stuff here; trace evidence. Look for marks, a faded patch on the tiles, an impression on the underside of the block, that sort of thing. Take some pictures in UV or oblique light; you know more about it than me. My team will be looking for other possible links. Were the knives a present from the Silkstones, or were they bought specially for the job? Count the knives in both houses, does one of them have too many or too few? Look for a receipt, trace the supplier, who bought them?"

"Perhaps there are photographs taken in their kitchens that might show the knives," the youngest of the SOCOs suggested. She was an Asian girl, with huge dark eyes. A SOCO's greatest asset is his or her eyes, and hers were belters.

"Good thinking," I said. "Find their photo albums. And while we're talking about photos, I'm going to ask Somerset to give the picture of Caroline Poole we found in Latham's bedroom a going over: does it carry any prints, inside or out, and what was used to trim it down to size? You know the score, so have a look at his scissors."

"All this should have been done before," Sparky declared.

"You're right, Dave," I said, "but Silkstone confessed to murder and we believed him. We believed what we saw and what he told us. Any tests we did were to confirm his story, because we had no reason to do otherwise. What we are saying now is that perhaps he was involved also with the death of his wife and the whole thing was premeditated. This is a murder enquiry, and not Confessions of a Salesman.

Without witnesses the odds are stacked against us, but let's give it a try."

They closed their notebooks and stood up, looking slightly more enthusiastic than before but not exactly over-flowing with optimism. The young scientist from the lab hung back as they drifted away.

"So where are the, er, whatsits?" he asked.

"Here," I said, passing him a manila envelope.

"There's a hundred in here?"

"A hundred and two."

"Do you realise how long it will take?"

"It could be up to three hours," I replied, "but just do as many as you can. The more the merrier. What I mainly want from you is an unbiased report, nice and scientific, that nobody can argue with."

He reached inside the envelope and extracted a dispenser of aloe vera liquid soap. "And what's this for?" he asked.

"Um, use your imagination," I replied.

"Present for you," I said, opening the car boot.

"What is it?" Dave asked, coming over to me. It was seven thirty in the morning and a light drizzle was falling. We hadn't met for a pint the night before, so I'd spent the evening shopping and doing chores.

"My old microwave," I told him. "You can have it for Sophie, if you want. You said she needed one. The bulb's gone, but otherwise it's OK."

He turned up his collar and looked at it for a few seconds before saying: "And what about you? I thought you lived out of the microwave."

"I bought a new one last night. A Mitsubishi. It does everything, including the washing up, so this is now going spare. Any good to you?"

"Charlie…" he began, "I'd be annoyed if I thought you'd gone out and bought one just so Sophie could have this."

"I didn't," I assured him. "Sainsbury's have started doing

these ready meals for the healthier appetite, like mine, and this isn't large enough for them. They get stuck corner-ways on when they rotate, so I bought a bigger one. Now I'm getting flippin' soaked, so do you want it or not."

"Yeah," he nodded. "Thanks a lot. I believe you like I believe the Prime Minister, but thanks. It'll save me a bob or two."

"And these are expensive times," I said.

"You can say that again."

I helped him carry it to his car and we walked into the nick, brushing the raindrops from our jackets. Dave is paid for the overtime he works, but it is strictly limited. I have to ration it out and try to be fair to everyone. The younger DCs have expenses, too: mortgages and young children if they're married; flash cars with big payments if they're single. "What a miserable day," I complained.

"Yeah," he agreed with a grin. "What we need is a nice juicy interview, to brighten it up."

"I'll see what I can arrange, Mr Nasty," I said.

"I'll wait for your call, Mr Nice," he replied.

Jeff attended the briefing while I read the night reports. He was wearing blue trousers with a logo tab sewn to a pocket, a short sleeved white shirt and a green tie with multicoloured triangles in a random pattern. Annette waved a coffee mug at me across the office and I nodded a *Yes please* at her. She was wearing a lime green T-shirt that managed to look expensive, black trousers with a slight flair and chunky-heeled granny boots. She looked sensational and I let my eyes linger on her, catching the curve of her breasts as she reached to plug in the kettle. Jeff, in contrast, looked quite ordinary.

Just before ten, front desk rang to say that Mr Silkstone and Mr Prendergast had arrived and were now in interview room number one. We gave them five minutes to decide where they were sitting and went down to join them. Silkstone looked leaner than I remembered him, and had worked on his tan. He was wearing a stone-coloured light-weight suit that was inappropriate for the weather and made him look like Our Man in Havana. Prendergast was in solic-itor blue, and two large umbrellas leaned in the corner, each standing in a small puddle. I wondered if they had licences for them.

"Nasty morning," I said, brightly, as I sat opposite Silkstone. They both glanced at me without replying, Silkstone giving me the look he normally reserved for flat tyres and dodgy oysters. Dave placed two cassettes in the recorder and announced that we were off.

I thanked them for coming and did the introductions, adding that DS Sparkington would have to leave us in a few minutes to make a phone call. "The principal reason we are here," I continued, "is to make what we call a definitive activity chart of Mr Silkstone's exact movements through the house on the day that Mr Latham died. It's not a new idea, but the prosecution service has started asking for it in all cases. Up to now we've only done one if we thought it relevant. I know you have told us most of it before, but I'd be very grateful if we could run through it again." I extract-ed a plan of Latham's house at West Woods from the papers on the table in front of me, and slid it towards Dave. He squared it up and laid a pencil across it. "So," I went on, "if you can describe your movements from when you parked on his drive to when the police arrived, DC Sparkington will mark them on the diagram."

Prendergast looked as if I were trying to sell him a time-share in Bosnia, which is about how I felt, but he stayed silent. Silkstone didn't know any better and leaned back in his chair, rehearsing his words as he drew on a cigarette. He had nothing to hide. He was the first person I'd met who could swagger sitting down.

"Er, Boss," Dave said.

"Mmm?"

"Don't you think we ought to start before then?" he

asked.

"Like when?"

"Well, when Mr Silkstone went home and found Latham with his wife."

"You mean a week earlier, at Mountain Meadows?"

"That's right."

"Why?"

"Because CPS will ask for it. It might not be relevant, but it's all part of the big picture. And then we want another one for a week later, when he found Mrs Silkstone's body. After that we can go to Latham's place."

I clenched my fists and stared down at the desk, breathing deeply. After a few moments I said: "OK, OK, if you say so. Do we have drawings of Mr Silkstone's house."

"It's The Garth," Dave replied. "There should be some in there." I found one and pushed it towards him. "Sorry about this," I said to the other two, "but my DC likes to do things by the book."

Dave turned towards the tape recorder and said: "I am now looking at a drawing of The Garth, Mountain Meadows." He announced today's date and the date that Silkstone first went home early, writing them both on the diagram. "Right," he declared, looking expectantly at me and then at Silkstone. "Let's go."

"Where did you park the car?" I asked, and Silkstone leaned over the table and showed Dave exactly where he'd left his £40,000 Audi A8.

"And by which door did you enter the house?"

"The kitchen door."

Dave traced a straggly line down the drive, around the corner to the side door.

"And then?"

"I walked through into the lounge," Silkstone informed us, exhaling a cloud of smoke towards the ceiling, "to where Margaret and Peter were sitting."

"Which was where, exactly?" I asked.

"Margaret was on the settee and Peter in the easy chair nearest the fireplace."

"And did you join them?"

"No. I was bursting to go to the toilet. That was mainly why I'd gone home. I put my briefcase down and went for a piss."

"Which bathroom did you use?" Dave asked, his pencil hovering over the plan.

Prendergast yawned and twisted in his seat, trying to see out through the little window. Relax while you can, I thought. We'll brighten up your morning in a minute or two.

"Upstairs," Silkstone replied. "The family bathroom."

"Why not the one downstairs," I asked, "if you were so desperate?"

"Never occurred to me," he said. "We only use that one when we entertain, and I don't suppose I was that desperate. Generally speaking, I use the family room all the time, and Margaret uses – used – the *en suite* one. I just went up there out of habit."

"Inspector…" the lawyer began, his face twisted by a pain that expressed his disdain for what we were doing. "Is this really necessary?"

I turned to Dave, saying: "Isn't it about time you made that call, Sunshine?"

"Yeah," he replied, pushing his chair back and standing up. "'Scuse me."

"DC Sparkington leaves the room at ten thirteen," I said, as if anyone cared, but it sounded professional. I reached for the incomplete diagram and turned to the brief. "My DC is right," I told him. "It might all look unnecessary, but we have a list of forms to fill in and if any are missing the CPS start chasing us. It's nice if we can get it right first time: saves us having to bother you again. So, Mr Silkstone, you presumably came downstairs again and joined the others?"

I convinced them, I'm sure of it. We join the police because we are honest, but it's a licence to lie through our teeth. You have to be careful, though. Evidence obtained by trickery is inadmissible, like almost anything else that works against the defendant. I don't care. Silkstone might get away with having been there when his wife died, and God-knows what else, but the newspapers would have a field day when they saw the pile of shit I'd bulldoze into court.

I galloped through the rest of his movements and was just at the point where he stabbed Latham when Dave returned. He handed me a manila envelope and I told the machine that he was back. When we'd finished we asked Silkstone to sign the diagrams and told him that he would be given photocopies, along with the tape.

"And finally," I said, "there's just a little matter of this." I pulled the warrant from its envelope and slid it across the table.

"What is it?" Predergast asked, as they both leaned forward.

"A warrant to search The Garth, Mountain Meadows, and make certain tests. A team of officers is there at this moment, waiting to start. You may go along to witness things, Mr Prendergast, but there is also a codicil to Mr Silkstone's bail conditions, saying that he must stay out of The Garth while these tests are being made. It expires at four p.m. today."

Silkstone looked as if the MD had just had him in to say that from now on the company's cars would be Reliant Robins, and Prendergast did a passable impression of an oxygen-starved koi carp.

"This is preposterous!" the brief eventually opined.

"It's legal," I stated, rising to my feet.

Dave said: "I'll tell them to get on with it."

"Yes, please," I affirmed, and he left the room again.

"What you are doing, Inspector," Prendergast spluttered, "is…is…highly irregular and…and…of doubtful validity. First of all, there is the question of security." He was getting himself back together. "It is normal procedure for a responsible representative of the defendant be present when a search is made. My client may have large sums of money, or other valuables, in the house. And then there's the question of the admissibility of any so-called evidence your men may purport to have discovered. The situation is outlandish and should not have been sprung upon us in such a precipitate manner. I feel obliged to take this up with your superiors, and am considering a formal complaint. The whole thing is completely out of order."

I turned to Silkstone. "Are there any large sums of money in the house?" I asked, and he shook his head before Prendergast had time to advise him otherwise. "My men, as you call them," I continued, "are accompanied by several civilian scenes of crime specialists and one of Her Majesty's scientists. I am confident that they will conduct themselves with their normal integrity and impartiality. As I have said before, their findings may corroborate your story and you will have full access to them. If you are concerned about your property you may go along and watch, but you will not be allowed in the house."

"So what am I supposed to do?" Silkstone demanded. "Stand in the garden in the rain?"

"I suggest you go about whatever you intended to do. Now, if you'll follow me to the front desk I'll sign a copy of the tape and photocopies of these diagrams over to you. Don't forget your umbrellas."

Prendergast complained all the way there and was still berating the custody sergeant as I danced up the stairs, three at a time, towards my little kingdom and a well-earned pot of Earl Grey. All we needed now was some evidence.

Jason Lee Gelder said that the food at the remand centre was really good. It was next door to Bentley prison, catering expressly for under-twenty-ones, and still came under Gwen Rhodes' authority. They had sausages and beans for breakfast and something different every day for dinner. He shared a room with another youth and they got on well together. The duty solicitor joined us, complaining about his beaker of tea, and I said: "Right, Jason. Let's talk about this girlfriend of yours. Have you remembered her name?"

"No," he replied.

"Have you tried to?"

"A bit, but I can't."

"I've checked the families of every police officer at Heckley," I told him, "and nobody has a daughter of that age who goes in the Aspidistra Lounge. Your girlfriend definitely wasn't a cop's daughter, so you have nothing to fear there. You are wrong about that, Jason, so who is she? Either you are lying to me or she was lying to you. Which is it?"

"Actually," he could have said, "it's you who are lying to me," but he wasn't to know that. Instead he coloured up and shrank into himself, like a child scolded by a grown-up.

I eventually broke the silence by saying: "Come on, Jason, start telling me about her. It can only help your case."

"Tell the inspector what you know," the solicitor urged.

"Let's start with a description," I suggested, rising to my feet. "How tall was she. You danced with her, so where did she come up to?" I took hold of his arm and helped him stand up. "Up to here?" I said. "Or here?"

"'Bout 'ere," he told me, holding his hand, palm down, level with his Adam's apple.

"About five feet four," I said. "Well done, that's a start. And what about her build? Was she slim, overweight, or in between?"

"She was a little bit fat."

"Good. What colour was her hair?"

Simple questions that he could answer, that would have saved me a sleepless night if I'd asked them earlier. Sometimes even the toppest cops get the basics wrong. After they'd had sex he took her home, which was somewhere in the Sylvan Fields estate. Not right to the door, because she was afraid that her dad would see her coming home in a car and cause some grief. And he was glad to oblige because dad was a cop, wasn't he?

We went through the whole sordid scene, and little flashes came back to him. She had a tattoo on her shoulder. He couldn't see it properly in the dark, but she said it was a spider. Her favourite group was Boyzone and her previous boyfriend drove a Mazda, but it was stolen and he lost it. She didn't go in pubs but went to the football, sometimes. Her mam and dad were always fighting and kept breaking up. She didn't think he'd stay much longer. They did it twice, and she helped him the second time. He only had one condom with him, but it was OK because she had one. Everything but a name. I could have asked him what I wanted to know, what I *really* wanted to know, but it would sound better coming from someone else.

"So you sat and talked for a few minutes before she got out?" I repeated for the third time.

"Yeah, a bit."

"What about?"

"Dunno. This and that. What I just told you, I s'pose."

"Did you arrange to meet again?"

"I told you, yeah."

"Tell me again."

"At the club, I think."

"You just left it loose. You had brilliant sex with this girl and then you said: 'OK, perhaps I'll see you again sometime.' I don't believe you Jason. I don't believe that you are getting it so often that you can afford to be choosy. I think you desperately wanted to see her again, as soon as possible, and you arranged to do so. Maybe you promised to phone her. Was that it? Did she give you her phone number?"

Jason slowly straightened in the chair, his brow furrowed and his lips pursed. He had the looks of a film star, but he'd have needed a stuntman to do his dialogue. "Yeah," he said, the light of remembrance lighting his countenance with all the illumination of a male glow-worm. (It's the females that glow, wouldn't you just know it.) "Yeah, that's what she did, she gave me her phone number."

"Great," I said. "That's great." Now all I had to do was prise it from him. Given the choice, I'd have preferred trying to take a banana from a rabid baboon. "So did she write it down for you, or did you try to remember it?"

"We didn't 'ave a pen," he told me.

"Well you wouldn't have, would you?" I replied with uncharacteristic understanding. With a combined IQ that was lower than the number of left legs at an amputees ball, it was unlikely that either of them would want to scribble down a sonnet, or even a haiku or two, after a moonlit shag in a Ford Fiesta. I waited for someone else to speak and wondered what to have for lunch.

"It wasn't then…" Jason began.

"Wasn't when?" I interrupted.

"Then. When I dropped her off. It was before that, at the brickyard, just after, you know…"

"Just after you'd had it?" My mind kept returning to the two of them bonking like a pair of ferrets in the front seat of his car. It was worrying.

"Yeah, then," he confirmed. "She told me 'er number and I asked 'er to write it down, on a parking ticket. Not a parking ticket, one from a machine, you know."

"A pay and display ticket," I said.

"Yeah, that's right. Pay an' display. But she didn't 'ave a pen."

"And you didn't, either."

"No. So she wrote it on the win'screen, with 'er finger. Up at the top. It was steamed up, y'know. Then she pulled the sun flap down, 'To protect it,' she said. I'd forgotten all about it."

"Alle-flippin'-luia," I sighed, burying my head in my hands.

Chapter Twelve

Jason's car was still in our garage at Halifax, emblazoned with stickers saying that it was evidence and not to be touched. Fingerprints had found the last three digits of the number on the windscreen when they gave it a good going-over, hoping to find evidence that Marie-Claire had been in there. The numbers were meaningless, so no action was taken on them. "It's a phone number for someone who lives in the Sylvan Fields," I told Les Isles, over a coffee in his office.

"So it probably starts with eight-three, followed by an unknown number," he stated.

"Which narrows it down to ten possibilities."

An hour later BT had furnished me with five names and addresses, and after fifteen minutes with the electoral roll I found myself drawing a big circle around 53, Bunyan Avenue; home of Edward and Vera Jackson, and their daughter Dionne.

I rang the number, but it was engaged. Les had left me to have a meeting with somebody, so I wrote him a note and headed for the exit. They have a visitors' signing in and out book at HQ and a young man in a Gore-Tex waterproof was bent over it. He looked at his watch and entered his leaving time in the appropriate column.

"Could Mr Isles help you, Mr Hollingbrook?" the desk sergeant asked him.

"Not really," he replied. "he was very kind, as always, but said that all he could do was have a word with the coroner. He has to make the decision."

He slid the book towards me and I put ditto marks under the time he'd written.

"I'm afraid that's always the case," the desk sergeant stated. "But the coroner's a reasonable man, and I'm sure he'll do what he can. I'd have liked to organise a lift back for you, but everybody's out at the moment."

The visitor was Marie-Claire's husband, I gathered, come in to ask about the release of his young wife's body for burial. He only looked about twenty. I caught the sergeant's eye and said: "I'll give Mr Hollingbrook a lift, Arthur. No problem."

"There you are, then," he said, and introduced me to the visitor. We shook hands without smiling and I opened the door for him.

His first name was Angus. He was twenty-four years old and a student of civil engineering at Huddersfield University, sponsored by one of the large groups that specialise in motorways and bridges. Marie-Claire had died on the Saturday or Sunday of the holiday weekend, while he was seconded to Sunderland to help in the replacement of an old stone bridge over a railway line by a modern pre-stressed concrete structure. He'd come home on Wednesday and found her body. I told him that I wasn't on the case, but I was interested because the assault was similar to the one on Margaret Silkstone at Heckley, back in June. I explained that we had somebody else for that murder, but there was a possibility that Marie-Claire's was a copycat killing. That was the official line, so I stayed with it. No point in stirring up the gravel with my own private paddle just yet. There'd be plenty of time for that: there's no statute of limitations on murder.

"Lousy weather," I said as the windscreen wipers slapped from side to side.

"Mmm," he replied, not caring about it, his thoughts with the beautiful girl he'd loved, wondering if he'd ever forget her or find her like again.

"It's next left, please," he said.

I slowed for the turn, then stopped to allow a bus out. It said *Heckley* on its destination board. The driver waved his thanks to me and when he was out of the way I turned into Angus's street.

"It's the last house on the left," he told me.

They were Victorian monoliths in freshly sand-blasted Yorkshire stone, with bay windows and stained-glass doors, built for the middle-management of the day but now converted into flats or lived-in by extended families. The street was lined both sides with parked cars, because, like the pocket calculator, nobody predicted the advent of the automobile.

"This is rather grand," I said, parking in the middle of the road.

"It is, isn't it. We just have the top floor. Marie loved it. Great big rooms and high ceilings. Lots of room for her hangings – she was in textile design – but a devil to heat. We…" He let it hang there, realising that there was no *we* anymore.

"Will you stay?" I asked.

He shook his head. "No, no way. Our lease runs out at Christmas but I don't think I could stay that long. We'd wondered about buying it, but it didn't come off. Fortunately, now, I suppose."

A car tried to turn into the street, but couldn't because I had it blocked. Angus opened the door and thanked me for the lift. "No problem," I replied, and drove round the corner, out of everybody's way.

John Bunyan would have loved the avenue they named after him on the Sylvan Fields estate, although the satellite dishes would have had him guessing. He'd have called it the Valley of Despondency, or some such, and had Giant Despair knocking seven bells out of Christian and Hope all along the length of it. I trickled along in second gear, weaving between the broken bricks, sleeping dogs and abandoned baby-buggies until I found number 53. At least the rain had stopped.

The front garden looked as if it had hosted a ploughing match lately, but the car that evidently parked there was not to be seen. I took the path to the side door and knocked. The woman who answered it almost instantly had an expectant look on her face and a Kookai carrier bag in her hand. She wore a tight leather jacket with leggings, and her halo of hair faded from platinum blonde through radioactive red to dish-water grey.

"Mrs Jackson?" I asked, holding my ID at arms length, more for the benefit of the neighbours and my reputation than the woman in front of me. I had a strong suspicion that male visitors were quite common at this house.

"Er, yes," she replied, adding, as she recovered from her initial disappointment: "'Ave you come about the fine?"

"No," I replied, "I haven't come about a fine. I believe you have a daughter called Dionne."

"Yes," she said. "What's she done?"

"Nothing," I told her, "but we believe she may have recently witnessed something that will help us with certain enquiries. When will it be possible for me to speak to her?"

"You say she 'asn't done nowt? She's just a witness?"

"That's right. She may be able to clear something up for us. When will she be in?"

Mrs Jackson turned, shouting: "Dionne! Somebody to see you," into the gloom of the house, and stepped out on to the path. "She'll be up in a minute," she told me. "I 'ave to go to work."

"Well," I began, "I would like to talk to your daughter on her own, but because of her age she is entitled to have a parent with her."

"But I don't 'ave to be, do I?"

"No, not really."

"Right, I'll leave you to it, then. Bye." She staggered off down the path, her litter-spike heels clicking and scraping on the concrete.

When daughter Dionne appeared she was wearing a tank top whose shoulder straps didn't quite line up with those of her bra and the ubiquitous black leggings. She was whey-faced, her hair hastily pulled together and held by a rubber band so it sprouted from the side of her head like a bunch of carrot tops. Hardly the sex bomb I'd expected. Her expression changed from expectancy to nervousness as I introduced myself.

"May I come in?" I asked, and she moved aside to let me through. I took a gulp of the chip-fat laden atmosphere and explained that she was entitled to have a parent present but as my questions were of a personal nature she might prefer to be alone. The carpet clung to my feet as I walked into the front room and looked for a safe place to sit. The gas fire was churning out more heat than an F14 Tomcat on afterburner and in the corner a grizzly bear was laying about a moose with a chainsaw, courtesy of the 24-hour cartoon channel. Dionne curled up on the settee as I gritted my teeth and settled for an easy chair. There was a plate on the table, with a kipper bone and skin laid across it.

"Kipper for breakfast," I said, brightly. "Smells good."

"No," she replied, her attention half on me, half on the moose who was now minus his antlers, "that was me mam's tea, last night."

I decided to axe the preliminaries. "Right. Your mother said she was off to work. Where's that?" I asked.

"Friday she cleans for someone," Dionne replied. The moose was fighting back, holding his severed antlers in his front feet.

"What else does she do?"

Dionne wrenched her attention from the screen and faced me. "I don't know what they get up to, do I?" she protested.

"I meant on other days," I explained. "Does she have a job for the rest of the week?"

"Yeah, 'course she 'as. She cleans for a few people. Well, that's what she calls it. Posh people. A doctor an' a s'licitor, an' some others."

I looked around the room, taking in the beer rings on every horizontal surface and the window that barely transmitted light, and tried to recall the proverb about the cobbler's children being the worst-shod in the village. "And what about your dad, Dionne?" I asked. "Where's he?"

"'E left us, 'bout two weeks ago."

"Oh, I am sorry."

"Don't be. 'E'll be back, soon as 'is new woman finds out what 'e's like." The moose had gained the initiative and the bear was in full flight.

"Can we have the telly off, please," I said, and she found the remote control somewhere in the sticky recesses of the settee and killed the picture.

"Thank you. Four weeks ago," I said, "On the Friday night of the holiday weekend, you were out with a boy. He says you can give him an alibi for that night. Can you?"

"Dunno," she replied. "What was 'e called?"

"I was hoping you would tell me. You met him at the Aspidistra Lounge, and he brought you home." She looked vacant, so I added: "You called at the brickyard on the way," not sure if that would narrow the field.

"Friday? Of the 'oliday weekend?"

"That's right."

"Does 'e look a bit like Ronan in Boyzone?" she asked. "Y'know, dead dishy?"

"He's a good looking lad," I admitted.

"Yeah, I remember 'im. 'E's called Jason. I can give 'im a nalibi for Friday night, if that's what you mean."

"Good, thank you. Did you arrange to see him again?"

"Yeah, but 'e 'asn't rung me."

"You gave him your phone number?"

"Yeah."

"Did you write it down for him?"

"No, well, yeah. We didn't 'ave a pen, so I writ it on the front window of 'is car, in the steam. Mebbe it got rubbed off."

"Perhaps it did. When you were talking to Jason did you mention your father at all?"

"No," she replied. "Why should I?"

"I thought you might have mentioned, for some reason, that your father was a policeman. Did you?"

Her podgy face turned the colour of my white socks after

I washed them with my goalie sweater, and one hand went to her mouth to have its nails nibbled.

"It's not a crime, Dionne," I assured her. "You're not in trouble for it, but I'd like to know what you told him."

"'E's a bit dense, isn't 'e," she stated.

"Jason? Yes," I agreed, "he does have a few problems in the brain department, like not being able to find one. Go on, please."

"Well, it were like this. We were just passing 'Eckley nick – the cop station – an I said: 'Me dad's in there.' Someone, a cop, 'ad rung me mam, earlier that night to say that 'e'd been done again for drunk and disorderly an' they were keeping 'im in t'cells until 'e sobered up. 'E was jumping up an' down in t'fountain, or summat, but I didn't tell 'im that."

"And what did Jason have to say?"

"'E got right excited, daft sod. 'What, your dad's a cop?' 'e said. 'Yeah,' I told 'im. ''E's a detective.' 'Blimey!' 'e said. That's all. I think it…you know."

"Know what?"

"Nowt."

She clammed up, and I knew she'd reached some indeterminate limit that I wouldn't push her past no matter how hard I tried. Everybody has one. I could only guess what she'd been about to say. That Jason became excited at the thought of shagging a detective's daughter? Probably.

"That's very useful, Dionne," I told her. "And then you went to the brickyard, I believe."

"Yeah."

"Right. Now this is where it gets a bit personal, I'm afraid. Not to put too fine a point on it, Dionne, and not wanting to pry into your private life, I have to ask you this: did the two of you make love that night, at the brickyard?"

"Yeah," she replied, as readily as she might admit to sneaking an extra chocolate biscuit. "We did it in the front of 'is car."

"Right," I said, nodding my approval at her answer, if not

her morals. "Good. And can I ask you if he wore a condom?"

"Yeah, I made sure of that."

"Good. I don't suppose you remember if you did it more than once, do you?"

"Yeah, we did it twice. 'E was dead eager." I swear she blushed again at the memory, or maybe the gas fire was reaching her.

"And he had two condoms with him, had he?"

"No just one, but I 'ad one. We used mine the second time."

"Very wise of you to carry one," I told her. "You can't be too careful, these days."

"You're telling me," she said, swinging her legs off the settee and facing me. "You won't catch me risking it. Did you know," she asked, "that when you 'ave sex with someone it's like 'aving contact with everyone that they'd ever 'ad sex with? Miss Coward told us that in social health education. Put the wind up me, it did. So if you 'ave sex with, say, ten people, its like you've really 'ad it with a 'undred."

"Gosh!" I exclaimed.

"An worse than that, if you did it with twenty, that's like doing it with four 'undred. Four 'undred! In one go! Can you believe that?"

"No," I admitted. "It's frightening. But I'll say this, Dionne: you're good at maths."

"Yeah, 'S'my best subject. Nobody cheats me."

"Good for you. So, when you'd finished, you know, doing it, what did Jason do with the condoms?"

"What did 'e do with them?"

"Mmm."

"Well, what d'you think?"

"You tell me."

"'E just dropped 'em out of the window, that's all."

And when you'd gone, I thought, somebody waiting in the shadows picked them off the dew-laden grass, and the following day he smeared their contents on the rapidly cooling thighs of Marie-Claire Hollingbrook.

"Thanks, Dionne," I said, rising to leave. "You've been a big help." I couldn't dislike her, or feel anything bad about her. Just sorrow for the world she'd grown up in. At the door I said: "These condoms you carry. Are you embarrassed when you buy them, like I am?"

"No," she replied. "I pinch them out of me mam's 'and-bag."

I smiled and flapped a wave at her, and walked back to the car, wondering how on earth I could have confused her with Sophie, my beloved Sophie. Cursing myself, hating myself, ashamed of myself. Les Isles wasn't surprised when I phoned him to say that he probably had the wrong man. He'd wondered about something like this, but Jason was still number one in the frame. "Let's just say that our enquiries are continuing," he admitted.

I could help you there, I thought, but I held my tongue. Instead, I drove all the way back to Halifax, to the street where Angus Hollingbrook expected to live happily-ever-after in a dream home, until his wife was murdered. He'd removed their name from the little space at the side of the bell, but there were only two of them and I assumed that the top one was for the upstairs flat. Sometimes you have to make these judgements.

I pressed the button several times, retreating to the gate after each burst and looking up at the windows. Eventually I saw a face and he gave me a wave of recognition. "Sorry to trouble you, Angus," I told him when he opened the door, "but a thought occurred to me. Can we have a word?" His eyes were rimmed with red and he was wearing a dressing gown over a T-shirt and jeans.

"I was having a snooze," he said. "Come in." Halfway up the stairs he turned to say: "It's a bit of a mess. They allowed me back in a week last Monday, but I haven't done anything. I'm still finding grey powder all over the place."

He opened a door and we moved into a big white-walled room that could have been the annex to a gallery. Half of the wall opposite the window was covered with a hanging that had me spellbound. It was a kaleidoscope of textures in all the colours of the moors, changing and drifting as cloud shadows passed over the earth's surface and the wind stirred the heather. "That's gorgeous," I whispered as I stood before it, smelling the wet peat, hearing the call of a curlew.

"That's all I have of her now," he said. "That and some photographs."

"Your wife was a very talented lady," I told him, relieved that we'd brought her into the conversation but hating myself for it.

"Would you like a coffee, Inspector?" he asked.

"No thanks, Angus. I'll just ask you a couple of questions, then get out of your way." He gestured for me to sit down and I sank into a chromium and leather chair that was surprisingly comfortable. How it would feel after an hour was another matter, because there was nowhere to hook your leg, loll your head or balance a glass. The room didn't have enough stuff in it to look untidy. Everything was clean-cut almost to the point of being clinical, but they'd started from scratch and stayed with a style. Only the wall hanging brought a touch of softness to the room, and I suspected the contrast was deliberate, to increase its impact.

"The grey stuff you keep finding is aluminium powder," I explained, glad to be on familiar territory. "The fingerprint people use it. The particles are flat, like tiny platelets, so they don't distort when it's lifted with sticky tape."

"I thought it must be theirs," he said, lowering himself onto a matching chair. "So, er, what is it you wanted to ask me?"

"When we were sitting in the car," I began, "you said that you and Marie were considering buying this place. I'd like to know how far you went along that route."

He looked puzzled, shrugged his shoulders, opened his

mouth to speak and closed it again. He was upset because another cop was bandying his wife's name – his dead wife's name – as if he'd known her for years. I'm afraid there's no way around that one. "It was Marie's idea," he said. "I wasn't keen because I'm not earning much, just expenses, and Marie's earnings were erratic, so we weren't a good risk for a mortgage."

"So who did you approach?" I asked.

"Well, we, er, tried all the building societies," he told me, "but they didn't want to know."

"Here in Halifax?" I asked. Home of the daddy of them all. Once they were a mutual society, existing for the benefit of members, whether they be investors or borrowers. Now they are part of the big conspiracy, doing it for shareholders and the Great God Profit.

"Yeah." He gave a little smile at the memory. "You know how it is," he went on, "these days they'll give you a loan to have the cat neutered, as long as they're sure they'll get their money back, or that you don't really need it. Everybody was very polite, but they were all sniggering behind their hands. We wanted a repayment mortgage, because of all the trouble we'd read about with endowment policies, but nobody would give us one. 'Open an account and come back in two years' was the best offer we had."

"So what did you do?"

"Nothing. Marie cut some adverts out of the papers and sent away for an application form, but when I explained to her that a secured loan meant that it was them that were secure, not us, she lost interest."

"Who was that with?"

"No idea. Some company I'd never heard of."

"Which papers do you take?"

"The *Telegraph*, usually, but I switch around a bit. Oh, and the *Gazette*."

"The Halifax edition of the *Gazette*, I presume."

"Yes, that's right."

"No tabloids?" I asked.

"No, not usually."

"And did she receive the application form?"

"Yes. I didn't want to send it back, but Marie said it couldn't hurt to find out what they offered."

"And would they give you a mortgage?"

He shook his head. "We didn't hear back from them, and then…"

And then all this happened. "Do you still have any covering letter that came with the application form, or the advert from the paper?" I asked.

"I imagine so."

"I'd be grateful if you could find them for me."

"Why, Inspector? What's it all about. You've caught the…the person who killed my wife, haven't you?"

"Yes," I replied. "A young man has been charged, as you know. Let's just say that I'm following a certain line of enquiry. These days it's not enough to prove who did the deed, we have to show that nobody else could have done it. We have to pre-empt any suggestions by the defence that another party, a mysterious unknown party, could be involved. You'd never believe the stories they'll concoct to sow a few seeds of doubt in the jurors' minds." And I'm not bad at concocting a few of my own, I thought.

He believed me and went to find the documents. I wondered if there was a room next door where they kept everything: piled up to the picture rail with cardboard boxes, over-flowing bin liners and bulging suitcases, but he was back in thirty seconds, carrying a thin file. "They should be in here," he said, pulling a sheaf of papers from it.

They weren't. I recognised a couple of bank books, an insurance policy and what looked like their tenancy agreement, but there was nothing relating to a mortgage application. "Sorry," he said. "Marie must have thrown it away. Like I said, I tried to discourage her."

As I walked back to the car I saw another Heckley bus

leaving the kerbside, the front of it swinging out only inches from the car parked adjacent to the stop. I caught up with
it on the climb out of town, and tucked in behind.

It did the grand tour, leaving the main road to call at
every village, dropping off pensioners who'd strayed past the
cheap fare deadline, picking up schoolchildren who had
stayed behind and office workers carrying briefcases and
shopping. When the bus stopped, I stopped. When it
crawled up hills, I dropped into first gear and followed it.
When it swooped down into the valley, swaying wildly and
leaving a cloud of dust and gutter debris billowing in its
wake, I hung back, waiting for the disaster that never came.

It took nearly an hour to reach the outskirts of Heckley,
where I abandoned the chase, turning off the ring road near
a fast bend where a tattered bunch of plastic flowers and a
teddy bear marked the spot where young Jamie What's-his-
name died, three months ago. Why would anyone want to
commemorate such a place? It's one of those little mysteries
that haunt my sleepless nights, like why do Volvo cars have
their lights on during daylight hours, but Volvo lorries
don't? I parked in a lay-by, near a fingerpost that said:
Footpath to Five Rise Locks. It was twenty-five minutes past
five, but good ol' Dave Sparkington was still at his desk
when I rang him. A little bit of me was wishing that Annette
would answer the phone, but it was Dave I needed right
then.

"It's past your home time, Sunshine," I said. "What are
you up to?"

"I'm doing police work. What are you up to is more like
it."

"You'd never believe me. Listen, I'm at Five Rise Locks
and could be in that pub called the Anglers in five minutes.
It's two for the price of one before six. Did I hear you say
that Shirley had gone to her mother's today?"

"I'll be about half an hour. See you there."

Evidently she had. "What about the kids?" I asked.

"Never mind them, I'm on my way."

"OK, but don't be late, I'm famished."

"I'm coming."

I strode up the hill to the canal side, where five locks in rapid succession lift the waterway a hundred feet, and crossed over by the footbridge. A narrow-boat was waiting for a companion, before moving up to the next level and sending ten million gallons of water in the opposite direction. The people on the boat wished me a good afternoon and the smell of their cooking made me feel even hungrier. I hadn't eaten since breakfast. Turn left to the Anglers, a hundred yards away, right towards Mountain Meadows, home of Tony Silkstone, less than half a mile up the towpath. I looked at my watch and headed right.

There were two pot-bellied ponies in the paddock between his house and the canal, and one of his neighbours was using a strimmer or a chainsaw, or some other implement with an engine that made more noise than horsepower. Further along, four cormorants were perched in a dead tree, one of them spreading his wings to catch a brief burst of afternoon sun, the others hunched like judges. The fishermen are always writing to the *Gazette* to complain about the cormorants eating all the fish. The birds have been driven inland because there is nothing left for them in the coastal waters, their natural habitat, and the anglers are too dumb to realise that if there were no fish in the canal the cormorants would leave. The birds are just better at catching them than they are. I think they're cormorants, but they might be shags. I checked the time again and started back towards the pub. Halfway there I saw Silkstone's car coming up the lane at the other side of the field. Maybe he'd join us, I thought.

Dave pulled into the car-park at the same time as I arrived, and uncurled his bulky frame from the car. "What's the difference between a cormorant and a shag?" I asked him as we walked in together.

"A cormorant and a shag?"

"Yep."

"Um, is it that you don't feel like a cigarette after a cormorant?"

It was gloomy inside, but warm and friendly, even though it was a large place, recently given a makeover, and we were the only customers. A young woman in uniform blouse and skirt greeted us as if we were an endangered species and asked what we'd like. *Here to serve you* said the badge on her blouse and a blackboard behind the bar told us that the guest beer was Sam Smith's.

"Pint of Sam's?" I suggested, and Dave nodded his agreement. "Make that two, please," I said, and she started pulling the pints, lifting them on to the bar after a few moments while the froth subsided.

"Will there be anything else, sir?" she asked.

I studied the chalked-up menu. "Yes, please. We'd like to order some food. Is it still two for one?"

The young woman looked at the clock. "Yes sir. Which table are you at?"

As we'd just walked in and were standing at the bar, I wasn't sure of the answer to that one. Dave came to the rescue. "Over by the window," he said, pointing, and the girl said it was table number twelve.

"Twelve," I repeated. "Remember that, Dave. Number twelve."

"Twelve," he said. "Right. Twelve."

"What would you like, Sir," she asked, still smiling.

"Er, I think the gammon and pineapple," I said, "with a jacket potato, and, um, the half a chicken, again with a jacket potato."

She tapped the order into the till. They don't have numbers on the keys, these days. Instead it says: *chicken and chips, egg and chips, ham and chips, ham eggs and chips,* and so on.

"Is that everything?" she asked, her finger poised over the

give them the bill key.

"No," Sparky interjected. "I'd like some food, too. I'll have the steak and kidney pie and…oh, half a chicken, both with chips."

It's hungry work, being a cop, and we're growing lads.

Saturday morning we told Silkstone that we'd be interviewing him again on Monday, so come prepared. I had long conversations with Mr Wood and Les Isles and they both agreed with what I was doing. Les wanted to be present, but we haven't worked together since we were constables and I gave it the thumbs down. Besides, I wanted Dave with me. Dave and I go together like rhubarb crumble and custard, or mince pies and Wensleydale cheese. Mmm! There's none of this nice and nasty routine with us; we're both our normal, charming selves, most of the time. In the file I found an advert for Silkstone's company, Trans Global Finance, clipped from the *Gazette*. It said: *Can't get a mortgage? Low earnings? County court judgements? No problem! Secured loans available on all types of property. Send for an application form. Now!* More or less what I'd expected.

Sunday I went through it all, over and over again. Sometimes in my mind, sometimes scrawling on an A4 pad. I don't have hunches; I don't follow lines of enquiry. Not to start with. I gather information, everything I can, without judgement, as if I were picking up the shattered pieces of an ancient amphora, scattered on the floor of a tomb. Some bits might link together, others might be from a completely different puzzle. When I've gathered them all in I join up the obvious ones, like the rim and the handles, and then try to fill in the gaps until I have something that might hold water. Ideally, when I have a possible scenario in mind, it would be possible to put it to the test, devise an experiment, like a scientist would. But liars and murderers are not as constant as the laws of physics, and it's not always possible. Instead, we turn up the heat and hope that something cracks.

"Did you know, Mr Silkstone," I said as Dave and I breezed into interview room number one, ten o'clock Monday morning, "that you have very good water pressure at Mountain Meadows?"

Prendergast looked up from the pad where he was adding to his already copious notes, shook his head and continued writing. Silkstone, sitting next to him, looked bewildered and reached for his cigarettes.

Dave removed the cellophane from two cassettes and placed them in the machine, watching them until the leader tape had passed through and nodding to me to say we were in business. I sat diagonally across from Silkstone and did the introductions, reminding him of his rights and informing him that he was still under caution. When prompted, Prendergast said that they understood.

"Let's talk about Margaret, your late wife," I began. "Word has it that you quarrelled a lot. Is that so?"

Silkstone drew on his cigarette and sent a cloud of smoke curling across the table. "No," he replied. "We had an occasional argument – what married couple doesn't? – but that was all."

"What, no vicious slanging matches? No slinging your clothes out of the bedroom window?"

"Inspector," Prendergast interrupted. "This sounds like hearsay to me."

"Of course it's hearsay," I agreed. "We talked to the neighbours: they heard it and they said it. It's a simple enough question, let Mr Silkstone answer."

Silkstone sucked his cheeks in and licked his lips. "That was nearly two years ago," he replied. "It only happened once, like that."

"What was it about?"

"Money."

"You were having problems?"

"No, not really. We just had to be a bit more careful than Margaret was used to."

"But it's true to say that you stand to prosper by Margaret's death, is it not?"

Prendergast shook his head vigorously and banged his hands on the table. "That's a preposterous thing to say, Inspector," he exclaimed. "My client did not profit in any way from his wife's untimely death."

Addressing Silkstone, I said: "But your mortgage will be paid off to the tune of a hundred and fifty thousand pounds, won't it?"

"Yes," he hissed, "but that's perfectly normal practice."

"Indeed it is," his solicitor affirmed. "My own mortgage is covered by a joint life, first death policy, as is anyone else's if they have any sense. You can't call that evidence."

"No," I agreed, "but we can call it motive."

"In that case, we all have motives to murder our spouses, and they us." He sat back in triumph.

"Would you say, Mr Silkstone," I asked, "that you and Margaret had a normal sexual relationship?"

He looked straight at me, then said: "I don't know, Inspector. How would you define a normal sexual relationship?"

"OK, let me put it another way. Were you and Peter Latham having joint sessions with your wife, three in a bed, that sort of stuff?"

"No."

"You married sisters, didn't you? And you shared girlfriends, in the past. Latham had known your wife as long as you had. Was he the one who used to pull the birds, and you always ended up with the friend? Were you sharing her – Margaret – with him?"

"No," he said, and crushed his cigarette stub into the ashtray.

Prendergast leaned forward, saying: "This sounds like pure conjecture on your part, Inspector. Have you any evidence to corroborate these suggestions?"

"Evidence?" I replied, shaking my head. "No. Not a shred." I pulled the report that the lab scientist had done for me from its envelope, pretended to read the introduction, then pushed it back inside.

"No," I repeated. "We don't think you were having a three-in-a-bed sex romp that went wrong. It was a theory, but we have no evidence to support it." I glanced sideways at the big NEAL recorder on the wall, seeing the tapes inside relentlessly revolving, making a copy of the words that passed between us. I'm a student of human behaviour, body language. When people lie they resort to using certain gestures: hands fidget and often cover the face; legs are restless; brief expressions are quickly suppressed. But Silkstone was chain smoking, and that has a language all of its own, disguising his real expressions. I was relying on the tape to unmask him.

"We have another theory now," I began. "And this time we do have some evidence. This one says that Peter Latham wasn't present when Margaret died. He'd left, shortly before. This one says that you, Anthony Silkstone, killed her all by yourself." They were both silent, stunned by the new accusation, wondering what the evidence could be. Sadly, it wasn't much. Prendergast shifted in his chair, about to come out with some double-speak, but I beat him to it. "Let's go back a week," I continued, "To when you came home and found Latham and Margaret together. You are on record as saying that you went straight upstairs to the bathroom. Is that correct?"

"That's what I told you," he replied.

"The family bathroom?"

"Yes."

"And what did you do there?"

"I had a piss, washed my hands and went back downstairs."

"Really? Are you sure you didn't see something floating

in the water in the toilet, Mr Silkstone?"

He reached for his cigarettes and made a performance of lighting one. It wasn't a smooth performance, because the flame from his lighter was flickering about, magnifying the shaking of his hand. *My* hand would shake if I were being grilled for a murder. "I don't know what you're talking about," he replied.

"Are you sure you didn't see a used condom in there, Mr Silkstone? The one that Peter Latham had discarded and tried to flush away after having sex with your wife, earlier that afternoon?"

"Inspector," his brief said, interrupting. "You mentioned evidence. Will you be offering any, or is this another fanciful tale without any substance?"

I pulled the report from its envelope again. "I talked to someone," I said. "A life-long philanderer, and he told me that when you deposit a French letter down the bog you have to be very careful to ensure that it goes right round the bend. He went into great detail on how to do it." I smiled and said: "We meet some terrible people in this job." I didn't mention that I was talking about a fellow DI. "So," I continued, "we did some tests. Last Thursday, while you were here, we dropped a condom down the toilet in your upstairs family bathroom and flushed it. Then we repeated the experiment a hundred times. To simulate used condoms we squirted a couple of shots of liquid soap into each one." I slid the report across the desk. "That's your copy. As you will see, it takes one minute and forty-three seconds for the cistern to fill again. That's very good. Each of the condoms went out of site, round the bend, but then, lo and behold, a few seconds later thirteen of them popped back into view. Just like the one that Latham had used did."

Prendergast looked across the table as if he'd just witnessed me kick an old lady. A very old lady. "Is *this* what you call evidence?" he asked, waving the report. "*This!*"

"It'll do for the time being," I replied.

"May we go now?" He rose to his feet. "Or have you some other fairytale to amuse us with?"

Silkstone blew another cloud of smoke across the table. I held his gaze and refused to blink, although my eyes were watering. "Sit down," I said. "I haven't finished." Prendergast scraped his chair on the floor and sat down again.

"What did you do with it?" I asked Silkstone.

"Do…with…what…Inspector?" he asked, enunciating the words, chewing on them and enjoying the taste. He was growing cocky.

"The condom."

"There was no condom."

"I think you took it downstairs. After drying it off, of course. You wrapped it up in, say, cooking foil, and placed it in the fridge. At the back, behind the half-eaten jar of pesto and the black olives." There was a flicker of recognition across his face as I recited the contents. I do my research. "At that stage all it meant to you was proof of your wife's unfaithfulness. Maybe you were pleased to have the evidence or maybe you were devastated by it. Which was it? Pleased or devastated?"

"It didn't happen."

"But as the days passed," I continued, "you thought of a better way to use it, didn't you? And a week later, after Latham had gone home, you murdered your wife, did things to her that she wouldn't let you do when she was alive – maybe you *couldn't* do them while she was alive – and then went round and stabbed Latham to death. After, of course, leaving the contents of the condom on Margaret's body. That's what happened, isn't it?"

Now he looked nervous, scared, drawing on the cigarette before deciding it was too short and fumbling in the ashtray with it. Prendergast said: "Your theories become more fanciful by the minute, Inspector. Now, if you have nothing to offer that bears the imprimatur of the truth, I suggest we bring this farce to an end."

I gave Dave the slightest of nods and he leaned forward, elbows on the table, thrusting his face towards Silkstone. "Tell us about Marie-Claire Hollingbrook," he said.

"Never heard of her," Silkstone replied, switching his attention to his new adversary.

"She was murdered in circumstances remarkably similar to Margaret's death. A month ago, on the Saturday before you did your sales conference."

"I've read about it, that's all."

"Bit of a coincidence, though, don't you think. Latham couldn't have done this one; he was dead."

"Sergeant," Prendergast interjected. "The modus operandi of Mrs Latham's murderer was in all the newspapers. As you know, certain sick individuals often emulate murders they have read about."

"It's constable," Dave said.

"I'm sorry. Constable."

"That's all right. And as you know, Mr Prenderville, sex offenders rarely stop after the first time. They get a taste for it, go on and on until they are caught." He turned towards Silkstone. "Is that what you did? Get a taste for it? It was good was it, that way? You strangle them, I'm told, until they lose consciousness, then let them revive and do it all over again. And again and again. Is that what you did to Margaret, and then to Marie-Claire Hollingbrook?"

Silkstone looked at his brief, saying: "Do we have to listen to this?"

Prendergast said: "Let them get it off their chests. It's all they can look forward to." He wanted to know how much, or little, we knew. And maybe, just maybe, he had a wife and daughters of his own, and was beginning to wonder a little about his client. Not that it would interfere with the way he handled the case. No chance.

"You'd done the perfect murder," Dave told Silkstone. "Got clean away with it. OK, you might have to do a year in the slammer for killing Latham, but the nation's sympathy was with you and it was a small price to pay for having all your problems solved." He paused to let the situation gel in their minds, then continued: "But the urge wouldn't go away, would, it? And when the application form from Marie-Claire plopped on your desk, it became too much to bear. What did it say? Name of applicant: Marie-Claire Hollingbrook. A lovely name, don't you think. Makes you wonder if she's as attractive as it sounds. Age: twenty-one; occupation: self-employed textile designer. Young and clever. It's more fun humiliating the clever ones, isn't it? Daytime telephone number and evening telephone number identical, so she must work from home. And then the same questions about her partner. Age: twenty-four; a student; and, would you believe it, not available during the day. You'd committed the perfect crime once, what was to stop you doing it again? Did you ring her at first, to see when her husband would be there? Or, hopefully, not there?"

"BT are checking all the phone calls," I interjected.

"Or did you just visit her on spec? Which was it?"

"You're mad," Silkstone replied.

"She invited you in and you asked to see the letter you'd sent her, and the advert from the *Gazette*. You carefully folded them, placed them in your pocket, and then the fun started. Except it wasn't much fun for that girl, because you were better at it by then, weren't you? And when you'd finished, you left your trademark: the semen you'd collected the night before, from the brickyard." Dave sat back and wiped his mouth with the back of his hand.

I said: "On the day of the murder none of your neighbours saw you leave home in the car, but you were seen out walking. There's a bus route from the other side of the canal to near where Marie lived. We're tracing everybody who used the route that day. Also, we've appealed for anyone who was at the locks to come forward. Prints of your tyres have been taken and will be compared with those we found at the brickyard. If you've ever visited there you'd be wise to admit it, now."

They sat there in silence, Silkstone with one arm extended, his fingers on the table; Prendergast upright, hands in his lap, waiting. The smoke from his client's cigarettes was layering against the ceiling, drawn there by the feeble extractor fan, and shafts of light from the little armoured glass window shone through it like searchlight beams.

"Is there anything you wish to say?" I asked him.

"Yes, you're a fucking lunatic," he snapped.

"Inspector," Prendergast began, placing a hand on his clients arm to silence him. "These are very serious allegations you are making. My client admitted killing Mr Latham, as we all know, but now he is being accused of these other crimes. First of all the death of his wife, the woman he loved, and now a completely unrelated murder. Either you must arrest my client and substantiate the charges against him, or we are leaving."

"No," I said wearily. "We won't be arresting him." I turned to the man in question. "Do you remember Vince Halliwell?" I asked.

"Who?" he replied.

"Vince Halliwell. He was in Bentley Prison same time as you, doing ten years for armed robbery. Says you had a chat on a couple of occasions."

"I never heard of him."

"What about Paul Mann?"

"Never heard of him, either."

"He's what we call a nutter. Poured paraffin over his girlfriend and hurled their baby out of a seventh story window. Said it was an accident and is appealing against sentence. He got a double life, with twenty- and thirty-year tariffs. Claims he dropped the baby, but unfortunately for him her body was found forty feet from the foot of the building. Kevin Chilcott, known as the Chiller, you ever hear of him?"

"No."

"Never?"

"Never."

"That's strange. Someone paid him fifty thousand pounds to kill me, and we thought it was you. Paul Mann arranged it, or is supposed to have done. Nasty people in prison. Wouldn't think twice about cheating a fellow inmate, especially one who thought he was a bit cleverer than them. Still, if it wasn't you there's nothing lost, is there? Fifty grand! Phew! I thought I was worth more than that."

That's the bit we should have had on video. Silkstone's eyes narrowed and his face paled as all the blood drained from it. He crushed the empty cigarette packet in his hand and for a second I thought he was going to come over the table at me. Accuse him of rape, murder, buggery and he can handle it. Suggest that a bunch of no-hopers have cheated him out of his nest-egg and you really hit a nerve.

"Interview terminated at...eleven-oh-two," I said, and pushed my chair back.

Dave and I trudged up the stairs in silence. He went to fill the kettle and I sat at my desk. There was a note saying that the SOCOs had failed to find anything useful at either of the houses. I closed my eyes and leaned back, massaging my neck to ease the tension in it. The door opened and I thought it was Dave, but it was Annette's voice that said: "Shall I do that for you?"

I grinned at her. "I'd love you to, but it might look bad. People would get the wrong idea."

"That's their problem."

I shook my head. "No, it's my problem. You leave this?"

"Yes. Came through ten minutes ago. Sorry."

"Damn."

"What did Silkstone have to say?"

"Nothing. We told him everything we knew, he told us nowt."

"Everything?"

"Nearly everything. We didn't mention Caroline Poole."
I pointed at her note, saying: "I was hoping this might give us some ammunition."

Dave came in with two coffees and placed one in front of me. "'Spect you've been drinking all morning," he told Annette, by way of apologising for not making her one.

"Most of it," she agreed.

"So what do you think?" I asked him.

"About Silkstone?"

"No! About Annette drinking coffee all morning."

He had a long sip, then said: "He did it all, as sure as shit smells. There's no loose ends, no coincidences, no far-fetched theories. It all ties in, perfectly. You might not convince a jury, Chas, or even Annette and she hangs on your every word, but you've convinced me."

Annette's cheeks turned the colour of a Montana sunset. I said: "Well, that's a start. It gives us something to build on." I felt like the Leader of the Opposition, after being wiped-out by a landslide.

They fought back and they fought dirty. We had the tape transcribed and sent a copy to Superintendent Isles. As I left the office that evening I was confronted on the steps by a reporter and a photographer. I referred them to our press office and fled. Tuesday, Dave and I had a meeting with Les Isles and Nigel at their place, and they made sympathetic noises but agreed that we weren't any further forward. Les's big problem was what to do with Jason Lee Gelder. He eventually decided to keep him inside for the time being, which I interpreted as a vote of no confidence. The HQ team was reconvened, however, and diverted to investigations that might place Silkstone near the lock or on a bus, that Saturday afternoon. As long as someone was in jail, the press would keep off our backs. That was the theory. As theories go it ranked alongside the one about the world being carried on the back of a giant tortoise.

Wednesday I decided to go in early and start the day with breakfast in the canteen. I wasn't sleeping well, too much on my mind, and it's a good atmosphere in there, early in the morning. The place is warm and steamy, loud with banter and fragrant with the smells of crispy bacon, sausages and toast. It's a good way of meeting the troops – the PCs who do all the real policing – and I always leave with high blood-sugar levels and a smile on my face, armed with a couple of new jokes to tell the boys. Except it didn't work out that way.

I was still at home, having a mug of tea and listening to Classic FM when the phone rang. It was Sparky. Sparky ringing me at six thirty means only one thing: he can't sleep, either. "Tell me all about it," I sighed.

"You seen *TV AM* this morning, Charlie?" he asked.

"No." Sad though my life was, I still had a bit left before I was that low.

"Just before the news headlines they do a round-up of all the papers," he explained. "I usually watch it, just to catch up."

"And…" I prompted.

"Well, this morning, you're all over the front page of the *UK News*."

"Eh? Me? Why, what does it say?"

"I'll see you in the office, and bring one in with me."

"I could collect one at…"

"No," he interrupted. "You'd better go straight in. Believe me, it's not nice."

Chapter Thirteen

There was a sprinkling of early birds in the office when I arrived. They raised their heads from their newspapers and followed me to my little enclave, where Dave was waiting. He closed the copy of *UK News* that he was perusing and spun it round for me to read.

One photograph took up most of the page. It was of Tony Silkstone, head bowed, tears glistening on his cheeks. But it was the caption that caught my attention. In the biggest typeface that the page could accommodate it said:

HOUNDED
BY KILLER COP

Inside was a photograph of me, taken when I left the office, Monday evening, with *World Exclusive* emblazoned across my forehead. A panel in large print informed the nation that I once shot dead an unarmed man, and now I was persecuting Tony Silkstone, the hero who did what the police had failed to do by ridding society of scumbag sex murderer Peter Latham, also pictured. On the next page but one, after a full-page special of a naked seventeen-year-old girl nibbling at a Cadbury's Flake, the editorial called me a renegade and a vigilante. *Is this the kind of police force we want?* it asked.

"The bastards," I heard a voice behind me say.

"Yeah," I agreed. "The bastards." I turned back to the photo of me and carefully folded the paper. "Look," I said, holding it towards the speaker. "They didn't even get my best side."

Willy O'Hagan was no-hoper mixed up in a drugs ring that we investigated. We raided a doss house one morning and he fired at me with a shotgun. Foolishly, I was alone at the time, and armed only with a little Walther two-two. There's a maxim among security forces that says minimum violence requires a maximum show of force. I got it wrong. I thought I knew best, but I got it wrong and I've reminded myself of that mistake almost every night since. O'Hagan swung his gun my way and blew a great chunk out of the chipboard wardrobe I was trying to hide behind, inches from my face. I loosed off three quick shots at him and he died a few minutes later. Then we noticed that his shotgun only had one barrel, and it wasn't a repeater. I'd killed an unarmed man.

The inquest was a whitewash, but I went along with it. He'd fired first, at an un-named police officer and that officer had returned fire. Lawful killing, justifiable homicide, call it what you will. I thought I'd heard the last of it, apart from the voices in the night, but Prendergast had done his homework. Like I said, they were fighting dirty.

Notoriety has its compensations. I laid low for the rest of the day, drinking coffee, catching up on paperwork and talking to our press office. They issued a statement, putting my case forward, and released a photograph that was used at the inquest, showing a uniformed PC standing where I'd been standing in O'Hagan's bedroom, with the corner blown off the cheap wardrobe. I blinked when I saw it, feeling the sting of debris hitting my face and eyes, seeing O'Hagan's form swimming before me, then falling to the floor.

I had a night in and watched the England game on TV, a couple of cans of Newcastle Brown at my elbow, like any good detective would do. The beer went down better than the football. With no goals scored and ten minutes to go our golden boy striker booted their dirty sweeper right in the penalty area and was sent off. One-nil to them, and that's how it ended. I bought a *UK News* on my way in next morning, but it was all football and ladies' chests; nothing at all about the Killer Cop. We were yesterday's news.

There was a big pink envelope on my desk, and the office was full. Was I missing something? I opened it and pulled out the card it held. It said: *Congratulations on your 100th birthday*. Inside, someone had written in a decent italic script: *To Charlie, just to let you know that we're all with you,* and everybody in the station had signed it. I walked out into the big office and flapped it at them. "Thanks," I said. "I appreciate it."

"Did you organise this?" I asked Annette, after the briefing and morning prayers, when she brought me a coffee. The big card was propped on my windowsill.

"Not guilty, Sir," she replied.

"Well it was good of someone to go to the trouble. Tell whoever it was I said so, will you?"

"Will do."

"Fetch your coffee and join me, please," I said. "I need some company."

She came back and sat in my visitor's chair, crossing her legs at the ankle, like any well-brought-up girl should. She was wearing a pinstripe suit with a knee-length skirt and a white blouse but no jewellery. "Don't suppose you watched the football last night?" I asked.

"No," she laughed. "Did you?"

"It was pathetic." After an awkward silence I added: "But at least it kept us out of the papers."

"Charlie…" Annette began. I looked at her, inviting her to continue. "Are you all right? We all know the truth about what happened, but it doesn't seem fair that…you know, that only one side of it gets published."

"Yeah," I agreed. "I half hoped that there'd be a more balanced report this morning, but I should have known better. Never trust the press, Annette. Never."

"What you need," she told me, "is a really hot curry, with a few lagers to cool it down. It's Thursday – my treat, my car. OK?"

I shook my head. "I'm sorry," I replied, "but I've something on tonight."

"Oh," she said. "Well, never mind. Some other time, perhaps."

"Yeah," I said. "Some other time."

We finished our coffees and she picked up the mugs. As she left I said: "The Deputy Chief Constable's coming to see me at eleven, so spread the word. Either be busy or be gone."

I was waiting in Gilbert's office when the DCC arrived, a great bundle of newspapers under his arm. "This is a pretty pass, Charlie," he said, unrolling them on to Gilbert's desk. At least I was still Charlie.

"Anything in them?" Gilbert asked.

"Not a bloody sausage from our point of view. All flaming football in the tabloids and a couple of the broadsheets have picked up on the *UK News*'s original story. The *Mirror* and the *Sun* will pretend it never happened, because they didn't get there first, and the others might eventually print something if there isn't a more important scandal on offer, like a pregnant soap star."

I grinned, saying: "You have a highly jaundiced view of our free and fearless press, Mr Pritchard."

"From years of experience dealing with 'em, Charlie. Now, what are we going to do?"

Don't you just love it when they ask you before telling you? He was retiring in a few weeks, so could afford to be generous and one of the boys. He'd come to the odd reunion or retirement party, but his authority would have gone and any influence he may have held would soon evaporate. What he'd like, all that he could hope for, was that people like me would talk about him with respect. "He wasn't a bad old stick;" "You always knew where you stood with him;" "He was firm but fair;" or perhaps even: "We could do with him back."

He didn't take me off the case, he just destroyed the case. I'd done a good job, he said, had seen possibilities that were not immediately evident to other officers and pursued them with my usual diligence. The story, as I had related it, certainly had credibility. But the time had come to draw back, reconsider our position. Without forensics to link Silkstone with the death of his wife and Marie-Claire, we were leaving ourselves open to criticism. Silkstone had killed Latham, a known sex offender, and a vociferous amount of public opinion was behind him. We needed to channel that opinion so that it was with us, the police service, and not provoke it.

"We can only do our job with the consent of the people, Charlie," he said. "Never forget that." I think he read it on a fortune cookie.

"So what do you want to do? Close the case?" I asked.

"*Close* is rather an extreme way of putting it," he replied. "Why not allow things to settle down somewhat and see what transpires, eh?"

"Put it on the back burner?" Gilbert suggested.

"Yes, put it on the back burner. And then, if anything else turns up, you can always re-open the investigation. But keep a low profile, the next time. I always find that the softly-softly approach has a lot going for it."

"How long would you suggest before we looked at it again?" I asked.

"Oh, a couple of years?" he replied.

"And what about Jason Gelder?"

His smile turned sour for a moment, then returned in all its supercilious smarm. "I think we should leave that for Mr Isles to sort out, don't you?"

I clumped down the stairs one at a time, dragging my hand on the polished banister, banging each foot on to the next step. I was hoping a friendly face would come the other way so I could shout at them, yelling: "What's it got to do with you how I am?" but none came. I thrust my hands deep in my pockets and skulked back to the office.

Jeff Caton was the only person there, his head deep in that morning's *Gazette*. "That all you've got to do?" I asked.

"Hi, Chas," he said, looking up. "Nothing in it, I'm afraid. Nothing about us, that is. The release will have gone out too late for this edition."

"But?"

"But there's something in the free ads that might be worth looking at. Bloke selling a box of fifty King Edward cigars for fifty quid. Says they're an unwanted gift."

"Maybe he's stopped smoking."

"Maybe, but it's the seventh week the advert's been in."

"Really? What are they worth?"

"About twice that."

"I'm convinced. Let's go round in the morning and kick his door down. On second thoughts, let's go round now, just the two of us. I feel like some aggro."

Jeff laughed. "I'll call round later, posing as a buyer. What's brought this on?"

"Oh, Pritchard," I told him. "Wants me to drop chasing Silkstone. He hasn't taken me off the case, but I've to leave him alone. It's back to keeping the fair streets of Heckley safe enough for decent people to go about their business. Who cares if one of them just happens to be a psychopath?"

"Maybe he's a fellow lodge member."

"No, it's just bad public relations. I'm the ugly face of the police force."

I went into my office and gathered up all the papers on my desk, piling them in the in-tray. I slumped in my chair and put my feet on the desk, pushing the chair back until the angle was just right. You can make yourself surprisingly comfortable like that. I checked the position of the big hand on the clock and closed my eyes. With a bit of luck the phone wouldn't ring for ten or eleven minutes.

Three minutes, but it was Annette, so I didn't mind. "Boss, I'm at the front desk," she said, sounding breathless.

"Well, you see those stairs on your left? Go up the first flight and your…"

"I'm interviewing a girl in number two," she interrupted. "Says she was followed by a stalker. I think you should come down and hear what she says."

"I'm a bit busy," I lied. "Can't you deal with it?"

"I can deal with it, no problem," she replied, "but I think you'd like to hear it for yourself. Believe me, Boss, you would."

"OK, I'm on my way." I swung my feet down on to the plain but functional carpet and reached for my jacket.

She was a big girl, with a bright, open face. Her hair was swept straight back into a ponytail and her complexion wasn't too good, but she had a nice smile and that makes up for a lot. Her school skirt was short, stretched tight around her crossed thighs, and she wore a blue V-necked pullover with a school badge on it. Apart from all that, she was sitting in my chair. I smiled at her and moved round the table to where the prisoner usually sits.

"This is Debbie Collins," Annette said, "and this is Inspector Priest. He's in charge of the case."

"I know," Debbie replied. "I saw your picture in the paper."

"That's me," I told her. "Now what can I do for you?"

Annette answered for her: "I've recorded an interview with Debbie, but she said she doesn't mind going through it again."

"OK. Let's hear it, then, Debbie, in your own words, at your own speed."

She leaned forward, placing one hand on the table. "It was one morning last June," she began. "I was going to school."

"Which one?" I interjected.

"Heckley Sixth Form College. This man waved to me, from a car. I waved back, sort of instinctively, if you follow me. But when I thought about it I hadn't a clue who he was."

"I know what you mean," I said. "Somebody waves and you wave back. It happens to all of us."

"Yeah, well, a few mornings later I saw him again. I was waiting to cross the road and he drove by. This time he smiled and gave a little wave, like that." She raised a hand, as if off a steering wheel. "I didn't smile back, I don't think. Next time I saw him was in the afternoon, as I walked home, and he smiled again."

"Did you take his number?" I asked.

"No, sorry. I didn't think too much about it. Then, a couple of weeks later, after we'd had our French exam, he stopped his car. I was smoking a cig. I don't normally, it's a stupid habit, but we were in the middle of exams and I was nervous. I took one of my dad's to school with me, to have afterwards, and I was smoking it on the way home and he asked me for a light."

"He stopped the car and asked you for a light?"

"No, not quite. I saw him drive past and he pulled into the shopping precinct and dashed into the newsagents. He came out with a new packet of Benson and Hedges, and that's when he asked me. He sort of pretended he wasn't in a car and walked out on to the path, in front of me. Said he'd lost his matches and could he have a light."

"Were you frightened?" I asked.

"No," she replied. "I was bigger than him. I'd've socked him if he'd tried anything." Her face lit up in a smile, and she looked lovely.

"Did he say anything else?"

"Well, just something, you know, suggestive."

"He propositioned you?"

"Not quite. He held the cigs out and said: 'Can I give you one?' but it was obvious he didn't mean the fags." She smiled again and this time Annette and I joined her. She'd done the right thing, coming to us, but fortunately her experience, if this was all there was, hadn't troubled her.

"And what happened next," I asked.

"Nothing. I said no and he went off. After that I started walking home with some other girls. I saw him once, the following week, but I ignored him."

"Would you recognise him again?" From the corner of my eye I saw Annette smile.

"Oh, yeah," Debbie replied, sitting up. "I'd recognise him all right. It was him in the paper, with you, yesterday. Him who did that murder."

"Oh," I said, caught off guard. I hadn't expected this. I sat up straight and placed both hands on the table. It shows that I'm being honest and concerned. "That must have been quite a shock for you."

"It was."

"Well, I'm pleased that your ordeal doesn't appear to have frightened you too much, Debbie, although it must have been pretty scary at the time. You handled the situation very well, but if it does start to bother you at all, have a word with us. Come and see Annette or myself, anytime. Meanwhile, as you know, he can't hurt you now, because…well…he's dead."

Her eyes widened and I heard Annette clear her throat. "No!" Debbie insisted. "Not him! Not Peter Latham. It wasn't him who followed me, it was the other one: Tony Silkstone."

I sat looking at her for an age, she returning my gaze from small blue eyes and her cheap scent spreading out across the rickety table. I glanced at Annette, whose grin looked as if it might bubble over into joyous laughter at any moment.

"When?" I managed, eventually. "When did you see him the first time? You said it was June. June the what?"

Annette said: "Debbie has checked when her French exam was, and believes it was on June the ninth."

"One week before Margaret Silkstone died," I stated.

"And probably the day Silkstone came home early and caught them together," Annette added.

"Debbie," I said, turning to her. "What you have told us may be very important. Do your parents know you are here?"

"Yes. My mum told me to come. She wanted to come with me, but I said it was all right."

"Good. I'm really pleased you did but I'd be grateful if you'd not discuss this with anyone else, OK?"

"Yeah, no problem."

"Smashing. And meanwhile, DC Brown – Annette – will take you on a tour of the police station before driving you home. If you're hungry she might even call in McDonalds and treat you to a burger."

"Great!" Debbie said, beaming one of her gorgeous smiles at me and uncurling those sapling legs.

I stopped at the front desk and dialled Mr Wood's number. "It's Charlie," I said when he answered. "Is Mr Pritchard still with you?"

"No, he left about half an hour ago. Why?"

"There's been a development. Give him a ring, please, Gilbert. Tell him Charlie Palooka is back on the case."

I rang my DI friend in Somerset and asked him to oil a few wheels for me. I wanted to see the file for the Caroline Poole murder, and then I wanted the files on all other associated cases. In a crime like that there are always similar offences which may or may not have been perpetrated by the same person. Caroline's death stood alone, shocking an otherwise safe community, but rapists and murderers go through a learning process, and usually have a few false starts before they hit the big time. I needed to know who might have had a lucky escape while the killer was developing his technique, and from them I needed a description.

Caroline's death pre-dated DNA fingerprinting by a couple of years, and there were no samples from her attacker that could be resurrected and tested, but the thought of sticking Silkstone in a line-up excited the Somerset DI. "When were you thinking of coming down?" he asked.

"It will have to be Saturday," I told him.

"Damn! I'm a bit tied up. I'll have to let you have Bob. You remember Bob?"

"I don't need any help," I protested. "Sit me in front of the files and I'll work my way through them."

"No disrespect, Charlie," he replied, "but I'd like us to

keep abreast of this one. We already have Caroline's file here in the office. I'll let Bob spend tomorrow on it and he'll identify the associated files and have them brought to Frome from HQ. He knows his way around them; with a bit of luck he'll have it done for you. What time will you be here?"

"Umm, ten o'clock," I said, thinking that I'd work out the details later.

"Right. He'll be waiting for you."

When I looked at the map I wished I'd said twelve noon. If I'd had the gift of second sight I'd have said: "Make it Monday," but I don't, so I didn't.

It was microwave chicken casserole for tea, with pasta and green beans. After doing two-days worth of washing up I ran the car through the car wash and checked the tyre pressures and oil and water levels. My energy level was high, things were moving, looking good. I had a shower, put some decent clothes on and went out. It was nearly dark.

I drove to the brickyard, where the lovers meet. It was early for the normal trysts, but one car was parked up, windows grey with condensation. I drove to the opposite corner and parked so I could see it in my mirrors. It was a Vauxhall Vectra, brand new, with a mobile phone aerial on the back window. Later, after the pubs closed, the cars would be cheap Fords and Peugeots owned by the youth of Heckley who had no homes worthy of the name to go to, nobody to ask questions. Right now, it was the time for married men, having a drink with the boys or working late at the office.

I saw the interior light come on as a back door opened. A right-angle of white leg reached out, testing its strength before trusting it with the full weight of the attached body. Sex does that to your legs. A pale dress, flash of peroxide hair as she transferred to the front seat and made herself comfortable behind the steering wheel. Ah well, I'd got the details wrong. The man extricated himself from the back, glanced over towards me as he adjusted his clothing and took his place next to the woman.

They drove away, back to their respective partners. "Had a hard day, Darling?" "Yes, you could say that." Unless they were married to each other of course, and trying to recapture love's young dream. Whatever turns you on, I say. I didn't check to see if he'd dropped anything in the grass. I drove straight into town, not knowing why I'd been there, wondering if sometimes I take my job too seriously.

I couldn't park in my usual place because next week was Statis week. In mediaeval times it was the annual thanksgiving and excuse for a piss-up in celebration of another successful year's wool harvest. When nobody needed an excuse any more it fell out of favour for a while, but has recently been revived as part of the culture boom. The fair has been relegated to the park and the town square now hosts a series of open-air concerts, sometimes followed by a firework display across the canal. It brings money into the town and causes traffic havoc, but this is how they do things in Europe and our councillors like to show how cool and young-at-heart they are. Council workmen were busily erecting a stage and seating where I normally park, so I drove into the multi-storey. All leave would be stopped for the woodentops this weekend.

Buddy Holly was still on the door at the Aspidistra Lounge but his hair was growing again, and the ticket girl hadn't finished her gum. I paid my money, picked up my change and waited for him to open the door.

The steady boom-boom I'd heard outside threatened to do me brain damage now I was in. Blue whales in the South Atlantic probably had their flippers over their ears. The place was as empty as usual and Georgie was behind the bar, surveying his monarchy. In his position, I'd have considered abdication.

"My my, it's Mr Priest," he said. "Your usual, is it?" I nodded and he reached into the chiller cabinet for a Foster's Ice. He flipped the top off and slid the bottle towards me. "This is getting to be a habit, Mr Priest," he went on. "Your little friends are in, not that they're little, of course. Young, perhaps, but not little. Like them young, do you, Mr Priest?"

"Glass," I said, and he lifted one down from the rack above the bar. I carefully poured the over-priced, over-rated lager into it.

"Personally," he said, "I prefer them slightly older. More mature. But I can see what the attraction is. At their age they still have that innocence, don't you think? That openness, like a blank page that's waiting to be written on. I can understand how that might appeal to someone like yourself, Mr Priest."

"George," I began. "I'd like you to know that you're talking family. If ever you or one of your goons as much as makes an approach to any of them, you'll be taking your sustenance through a tube for the next month."

"Ooh, I love it when you talk tough," he said.

I picked up my change and turned away. He called after me: "You know what they say, Mr Priest, *vice is nice, but…*" The rest of it was lost in the mindless drumbeat, but I knew what he meant: *Vice is nice, but incest is best.* It rhymes, which is the sole reason for its memorability.

There were only three of them. Shani saw me first and waved, causing Sophie to look up from her glass and give me a smile that did more for me than the lager ever could.

"Who's missing?" I asked, sitting down.

"Josie," Sophie told me. "She's doing a year in Italy before university."

"And next week you'll all be gone, will you?"

"Week after is Freshers' week for me," she explained. "But this is our last night out." Shani was going to London and the other girl, Frances, to Keele.

"Looks like I'll be here on my own, then," I said, pulling a face.

"Aw!" they cried, in sympathy, and Shani reached out and put her hand on mine. "We'll make a special point of coming to see you during vacation," she promised.

Sophie thanked me for the microwave and I mumbled something about having a new one. I offered to buy drinks but they said it was their turn and Frances went to fetch them. While she was gone Shani said: "We're sorry about what it said in the papers, Charlie. They don't care what they print, as long as it sells."

Sophie looked at me, blushing slightly. "I told them what happened," she began, "when you and Dad…you know."

"That's all right, Sophie," I told her. "They have to print something."

"But it doesn't seem fair," Shani said.

"Fair!" I retorted with mock indignation. "Fair! What's fair got to do with it? It isn't fair that you're all going to university while I have to stay here. It isn't fair that you have looks and brains, while I have to make do with just looks. And you're ten years younger than me. What's fair about that?"

We had a dance and another drink, staying longer than before because it was a special occasion. I politely asked if I was in the way, offering to leave them to it, but they glanced round at the local talent and begged me to stay, hanging on to my arms, making a production of it. We left when they started playing something called garage music, recorded in the panel beating shop by the sound of it.

It was the obligatory hot dogs at the stall outside, smothered in ketchup and mustard. I declined, sitting on the wall upwind of the smell until they'd finished. I watched them as they told stories about their teachers and boyfriends, and threw their heads back in girlish laughter.

We dropped Frances off first. She was a shy, polite girl, and thanked me for the drink and the lift. I wished her well at Keele and told her that if she ever needed anyone sorting out she'd to let me know. She smiled and said she would.

Shani lived less than half a mile from Sophie. Outside her house she gave me a kiss on the cheek and said: "I hope you catch 'em, Charlie, whoever they are."

"Good luck, Shani," I replied, "and keep in touch." I waited until she was safely inside before driving off.

We didn't speak for the last leg of the journey, both probably engrossed in our thoughts. At the top of Sophie's street I switched off the engine, doused the lights and coasted like a Stealth bomber towards her home, which was in darkness. I slowed on the brakes, very gently, and came to a silent stop outside her gate. I pulled the handbrake on and turned to face my passenger, my best friend's daughter, my goddaughter.

I could smell her perfume. It was Mitsouko by Guerlain, as used by Annabelle, my last love. Annabelle was accepted for Oxford when she was Sophie's age, but went to Africa instead and married a bishop. Sitting there, in the dark, it could have been Annabelle next to me.

"Sophie," I began. She turned to face me, leaning her head on the back of her seat. I reached out and her hand found mine. I heard myself exhale a big breath, not knowing where to begin. "Cambridge, next week," I tried.

Sophie nodded. "Mmm," she mumbled.

"I just want to say that, you know, it's a whole new world for you. It is for anyone. If you have any, you know, difficulties…"

"If I have any problems," she interrupted, "if anyone gives me any hassle, let you know and you'll come down and sort them out."

"Well, that's part of it."

"It's all right, Charles," she continued. "Nobody will give me any hassle, and Dad's said the same thing to me already."

"It's not just that," I told her. "What I really meant was, well, money's bound to be tight. Impoverished students, and all that. Don't do without, Sophie. And don't keep running to your dad. I wanted to buy you something special, but I didn't know what. There'll be books you'll need, and other things. You're my family, too, you know, all I've got, so come to me first, eh?"

She bowed her head and put her other hand on mine.

After a few moments she looked up and said: "That's really lovely of you, Charles. Dad had told me that, too, but..."

"What?" I interjected. "He told you to come to me if you were short of money? Wait 'till I see him..."

She squeezed my fingers, saying: "No, silly, he told me to go to him first, not Mum."

We sat smiling at each other in the dark, our fingers intertwined. After a while Sophie asked: "Is it true you saved Dad's life?"

I shook my head. "No."

"He told Mum you did. She said he won't talk about it but that's why you are such good friends."

"I hope we're good friends because we get on well together," I replied. "We've had a few adventures, like all policemen, that's all."

"She said it was a long time ago, when you were both PCs."

"Oh, I remember," I declared. "Yes, it was when we were both PCs. We were at Leeds Town Hall Magistrates' Court, and your dad had to go in the witness box to give evidence. Someone pinned a note on his back that said: *I am a plonker*. Everybody would have seen it when he went to the box, so I told him about it. He said: 'Thanks, Charlie, you saved my life.' That must be what he means."

Sophie squeezed my fingers. "I don't believe you," she giggled.

"Well it's true."

"Charles..."

"Mmm?"

"I...I love you."

It was a tiny, hesitant voice, but the words were unmistakable, what we all long to hear: I love you. What do you say: "Don't be silly" or "You'll get over it"? I never subscribed to the views that babies don't feel pain, or that the emotions of the young are less valid than those of their parents. Love at eighteen is probably as glorious – or as agonising – as it gets.

"Yes, I know," I replied, softly, aware that I hadn't used the words myself for a long time, not sure how they would sound. "And I love you." There, it was easy, once you took the plunge. The pressure of her fingers increased. "I loved you when you were a baby," I explained, but it was not what she wanted to hear and her grip loosened. "And when you were a moody teenager."

"I was never a moody teenager," she protested.

"No, you weren't. You've never been anything less than delightful. And I love you now, as a beautiful young woman. Love changes, and it's a different sort of love." She was squeezing my fingers again.

"But," I went on, "this is as far as it can go. You realise that, don't you?"

She looked at me and nodded. We held each other's gaze for a few moments until, as if by some secret signal, we both moved forward and our lips met.

We pressed them together, held them there, and then parted. I disengaged my fingers from hers and sat back. Her mouth had stayed closed, no tongue sliding out like a viper from under a stone to insinuate its way into my mouth and check out my fillings. She was still her daddy's little girl. "That was nice," I whispered.

"Mmm." She agreed.

"Remember what I said."

"Yes." She reached for the door handle, then turned, saying: "I think Annabelle is a fool." From the pavement she added: "And I hate her," and reinforced her words by slamming the door so hard that the pressure wave popped both my ears. Why do women do that? I watched her into the house and drove home. I don't know why, but there was more joy in my heart than I'd felt in a long time.

Somerset Bob rang me Friday morning and I told him what I wanted. He was pleased and eager to be on the case and suggested I come down the A420, M4, and A350, but not the A361. I began to worry that we'd spend most of Saturday discussing the merits of the motorway versus those of A-roads, in which case I'd have to remind him of why I was there, but he was just being helpful and I needn't have worried. He invited me to stay the night with himself and his wife if we had a long day and I couldn't face the journey home, which was thoughtful of him.

I pulled everything that might be useful from the Silkstone file and made copies for Somerset. I was extricating details of his early life in Heckley from the photocopier chute when Annette joined me, holding a letter she wanted duplicating.

"What's all that?" she asked.

"Stuff about Silkstone, for Somerset," I replied. "I'm going down there tomorrow to look at their files."

"There looks to be a lot."

"There is."

"Why didn't you ask? I could have done it for you."

"Because: a, you were busy; and b, you're a detective, not a clerical assistant."

"Sorry," she replied. "Put it down to a hundred thousand years of conditioning."

"Pull the other one," I responded, lifting the original off the bed and gesturing for her to put her document on it.

"Thanks, I only want one copy." I pressed the button for her. "Are you driving down?" she asked.

"'Fraid so. Early start, about six o'clock."

"Do you want me to come with you?"

The light tube moved across and back again, and I lifted the lid. "Why?" I asked. "Aren't you going to York?"

"No. He's taking the girls to see their grandma. It's her birthday, and I'm not invited."

"Damn!" I cursed. "I wish I'd known. I've arranged to stay the night at Bob – the DC's – house. It would have been a good day out, and you could have shared the driving."

"Tell him there's been a change of plans."

I thought about it. "How were you going to spend the day?" I asked.

"Shopping in Leeds, and a hair-do," she replied.

"Harvey Nick's? House of Fraser?" I suggested.

"That's right."

"Treat yourself?"

"You bet!"

"Made an appointment for the hair-do?"

"Yes. What's all this leading to?"

"No," I said. "Thanks for the offer, Annette, but you have your day out in town. You've probably been looking forward to it, and you deserve it."

"I don't mind cancelling," she offered.

"No, but there is one thing."

"What's that?"

"Don't let him cut too much off. I like it how it is." She blushed, so I followed up with: "And as it's an early start for me in the morning I won't feel like cooking tonight, so I might pop out for a meal somewhere. Some company would be nice."

She tipped her head on one side and gave a little tight-lipped smile. "Would I do, Mr Priest?" she asked.

"You'll do just fine, Miss Brown," I replied.

I decided to splash out, demonstrate that I know how to treat a girl. Annette protested, said it was her turn, offered to at least split the bill, but I asked her to indulge me. I laid it on a bit thick, said I felt like a treat, something more special than our usual curry or Chinese. I drove us into Lancashire, to a place near Oldfield that Jeff Caton had discovered, run by a French-Persian couple and attracting rave reviews.

We started with kebabs and I followed them with lamb done in goat's milk and smothered in a spicy sauce. Annette had chicken in a fruity sauce with lots of chutneys, which I helped her with. We washed it down with a full-bodied Bordeaux. The proper stuff, all the way from France. The reviews, we agreed, were well deserved.

"Phew!" Annette exclaimed, dabbing her lips with her napkin. "That was good."

I finished my coffee. It came in tiny cups and was strong enough to drive a nuclear reactor. They didn't throw the grounds into the waste bin; they sent them to Sellafield for re-processing. A waiter appeared with the coffee jug but I held my hand over the cup and shook my head. "Any more of that and I'll be awake all night," I said.

"And you've an early start in the morning," Annette reminded me.

"Six o'clock," I groaned. "As much as I'd like to take you for a night on the town, it had better be some other time." I paid the bill, which went a long way towards compensating the proprietor for the oil wells he lost when the Shah was deposed, and we left.

It was raining and dark, but I decided to take the scenic route back, over the tops rather than the motorway. I pushed the heater control over to maximum and pressed the Classic FM button on the radio. Rodrigues, excellent. I'd thought about pre-loading the cassette with a romantic tape, but it had felt corny, even for me. And what could be more romantic than Rodrigues? Annette wriggled in the passenger seat, making herself comfortable, and hummed along with Narciso Yepes.

A sudden flurry of sleet had me switching the wipers to maximum, but it only lasted a few seconds. "Where does Grandma live?" I asked.

"Scarborough," she replied.

"And does she know about you?"

"Yes. I think so."

"So why aren't you going with them?"

"Because they're staying overnight, and there isn't room for me."

"I see."

More sleet splotched on to the windscreen, blobs of shadow that slithered upwards until the wipers swept them to the sides, where they clung to each other for security. "Brrr!" Annette exclaimed. "It looks a bit bleak out there."

"Ah, but…" I argued, raising a finger to emphasise the point I was about to make, "we're not out there."

"Do you think…" she began, then stopped herself.

"Do I think what?"

"Do you think he is, out there?"

"Who?"

"Chilcott. Chiller."

I hadn't forgotten him, just pretended to myself that he'd gone away. "Somewhere, I suppose," I replied. "Probably where it's a little warmer than this, if he's any sense."

"Have you heard anything about him, since he escaped?"

"No, not a word since the Calais sighting. When we interviewed Silkstone we made it clear that they'd conned him out of his money. That's probably what happened. Shooting me was never on the agenda."

"I don't believe you," she stated.

"Well I'll be off it now, that's for sure. All he'll want to do is survive. If the look on Silkstone's face was anything to go by he'd been paid in full, and there's no honour among thieves. None at all." Apart from the odd fool like Vince Halliwell, I thought, doing ten years for someone whose name he "couldn't remember." Except that a hit man who ran off with the money without delivering the goods would very soon be an ex-hit man, but I kept that to myself.

I changed gear for the hairpin bend at the end of the reservoir and let the car drift over to the wrong side of the road. We were the only people up there, and it was easy to imagine, after just a few minutes, that we were completely alone in the world, snug in our private cocoon of warmth and music. Now it was Samuel Barber, *Adagio for Strings*. Someone was making it easy for me.

I slowed and turned off the road. A length of it, right on the top, has been straightened, but the old road is still there, used as a picnic place for day trippers from both counties, risking ambush by the old enemy.

"Don't panic," I said as we came to a halt. "I bring all my female friends here to admire the view." Usually it's the sky, ragingly beautiful as the sun sinks somewhere beyond the Irish Sea; or the lights of the conurbation, spread out below in a glowing blanket. Tonight it was a streak of paler sky marking the horizon, with indigo clouds bleeding down into it. Ah well, I thought, at least I got the music right. As I killed the lights I noticed the time. Twenty-two hours earlier I'd parked up with young Sophie sitting next to me. This was beginning to be a habit.

"I'm not panicking," Annette said, turning towards me.

"I just thought we should talk more," I began. "It would have been really nice to have had you along, tomorrow."

"We could have had a cream tea in the Cotswolds," Annette suggested.

"Or Bath buns in Bath," I added. The music paused, hanging there like an eagle over the edge of a precipice, held by the wind. It's moment, near the end of the adagio, when the silence grips you, forbidding even your breath to move. We sat quietly until the end of the piece, when I pressed the off button. Nothing could follow that.

"What will you do?" I asked, breaking the silence.

After a moment she said: "He wants to marry me."

The rain on the windows had completely obscured the view and a gust of wind rocked the car. Who'd believe we were just into October? "Do you want to marry him?" I asked.

"Yes, I think so."

"Will you leave the police?"

"Yes. If I go back to teaching we'd all have the same holidays. It would be an ideal situation."

"You tried teaching, once."

"I was twenty-two. I've learned a lot since then."

"Like karate," I said. "How to disarm an attacker, or use a firearm."

She didn't reply. I said: "I'm sorry, I shouldn't be trying to dissuade you."

"What would you do, Charlie," she asked, steering me away from the private stuff, "if you weren't a policeman?"

"Same as you, I suppose," I replied. "I was heading for a career in teaching. Physical education and art. Non-academic, looked down upon by all the others in the staff room, with their degrees in geography and…home economics. The police saved me from that."

"What would you really like to do? If you could do anything in the world, what would it be?"

"Cor, I dunno," I protested, my brain galloping through all the fantasies, searching for a respectable one.

"There must be something."

"Yeah, I think there is."

"What? Go on, tell me."

"Swimming pool maintenance," I announced.

"Swimming pool maintenance!" she laughed.

"That's right. In Hollywood. I'd have a van – a big macho pickup – with *Charlie's Pool Maintenance* painted on the side, and I'd fix all the stars' pools." I liked the sound of this and decided to embroider it. "When I'd finished checking the chlorine levels, cleaning the filters or whatever," I continued, "the lady of the house would come out with iced lemonades on a tray, and she'd say: 'Have you fixed it, Charlie?' and I'd reply: 'No problem, Ma'am.' 'What was the trouble?' she'd ask, and I'd say: 'Oh, nothing much, only your HRT patch stuck in the filter again.'"

Annette collapsed in a fit of giggling. When she'd nearly stopped she said: "Oh, Charlie, I do…" Then she did stop.

"You do what?" I asked, but she shook her head. I reached out, putting my arm across her shoulders and pulling her towards me, meeting no resistance. I buried my face in her mass of hair, smelling it that close for the first time. "You do what?" I insisted. "Tell me."

"I...I...I do enjoy being with you," I heard her muffled voice say.

"That counts for a lot," I told her, and felt her nod in agreement. I tilted her chin upwards and kissed the lips I'd longed to kiss for a long time. A grown-up kiss, tonight, with no holding back. She broke off before I wanted to.

As I held her I said: "I've dreamed of that ever since I first saw you."

She replied with a little "Uh" sound.

"It's true. I'm not looking for a one-night stand, Annette, or a bit on the side. You know that, don't you?"

"Aren't you?" she replied.

"No. I want you to believe that."

"Take me home, please."

I started the engine and pulled my seatbelt back on. We drove most of the way to Heckley in silence. As we entered the town I said: "If luck's on our side we'll find something tomorrow to link Silkstone with other attacks in Somerset."

"Do you think you will?" Annette asked.

"Depends whether he did them," I replied. "And even then, it's a long shot." As we turned into her street I said: "I don't know what to think. About anything. Sometimes I wonder if it's worth bothering." We came to a standstill outside the building which contains her flat. "Here we are," I said. "Thank you for a pleasant evening, Annette. Sorry if I stepped out of line. It won't happen again."

She shook her head, the light from the street lamps giving her a copper halo that swayed and shimmered like one of van Gogh's wind-blown cypress trees. "You didn't step out of line, Charlie," she told me.

"Honest?"

"Mmm. Honest."

"Good. I'm glad about that."

She reached for the door handle, like Sophie had done,

then hesitated and turned to me in exactly the same way. "What do you have against one-night stands and a bit on the side?" she asked.

"Nothing," I replied. "Nothing at all."

I held her gaze until she said: "Would you like to come in?"

"Yes," I told her. "I'd like that very much."

Chapter Fourteen

I blamed the traffic for being late. Bob asked if I'd come down the Fosse Way or Akeman Street, but I said: "Oh, I don't know," rather brusquely and asked him what he had for me. I realised later that it was an office joke, probably imitating one of the traffic officers who always swore that the *quickest* way from A to B was via Q, M and Z.

Plenty was the answer. I wanted to see the basic stuff first and then move on to the specific. I asked myself, as I looked at the ten-by-eights of poor Caroline's body, if this was necessary. Couldn't I have gleaned the information I wanted from someone's report? No doubt, but this way was quicker. Caroline had been strangled and raped, from the front and not necessarily in that order. Also, the deed was done outdoors. Serial rapists develop a style, like any other craftsman. Some, who often have a record for burglary, prefer to work indoors. Others, quicker on their feet, strike in parks and lonely lanes. If Silkstone was our man he'd changed his style. Caroline's body was left in a shallow stream and not discovered for two days, hence the lack of forensic evidence.

Bob had extracted a list of statistics from the pile of information, to show how extensive the enquiry had been: fifteen thousand statements; twenty thousand tyre prints; eighteen thousand cars. He fetched me a sandwich and percolated some decent coffee while I read the statements made by the officers who had interviewed the Famous Four: Silkstone, Latham, Margaret, and Michelle Webster. What could they have said to differentiate themselves from all those thousands of others, short of: "I did it, guv, it's a fair cop?"

But they didn't, and were lost in the pile of names just like others before them and a few since.

"Cor, that's good," I said, taking a sip of the coffee. "Just what I need."

"Late night?" Bob asked.

"Yeah," I replied.

"Working?"

"No, er, no, not really. It was, um, a promotion bash. Went on a bit late." I liked that. A promotion bash. He was a detective, so he could probably tell that I was smiling, inside.

There were twenty-one reported attacks on women in the previous ten years that may have been linked to Caroline's death. Seventeen of them were unlikely, two looked highly suspicious. I started at the bottom of the pile, working towards the likeliest ones. Had I done it the other way round I might have become bogged down on numbers one and two. Some had descriptions, some didn't. He was tall, average height – this was most common – or short. Take your pick. He wore a balaclava, was clean shaven and had a beard. There were three of them, two of them, he was alone. He spoke with a local accent, a strange accent, never said a word. He had a knife, a gun, just used brute force. He was on foot, rode a bike, in a car.

Which would the good people of Frome prefer, I wondered? A serial rapist in their midst or twenty-one men who'd tried it once, for a bit of fun? Most of the attacks occurred on the way home from a night out, after both parties had imbibed too much alcohol. Some of the reports appeared frivolous, some hid tragedies behind the stilted phrases of the police officers. This was fifteen plus years ago, when the courts believed that a too-short skirt and eye contact across a crowded room meant: *take me, I'm begging for it*.

I'd placed the four favourites to one side. I untied the tape around the top one and started reading. She was a barmaid, walking home like she did every night. Someone struck her from behind, fracturing her skull, and dragged her into a field. She survived, after a December night in the open and three in intensive care, but never saw a thing of her attacker. One year, almost to the day, before Caroline.

Bob was busy at another desk. I raised an arm to attract

his attention and he came over. "He had full penetrative sex with this one," I said. "Do we know if she became pregnant?"

Bob lifted the cover of the file to look at the name. "The barmaid," he said. "On the Bristol Road. She nearly died. Of these four she was the last and the only one where he managed it. We've thought of that so she can't have been."

I didn't curse. I felt like it, but I didn't. It was good news for her. All the same, if he'd made her pregnant and she'd gone full term we could have done a DNA test, introduced someone to his or her daddy, perhaps.

The next one I looked at happened eighteen months earlier, in the summer of 1981, and he drove a Jaguar. "Bob!" I shouted across the office.

"What is it?" he asked, coming over.

"This one," I told him, closing the folder to show the name on the front. "Eileen Kelly. In her statement she says that the car she accepted a lift in was a Jaguar. On the wall of Silkstone's bedroom is a photograph of him posing alongside a Mk II Jag. You can read the number and it's in the file somewhere."

"I'll get on to the DVLC," Bob said. "When are we talking about?"

"She was attacked in August, '81."

He went back to his telephone and I read the Eileen Kelly story. She was sixteen, and had just started work at the local egg-packing factory. At the end of her second week the other girls invited her out with them to a disco. They met in a pub and Eileen was disappointed to discover that they stayed there, drinking, until closing time. As soon as they entered the disco the other girls split up, each appearing to have a regular boyfriend, and Eileen was left on her own. The last bus had gone and she didn't have enough money for a taxi. The thought of rousing her parents from their bed to pay the fare didn't appeal to her.

An apparent knight in shining armour appeared on the

scene and after a few dances offered her a lift home, which she gratefully accepted. Except he didn't take her home. He drove almost thirty miles to a deserted place called Black Heath, on Salisbury plain, and dragged her from the car.

Eileen put up a fight and escaped. He chased her, but some headlights appeared and her attacker changed his mind and fled, leaving her to walk two miles down a dirt track in her stocking feet. She survived, and he graduated to the next level of his apprenticeship. He was on a learning curve.

The description she gave was fairly non-committal. It's broad terms certainly included Silkstone, who would have been twenty-five at the time, but it could equally have been anyone that you see at a football match or leaning on a bar. She was certain about the car, though: it was Jaguar.

"Bad news," Bob said, placing a sheet of paper in front of me. "Anthony Silkstone owned a Mk II Jag from September '76 to December '78, which is over two years too early for us."

"Bugger!" I exclaimed.

"Steady," Bob protested, "I'm a Methodist."

"Well sod and damn, too."

"Maybe…" Bob began.

"Go on."

"He'd be what, in his early twenties?"

"When Eileen was attacked? Twenty-five, maybe twenty-six."

"But he'd only be…what, twenty-one…when he bought the Jag?"

"That's right."

"A bit young, I'd say, for a car like that, expensive to run. Maybe he couldn't afford it, and sold it to a friend, Latham perhaps, but still had access to it. And if you were up to mischief it would make sense to use somebody else's car, wouldn't it?"

"I don't know," I replied. "I'm just a simple Yorkshire lad. Find out what happened to it, Bob, please. He may even have traded it in for another Jag. We need a rundown of every car he and Latham have owned, and a full history of the Jag after he sold it. Let's see if we can get some justice for Eileen, we owe her that much."

I carried on with the file. Poor Eileen had been taken and seated in the passenger seat of every model that Jaguar, formerly Swallow Sidecars, had made. They changed their name at the outbreak of World War II, because SS, the abbreviated form, wasn't good PR in 1939. Eileen couldn't identify the actual model, but was adamant it was a Jag because it had the famous mascot on the bonnet and when she was little she'd seen a Walt Disney film about the animal.

I closed my eyes and leaned back in the chair. We were in the main CID office, but the place was deserted on a Saturday afternoon. I'd thanked Bob for his consideration but told him that I'd prefer to go home if we finished at a reasonable hour. Staying overnight would take another big chunk out of the weekend. Barber's *Adagio* is one of those tunes that I can hear in my head but can't reproduce with a whistle or hum. I imagined it now, with its long mournful descants and soaring chords. I saw a car, a Jag, revolving on a plinth. First it was sideways on, sleek and elegant; then it slowly turned to three-quarter view, radiating power and aggression with its rounded air intake and fat tyres; and then nose on, looking like it was coming at you from the barrel of a gun. People fall in love with their Jags, and I could understand why. Parting with it must have broken Silkstone's heart.

I collected Bob's mug and made us another coffee. He was talking on the phone and scribbling on a pad. I placed the replenished mug on his beer mat and tried to make sense of his notes.

"Thanks a lot," he said. "You've been a big help. I'll come back to you shortly."

He pushed himself back and turned to me, throwing his pencil on the desk. "According to Swansea the Jag was written off," Bob told me. "After that he owned an MGB, presumably bought with the proceeds, but three years later that was written off, too."

"Writing off one sports car is unfortunate," I said. "Writing off two is downright careless. So he had an MGB at the time of the Eileen Kelly attack?"

"That's right."

"According to the file she was shown and seated in every Jag produced, but couldn't recognise the precise model. I wonder if she was shown an MGB?"

"I don't know," Bob replied, "but we'll be on to it, first thing Monday."

"Do you know where she is?"

"We'll find her."

I pulled a chair closer to Bob's desk and took a sip of coffee. He shoved a sheet of paper towards me, to stand my mug on. "I used to have a Jaguar," I began. "An E-type. My dad restored it and it came to me when he died. It was a fabulous car, but wasted on me. I like one that starts first time, and that's about it. We used to go to rallies, and I was amazed at the attention and devotion that some owners lavished on their vehicles. Love isn't too strong a word." I paused, remembering those good days, some of the best I'd ever had. "Imagine, if you can," I continued, "that you are in your early twenties and you own your dream car. It's fast and desirable, it turns heads and it pulls birds. What more could a young lad want? Then, one day, you write it off. It's beyond repair, a heap of scrap. What would you do?"

"Look for another, I suppose," Bob replied.

"There isn't another. They've stopped making them and those who own 'em aren't parting."

"Look for something similar, then."

"Yes, but what about the old car. How would you remember it?"

"Photographs?"

"Perhaps. What about something more substantial?"

"You mean, like a momento?"

"That's right."

"The jaguar!" he exclaimed. "The mascot off the bonnet. I'd save that."

"Good idea," I told him. "And if you just happened to own an MGB? It's a very nice car, but not quite in the same class as the Jag you once had. Might you not be tempted to…you know…so you could relive your dreams…?"

"Put the mascot on the MG," Bob suggested.

"Exactly. And Eileen Kelly said the car was a Jag because of the mascot on the bonnet."

"Fuckin' 'ell, Charlie," he hissed. "It's a bit far-fetched, don't you think?"

"I thought you were a Methodist," I reminded him.

"Only in leap years." We drank our coffee, reading the notes he'd made. "A more likely explanation…" Bob began, "…is that it really was a Jaguar, driven by someone unknown to us."

I nodded and placed my empty mug on his desk. "I know, Bob," I agreed. "But humour me, please. We can either go back to the beginning and start all over again, which will take us nowhere all over again, or we can run it with Silkstone in the frame. So let's do it, eh?"

"That's fine by me, Chas."

"Thanks. I'm going home."

Sunday I stayed in bed until after ten, had a shower and went out for a full English breakfast. I brought a couple of heavies back in with me and spent the rest of the day catching up on the latest hot stories, a neverending supply of tea at my elbow. Heaven. Annette had said she might go to her mother's, in Hebden Bridge, and I'd said that I might stay overnight with Bob, so there was no answer when I tried her number. Another communication breakdown. The weather system had swung right round and the day was warm again, with just enough threat of rain to put me off doing some gardening. A quick run-around downstairs with the vacuum cleaner gave me sufficient Brownie points to justify an evening watching television and listening to music. I brought the Chinese painting in from the garage and propped it in a corner, where it caught the light, so I could study it. You are supposed to leave oil paint for about a year to dry before varnishing it, but a month or two is usually enough. A few touches of black contour, I thought, on some of the images, and that would be that. I can't justify black contours, but they can transform a picture, and V. Gogh did it all the time so why shouldn't C. Priest? I was pleased with the painting and it was good fun having a whole day to myself. At nine o' clock I gave Annette's number another try, and this time she answered.

"You were lucky to catch me," she said. "I've only been in two minutes, and I've put my waterproof on to go straight out again."

"Fate," I told her. "Fate, working in sympathy with our circadian rhythms as part of some great master plan to bring us together. On the other hand, I could have tried your number every minute for the last two days."

"Oh, and which was it?"

"Fate, definitely fate. So where are you going, young lady, at such a late hour. Didn't you know that the streets are not safe in this town?"

"It's the start of Statis week," she reminded me. "There's a concert in the square, followed by fireworks. Why don't you come? I could see you there."

"Who's playing?" I asked, as if it mattered.

"It's an Irish band, called Clochan. They're pretty good."

"Right. Great. Where shall I meet you?" I like Irish bands, but I'd still have gone if it had been Emma Royd and the Piledrivers.

Annette was standing at the edge of the audience, near the Sue Ryder shop as arranged, with the hood of her waterproof down even though it was raining. She looked pleased to see me, and I kissed her on the lips and put my arm around her.

"Good weekend?" I shouted into her ear, in competition with 'Whiskey in the Jar.'

"Mmm," she mouthed in reply. "And you?"

"So so. They are good, aren't they." I sang along with them, to show how hip I'd once been: *As I was going over the Cork and Kerry mountains, I met Captain Farrel…and I shot him with my pistol.*

We caught the last three songs, finishing with a *tour de force* rendition of 'Marie's Wedding' that slowly built-up and carried the audience along with it: first swaying to the tune; then clapping and foot-stamping; and eventually dancing wildly, arms and legs flailing. Annette and I looped arms and dozey-do'd, exchanging partners with the couple next to us, until the music stopped and we all ground to a breathless halt. I stood with my arms around her and the rain running down my face as she and the others applauded them from the stage. If the devil really does have all the best tunes he must be a Celt.

The bang startled me. I spun round, heart bouncing, but all I saw was a sea of upturned faces, washed in pink and then lilac as the firework filled the sky with spangles. Annette joined in the chorus of "Ooh" and "Aah" as chandeliers of fire blossomed above our heads, each burst of light a giant chrysanthemum, illuminating the smoke trails of its predecessor until it faded to make way for something even brighter. I looked around at the jostling crowd, their eyes shaded by hoods and hats, as explosions rippled and crackled through the sodden sky. The noise of a machine gun, never mind a .38, could easily have gone un-noticed amongst all that cacophony.

A single desultory bang signified the end, leaving us with fading images on our retinas and the smell of cordite in our nostrils. "Thank you for the dance," I said to the complete stranger that I'd been whirling around two minutes earlier.

"I'll save one for you next year," she laughed, and her

husband looked embarrassed, as if he couldn't believe it had all happened.

Annette and I picked our way through the crowd heading towards the car parks until I eased her into a side street and steered a course down towards the canal, where it was quieter. "I'm in the multi-storey," I explained. "But let's take the romantic route."

"I'd hardly call Heckley Navigation romantic," she laughed.

"I know, but it's the best I can do. I think hot cocoa at your place is called for. How does that sound?"

"It sounds very inviting," she agreed, squeezing my hand.

The alley down to the canal is the one where Lockwood and Stiles had come to grief, four months earlier. As we approached the end I sensed Annette looking around her, realising where we were.

"This is Dick Lane, isn't it?" she asked.

"Mmm," I replied.

"Where Martin Stiles got the panda stuck?"

"That's right." Through the day it is blocked with delivery vehicles servicing the shops that back on to it, but at night only courting couples and glue sniffers use it, sheltering in the doorways and behind the dumpsters. Tonight the rain had kept them away, but it was still early. We'd reached the iron posts that prevent the egress of anything wider than a stolen Fiesta. "And these," I said, fondling one of the rounded tops, "are the items in question."

"Oh God!" Annette giggled, letting go of my hand.

"What?" I laughed.

"I just...I just..."

"What?"

She shook her head and made gurgling noises.

I put my hand on her shoulder to steady her. "You just what?"

"Nothing!"

I engulfed her in my arms and felt her body shaking as

she tried to control her giggling. It was a pleasant experience. "What?" I demanded, turning to shelter her from the rain.

"I just...I just..."

Now I was giggling. "You just what?"

"I just realised...I just realised why they call it...Why they call it..."

I completed the sentence for her. "Why they call it Dick Lane? It was named after the Methodist minister who built this church." I flapped a hand at the building to my left.

A respectable stream was running down the middle of the alley, and up at the top the cobbles shone yellow and orange with the lights from the square. Halfway along a movement caught my attention, so brief that I wondered if I'd imagined it. A figure stepped out of the shadows and stepped straight back into them.

"If you say so," she replied, finding a tissue and blowing her nose. "But I don't believe it."

"I'm appalled," I told her. "I can't imagine what sort of people you mix with. C'mon, I'm soaked." I grabbed her hand again and pulled her towards the towpath.

The canal was a black hole, devoid of movement or form apart from where an occasional rectangle of light fell on to it and the surface became a pattern of overlapping circles, piling on to each other as the rain increased in force. I stepped into a puddle and said: "I think this was a mistake."

Annette stopped, saying: "That's where Darryl Buxton lived, isn't it?" She was looking at a mill across the canal, converted into executive flats. Buxton was a rapist that we jailed.

"That's right," I agreed, looking behind us. I hadn't imagined it. A figure stepped cautiously out of the end of Dick Lane and merged into the shadows again. He was hugging the wall, gaining on us, and the next opening was nearly a hundred yards away. "Do you have plenty of milk?" I asked, tugging at her arm.

"Milk?"

"Mmm. You know, comes from cows. I like my cocoa made with milk."

"Oh, I think we'll be able to manage that. Except mine comes from Tesco."

"That'll do. C'mon."

"The canal looks spooky, doesn't it?"

"Yes. Not as romantic as I'd thought. Perhaps I was confusing it with Venice."

"How deep is it?"

I looked back but couldn't be sure if he was there. "I don't know."

"Did you swim in it when you were a child?"

"No."

"You didn't?"

"No. We went to the baths." This time I saw him, and he was much closer, moving purposefully but still keeping to the shadows. I stopped to pick up a stone and tossed it towards the water. It splashed somewhere out in the blackness. When I looked, he'd stopped too.

We were nearly at the end of the next alleyway, similar to Dick Lane but without the dicks. It was another service road, cobbled and narrow, and not illuminated. I patted my pockets, feeling for my mobile phone, knowing I wouldn't find it. "Do you have your phone with you?" I asked, but she didn't.

"Listen, Annette," I said as we approached the end of the wall. "When we reach this corner I want you to do exactly as I say."

She sensed the urgency in my voice. "What is it, Charlie?" she asked.

"Just do as I say. When we get round the corner I want you to run as fast as you can towards the town centre. There's a pub called the Talisman at the top of the street. Go in and go straight to the ladies'. Lock yourself in for five minutes. Then come out and order two drinks at the bar. I'll join you about then."

"What are you talking about?" she demanded.

"Just do as I say."

"Why? What is it?"

"We're being followed." We reached the corner and turned it. Two big green dumpsters were standing there, just as I'd hoped. "Now run!" I hissed, pushing her towards the lights.

"And what are you doing?" she asked.

"Just run!"

"I'm not running without you."

I heard the *tch tch* of his trainers on the wet floor, fast at first, as if he were jogging, then slower, cautious, as he reached the corner. I grabbed Annette's arm and pushed her behind the dumpster, bundling her deep into the corner. A rat squealed a protest and scuttled away.

The footsteps paused as he surveyed the empty street, then started again, striding out. I heard his noise, sensed his shadow as I anticipated his position, predicting the exact moment he would emerge. As he passed the dumpster I took two rapid strides forward and hurled myself at him.

Priority was to stop him finding his gun. I threw my arms around him in a bear hug and knocked him to the ground. He kicked wildly and we rolled over, first me on top, then him, followed by me again. As he rolled over me I felt water running down my neck. He shouted something I didn't catch and Annette joined in, flailing at him with her fists, trying to hold his head. Next time he was on the bottom I risked letting go with one hand for sufficient time to smash his face against the cobbles. He jerked and went limp.

Neither of us had handcuffs with us. I felt his clothing for a gun but he was unarmed. I rolled him over and moved to one side so my shadow wasn't on him. His lips were moving and a trickle of blood ran from his forehead until the rain diluted it to almost nothing.

"Oh shit!" I said.

"It's me," he mumbled. "It's me, Mr Priest."

"Do you know him?" Annette asked.

"Yeah, I know him." I grabbed his lapels and pulled him, still mumbling, into a seated position. "I know him all right. I'd like you to meet Jason Lee Gelder: until recently chief suspect in the Marie-Claire Hollingbrook case."

It was Les Isles' fault. We led Jason to where there was more light and cleaned him up. He was more apologetic than I was, and refused to be taken to Heckley General for a check-up. He wouldn't even let us give him a lift home. "It's my fault, Mr Priest," he kept insisting. "I shouldn't have followed you like that."

When they'd decided not to oppose bail, poor old Jason had interpreted this as implying that he was no longer in the frame for Marie-Claire's murder. He'd attempted to thank Les, who'd said: "Don't thank me, thank Inspector Priest," and told him that he owed me a pint. Jason took him literally. When he saw us at the fireworks he thought he would pay his debts, and followed us into Dick Lane. He said he was going to catch up with us there, but when we stopped "for a snog" he thought better of it and waited.

I believed him. Jason wasn't a crook, but he certainly qualified as a *client*, and some of them get funny ideas. They come into the station and see us in court, and start to see themselves as part of the organisation. We see them as the enemy, they regard themselves as our colleagues. I told Jason to call into the nick tomorrow and report the incident. He said it didn't matter, but I insisted. I'd do a full report, to keep myself and Annette in the clear. He was slow but well-meaning, and destined for a lifetime of holding the dirty end of whatever stick was offered him. I imagined him at the slaughterhouse, doing every obscene job that his sick workmates could find, and felt sorry for the Jasons of the world.

It was only a five-minute drive to Annette's, and we did it in silence. I doused the lights outside her flat and turned to face her. She stared straight ahead, unsmiling and pale in the harsh light. Under the street lamps the rain was falling like grain out of a silo.

"You're soaked," I ventured, and she nodded in agreement.

"The, er, evening didn't quite turn out as I intended," I said.

"No," she replied.

"But the music was good. I enjoyed that." Annette didn't respond, so I went on: "We used to go to the Irish Club, years ago. Had some great nights there. It was the headaches next morning that put a stop to it."

She turned to face me, and said: "You thought it was him, didn't you?"

"Who?" I asked, all innocence.

"Him. Chilcott. The Chiller, whatever you call him. You thought it was the Chiller following us."

"No I didn't."

"I don't believe you."

"I thought he was a mugger. He'd seen us and decided we'd be easy prey, so he followed us. I thought we'd give him a surprise."

"So I had to run as fast as I could to the pub and lock myself in the toilet? For a mugger? I don't believe you."

"Yeah, well," I mumbled.

"I saw the look on your face, Charlie," she told me. "When we were behind the bins. You were...*eager*. You were enjoying yourself. You were about to tackle someone you thought had a gun, who wanted to kill you, and you were enjoying yourself."

"I wasn't enjoying myself," I protested. "I was scared stiff and I was worried about you."

"But you admit that you thought it was Chilcott?"

"It crossed my mind, Annette, in the heat of the moment. But now I see the idea as preposterous. He's a long way away and I'm just history to him, believe me."

"I don't know what to believe."

After a long silence I said: "Shall we cancel the cocoa?"

"I think so," she replied. "If you don't mind."

I shrugged my shoulders. I minded like hell. I minded like a giant asteroid was heading towards Heckley, and only a cup of cocoa in her flat, listening to George Michael CDs, would save the town. But who was I to make a decision like that?

As she opened the door I said: "You're upset, Annette. It was a frightening experience. Go have a nice hot bath and stay in bed until lunchtime. I'll make it right. Have the whole day off, if you want."

She looked at me and sighed. "I think it's you who needs some time off, Charlie," she said, opening the car door and swinging her legs onto the pavement. "I'll be there," she stated. "Bright and early, as always."

I braced myself for the inevitable door slam, but it didn't come. She held the handle firmly and pushed it shut, so it closed with a textbook *clunk*. She didn't slam it. I watched her sashay across the little residents' car-park and punch her code into the security lock. A light came on and she went inside. She didn't slam that door, either, but turned and held the latch. For a few seconds I could see her shape through the frosted glass and then she faded away, as if she were sinking into a deep pool. She didn't slam the door, and that's the moment I fell in love with her.

On Tuesday afternoon, when Somerset Bob sat her in an MGB, Eileen Kelly went bananas. The poor woman had never really recovered from the attack and had drifted from one unhappy relationship to another. At the moment she was alone, living in rented accommodation and working in the kitchen of a department store in Bath. He said that she was pleased, at first, to have a change in her routine and go along with him to the house of a Bath traffic cop who had a much-cherished model of the car. On the way there she reiterated her story, glad that at last someone was listening, and no doubt encouraged by the change in attitude over the last eighteen years.

Her attacker's car had been parked at the roadside, and she hadn't realised which it was until he opened the door for her, so she never really saw it from the outside. Bob said he opened the passenger door and beckoned her to get in. As soon as she dropped into the low seat she started shivering and shaking. He climbed in next to her and saw that she had turned white, her wide eyes taking in the instrument panel, glove box and everything else.

The traffic cop's wife made them tea and Eileen slowly regained her composure, sitting in their kitchen. "I'm sorry," she'd sobbed, blowing her nose.

"There's nothing to be sorry about," Bob had assured her. "What can you tell me about the car?"

"It was one of them," she'd declared. "Definitely, but it had a little animal on the front, like a Jaguar does."

"Find it, Bob," I ordered, when he finished his story.

"Might not be easy, it was written off."

"Well find where the bits went. We need that car."

There was a note on my desk from the twilight detective, who just happened to be Rodger. Two of them alternate, afternoons and nights, because their wives work shifts at the General Hospital, and it suits them. I'd asked for a watch to be kept on Silkstone, when times were slack, and the note said that he'd fallen into the habit of strolling along to the Anglers for a meal, usually between six and seven. I grow restless when a case stagnates, like to jolly things along a little. It was time to go pro-active, I decided. We're big on pro-active policing at the moment. First thought was to take Annette with me, but I changed my mind. It would be better if I was alone, my word against his. Except I would have a witness. I rang our technical support people and asked to borrow a tape recorder.

Annette came into my office just before five, carrying a coffee. "Hi, Annette," I said, pointing to the spare chair. "Sit down and talk to me."

"Coffee?" she asked.

"No thanks."

"You've been after me."

"Yes," I replied. "I rang you because I'm going to accidentally-on-purpose bump into Silkstone, in that pub near his place, and I thought it might look more natural if you were with me."

"No problem," she replied. "What time?"

"It's OK, there's been a change of plan. I've decided to be alone, in the hope that I can tempt him into the odd indiscretion."

"But it won't be worth a toss," she informed me.

"I know, but if it were he wouldn't say it, would he? We could have a drink after," I suggested.

"Socially?"

"I suppose so. You've been avoiding me since…since the weekend."

"I don't think so, if you don't mind, Boss."

"It's Boss again, is it?" I said.

"I'm sorry, Charlie," she replied, shaking her head. "I don't know what to think." She looked more unhappy than I've ever seen her.

"I cocked-up on Sunday," I admitted. "I know I did. Something just happened inside me. I was scared, but for you, not myself. I thought I'd got you into something. Maybe it was the music, or the words of the songs. I don't know. We need to talk, but this isn't the place. Let me come round to your place, later."

"I don't know." More head shaking, her hair covering first one half of her face, then the other, as it tried to keep up. I glanced out of the window across the big office. Nobody was watching us, trying to decipher the touching scene between the DI and the attractive DC.

"Friday night," I began. "I thought it was rather special. I thought that, you know, it said something about how we felt for each other."

"So did I, but…"

"But what?"

She gave a violent shake of the head and started sobbing. I looked out and caught David Rose glance across. He quickly looked away. "I'm sorry, Annette," I said. "Maybe I read too much into it. OK, it's back to strictly a working relationship, if that's how you'd prefer it. I don't want to lose you as an officer and I can switch it off, live a lie, if you can. Shall we just…call the whole thing off?"

She sniffed and looked at me for the first time. "Yes, I think we should," she replied.

"Right."

"I'm sorry, Charlie."

"Me too, Annette. Me too."

I did paperwork until just after six, then hared off to the Anglers. In the car park I tested the tape recorder, running the tape back to the beginning and pressing the *play* button.

Male voice: "Hi, Annette. Sit down and talk to me."

Female voice: "Coffee?"

Male voice: "No thanks."

Female voice: "You've been after me."

Male voice: "Yes, I rang you because…"

I pressed the *stop* button and ejected the cassette. There was nothing there that I wanted to save for posterity; nothing I could play back to her later, and watch the colour rise in her cheeks until I reached out and cooled them with my fingertips. I hooked a thumbnail under the tape and pulled it from the spools, heaping it on the passenger seat until no more was left and ripping the ends free. I clicked the spare cassette into position and concealed the tape recorder in my inside pocket. The microphone was under my tie. It worked, and that was all that mattered. I locked the car and went into the pub.

I tried the steak and kidney pie but didn't enjoy it. I was stabbing a perfunctory chip with my fork – there's something oddly irresistible about a plate of cold chips – when a movement outside caught my eye. Another Ford Mondeo had joined mine in the car-park, and it was closely followed by a Peugeot. The place was getting busy. My phone rang and I grabbed it from my pocket. "Charlie," I whispered into it.

"He's with someone," I was told, "in a Ford like yours. I've done a vehicle check and it's owned by a Julian Maximillian Denver."

"Cheers, I know him." I looked up at the door as I slipped the phone back into my pocket and saw Silkstone, accompanied by Max Denver, ace reporter of the *UK News*, heading my way.

Denver, a grin on his face, was all for joining me, but Silkstone didn't want to. I'd never been formally introduced to Denver, but recognised him as the character who'd confronted me outside the station a week ago, and his name was plastered all over the articles. He was wearing a belted leather coat a size too big, faded jeans and a slimy smile on one of those faces that has *punch me* writ large across it. I scratched my armpit and switched the tape on. If Mohammed wouldn't come to the mountain...

They ordered drinks and food at the bar and took a table several places away from me. I waited until they were settled and wandered over, glass in hand.

"Well well," I said, pulling a chair from an adjoining table and placing it at the end of theirs. "I'd have thought this was a bit downmarket for a pair of hotshots like you two."

"I was thinking the same myself," Silkstone sneered.

"Sit down, why don't you," Denver invited, somewhat superfluously as I already had done.

"Thanks. On the other hand, in your reduced circumstances, Silkstone, I'd have thought you'd have taken advantage of the two-for-one, before six o'clock."

He turned to Denver, asking: "Do we have to listen to this?" but Denver would listen to anyone, and the more aggro the better.

"Or is this little treat on your new-found friend's expense account?" I asked. "Signed a contract with him, have you?"

Denver said: "Killed any unarmed men today, Priest?"

"No," I replied, "but there's time." I turned back to Silkstone. "How much is he paying you then? Enough to replace the fifty thousand you donated to the Kevin Chilcott holiday fund?" A red shadow spread from Silkstone's face, stopping as it reached his bald head, like the British Empire on an old map of Africa. Denver looked from me to Silkstone and back again, his brow beetled in mystification. "What!" I exclaimed, "hasn't he told you about the fifty thousand?"

"Because it's a pack of lies," Silkstone hissed. "Another of the stories you invented to blacken my name because…because…because you haven't got a leg to stand on and you know it. Why don't you leave me alone and…and…"

"And go out and catch a murderer?" I suggested. I drained my glass and placed it on their table. Denver twisted in his seat and raised a hand to the girl behind the bar, but she turned away because they don't do waitress service.

"Ah, maybe you're right," I conceded. "It's this job."

Denver got to his feet and shouted to the barmaid, asking if he could order some drinks, but she ignored him again. He wanted a drink in my hand, but he didn't want to leave my side, in case he missed something. "Don't worry," I told him, "I'll get it." I strolled to the bar and ordered myself another pint.

"You know," I began, when I'd rejoined them, "I took an instant dislike to you, Silkstone." I looked at his companion and explained: "You have to, when you're investigating a murder. But then, as I looked around your house, I decided that you had at least one redeeming feature." I picked up my glass and drained nearly half of it, licking my lips and pretending it wasn't as unappetising as the cold urine it resembled.

"And what was that?" Denver prompted.

"He's a Jaguar man," I replied. "Had a 1964 Mark II.

Great car, highly desirable." I had another drink, before
adding: "Can't be much wrong with a man who owned a car
like that, I said to myself."

"It hasn't stopped you persecuting me," Silkstone
declared.

"Top brass," I told him. "You know how it is." I finished
my drink and Denver snatched up the glass almost before
my fingers had left it.

"Another?" he asked.

"Why not?" I replied.

"Lager?"

"Please."

"Which one?"

"Labatt's."

He dashed off to the bar as I said to Silkstone: "Once
upon a time I had an E-type. A three-point-eight. Fabulous
car. I loved it. Drove it to southern Spain, once. Boy, did that
machine turn heads. And pull birds. Felt like a bloody film
star when I was in it."

Denver placed the replenished glass in front of me and I
thanked him. "I was just telling Mr Silkstone that I owned
an E-type Jag, a long time ago. It nearly broke my heart
when it was stolen. A scrote from Sylvan Fields took it and
torched it. I'd have strangled the little bastard if I'd got my
hands on him." I took a sip of the Labatt's. It was a big
improvement. I'd sold the car when prices were at their
highest and made nearly ten grand profit, but they didn't
need to know that. "What happened to yours?" I asked.

"I crashed it," Silkstone informed me.

"Crashed it? Were you hurt?" Some men are embarrassed
if they have the misfortune to crash their car, see it as a mistake; others never accept the blame and enjoy relating all the
gory details. I had little doubt which group our friend
belonged in.

"No. I was lucky."

"What happened?"

"Hit a patch of black ice on the A37. The gritters hadn't been out."

"And it was written off?"

"Yeah. I rolled it over three times. Would have cost too much to repair, so it went for scrap."

"And you walked away from it?"

"Without a scratch."

"Blimey." I had another drink.

"So what's the state of the investigation now?" Denver asked, trying to drag the conversation back to something he might be interested in.

"The file's with the CPS," I told him. "It's up to them."

"But aren't you following any lines of enquiry?"

"No," I lied. "It's up to them, now," and I gave a little belch, for emphasis.

"Why don't you charge Mr Silkstone?" Denver challenged me.

"What with?" I asked.

"You're the one making all the wild accusations. Saying he murdered his wife and that woman in Halifax."

"Marie-Claire Hollingbrook." I said. "She has a name, Denver – God knows, you've typed it often enough."

"So why don't you charge him?"

"I told you, it's the CPS's decision. Me, I'm just here for a quiet drink. Can I remind you that I was here first. But as we're all together I thought that talking about cars might be a pleasant diversion. I thought that was what people like us were supposed to do. You know, lads' talk. Did Silkstone ever tell you that he had an MGB after the Jaguar?" I turned to him saying: "That's right, isn't it?"

"If you say so," he replied.

"Not me, the DVLA," I responded. "I had to check your records. Was it any good?"

"The MG?"

"Mmm."

"It was alright."

"But not in the same league as the Jag?"

"No."

I decided to backtrack, not pursue the MG. Maybe it was a mistake, bringing it into the conversation. I looked at my glass, studying the bubbles clinging to the sides, wondering whether they brought the lager all the way from Canada or just the name. Outside, a narrow boat glided by, heading for the open canal, fulfilling someone's long-held dream. I hoped it wasn't a disappointment. "When my car was burnt out," I began, "I salvaged the little pouncing jaguar mascot from the bonnet. Actually, the garage where it went took it off and saved it for me, which was thoughtful of them, don't you think?" The expressions on their faces suggested they didn't, but I pressed on. "I still have it. I mounted it on a piece of mahogany and had a little metal plate engraved for it. It stands on my mantelpiece, reminds me of the life I once led." I smiled at the memory, a little wistful smile, which was difficult because I'd just invented the whole story. "What about you?" I asked, looking at Silkstone. "Weren't you tempted to do something similar?"

"What's all this about?" he snapped. "Why all this interest in my cars, all of a sudden?"

"It's just conversation," I protested, turning to Denver as if appealing to him to intervene on the side of reason. "I just wondered if he'd removed the mascot from his car, like I did."

"Fuck off!" Silkstone growled.

"Nice friend you have," I told Denver.

"He's right," Denver said. "Just what are you after, Priest?"

"He wants me to say something he can twist round, for his own purposes," Silkstone declared. "While my brief isn't here. Well, I'm not saying another word. Why don't you just piss off, Priest, and leave us alone. You're not welcome."

I'd blown it, that was for sure. Ah well, I thought, if he wasn't going to say anything incriminating the least I could do was give him something to ruin his sleep, and maybe sow a few doubts in his new friend's mind. Perhaps I could provoke Denver into doing some investigating of his own. He had resources that I didn't possess, and could take liberties that would have me carpeted. With luck, he'd do my job for me. "There was an attempted rape in Somerset," I told Denver, "two years before the girl called Caroline Poole was murdered; and another extremely serious assault just a year before. One of the victims has given evidence that suggests her attacker's car was an MGB." I paused to let it sink in. So what? they were thinking. "An MGB," I added, "that just *happened* to have a pouncing jaguar mascot screwed on the bonnet. Can't be many of those about, can there?" They didn't appear to have an opinion on that. Silkstone looked away and Denver was lost for words, so I pressed on. "Silkstone and Latham gave each other alibis for Caroline's murder," I said, addressing Denver. "Margaret Silkstone and a woman called Michelle Webster verified their stories." From the corner of my eye I saw Silkstone flinch at the mention of Michelle's name. "She sends her regards," I told him. "She also says that she lied about the alibi. Her new story is that Margaret asked her to cover for you and Latham. I was being less than truthful a few seconds ago when I said that we weren't following any new lines of enquiry. We now think that you killed Caroline Poole, too, as well as Margaret and Marie-Claire."

Denver shook his head and laughed. "Kick a dog while it's down, eh, Priest?"

"He was besotted with Caroline," I went on, "after he saw a photograph of her in the local paper, as a twelve-year-old. He saved the photo, bought a glossy print from the paper and kept it as a souvenir, until he planted it in Latham's bedroom to throw suspicion on him."

Denver said. "Let's face it, Priest, you've got Tony for doing a scumbag like Latham and now you're trying to pin every unsolved crime on your books on him. Makes your figures look good but meanwhile the real killers go free. A confession for manslaughter isn't good enough for you, is it? No glory in that for Charlie Priest the Killer Cop, is there? You'll have to do better than that, Squire, you really will."

"We'll see," I replied, standing up to leave.

"You haven't finished your lager," Denver said, eagerly gesturing for me to sit down again. He wanted more.

"I'd rather drink from the drip tray at the path lab, where I have to watch the results of his handiwork being dissected. You deserve each other." I turned, then turned again. "Think about this," I said. "Their marriage was on the rocks. Maybe he wanted to leave Margaret. Perhaps, just perhaps, she didn't want him to go. She suspected he'd done the Caroline job and was threatening to confess to lying about it if he did leave her. That makes another good reason for wanting her dead." I found my car key in my pocket and pointed it at Denver. "And just for the record," I added before striding away from them, "the first two pints were non-alcoholic, and they tasted like piss."

On my way out I winked at the only other customer, sitting at a table near the door. Rodger, the shift tec' gazed implacably through me as he lifted a square of gammon towards his mouth. Outside, the rain had started again.

Chapter Fifteen

Peddling drugs is a serious offence, as serious as it gets, and some people believe that tobacco is as pernicious as any. Jeff Caton posed as a buyer of King Edwards and brought their advertiser back in with him. We sat him in a cell for an hour and decided to let him off with a caution, this time. Selling tobacco isn't illegal but importing cigars, other than for your own consumption, is. He'd brought a thousand back from Spain and was a non-smoker.

I put on my jacket, straightened my tie, and went downstairs to give him his bollocking, arranging my expression to one of suitable solemnity. He stood to make about a tenner per box of fifty, which would give him a grand profit of two hundred pounds. Somehow, I just couldn't take it seriously. I told him that he was robbing the exchequer of their cut, reminded him that if he was prosecuted we could seize his assets, and suggested he didn't waste my time again.

"What about the rest of the cigars?" he asked. He was a real professional.

"How many do you have left?"

"Four boxes."

"Well put them on the compost heap."

Somerset Bob had left a message for me when I arrived back in the office. I tried his number but he'd gone out. "After the Eileen Kelly attack," I asked him, when we finally crossed wires on Wednesday afternoon, "was the information released that you were looking for a Jaguar?"

"Um, not sure," he replied. "I'll have to check the cuttings. Why do you need to know?"

I told him about my little talk with Silkstone. "He clammed up as soon as I mentioned the mascot, as if he knew it had been a mistake. If he saved it, afterwards, we never found it when we searched his house."

"I'll check. Want to know what I've dug up?"

"Yes please."

"OK," he began. "I've checked his insurance records and discovered a bit about the accidents. It wasn't easy – they've had several take-overs since the time we're talking about. The Jag was written off and sent to the crusher. Apparently it was vandalised after the accident and set alight. The MGB went to somewhere called Smith Brothers Safe Storage, which is one of those places where insurance cases are stored until a settlement is made. They're at Newark. Silkstone's occupation is down as area manager with a company called Burdon Developments and he covered the Midlands, which is probably why he was over there."

"Bet it wasn't his fault," I said.

"No," Bob agreed. "He was dead unlucky. An old lady stepped off the pavement right in front of him and he skidded on loose gravel avoiding her. Lost control and sideswiped a telegraph pole."

"Another write-off?" I asked.

"No, the electricity board straightened it up and dabbed some creosote on and it was as good as new."

"That's a relief. And what about the MG?"

"Oh, that was a write-off. Bent the chassis beyond repair."

"It could happen to anyone. Have you taken it further?"

"Haven't managed to raise anyone at Smith Brothers, but I'll keep trying."

"Do that, please, Bob," I told him. "Who knows, somebody may have bought the wreck and rebuilt it. We're getting warm, I can feel it."

Nigel had a date with a sister from St James's, so he wasn't at the Spinners that evening. I assumed he meant the hospital, but with my luck she'd probably be from a convent of the same name. Dave brought Shirley to make up the number, and we sat looking miserable, hardly speaking. On the Saturday they were taking Sophie and her belongings to Cambridge in a hired Transit, hence their gloom. I had no excuse. I told them that Annette and I had decided not to have a future together, but didn't mention her other boyfriend; the one with the two daughters. I said that she wanted to stay with the CID and being linked romantically with the boss might not be a good career move. They made sympathetic sounds and Shirley said: "Oh, Charlie, what are we going to do with you?"

I smiled, saying: "Looks like I'll just have to wait for Sophie getting her degree," and was rewarded with a growl from Dave as he picked up his glass. I'd touched his weak spot.

Bob rang me in the middle of Thursday morning, in a state of high excitement. "The Smiths've still got records, Charlie," he told me, "after all these years. I talked to the son of the original proprietor. He found the file, eventually, and it said that the MGB was sold as scrap to someone called Granville Burgess-Jones, who owns a small motor museum just outside Newark. He's a regular with them, builds and restores vehicles. Sometimes they're not always roadworthy, or might not have an engine in, but they look good. Most of them are just for show. We might be in with a chance, Charlie. You know what these collectors are like – never throw anything away. If the bonnet wasn't damaged," he gushed, "he might still have it."

"That's fantastic," I agreed. "Any chance of you getting over there?"

"It's a bit awkward for me," he began, "and you're quite a lot nearer…"

"I understand, Bob," I told him. "Give me all the names and numbers and leave it with me."

"There's a couple of other things."

"Go on."

"Well, after the Eileen Kelly assault we issued a statement saying that her attacker drove a dark sports car, possibly a Jaguar, so Silkstone would have known what we were look-ing for."

"And destroyed the mascot."

"Exactly."

"Mmm. Did you say a couple of things?"

"Yeah. I've been thinking. Even if we find the actual bonnet, it won't have a serial number on it, or anything. The only link between it and Silkstone is the paperwork. It's vital we maintain the integrity of that."

"God, you're right," I told him. "Good thinking. OK, here's what we do. I'll set off for Newark in about, oh, an hour. Any chance of you ringing the local police and having someone meet me at the Smith Brothers' yard, just to witness things? It'll take me about two, two and a half hours to get there."

"No problem. Good luck, and let me know what you find."

"Thanks, Bob, you'll be the first to know. Meanwhile, I've another job for you. Put it all down in writing, particularly this conversation. Make it read as if we have a hypothesis, and all we have to do to prove it is examine the bonnet of that MG. That's what our entire case revolves around."

Five minutes with the map can save you fifty on the road. I just made that up. It needs working on, but it's true. Head for the M1, A57 at J31 and then the A1 down into Newark. Smith Brothers were on a trading estate on the south side, as you left town, I was told. I memorised the route and set off.

I reached my destination half an hour earlier than expected thanks to clear roads and a reckless disregard of speed limits, but I was still overtaken by a procession of expensive cars on the motorway, heading for the next appointment. They can't all have believed that they'd be able to sweet-talk the traffic cops because they were on their way to nail a murderer, but they drove as if they did.

I lost the half-hour looking for the yard. It was well outside town, at an old World War II bomber station, and the business was based on the storage capacity of three huge hangars. There were wrecked cars everywhere: piled in heaps outside; stacked neatly on pallets inside. Multi-coloured conglomerates of twisted metal, chrome and glass; each one, I thought, bringing misery to someone. About ten people a day are killed on our roads, dotted about the country like a mild case of chicken pox, but this was where the evidence came together in one great sore. Some were hardly damaged, awaiting the assessor's go-ahead to repair; others – many of them – were unrecognisable, and you knew that people had died in there. Once these hangars had housed the bringers of carnage, now they housed the results. A corner was reserved for bent police cars, gaudy in their paintwork but strangely silent, like crippled clowns. Wandering down the first aisle, between the neatly shelved wrecks, I saw abstract images, paintings and photographs, everywhere I looked. I tore myself away and knocked at the office door.

A uniformed PC was inside, drinking tea with a man in a blue shirt and rainbow tie. A woman in a short skirt with a ladder in her tights, a small-town siren, was typing in the corner. "DI Priest," I announced to all present, "Heckley CID. Hope I haven't kept you waiting."

The PC stared at me, open mouthed, and the man in the shirt coughed into his hand. "Lost your tongue?" I asked the PC.

"No, er, Sir," he mumbled, reaching for his hat.

"Never mind that," I said, turning to the other person and asking: "Mr Smith, is it?"

"Um, yes," he replied uncomfortably.

"Good. I understand you have some records for an MGB that was brought into here back in 1982." I told them the registration number and continued: "A colleague in Somerset has rung you, hasn't he?"

The PC unwound himself from the chair and stood up. He was only about twenty-two, but even taller than me.

"Could I, er, see your ID, Sir, if you don't mind, please?"

"Sure." I already had it in my hand. He took it from me, studied it carefully, then said: "Oh, heck."

I pushed some papers to one side on a desk against the opposite wall and perched my backside on a corner of it, saying: "I think you'd better tell me all about it." I folded my arms in the pose of a patient listener and waited, except my patience was rapidly evaporating.

"I've just arrived, Sir," the PC stated, and introduced himself. "I came straight here when I received the message, but thought I must have missed you. Mr Smith had better explain."

I turned to Mr Smith. When Bob had described him as the son of the proprietor I'd immediately formed an image of a young man barely out of college, but he was probably in his late forties. Another reminder of the passing years.

"Well," he began. "I, er, received this telephone call, yesterday, I believe it was, from the police about the MG. Nothing new in that, it's always happening, except usually it's about something that came in recently, not twenty years ago. I said that we kept all the record cards and that we would probably have it somewhere if he gave me the dates." He turned to the woman, who had stopped typing and was listening to our conversation. "Glynis here found it, didn't you, duck?"

"Got black bright," she complained. "It's filthy in there, that far back." She was wearing false eyelashes that a Buddhist monk could have raked the gravel with.

"And then what?" I asked.

"I was saving it," Smith continued, "here in my drawer. He rang me again this morning. Twice, in fact. First time I told him we'd found the card, second time he said that you," – he showed me the pad he kept alongside his telephone, with my name written on it – "would be calling to collect it. Then, about five minutes later, this man came in. Blimey, I thought, that was quick. Thought he'd said you'd be coming down from Yorkshire. This feller asked about the MG, gave me the number, and I said: 'Are you DI Priest?' and he said he was, so I gave him the card."

"Can you describe him?" I asked.

"Well, he wasn't very tall. Didn't look like a cop, now you mention it. Dark hair, slim build, wore a leather raincoat."

"I know him," I said. "He's a reporter."

"A reporter!" Glynis exclaimed, clasping her hand to her mouth, as if I'd announced that the Son of Beelzebub had walked amongst them. I couldn't imagine what she might have told him.

"Did you ask for a receipt for the card?" I asked.

"No, I'm sorry," he replied.

"Or make a photocopy?"

"No, sorry. After all these years…"

"Nothing for you to be sorry about, Mr Smith," I interrupted. "You were trying to be helpful and he took advantage. That's how he earns his living. He definitely said he was me, did he?"

"Yes. I said: 'Are you DI Priest?' and he said: 'Yes, that's right,' just like I told you."

"Can you remember what it said on the card?"

"No, not really, except that I remember telling the other policeman, the one who rang, that Mr Burgess-Jones had bought the MG from the insurance company. He's at Avecaster, on the Sleaford road, about fifteen minutes from here. Has a museum of vintage and classic cars. Used to buy a lot of stuff from us, but not so much these days."

"OK," I said, "here's what I'd like you to do. Our young friend here," – I gestured towards the PC – "will take a statement from you, putting in writing exactly what you've just told me, and anything else you remember. I'll be grateful if you could do that for me."

"Yes, glad to," he agreed.

I stood up to leave. "And Glynis can make a contribution, if she has anything to add. Towards Sleaford, did you say?"

"That's right."

"It's just off the A17," the PC explained.

"Then that's where I'm headed."

It's a different landscape to the one I live in: kinder to its inhabitants but two-dimensional and undemanding. Neat and fertile fields stretch away into the distance, outlined by lush trees, and in every direction a church steeple punctures the sky. Underneath the signpost pointing to Avecaster was one for Cranwell, home of the famous RAF college. I'd considered going there, once upon a time. The thought of roaring up and down the countryside in the latest fighter plane, silk scarf blowing in the wind, had a great appeal to me, but they changed the uniform and I lost interest. Avecaster was a typical Lincolnshire village: yellow stone houses; ivy-clad walls and an understated air of prosperity. Close-cropped verges fronted walled gardens. In the main street the houses crowded the road but on the outskirts they stood back from it: some quite modest; others with stable blocks jutting out to balance the triple garage at the other side. Mr Granville Burgess-Jones and his museum were at Avecaster Manor, probably known locally as the Big House. The gates were open so I drove in.

It was a respectable driveway, curving and lined with ornamental chestnut trees to hide the house until the last dramatic moment. A sign pointed left to the museum and car-park, with the information that it was only open at weekends and bank holidays. I went straight on, through an archway in a high wall, to where I could see several parked vehicles.

Denver's car was parked at the end of the line and I turned towards the space alongside it, gravel crunching under the tyres, making the steering feel heavy and imprecise. Away to the right a group of people turned to see who the new arrival was.

I was in a courtyard, with the house facing me and outbuildings down the adjacent sides. The sun was out and I felt as if I'd wandered on to the set of *Brideshead Revisited*. Denver had reversed into his parking place, but I drove straight in, so my driver's door was next to his. Why people reverse into parking places mystifies me, unless it's so they can make a fast getaway. I climbed out and stretched upright. The little group of them – I counted six – were still looking towards me, over the roofs of the other cars in the line. Denver was there, and so was Prendergast, which was a surprise. I didn't know the others.

I glanced down into Denver's car and saw his mobile phone on the passenger seat, plugged into the cigar lighter to have its battery recharged. I also noticed that his keys were dangling from the ignition lock. It's a funny thing about Fords. Because of the activities of some of the younger members of our society, they, along with all the other manufacturers, have spent millions of pounds trying to protect our beloved vehicles against theft. War, they say, brought about vast improvements in the field of aviation. Little scrotes like Jamie What's-his-name initiated the development of the car alarm and immobiliser, thus creating thousands of jobs in the security market. Thanks to him and his friends, the key I held in my right hand had a minute electronic chip built into it. It would only open a lock that had a certain combination of signals, and there were two hundred and fifty thousand possible combinations. My mind boggled at the thought of it. A thief had a 1-in-250,000 chance of his key starting my car, which made the odds against him guessing my pin number and emptying my bank account, at a mere 1-in-9,999, look a good bet.

What they don't tell you is that any Ford key will *lock* any Ford car. When it comes to locking the car, they're all the same. It was Sparky's sixteen-year-old son, Danny, that told me that. His dad had just bought an Escort, and Danny bet me a pound that his dad's key would lock my car. I lost the bet. That's what they teach them at school, these days.

The little group were still looking my way. Without taking

my eyes off them I felt for the lock of Denver's car with the tip of the key for mine. Years of practise, opening the car day after day, give you an instinct for it. The key slipped home and I turned it away from the steering wheel. I heard the whirr of electric motors and the *chunk* of the bolts slamming across as a glow of satisfaction welled up inside me. Denver was locked out, and that was the best quid I'd ever lost.

Two of them were TV people. Freelancers, armed with cameras and sound equipment and presumably hired by Denver. The other two were wearing blue overalls with *Avecaster Motor Museum* embroidered on the breast pocket. The taller of them had a gaunt face and was puffing on a cigarette stub, the other had a handlebar moustache and the complexion of an outdoor man who enjoys a tipple. The type who never hunts south of the Thames nor services the wife in the morning in case something better presents itself in the afternoon.

"Mr Burgess-Jones?" I asked.

"That's right," he replied. "I don't believe I've had the pleasure…"

"Detective Inspector Priest, of Heckley CID." I looked beyond him. "And that," I added, "is presumably the lady who brought us all here."

It was the MG, standing there gleaming in the sun. Flame red, black and chrome, pampered and aloof, like a thoroughbred at Crufts or Ascot. She looked good.

"The police, did you say?" Burgess-Jones was asking.

"Yes Sir. I'm afraid you've been mixing with some bad company." I turned to the others and pointed at Denver. "This gentleman here is under arrest for impersonating a police officer and interfering with an investigation. He also impersonates a journalist, but that's not an offence. And this gentleman…" I looked at Prendergast, "…is a solicitor."

Everybody spoke at once. Denver wanted to know why he was under arrest, Prendergast didn't know why he had been invited and Burgess-Jones was completely bewildered.

I raised a hand to silence them. "I don't know what you were planning to do," I told them, "but whatever it was, it's off. That car is evidence in a murder investigation and I am seizing it."

"Hey man," one of the TV people said. "We still want paying, y'know." He looked like one of the guitarists from Grateful Dead.

"The question is," Denver stated, "what will you do with the car?"

"We'll take it away and give it a thorough examination," I replied.

"For holes in the bonnet," he said, "where you say Silkstone fitted the Jaguar mascot?"

"That's right."

"In secret, and you'll fix it to suit your own ends."

"That's not true. Everything will be done in the presence of independent witnesses."

"Rubbish! You'll rig it."

I ignored him and turned to Burgess-Jones. "I'd be grateful, Sir," I said, "if you could move the car back into its garage until I can arrange for it to be either collected or examined here. You'll be fully compensated for any damage done to it."

"Not my problem," he replied. "Just sold it to Mr Denver for a very good price. It's his, now."

Denver smiled smugly. I resisted the urge to thump him and walked over to the MG. A Black and Decker angle grinder lay on the ground in front of it, ready to do business, with a bright orange cable snaking off into an outbuilding. I stooped to look inside the car and saw a thick photo album sitting on the passenger seat. "Is that a record of the restoration?" I shouted to Burgess-Jones.

"That's right," he replied, strolling towards me. "We do a full photographic history of the entire process."

"You built this car from two others, I believe."

"Yes. This one had a damaged front end, so we grafted the

front of the other on to it."

"Is it roadworthy?"

"I think our work would be frowned upon now, but at the time it was common practise. We've never tried to register it."

"Do the pictures show the other car at all?"

"Oh yes. It's all there."

"Was the bonnet from the other car? It's only the bonnet we're interested in."

"It looks like it. It was a green one, so we must have resprayed it. I vaguely remember, but not the details."

"Will there be any evidence of the original colour still there?" I asked.

"I would imagine so," he replied. "We'd fully strip all the top surfaces, but not underneath. The green paint should still be there, under the red, if it is the bonnet from the second car." The paintwork was superb, glowing like rubies in the afternoon sun. He obviously employed a craftsman.

Denver had joined us. "So let's do it," he suggested.

Grateful Dead shouted: "Look, you guys. We appreciate being here, an' all that, but we got places to go. Are we doing the fuckin' shoot, or what?"

"What's Prendergast doing here?" I asked Denver.

"I invited him."

"Why?"

"Because I decided to. We're not a police state yet, you know."

"You mean because you'd also invited Silkstone."

"So what. He's a right to be here."

"And it would have made a better story. Statements all round, from the injured party and his hot-shot lawyer. So where is he?"

"Don't know. Should have arrived an hour ago. We thought you were him."

"I'll tell you where he is. Collecting whatever money you paid him and waiting for a ferry to warmer climes. The next time you see Silkstone he'll have a coat over his head."

"So let's do it then, if you're so sure."

"We're doing nothing. Go home. The show's over." I shouted it, for the benefit of everyone: "That's it folks. Go home, the show's over."

"So what'll happen to the car?" Denver demanded.

"I've told you. We'll have it examined."

"So why not do it now? You've got independent witnesses. There's Mr Burgess-Jones, and Mr Prendergast. What more could you want? And the crew can film the whole thing. What are you scared of, Priest? The truth? That you're hounding an innocent man? Or are you just scared that you won't be able to fix it, like you did when you shot someone?"

"It's the truth I'm after, Denver," I told him. "I'm not interested in a media circus and all this *the public's right to know* bullshit that you hide behind."

"Then do it."

"When we do it we'll do it properly, in the presence of a magistrate."

Burgess-Jones coughed and took a step forward. "Um, I'm a JP," he announced. "Been on the bench twenty-three years, if it's any help."

The expression *painted himself into a corner* flashed up in my mind. Strange thing was, Denver was right. This was the perfect opportunity to put the hypothesis to the test. The big problem was that if I was wrong, it was in public. I wouldn't have twisted the evidence in any way, but I'd have sneaked off like a defeated stag and licked my wounds in private. What was my chief concern: the truth about Silkstone and the car, or my reputation? I remembered Sophie, and how I'd been scared to ask the right questions because I'd doubted her. Was I doubting myself, now? Everybody was looking at me.

"OK," I said. "We'll do it."

Chapter Sixteen

"Right!" Denver proclaimed triumphantly. "Right! You lot ready?"

"We've been ready a fuckin' hour," Grateful Dead told him.

"Not so fast," I said. "There's conditions."

"Conditions?" Denver echoed.

"Jesus H fuckin' Christ!" Grateful Dead cursed, throwing his hands in the air.

"That's right. Conditions. First of all, it won't be a TV show, with you doing the narration. We do it from a forensic point of view, for use in court."

"Well, fair enough," Denver conceded.

"And secondly," I added, "you pay, so the tape is yours, but I'm impounding it until it can be copied. OK?"

"It's a deal," he said. "Let's get on with it."

Prendergast, who hadn't spoken so far, decided to earn his fee. "Gentlemen," he said. "I really do think this has gone far enough. As my client isn't here I have to say, on his behalf, that we do not accept the entire premise upon which this allegation is based. Whatever is found on the car, it can have little bearing on what happened twenty years ago. Who knows who has tampered with things since then."

Burgess-Jones said: "Nobody has tampered with things, as you put it, Sir. Everything is as it was or as recorded in the photograph albums."

"Good try, Prendergast," I told him, "but over-ruled. We'll tell Silkstone you did your best." I turned to the film crew. "Listen up," I said, slipping my watch off my wrist. "This is how I want it. Can you focus down on that?" I propped the watch behind one of the windscreen wipers and stood back.

"No problem," Grateful Dead assured me.

"Good. I want to start and finish with a shot of the watch, close up. Then I want a wide angle, to include everybody present. After that you can zoom in and out as you like. The main thing is that I want the entire thing to be seamless, with one camera and no stops and no editing. Can you do that?"

"One take, beginning to end, starting and finishing with the time?"

"That's it."

"You goddit, no problem."

"Do we have sound recording?"

"Sure do."

"Right. In that case, I'll do the talking. Let's go."

I felt Burgess-Jones tug my sleeve and turned to him. "Nobody goes anywhere without some protection for their eyes," he said, placing a pair of safety spectacles in my hand. I put them on and the film crew found their Oakleys.

"OK, gentlemen," Grateful Dead said, taking over the role of director because he realised that it was the only way to get things done, "let's have you all together, at the side of the car. Take one, of one."

Burgess-Jones picked up the angle grinder and we stood there as the camera zoomed in at the watch and then encompassed us all in its impartial gaze. I introduced myself, feeling foolish, and invited the others to do so. Burgess-Jones's assistant was called Raymond, and he said he was chief mechanic and brother-in-law of the proprietor. He's married well, I thought.

"We will now lift the bonnet and attempt to establish its original colour, before any restoration work was done on it," I said, and Raymond reached inside the car and released the catch.

We all stepped back to allow him to walk round to the front of the car. He poked his fingers inside the front grill for the lever and lifted the bonnet. I could see pipes and wires, a drive shaft and exhaust pipe, all pointing towards a big void where most cars have an engine.

"There's no fuckin' engine!" Denver gasped. He turned to Burgess-Jones. "Hey! There's no fuckin' engine. You never said it didn't have an engine."

"I told you it was a museum piece," Burgess-Jones replied.

"Six fuckin' grand!" he ranted. "I just gave six fuckin' grand for a car with no fuckin' engine."

"Let's have a look at the underside of the bonnet," I said, and Raymond held it upright so the camera could zoom in. Burgess-Jones pressed the trigger on the angle grinder and applied it to the paintwork.

He moved it gently back and forth and we watched as the scarlet paint shrivelled and flew off in a spray of debris and smoke. First a grey undercoat was revealed, then a dark colour and then more primer. He stood back and the machine in his hand whined to a standstill.

"That should do it," he declared. "BRG, I'd say. British racing green."

Raymond stooped to look under the bonnet. "Yep, BRG," he confirmed.

Denver and I looked and agreed that the original colour was green. Prendergast declined.

"OK," I said. "Now lets have a look at the outside." Raymond slammed the bonnet shut and Burgess-Jones stepped forward, brandishing the Black and Decker.

Denver restrained him with an extended arm and positioned himself in front of the MG, facing the camera. "This," he began, "is a simple test upon which the life, the freedom, of a man depends."

I was standing alongside Grateful Dead, who glanced sideways at me. Had I tried to stop Denver it would be captured on film, and he knew it. "Keep filming," I told him through gritted teeth.

"Tony Silkstone," Denver continued, "stands accused of a series of crimes – rape and murder – going back eighteen years. Some would say the police have been over-zealous in their pursuit of Silkstone, their enquiry based entirely on the suspicions of one officer. Whilst we wish our police to be

diligent and thorough, there comes a point when these qual-
ities become vindictive and mean spirited. Hounding the
innocent should not be part of the police's role."

I thought he'd finished, and took a step forward. Denver
shot me a glance then looked back at the camera. "The bonnet of this car might hold the clue to the killer who murdered and raped sixteen-year-old Caroline Poole back in
1983, and who had sexually assaulted young Eileen Kelly
two years previously. Eileen says her attacker drove a Jaguar
car. The police, or, more accurately, one police officer with a
reputation for irresponsible action, say that the car was an
MGB, similar to this one behind me…" he stepped to one
side and gestured, "…that belonged to Tony Silkstone at the
time in question. This officer says that Silkstone had fitted a
Jaguar mascot to the bonnet of the car, thus causing Eileen
to believe the car she was abducted in was of that make.
Silkstone denies it. The proof, ladies and gentlemen, is
awaiting discovery. If this car ever had the Jaguar mascot fitted, there will be evidence of two holes, somewhere about
here." He touched the appropriate place. "Let's see, shall
we?"

I thought about going out in a blaze of glory. They'd have
put it down to post-traumatic stress, or something, and
given me a full pension. And it would certainly have made
good television, as I demonstrated how to reshape the front
of an MG by battering it with a journalist's head. They
might even have given me my own chat show. Instead, I just
turned away and took a few deep breaths. I'm growing either
old or soft, or both.

Burgess-Jones stepped forward again and the grinder in
his hands leapt from zero to three thousand revs per minute
with a yelp like a kicked dog. "About there," Denver
instructed him, pointing to a spot just behind the MG
badge. I walked forward to have a closer look.

He moved the spinning wheel across the pristine surface,
barely skimming the top layer away. We smelt burning paint

and saw flakes of it melt and then fly off. He gradually enlarged the patch, revealing the grey undercoat and a darker primer edging the scar, like woodgrain, or an aerial view of a coastline.

Sparks flew when he touched metal. The patch of bare metal grew as he moved the wheel across it. Silver steel, that's all. "Back a bit," I shouted to Burgess-Jones above the whine of the grinder, and he expanded the area he was attacking. The patch grew longer, but it was blank and inviolate.

There was one aesthetically pleasing spot where you could fix the jaguar, and we'd covered that. Anywhere else and it would have looked wrong. Too far forward and the cat would have been leaping downhill, too far back and it would cease to be a bonnet mascot. But Silkstone knew nothing about aesthetics, and I clung to that fact.

"Keep going," I said.

Denver gestured to Grateful Dead for him to move in with the camera and get a good close-up of the metal. Burgess-Jones was nearly halfway back to the windscreen when I saw him tense and stoop more closely over the car. "There's something here!" he cried.

There it was. A dissimilar metal, to borrow a phrase from my schooldays, peering out from under the paint and growing by the second. First one brass-coloured disc was revealed, then another an inch behind it, like twin suns blazing in the silver sky of a distant planet. Burgess-Jones enlarged the sky, gave it a neat finish, then stepped proudly back.

"You did it," I said to him. "You did it. Thanks. Thanks a lot."

"My pleasure," he replied, a big smile across his face.

Denver looked at where the holes had been, before some craftsman had filled them with braze and made the bonnet as good as new. "Are they the right size?" he asked.

"Yes," Burgess-Jones told him. "About a quarter inch

diameter at one inch centres. Exactly right, I'd say."

"Wow!" Denver exclaimed, recovering his equilibrium and doing a U-turn that would have overturned a Ferrari but didn't make his conscience even wobble. "Wow! Do I have a story! Do I have a fuckin' story!" He patted his pockets, feeling for his phone, then remembered it was in his car, being recharged.

Grateful Dead zoomed in at my watch and asked me if that would do. I nodded and he said: "Cut!" and stopped the camera.

Denver was heading towards the cars, so I followed him. When I arrived he was emptying his pockets, piling coins and mints and tissues on the roof of his Ford. Everything but keys. I unlocked mine and reached into the glove box for my mobile phone. "I've lost my keys," Denver muttered. "I've lost my keys."

I tapped out the Heckley nick number and pointed inside his car, asking: "Are they them?"

Denver stooped to look inside, pulling at the door handle. "Aw fuck!" he cursed. "I've locked them in. I've fuckin' locked them in. How'd I do that? I thought it was impossible. How'd I do that?"

"It's DI Priest," I said into the phone. "I want you to do two things for me. First of all I want an all ports warning issuing for the arrest of Tony Silkstone, and then I want to talk to the press department. I want a story circulating to Reuters and Associated Press, as soon as possible."

Denver had decided to enlist help. "Mr Burgess-Jones!" he called, turning and jogging back to the others. "Mr Burgess-Jones, can you help me, please?"

A voice on the phone said: "Heckley police station, how can I help you?"

"Hello George," I replied. "Where've you been? I've been talking to myself."

"Feeding the cat, Charlie. Where are you? That's more to the point."

"I'm down in Lincolnshire."

"It's all right for some."

"Work, George, work. Listen, there's two things. First of all I want an APW issuing for Tony Silkstone, and then I want to speak to the press officer."

"Silkstone?" George replied. "You got enough on him, have you?"

"Yes, George, I think we have. I really think we have."

After that, I got mean. I made Denver sit in my car and when Prendergast started making objections I reminded him that he represented nobody there and threatened to chuck him in the duckpond, whereupon he made an excuse and left. Burgess-Jones thought it all a hoot. I rang the local CID and eventually handed everything over to them, including Denver. The AA arrived with a set of Slim Jims, as used by the more professional car thieves, and opened Denver's car. Inside it we found the record card for Silkstone's MG, as made out by Smith Brothers and showing that it had been sold to Mr Burgess-Jones, so the chain was complete.

All the papers carried the story next day, but the *UK News* still claimed it as a world exclusive, even though we gave some of the best bits to the others. Lincolnshire police let Denver go, on their bail, and a week later he was given an official caution. No chance there of him claiming that we were heavy-handed with him.

Silkstone had made a run for it, as we thought. He panicked, and followed an elaborate plan to make it look as if he'd killed himself by driving the Audi over Bempton cliffs. Unfortunately several eye-witnesses and a few second's video footage revealed that he'd driven his late wife's Suzuki Vitara to York, travelled back to Heckley by train, taken the Audi to Bempton where he'd sent it over the edge, and then found his way back to York again and, he hoped, freedom. We picked him up two days later, lying low at a caravan site near Skegness. Dave and I went to fetch him – sometimes, I indulge myself.

Afterwards, in the in-between hours which are neither night nor day, I thought that perhaps it might not stick. A clever brief might cast doubts on my methodology, declare some evidence inadmissible, get him off. It would all be down to the jury, but I didn't care. The first time DNA profiling was used in a murder case it indicated that the person under arrest was innocent, even though he had made a full confession. The local police were outraged and Alec Jeffreys, the scientist who developed the technique, must have been devastated. But he stuck to his guns, had faith in the system, and eventually the real murderer was caught.

Looking back on it, freeing that innocent man must give Sir Alec much more satisfaction than pointing the finger at a guilty one. About a fortnight after Silkstone was committed for trial I received a letter from Jean Hullah, matron of the Pentland Court Retirement Home. She said that Mrs Grace Latham, mother of Peter, had died, but she was aware that her son had been cleared of suspicion of murdering Mrs Silkstone and had wanted to write and thank me. And young Jason Lee Gelder was off the hook too. He was too dense to realise how close he'd been, but now he was free to earn his living skinning dead cows and spend his earnings on evenings of passion in the brickyard. Even if Silkstone walked, and I didn't think he would, it was still a result.

I was sitting at my desk, feet on it, reading a report from Germany about how changing the diet of the inmates of a children's home from cola drinks and fish fingers to organically grown sauerkraut transformed them all from rebellious louts into adorable little cherubs when there was a knock at the door and Annette came in. I let my chair flop onto all four feet and smiled at her.

"Oh, I thought you'd brought me a coffee," I said, noticing that she was empty-handed and pushing the spare chair towards her.

"No," she replied, without returning the smile. "I

brought you this. I thought you ought to be the first to know." It was a long white envelope, addressed to me.

I took it from her and turned it in my fingers. "Is it what I think it is?" I asked.

"Yes."

"I hoped it wouldn't come to this," I told her, and she shrugged her shoulders. I placed it on my desk, propped against a box of paperclips, and looked at it. "You've some holiday to come," I stated.

"Three weeks," she confirmed.

"So you could be gone by the end of next week."

"Yes."

"You've accepted his proposal?"

"Yes."

We only have to give a month's notice to resign. The last thing you want hanging round a police station is a demob-happy disgruntled officer spreading doubt and disillusion about the job. A week, though. We'd been jogging along quite nicely, up to now. I'd behaved myself, Annette had done her job. We'd even had a drink together, after a particularly harrowing day, and I'd enjoyed seeing her around, half hoping that her friendship with the teacher might grow cold. It obviously hadn't.

"There's an alternative," I said.

She shook her head. "No."

"I could tear this up, drop it in the bin, and you could come to live with me."

She hung her head, one hand on her brow. "Don't, please, Charlie," she mumbled. "Don't make it more difficult than it is."

I looked at her, seeing for the first time the worry lines in the corners of her eyes that hadn't been there before she started seeing me. Now somebody else would have to soothe them away. I opened my mouth to tell her that she was making a mistake, then changed my mind. I've been through all that, before. "I'll miss you," I said, "and I hope it all works out for you."

"I hope it all works out for you, too, Charlie," she replied.

"Oh, it will," I told her. "It will. No doubt about that."

So the following Friday we had a "do" in the Bailiwick, with everybody there. Gilbert made a presentation and Annette said we were the best bunch of people she'd ever worked with. Embarrassing episodes in Annette's career were recalled and David Rose did his party trick, drinking a pint of beer while standing on his head. It's time to leave when David does his party trick.

I didn't have the opportunity to say a private goodbye to her, thinking that maybe I'd give her a phone call the next day, but suspecting that I wouldn't. Dave Sparkington and I shared a taxi home and I asked him if they'd heard from Sophie this week.

"Yeah, she keeps in touch," he told me.

"Is she enjoying her lectures?"

"She says she is. It's hard work, but she's coping."

"And the flat's OK?"

"Hmm, bit of a problem, there. She says the place stinks of garlic. The previous tenant must have eaten nothing else but."

I remembered the microwave I'd given her, and the exploding chicken Kiev. "Students," I said, by way of explanation.

"Yeah, students."

We rode the rest of the way in silence, apart from the hiss of the tyres on the wet road and the swish of the wipers. "I reckon you missed your way there, Chas," Dave said as we turned into his street.

"Where?"

"With Annette."

"Oh. No, not my type."

Rain, carried by a wind straight off the hills, was lashing at the windows as he slammed the car door and dashed for the shelter of his house. I gave the driver new directions and he took me home.

I over-tipped him and turned up my collar as he wished me goodnight. The postman had left the gate open and the bulb had failed again in the outside light. I'm sure they don't last as long now that we get our electricity from the gas people. I found the right key by the light of the street lamp then plunged into the shadow at the side of the house, shuddering with cold.

What was it to be, I wondered: a hot bath; some loud music; a couple of cans with my feet on the mantelpiece; or all three? Silkstone would probably be tucked up in bed in his nice centrally heated cell. Jason would be having it away with some totty he'd picked up at the Aspidistra Lounge. And what about Chilcott – the Chiller – where would he be? In a bar in a warmer clime if his luck had held. Somewhere where you can live like a lord on ten grand a year. Cuba, or Mexico.

Unless, of course, he was still out there, wondering about fulfilling his last contract. I doubted it, but it gave life a certain piquancy, knowing that somebody thought enough about you to pay money to have you killed. I was a cop, so I must be doing something right. The key found the keyhole third attempt and I turned it. I pushed the door open and reached inside for the lightswitch. No doubt Mexico's fine, but there's no place like home.